Time's a Thief

Time's a Thief

B. G. FIRMANI

Doubleday

New York   London   Toronto
Sydney   Auckland

All rights reserved. Published in the United States by Doubleday, a division of Penguin Random House LLC, New York, and distributed in Canada by Random House of Canada, a division of Penguin Random House Limited, Toronto.

www.doubleday.com

DOUBLEDAY and the portrayal of an anchor with a dolphin are registered trademarks of Penguin Random House LLC.

Jacket design by Emily Mahon
Jacket photograph © Eli Fendelman / 500px

Library of Congress Cataloging-in-Publication Data
Names: Firmani, B. G., author.
Title: Time's a thief / by B. G. Firmani.
Description: First edition. | New York : Doubleday, 2017. |
Identifiers: LCCN 2016021705 (print) | LCCN 2016029862 (ebook) |
ISBN 9780385541862 (hardcover) | ISBN 9780385541879 (ebook) |
Subjects: LCSH: Women college students—Fiction. |
Female friendship—Fiction. | Dysfunctional families—Fiction. |
Life change events—Fiction. | Self-actualization (Psychology)—
Fiction. | New York (N.Y.)—Fiction. | Psychological fiction.
Classification: LCC PS3606.I736 T56 2017 (print) |
LCC PS3606.I736 (ebook) | DDC 813/.6—dc23
LC record available at https://lccn.loc.gov/2016021705

MANUFACTURED IN THE UNITED STATES OF AMERICA

1 3 5 7 9 10 8 6 4 2

First Edition

This is for Damian

What will remain of us is cities and songs.

—Jane Jacobs, in conversation

Part I

I

Kendrick Löwenstein.

I'd heard her name for almost a whole semester before I ever saw her. I was taking a philosophy class, a terrible class actually, with a student-hating, prehistoric professor who never gave lectures or "unpacked" anything but instead read aloud to us for the entire hour, as if we'd gathered there for a bedtime story. To eat up some time before turning to his disintegrating notebook and intoning his notes on Epictetus—notes unchanged, was the word on the street, since the time of the '68 student protests, when a few subversive asides crept in, among them an oblique reference to the world actually having ended in 1908 due to the Tunguska Meteor Event—he would call the roll. There were certain people who never showed up, and on these he would hang, repeating their names over and over again, a dull needle stuck in a bad groove.

Kendrick Löwenstein, he would read. Getting no response, he would repeat: *Kendrick Löwenstein.* He'd look up, squinting his eyes under caterpillar eyebrows. *Kendrick Löwenstein!* he would demand, warning her that she risked giving offense and commanding her to appear. *Kendrick Löwenstein?* he would say finally, wistfully, lingering over the name as if he were a lover and she the one who got away.

I remember very clearly the first time I finally saw her.

It was about four in the morning, just after bar time, and I was trucking up Broadway with my motorcycle jacket stuffed with packs of Marlboros and a six of $2.99 Knickerbocker beer under my arm. I'm not even sure where I was going. Probably I'd been hanging out with Trina,

Audrey, and Fang-Hua and I'd volunteered to do the beer-and-cigarette run, or I'd been at a bar and I was out looking to prolong the mischief, but who can remember so many years down the line? Anyway, right there on the corner of Broadway and 116th was this *girl*. And she looked so dramatic, so absurdly exaggerated, that I almost laughed out loud. It was freezing cold, but the top of her coat was pulled down, swathed around her freakishly pale, almost alien-white shoulders, and held closed over her breastbone with one long-fingered hand. Worn like this it took on the aspect of an opera cape, or some last shred of grandeur clung to, literally, by deposed royalty. With her other hand she held by the corner an enormous clutch purse, which was covered in some kind of ancient linsey-woolsey needlepoint fabric and which sagged with (I'd learn only later) masses and masses of stolen dexies. I remember thinking she had a kind of arrogant, indolent lower lip, and I got the feeling she had just left some louche company. She was like a tragic heroine, worse for the wear—glamorous, haggard, in extremis— and she was made up like a silent movie star. Except that she had electric-blue hair.

There was something to this. The thing of it was, she was a mess, standing there with her lips parted, smudge-lidded and surprised at herself, with her sulky and offended face. But I knew from experience how much discipline it took to have blue hair. Green hair, we all knew, was easy. It was what you got when you tried to dye your hair blue. You'd bleach and bleach your brains out, but it was never enough, so your hair would go a crazy straw yellow. Then you'd slather on the Manic Panic blue dye and get . . . green hair. You had to have real patience, real technique, to have blue hair.

And so, looking at this girl standing on the corner of 116th and Broadway at 4:12 a.m. on a cold winter night in the late 1980s, I thought, Here's a girl who, all evidence to the contrary, has a backup plan.

"Got a light?" was the first thing she said to me.

Of course I had a light. I was born with a Zippo in my hand.

I lit her cigarette for her—it was almost the same blue as her hair, with a long gold filter, a Nat Sherman Fantasia, I would learn—and when it was clear she was going nowhere, I put down the six-pack, took out my own cigarettes, and lit one. It felt wrong to leave her standing there on the corner. I was still holding the lighter when she took it out of my hand.

"Cool," she said, turning it over and over and looking at it. "Why'd you paint it black?"

"They made them like that during World War Two. To save the brass. And you could light up in the trenches and the metal wouldn't reflect the light."

She flicked it open, lit the flame, snapped it shut.

"Can I have it?" she said.

I laughed.

"Um, no?" I said.

"Oh, come on, can't I have it?" she said. She was holding it up in front of her face, clicking it open, flicking the flame, snapping it shut again and again. I realized with this that she was a rich kid. Because middle-class people, let alone working-class, don't go around expecting stuff for free. I grabbed the lighter back on the last snap.

"It was my dad's," I said, putting it in my pocket.

"Your dad was in World War Two?" she said.

I said yeah.

"My dad's way old too," she said. "How old's your dad?"

"He's dead," I said.

"I *wish* my dad were dead," she said. She inhaled deeply on her cigarette, threw her head back, and exhaled. She tilted her head down and looked at me fiercely. "Actually, I wish my fucking mother were dead. I could chuck her down a *well*."

She was . . . theatrical. But there was also something strangely languid about her, distracted. She threw me off. I would later learn that her parted-lip, surprised look was what her face settled into at rest. I would go on to wonder if this might have had something to do with her having done lots of drugs since the age of eleven.

She took her hand from her coat and one side slipped down her shoulder, revealing a thin dress, cut '40s style, rhinestone clips pulling its neckline square. With her heavy-lidded, rounded eyes, her pouting mouth and long neck, she reminded me of a Pontormo Madonna. But without any calm, without any quiet.

"Aren't you fucking freezing?" is what I said to her.

5

She smiled.

"Don't you know," she said to me, "that crazy people don't feel the cold?"

She made no move to pull her coat back up again. She seemed rooted to the spot, smoking her blue cigarette there on the corner by the Chock Full o'Nuts with its perpetually sweating windows. I really was freezing and I had to pee, but I couldn't leave her there.

"You just hanging around out here?" I said to her.

"Yeah, whatever," she said.

Then she sang a line from "I'm Waiting for My Man."

It seemed like a weirdly public place to be meeting a drug dealer. Then I wondered if she meant something else and she was actually, what, a prostitute? But you really didn't see a lot of punk-rock prostitutes on the Upper West Side in the 1980s.

"You live here?" I gestured down 116th Street.

"Sort of," she said. "Do you?"

"Yeah," I said, and pointed. Then I abruptly retracted my hand, because the building I'd pointed to was a dorm.

She cocked an amused eyebrow at me.

"You go to Barnard?" she asked.

I cleared my throat, feeling deeply uncool.

"Yeah," I admitted.

She rolled her eyes in a complete 360-degree lunatic circle.

"So do I," she said.

And with this, our pretensions that we were as bad as all that melted into air.

"I'm Chess," I said, putting out my hand. "My name is Frances—Francesca Varani, actually. But everyone calls me Chess."

"Kendra," she said, "Kendra Löwenstein."

"Damn, girl—*you're* Kendrick Löwenstein?" I said. "You better get that shit to class!"

*

I should probably back up a moment and talk about what got me thinking of her.

It was another cold winter, some twenty years later, when I got a

6

piece of news that sent me right back to Kendra and her family. It was a pretty dire time jobwise, and I'd just stumbled into a new gig as a bid writer in a loony little office in the Garment District. The whole sick crew there sort of bears some words, as does where my head was at just about then, age thirty-nine and feeling blindsided by how quickly time was passing.

The Acme Corporation, as it was called, was a "language services" company that specialized in plucking consecutive interpreters out of the ether and dropping them into grim situations such as family court appearances, determinations of Medicaid fraud, and deportation hearings. As far as I could tell, though, no one in the Acme office did a lick of work. There was a sales guy, Walter, a friendly, mildly defeated fellow who dealt in uncontrollable sighs and who spent most of his days eating sad, crunchy snacks behind the privacy of his workstation divider. There was the team that dispatched the interpreters: a creepy manager (male) and four young and good-looking women, all with long and lustrous hair, as if they'd been hired because they fulfilled a type. The three who did any kind of actual work were constantly quivering with disgust or terror, while the fourth, Nikki, an elaborately lazy yet hot-tempered twentysomething from Staten Island, had the worst trash mouth I'd ever encountered at a job. She had near-screaming conversations with the lecher of a dispatch manager where she'd yell across the office, *You answer the fuckin' phone—my nails are wet!*

I could not believe I had to work in this place. This is no mere flimsy figure of speech: I just *could not believe* I had to work there. I kept waiting for Allen Funt to pop down through the acoustic tile and say, *Just kidding, hon! You can go now!* But this was right when the first shocks of the recession were rippling through Manhattan, and no one in the industry I typically freelanced for—architecture—had a crumb to spare. Everywhere around us industries were tanking, and just a month before, my best friend, Trina, had been laid off from a media company where she'd been a photo editor for sixteen years as print media seemed to go the way of the eight-track tape. And my own guy, Fitz, an artist who earned his bread in animation, had been thoroughly unemployed for months, as "outsourcing" and new technology killed off nearly every studio on the East Coast.

So the prevailing notion was that one was lucky to have a job at all. However, "lucky to have a job" was an idea that, dating back to my first reading of *Bartleby the Scrivener* as a cringing, glasses-wearing preteen, could only make me want to vomit.

But! We had rent to pay.

Fitz and I did have a little bit of savings, and he was getting $342 a week in unemployment, but the idea of blowing through this and having to tap a relative for a loan filled us with deep Catholic shame. Fitz ate himself alive trying to come up with something he could do to earn money, and went around the neighborhood picking up applications at every last Ukrainian grocer and taco shack until we did some basic math and realized that, going by the minimum wage of $7.15, after taxes he'd actually make more on unemployment. Plus, I reminded him—all the while feeling huge discomfort over having become a "reminding" type of woman—the most important thing for him was to get his degree. He'd reenrolled at CUNY, and ditching college again just to fry up buffalo wings on Avenue D seemed criminal. Besides, truth be told, with my many years of schooling and "wide breadth of work experience"— *porca miseria!*—I was the employable one.

Anyway, to get back to the story here, I'd got a random call from Acme telling me they'd just lost their bid writer and had something big in the pipeline. Could I come in for an interview?

I hadn't spent any real time in the Garment District for years, and getting out of the subway at Penn Station and walking west, I was surprised to pass into the ominous cloud of dinge that hung over the streets, something to do with decades of underpaid labor and the still-lingering scent of Gambino crime family stogies. I passed shops with names like Spandex House, Stretch World, Textile Kingdom, places that sold to the trade, *al por mayor,* their windows showing endless evidence of the strange trickle-down from haute couture to discount-bin *schmatte*. I was running early, and I stopped to look at a polka-dot catsuit trimmed with military insignia and then, farther west, a beautifully made portrait of Barack Obama rendered entirely in sequins. More than anything, the vibe of the sweatshop still hung heavy over the terrain, and I got to thinking of my various great-aunts who spent

8

thirty, forty, fifty years hunched over sewing machines on these very streets, trying to sew their way up the fabric of the American Dream.

I found myself in front of the building, a sooty old workhorse of a place with a retrofitted black-marble lobby dating from the 1980s. The security fellow, a melancholy Gujarati whose strange habits I would come to know well, immediately guessed where I was going, which somehow surprised me.

Upstairs on Acme's floor, I picked up the phone, and the man I'd spoken with, Mr. Walker—Acme's president—said he'd be right out. He'd sounded erratic earlier, voluble and strange, but I had no idea of the real degree of this until I saw the person who greeted me now.

The first thing I noticed about Mr. Walker was his hair. It was copious, sculptural, and uncommonly blond. The second thing was that his glasses were on upside down. When I looked closer, however, I realized the problem was that they were actually women's glasses, of the gold-braid-trimmed, peekaboo-stem variety. This idea was confirmed later, when I met his wife, Tootsie, who had exactly the same pair.

Besides the glasses, Mr. Walker wore a wrinkled dress shirt, buttoned crookedly in sight-gag fashion, and, one could not help but notice, overly tight trousers. He was lean and fit, with oddly bright eyes—*cokehead,* I thought—and he told me to call him, in all seriousness, Dee-Dee. He talked a mile a minute in a constant yammer, asking and answering his own questions: *So did you get here all right, of course you got here all right, you're here aren't you, you want a coffee, sure you want a coffee, it's free, I mean—who doesn't like something free?*

By now he'd taken me into his office and closed the door.

He told me they'd just got in a big Request for Proposal and unfortunately their bid writer, Mrs. Churtie-Matz, had been afflicted with a persecutory delusional disorder and split the scene. Bad news for them, because this proposal was due right after the holidays and there was plenty to be done on it. All this time as I listened to him yammer I was trying not to react to his oddly filthy play-grown-up office (cracked vinyl Chesterfield sofa, Wayne Gretzky inspirational poster, orange carpeting covered in violent burn marks) or to his ludicrous hair and overall hophead manner. But I guess I passed some test, because in a moment he asked me to meet his second-in-command, Petey, as well as Cissy, the ops manager, and Will, the "money guy."

All three spilled into his office immediately, as if they'd had their ears pressed to the door. Petey appeared at once paranoid and anesthetized and had the staring-into-the-abyss look of a late-career Francis Bacon, while Will seemed like some worried bear with a WTF look on his face (later I'd learn that he was amazed that anyone who had gone to "fancy schools" would want to work "in a dump like this"—even though, not to put too fine a point on it, I did *not* want to work there). Cissy freaked me out because of the mean, witchy cast she had to her face, not to mention her totally crazy-looking, seemingly Halloween-themed dye job. I thought maybe her scowl signified that she was always shunted aside as an older woman in this world of men, so I was careful to acknowledge her and greet her especially, at which point she smiled, and the witchy aspect disappeared entirely.

Well, we had a good meeting on the face of it. They told me they were partnering with a big D.C. firm on the proposal, because it was only together that they'd have the *manpower* to fulfill such *huge, lucrative* interpreting contracts. The D.C. firm already had the *huge, lucrative* contract for this or that arm of the Defense Department or the DOJ or Homeland Security—whatever it was, it was worth *billions*. Dee-Dee licked his lips. That was when I felt my back stiffen. From here the conversation took a different turn, and I began to understand why the place felt so sinister to me.

"So the idea is to get in while the getting's good," Dee-Dee told me, "because you know once Obama comes in . . ." He made a slice at his neck. Have I mentioned all this was taking place late in 2008? Dee-Dee meant, of course, that he feared once Obama took office, he would cut off their livelihood.

Oh, I realized, these people support the war. The war*s*. They support the wars because it's money in their pocket. They are Mutter Courage dragging their wares across the battlefield. I just didn't know people like this. I *did* know people who supported the wars for other bullshit "moral" reasons, but I'd never met anyone who got behind war because it was good business.

"But the other side's good for us too, you know," Dee-Dee went on, beaming his cokehead smile at me. "With Obama there'll be plenty of social services contracts: Medicaid, welfare—all that shinola. You see, Frances, it's a win-win for us. Interpreting's a recession-proof industry."

They were thrilled to make money off other people's misery.

I must get out here, I thought to myself.

"May I call you Franny?" Dee-Dee said suddenly.

"Absolutely not," I said.

After I shook hands with the others, Dee-Dee and I reconvened to talk turkey. I'd quoted him my usual rate on the phone, but in the next few minutes he slashed me down to an hourly rate that was less than half of that. Then he told me that sum was a lot more than what he'd been expecting to pay me, and named a figure that suggested I'd be better off frying up chicken wings on Avenue D. "I'll give you the good money," he said to me, "but don't expect a raise anytime soon—you've screwed yourself out of that." I sat gazing at him as if he were Gogo, the talking dodo.

He also told me they'd be interviewing other people, *so don't get too cocky*. It was hard not to make a flip comment at this, but I held my tongue, which is maybe what twelve years of Catholic school will do to you. He saw me to the door and shook my hand, which I immediately wiped off on my skirt.

I couldn't wait to get home and tell Fitz how wacko the whole place was.

When I got in it wasn't yet noon, and I found Fitz at the kitchen table, chin in hand, doing math calculations on the back of an envelope. He'd made us a big salad for lunch—he was a man who cautiously invited one to admire his handiwork—and even though it was early we were both ravenous, since anxiety had been causing us to pop out of bed fully awake and crazed with money worries at five every morning.

I told Fitz about freakazoid Dee-Dee, planet-struck Petey, witchy Cissy, and worried Will, dwelling for comic effect on the office decor, Dee-Dee's bait-and-switch stinginess, and the all-around hideousness of capitalizing on the misery of others, something *I* could never possibly do. Fitz, with a look of concern—he was a tall, skinny man, with a bit of a stoop and the kind of intelligent, sympathetic face that made women of a certain age want to take his arm—told me I didn't have to take the job. We'd find a way to get by. Well, I said, they probably wouldn't hire me anyway.

Just then the telephone rang, and when I picked it up, it was Cissy asking me could I start tomorrow at eight o'clock?

*

Thus I found myself actually working in that loony bin. I was Alice, abruptly fallen down the rabbit hole, all my nice ideas about myself smarting with insult.

On my first day there, as I sat reading the three-hundred-page Request for Proposal, I looked around at the nearly blank workstation where I sat. That Mrs. Churtie-Matz had been a desolate woman was abundantly clear. Heaped on her desk were manila folders covered with big, looping, I-am-so-angry-I-can-barely-keep-it-together hand-writing saying things like FORMS, FORMS, and OTHER FORMS. Looking inside, I found them all empty. On her overhead shelf, instead of books was a neat row of family-sized boxes of off-brand high-fiber cereal. But what got me was a little picture hanging at eye level directly in front of me. It was a gag picture of a cat sitting at a typewriter and wearing a pince-nez, with the words *You Want It When?* beneath it. What made this so bad—almost physically painful—was the fact that I'd seen this very same picture pinned up in the workstation at my first temp job, some twenty years before.

Twenty years. It seemed impossible.

Looking at that picture of that cat with its stupid pince-nez, I felt like anything I had done or gained or won for myself in those twenty years had vanished. That cat, with its stupid pince-nez, told me that those twenty years of living, of learning, were really just for shit. I was spinning my wheels. I was, for all intents and purposes, just the same clueless, self-deceived, hustling-after-chump-change person I'd been twenty years before. I still reeked of the working class, I hadn't magically become the wise, age-appropriate matron in a twinset making a gift of securities to my Seven Sisters alma mater. I was just twenty years older.

I quietly took the cat with its pince-nez down from the wall and, looking about me, crunched it in my fist and slammed it into the waste-paper basket.

As the days went on and I attempted to adjust to my life's new rhythms, an enormous lassitude came over me. Fitz would pack my lunch each morning, and every day at one o'clock I'd stop work to eat, there at my desk. But this took no time at all, and the monotony of Acme would creep over me, and inevitably I would grab my coat and flee.

On the west facade of Macy's was a big video screen, and sometimes—after hours of notating the RFP and its many hundred pages of addenda—I'd find myself stopping to stare at it and mumble aloud words like "The Macy's Bra Event" with Kaspar Hauser–like fascination. But standing too long on the sidewalk only meant getting violently shoved aside. People were shopping! In the stores on Thirty-Fourth Street you could buy shoes, exfoliators, basketballs, but I'd never been much of a shopper unless you're talking books, and I couldn't afford to buy anything anyway. So instead I'd find myself walking.

It was cold outside. I'd be bundled up in my big black parka, scarf swaddled around my face like Mort from *Bazooka Joe,* but as I walked along Thirty-Fourth Street the December wind blew right through me. Signs of the newly lean times were everywhere, from the heavy traffic in and out of Central Medicaid on the south side of the street, to the number of people lined up for the discount BoltBus to Philly on the north side, to actual signs, such as the sandwich board in front of Soul Fixins' advertising the Bail-Out Special (fried chicken and vegetable) for only $7.99—which seemed like a lot of cash to me.

It was on one of these early, gloomy days that I came upon a church just past Ninth Avenue. It was hemmed in by big buildings and faced in rusticated limestone, with a series of arched doorways leading inside. It was called St. Michael's, after the archangel. This seemed like a good sign, because Saint Michael was a favorite of mine from way back, perhaps because I started life as a child both fanciful and furious and I dearly wanted a sword with which to smite my enemies.

The door was open.

Inside was a big statue of Saint Michael in the famous pose, from Guido Reni: the saint stands *contrapposto* with his weight on his right foot, left foot on the head of Satan. In his hand he holds his sword, and he rears back to bring it down on the devil's writhing neck. I went over to Saint Michael and stood looking at him for a moment. Then I started to cry.

I was crying for my mother. I was crying for my friend Keith, who had died of an AIDS-related illness the year before. Linked in my mind to the death of Keith was the death of my friend Sal, who had died a similarly avoidable death by falling off his fucking roof. None of this I ever got over. I was crying for myself, and for the many things that had been lost.

I was crying for the past, and being young then, and having had expectations.

I realized mass was about to start, and though I was utterly lapsed, disgusted by the politics of the Church, and no sort of "good Catholic" at all, I wiped my face, went to a pew, and sat myself down.

Looking about me, I felt the beauty of the church thrilling me as it would any medieval peasant. It was decorated for Christmas, with great sprays of red poinsettias banking its altar, and though it was cold inside, the silver lamps that hung from the ceiling gave off an aura of comforting warmth. Sitting there, I really did understand how a serf in wooden shoes, covered in mud and wearing burlap underpants, could believe this was the house of God.

As the mass went on I spaced out, as I always had as a child, idly looking at the others in attendance: an older man in a pile-collar coat, a big lady in a yellow hat, a skinny auntie with a floral scarf. I started to fix on the back of a woman who sat a few rows ahead of me. The blue blazer she wore was strange—severely cut, with shoulders padded in an exaggerated style that wasn't really worn anymore. Plus, it was cold outside: where was her coat? I tuned in enough to hear the reading, which, I remember, was full of hectoring, repetitive verses: *I am writing to you, little children . . . I am writing to you, fathers . . . I am writing to you, young people . . .* In typically Catholic fashion I didn't know my Bible, and I found myself wondering if the reading was from Paul, because the guy was always such a dick. Suffer not a woman to teach! Better to marry than to burn! I was about to roll my eyes when I looked up at the very old man reading and saw that he was looking right at me.

He read:

. . . because all that is in the world (the desire of the flesh and the desire of the eyes and the arrogance produced by material posses-

*sions) is not from the Father, but is from the world. And the world
is passing away with all its desires, but the person who does the will
of God remains forever.*

I felt a prick of strange sensation, of odd familiarity. It was the strong,
beautiful language, but it was also the feeling given me by the words
the desire of the eyes. How can I explain this? I blinked through my own
wanting present and those words took me back to Kendra and her family. *The desire of the eyes.* Because my eyes in those days had been filled
with desire.

Kendra Löwenstein. Kendrick Marr-Löwenstein, properly speaking.
The Marr-Löwenstein family, out of the past.

My mind must have flown away thinking about them, because next
thing I knew it was the kiss of peace. I remembered that the handshake
had largely gone out of style since my childhood and more often than
not people would just sort of turn and wave. Each of us was alone on
our island. But the young woman in the blue blazer turned to me and
actually reached her hand across the pew. We shook hands warmly, and
that was when I saw the insignia on her arm and understood: she was
a cop.

Afterward, as I walked down Thirty-Fourth Street, another pair of
cops caught my eye. These were women too, walking arm in arm like
Europeans, both also wearing dress blues; one of them, sharp and cute,
had white gloves tucked under her right epaulette. And when I got to
Seventh Avenue it was as if a dam had burst. Hundreds of cops spilled
out all over the sidewalks outside Madison Square Garden in their
fancy blues, hundreds of them. The academy had graduated new cadets,
of course! And in my mind's eye I saw a thousand white gloves being
thrown into the air all at once, like a huge flock of birds taking wing.

The crush on the sidewalk was abruptly too much for me, and I got
bumped out onto Thirty-Fourth Street. I leapt back up on the curb just
as a bus sailed by, blaring its horn. I had instant crowd panic and I
was almost panting waiting for the light to change. It changed and
I ran across Thirty-Fourth Street, through the moving streams of people, and bounded up on the curb. There was a newsstand at the corner,
and as I turned I caught a glimpse of the front page of the *New York*

Times. I stopped in my tracks. What? What was this elaborate trick? What was this freaky, synchronic moment? Because I looked to see, on the front page of the newspaper, the obituary of Clarice Marr. Kendra's mother.

Oh my God, I thought. The old bitch finally died.

2

... which is not a word I kick around casually, needless to say.

Would it be strange if I told you I was surprised to read that all the kids were still alive? Besides Kendra, there were Bertrand and Cornelia and Gerhardt: four of them. Though none of them could rightly be called a kid anymore. I realized that Cornelia, the youngest, would be thirty-four now, and the eldest, Bert, over fifty. It seemed impossible to think of them as that old.

A song flooded my mind: *Love is pure gold and time a thief...*

But it was the other two who had mattered to me.

Kendra and Jerry.

Jerry and Kendra.

I'd been so fascinated by their names: Kendrick and Gerhardt, spiky little bundles to keep the world at bay. Back then those names had seemed to me so exotic, so cool, so different from the regulation Maureens, Eddies, and Jennifers of my childhood...

*

"That Kendrick Löwenstein," Trina said to me not a week after I'd first met Kendra, "is completely out of her tree."

I remember we were at the student center, McIntosh, waiting on the greaseburger line. They were really fantastically terrible, the burgers they had there, and it couldn't have been any kind of picnic for the women who worked the short-order grills, what with all these impatient entitled girls, some in tip-to-toe Moschino, glaring at the backs

17

of their heads as they waited for their grub. I remember particularly one lady there, whose heavy makeup would melt down her face as she worked the grill—she reminded me of Cruella de Vil—and how she would turn and slap your greaseburger down in front of you when it was ready, implying that it was actually her spleen and daring you to eat it. This might have been part of why Trina and I eventually became vegetarians.

"I swear," Trina was telling me, "the girl was doing the heroin nod in 'Joyce, Eliot, Pound.'"

It would take me a little time to really understand what an excellent judge of character Trina was. I simply hadn't known her long enough at that point. If I had, perhaps I would have listened to her better.

"Maybe she was just tired," I suggested.

"There's tired and then there's your sodden ragdoll head hitting your desk to the rhythms of 'The Hollow Men.'"

It also needs to be said that Trina was always socially smarter and more circumspect than I. The well-adjusted child of a military judge and beautiful Scandinavian mom, she never seemed to have anything to prove. Whereas I, in those days, had a chip on my shoulder the size of Alaska. I was embarrassed by my class background and very often I was fronting, but I had internalized this so much that I often lost track of where reality ended and fiction began. I wanted to be worldly and sophisticated, but really I dragged my peasant prejudices after me as if they were a big bag of deposit bottles.

I was impressed by money.

I was impressed by money, it should be said, for the things it protected you from.

But of course all of us were punk rock back then, and things like money were incompatible with our core beliefs of DIY-ism, smashing the state, going off the grid. Not being like our parents—our complacent parents—who were the root of the problem. Maybe the difference was that my parents were anything but moneyed. They were their own weird subset, the educated but luckless poor, so to be not like them would be to have a savvy career as a Wall Street broker.

Anyway, I remember this particular day was a Friday, because there was a show I wanted to see at the Ritz that night, and it seemed like all my friends were going home for the weekend even though winter break was only a few weeks off. Audrey was going to Pennsy to see her family, Fang was going down to Virginia for some kind of obligation involving her annoying sister, and Trina had decided to hitch a ride with Fang and get dropped off in D.C. to surprise her dad on his birthday. I did have other friends, but they were mostly more interested in reading Husserl in the original German than going to see the Cro-Mags—not that the two were necessarily incompatible—and I found myself staring at the prospect of a Friday night alone. Make no mistake, I was a pretty diligent student, but the idea of staying in and reading my Nochlin—have I mentioned that I was an art history major?—on a Friday night made me completely stir-crazy. It was a bad habit that our father had instilled in his children, I think. Friday was payday in our house, and on payday our dad would come home from work, from his week of teaching remedial reading to adjudicated youth at the county juvie known as Hell's Acres, with candy bars and money for us all. Then we'd pile in the car and tear off to Hoy's 5 & 10 so that we could run down its aisles to find shiny junk to blow the money he had just given us on. He wanted to give us a treat, see us pleased for once, and it's true that this was the most exciting thing in the world to me as a little kid—I still can remember the beautiful crap that I got at Hoy's—but it didn't exactly set up a responsible fiscal model for us.

My dad's favorite candy bar, needless to say, was the PayDay.

I had no love for where I'd come from, a place of haves and have-nots, but, I realize only now that I've lived in New York City for so long, I was still not quite down with how to live in Manhattan back then. Sometimes the wide, blank sidewalks of Broadway in the middle of the night—and somehow I found myself out in the middle of the night all the time—would send a tremor of the deepest aloneness through my body. Trash would blow right down the avenue, and every block or so you'd find a stoic homeless man, covered in a wretched blanket and often sitting up, miserably alert at the devil's hour of three a.m., as if there were no hope for even the escape of sleep.

After we ate our greaseburgers I said good-bye to Trina and, feeling distracted and unsettled, went back to my dorm room. My roommate and I didn't exactly hate each other but didn't exactly get along either. On her side of the room she had hung up hundreds of pictures of herself with millions of her friends in places like Vail, Acapulco, and downtown Dubuque, and oddly, in each of these photos she assumed the exact same smiling pose, as if she were some Zelig-like Bacardi Rum girl. This was a topic of fascination for my friends, who would come over, see the sharp delineation between the two sides of the room, study poor Jackie's photographs, and wonder aloud, *How the fuck did you get a roommate like this?* The answer was that I had been utterly flippant on my roommate form, and in a moment of high spirits wrote on it *I am an extremely silly person!* Truth is, I was a terrible roommate, an arrogant jackass and a smelly snob ready to make fun of anything that moved, so Jackie had a lot to put up with in me. She was a fundamentally decent person. Once when I came in drunk, lit a cigarette in bed, and promptly fell asleep, she knocked the cigarette out of my fingers and slapped down my flaming bedclothes with the copy of *Nueva Revista de Filologia Hispánica* she'd been reading. So it's maybe not such a leap to say that without Jackie Ebersole, I wouldn't be here today to tell this story.

Professor Ebersole, I am told, has an impressive career as a revisionist feminist critic of nineteenth-century Spanish fiction these days.

At any rate, that Friday Jackie had also gone away for the weekend—it could have been that my whole suite was empty, it was so quiet—so I found myself alone, sitting at the window that looked out onto the airshaft and smoking cigarette after cigarette. I tried to work a little. I remember taking out my copy of *Realism* and reading the chapter about death, but when I found myself just staring at a reproduction of Courbet's peasants bowing their heads at the Angelus bell, I put the book down. Eventually it was time for dinner, but I didn't feel like finding someone to sit with in the depressing and near-empty dining hall, so instead I went to the suite kitchen and made a big Dagwood sandwich out of someone else's cold cuts, which were just then starting to get all hard around the edges. I wrote a little note of apology, decorated with pictures of skulls and Jesus's bleeding heart, and put it in the refrigerator where the cold cuts had been.

Eight o'clock found me with the Columbia/Barnard Facebook in hand (which was an actual material thing in those days, a hardback on the order of a yearbook), staring at the entry for Kendrick Löwenstein. The image printed by her name was not Kendra at all but what I recognized to be a Man Ray photo of Kiki de Montparnasse.

She didn't have a campus phone extension listed, just a regular Manhattan number. Did she live with her parents? Did she have her own apartment? I stared at the number, hesitating for a long time, and then finally dialed.

"YES?" a very old, thickly accented voice answered.

"Um, I'm sorry, I think I have the wrong number," I said.

"WHO? YOU WANT WHO?" the very old man said.

"I'm sorry!" I called out.

"THIS IS ALGONQUIN FOUR EIGHT SIX TWO NINE."

I had called the Algonquin Hotel? I stared at the wall, flummoxed. But then I thought of the movie *BUtterfield 8.*

"HELLO, SIR, MY NAME IS CHESS. MAY I PLEASE SPEAK WITH KENDRA?" I yelled.

"HOLD THE LINE!" the very old man said.

There was a crazy amount of noise, as if the phone had been dropped into a bag of cats, and I could hear different voices yelling in the background. I thought about quietly putting the phone down. It seemed impossible that this could be anyplace where Kendra lived, and accidentally dialing into strange lives has always been a special nightmare of mine. But then I heard the receiver being picked up and Kendra's voice distinctly saying, *Zeyde, you know better than to answer the telephone!*

"Hey, Kendra, it's Chess," I said to her, something like amazed.

"Chess!" she called out—and I confess to a warm and sudden tap of feeling in my chest. "Did you have a chat with my gramps? The fella is *starved* for attention."

"You live with your grandfather?"

"Oh, we're all here, driving each other nuts."

It struck me that she seemed to be making an assumption that I knew what her life was like.

"Do you, I don't know, want to go with me to the Ritz and see the Cro-Mags?"

"When?" she said.

I looked at the clock.

21

"Like, now? Like, soon? Like in an hour, actually." I could almost feel myself sweating, as if I were asking her out on a date.

"Geez, I'd have to put my face on," she said, which was not the response I'd been expecting.

"I'm sure your face is fine," I said.

There was silence.

"Kendra?"

"I could meet you there a little after ten," she said.

"Cool!" I said, with real delight.

"But don't be late," she said.

"I never am," I said.

Instead, she was late. She was actually very, very late, and in fact I was drunk as a skunk by the time she got there, or at least by the time we found each other. I am in some ways a deeply shy person, and to overcome this, back in the old days especially, what I would do was drink. Drink my face off. I haven't been to the Ritz in years—it's since reverted back to Webster Hall and apparently it's much cleaner, brighter, and just more all-around fabulous now. In the '80s, though, I remember it as cavernous and dark, with sticky black surfaces and a sour-beer smell, a place where you could get into trouble. And as I remember this night, I was at the bar getting yet another beer with money I didn't have when I felt a yank on my arm, and there was Kendra.

"Hey!" we yelled to each other over the music.

She had made herself up in her exaggerated silent-movie way, but she seemed curiously subdued, or distracted. She was doing something weird with her mouth, sort of popping and clicking her jaw. At that point I didn't know Kendra's complex history of addictions, but I did have an older sister, Olivia, who was a precocious user of a different style of drugs—old-school hallucinogens instead of new-school amphetamines—and who had done herself a world of bad when I was still a kid, which put me off doing anything more than the occasional hit off someone else's bong. So even though I was drunk, I was aware that Kendra was very far away from me on some other high at that moment.

And in no time at all a guy joined us, a guy I always saw at shows at CBGB or at the eighty-five-cent pizza place on St. Mark's, who was

22

forever telling me all sorts of shaggy dog stories about being a roadie for Samhain, being a former member of Murphy's Law, or, incredibly, being the American cousin of one of the founding members of Can, even though when pressed he didn't know any of their names. I was such a confrontational so-and-so at that age that I thought he was challenging me to an I'm-more-punk-rock-than-you pissing contest when in fact what he was doing was hitting on me. I was blind to this, however, until I saw the flirty way Kendra was with him now. She did little head-tilting adjustments and things with her hands—she actually reached out and pulled his cigarettes from his shirt pocket at one point, and then, when he had to "go deal with something," offered to hold his flight jacket for him. It wasn't clear how well she knew him or what the story was, but I felt annoyed, and obscurely jealous. He wore the regulation nonracist skinhead outfit—red laces, red braces—and his name was Dan or Andy or Knucklehead. At any rate, this went on for some time, with him going off to mosh or do whatever important thing he was doing and then coming back to us like we were his waiting band bitches. My resentment was rising. Finally, when he was off again to *have a pee,* as he so descriptively put it, Kendra suddenly turned to me and yelled, "We're getting out of here."

"What?" I said.

"We're getting out of here *now.*"

"Why?" I said.

" 'Cause I totally stole his stash."

"*What?*"

"You heard me!" she said with glee.

I stood there blinking.

"Would you just *put it back*?" I said.

She threw her hands up joyously. What could she do? This time he'd taken his jacket with him.

"Come on!" she said.

She grabbed my hand and suddenly we were running through the club. Have I mentioned that Kendra was kind of a big girl? I mean like a statuesque girl, tall and handsome—no size two shrinking violet this. Everyone practically dove out of our way as we tore through the club, galloped down the steps, and beat it up the street. I had no history of stealing drugs from anyone—of stealing *anything* from anyone, unless you count the dollar I took off Eddie DeLuca's desk in the third grade, something I spent years feeling terribly guilty about—and I was completely freaked out and running for my life, while Kendra was practically hooting aloud and skipping by the time we got to the corner. Eleventh Street runs smack into the back of Grace Church at Fourth Avenue, and it was there that we suddenly heard a furious male voice bark *Hey!* from down the street. Kendra almost ripped my arm out of the socket and then we were tearing south. The girl could really hoof it, and even in the midst of my terror I thought, Geez—I should really cut down on the smoking. We were on the next street booking west and then turning another corner and another one still and I couldn't even tell you where we ran to when she said, *Quick! Duck in!* and we dove into some under-stoop entrance gate. I remember thinking it was crazy that the gate was open, but then somehow she quickly opened the inside door as well. She slammed it behind us.

"What the—?" I said.

"*Shhh!*"

We stood there in the dark, panting. What was this place? All of this seemed random and crazy, but it wasn't punk rock to ask lots of questions. There was a phrase people punted around: *Act like you know.*

And then—*click!*—the light went on, and Kendra was bathed in a jeweled light. Garnet and ruby and emerald on her powder-white face, her eyelashes fluttering long shadows on her cheeks.

"What is this place?" I whispered.

"It's my house," she said, fighting to catch her breath.

"It's your house?" I said.

She nodded vigorously, still catching her breath.

"My parents' house," she said. "Dad and Clarice . . . Clarice the Fabulous . . . who are—thank God—upstate for the weekend . . . Bertie's gone with them . . . but maybe we'll see Jerry if we're lucky . . . actually, we're in a fight right now, so fuck 'im . . . but you can meet Cornelia . . . Cornelia the Priss . . . and my gramps is home. They always try and stuff him in the car, but"—she stopped, gulping for breath—"Jews *hate* the country."

I stood there trying to take all this in when into the circle of jeweled light cast by a colored-glass lamp overhead came a big black cat, twirling itself around my ankles. I crouched down to pet her and she immediately collapsed on her side, offering up her belly for caresses.

"That's Agnes Smedley," Kendra said. "She's a total whore."

I remember laughing, looking up at Kendra. Not knowing then, at all, how important this house and these people would become to me, and how completely they would break my heart.

3

Working at the Acme Corporation, I felt like my world had shrunk to the size of a biscuit.

Mostly I kept my head down and did my work. *You sure are talkative, Frances!* Walt would say, poor, sighing Walt with his crunchy snacks, who, I learned, had earlier that year been downsized from a long-term sales job for a manufacturer of plastic storage devices. No matter the bedlam going on around us, Walt remained calm. On top of the obscenity-filled screaming matches between trash-mouthed Nikki and Vinny, the dispatch manager, sometimes the interpreter requests would come in fast and furious, and the three dispatchers who actually did any kind of work would be juggling receivers, hollering over workstation dividers, trading names and numbers to find interpreters to send to government offices, detention centers, courthouses, everywhere. Orders came in from all over the ravening prison-industrial complex, from all across New York State to as far west as Ohio, as far south as the Chesapeake Bay, and as far north as snowy Vermont. Most seemed to be for Spanish, sometimes with the slant of a certain area—*Colombian Spanish* or *Caribbean Spanish,* a dispatcher would shout—but there'd be orders for Mandarin, Russian, Urdu, Portuguese, Bengali. Sometimes requests would be for a language so obscure I'd find myself Googling it to find out what country it was spoken in. More than once this gave me a picture of a quaint little clapboard courthouse with some sad and specific tragedy playing out inside, half in English and half in Phla, Vepsian, or Kwerba. During one especially frenzied moment, the liveliest dispatcher hopped up on her desk and yelled into the frantic air, *"I need a Twi in Philadelphia!"*

Amid this chaos, Walt always spoke with a compassionate calmness and never said anything bad about anyone. In fact, before essaying any conversation, he seemed to dowse around in himself for a new reserve of goodwill to pull up to his defeated exterior. Walt was so gentle that sometimes I thought he was probably mad as hell—shrieking effing furious—but needed to swallow it lest he go totally berserk and beat the whole crew to death with his computer keyboard.

The owner, Dee-Dee, would come by every once in a while to give me a totally delusional, unwanted, and unnecessary pep talk—*Doin' pretty good, Frances, why this time next year we'll have a whole slew of proposal writers, with you overseeing all of 'em!*—after which he would run back into his office, stab on the speakerphone, and bark like a dog.

Mostly I dealt with Cissy. Since she was Acme's ops manager, I'd often have to go into her office with a question. She'd raise her head and have the angriest and most defensive face imaginable on, which would then blossom into fond smiles when she saw it was me. *What do you need, pumpkin?* she'd ask, and I would feel at once abashed, a little bit sickened, and yet perversely pleased at this. Because I hadn't had a real mother in years.

Anyway, one early visit to Cissy's office, I found her on the telephone, and I signaled that I'd come back. She arched her eyebrows—eyebrows that had been plucked out in their entirety round about 1969, and which she must have drawn on each morning with a fluorescent orange highlighter—and smiled at me, indicating that I should wait.

Suddenly she erupted in a fit of yelling: "I say fire their asses! *Fire their asses!* That girl does nothing! All she does all day is put on friggin' makeup! That whole department does nothing! *Grow a spine,* Dee-Dee!"

I left the room. Of course she was talking about the dispatch team. She had nothing but hatred for Nikki in particular, and not so much because Nikki was an ignorant, lazy dope, which she was, but (so it seemed to me) because Nikki was young and sexually attractive. I had the feeling that Cissy would have gladly thrown all ninety-six pounds of Nikki out the window with no regrets whatsoever.

Sitting there at my desk, thinking these thoughts, with the phones on the dispatch side of the office ringing off the hook, I heard Vinny yell at Nikki, "Answer the fuckin' phone!"

"Answer your fuckin' bald head!" she yelled back.

"Answer the fuckin' phone, you fuckin' piece a shit!"

A steam whistle of exasperation shot out from Nikki and up over the workstation divider that separated us. And then she picked up the phone.

"Yeaaah, Acme Corporation," she said. "What the *fuck*?"

When my first check from Acme came in, Fitz and I raced off to the Indian importer's on First Avenue and bought huge bags of brown rice, lentils, dry beans, and tea for a month, then walked home swaying under the weight of our bundles. We bought water filters, potting soil, jumbo containers of eco-friendly dishwashing detergent, reserve bottles of Dr. Bronner's Peppermint 18-in-1. Back home, we mapped out our meal plan for the week with Clausewitz-like precision. Then we went across town to Citarella and bought two dozen Wellfleet oysters for $37.98.

Have I mentioned that we lived in the East Village?

I'd never really planned on living in the East Village. Reflecting the changing fortunes of New York City neighborhoods, my tribe's place really was Williamsburg, mostly Northside but Southside too. Fitz had a few years on me, so he was more of that early '80s East Village generation, and when he and his old friends got together, they'd reminisce about long-gone things like Save the Robots, The World, Gracie Mansion's gallery, Dean and the Weenies, and the sad, strange career of Rockets Red Glare. But the low rents that had helped anything cool flourish there were pretty much gone by the time I graduated from college. Similarly, after my time in Williamsburg, it became mostly closed to new crops of cash-poor creative transplants, and Greenpoint had filled up too. New luxury housing gobbled up space and squeezed out everyone below a certain income level, so people moved east to Bushwick, up into Queens, or to parts of Brooklyn that felt to me so far-flung you might as well have been walking on the moon.

Anyway, I'd long ago planted my feet on the soil of Brooklyn and planned on keeping them there. But once I got with Fitz, it was easy enough to leave my Southside apartment and come back over the water for a fifth-floor walk-up. Even as the new brand of greed, the post-9/11 grab-the-shit-you-want-and-screw-these-loser-poor-people greed, started running amok through this city of ours and new buildings rose around us on all sides, making us feel like we were in "The Cask of Amontillado," getting bricked in alive.

The day we went across town to Citarella's, I asked Fitz if he wouldn't mind walking home along Eleventh Street. I didn't have to explain to him why, even though this stuff was ancient history. But what's funny is that for years I'd managed never to walk down that particular block. Past that particular house. I guess it's easy enough to avoid, but even so.

Even so.

When I saw it, I actually stepped back and put my hand to my chest. It felt like a physical blow. I stood looking up at the house and at the blue shingle hanging in front of it. The windows of the house once so beloved were filthy.

It was empty. It was up for sale.

I'd read that Clarice had been predeceased by her husband, Sidney, but somehow I thought . . . Oh, what had I thought?

I turned and kept walking. Fitz caught up with me, took my hand, and said nothing, leaving me to my romantic notions of loss. He had history there too.

"Why don't they wash the windows?" I found myself saying to him.

Why don't they wash the windows?

*

The morning after I first slept over, I remember, it was the light that awakened me, the winter morning light from the south-facing windows, French doors that gave out onto a terrace that overlooked a garden. I remember lying there, disoriented, feeling something curious going on with my scalp, almost as if it were actually rippling with my hangover in some articulated cartoon way. I opened my eyes to see a little girl with a serious face bending over me, attempting to comb my uncombable hair.

"Hi," I said to her, blinking.

"Who are you?" she wanted to know. She was kneeling on a chair pulled over to the bed, holding an enormous, antique-looking comb

29

and peering into my face with somber curiosity. She had a fretful, lop-sided look.

"Chess," I said.

"That's your *name*?" she said. She was ten or eleven, but she talked like a little schoolteacher.

"It's really Francesca, but nobody calls me that," I told her.

"That's really better," she decided.

"Are you Cornelia?" I asked her.

She tilted her chin up, as if to meet a challenge.

"I am," she said.

I am. She was like Kendra in that she seemed almost chillingly poised, used to being looked at. All the siblings shared this, I would see: the professional grace of children all but raised in public. She had the same pale skin as Kendra but a different demeanor—much less languid, less heavy-lidded and indolent. Her face had a cruel severity for a little girl and an almost planar smoothness. She looked like a stolid little businessman, worried because his train was late. But there was something odder to her still. I realized that she had different-colored eyes: one brown, one half green, half brown.

"Are you black?" she asked me.

"Black? Um, not so much," I said.

"You have very ethnic hair," she said to me.

"Is that a good thing?" I wanted to know.

I rolled over to sit up and found Kendra propped up and looking at a huge, illustrated copy of *Louise de la Vallière*.

"Sorry, she just does that," she said to me.

"Sorry, she just does what?" Cornelia wanted to know.

"Loves being the Annoyance Factor," Kendra said.

"You are so *fat* it's shameful," Cornelia said, resting back on her haunches and sliding into a sitting position on her chair.

"Hogface," Kendra said to her. She had her hair tied up in a tropical-print wrap and what looked to be cold cream lathered on her face, like someone's mother from the '50s. "Criminal hogface," she went on blithely, "revolting, stunted character. Wretched, horrid fussbudget."

Cornelia studied her as if to come up with the perfect insult.

"Hideous flower of rosacea," she finally said.

Kendra turned a shocked, sullen face to her.

"That was really very cruel," she said quietly.

Surprisingly, Cornelia was instantly crestfallen.

"Really beyond cruel," Kendra said, looking down.

"I'm sorry," Cornelia whispered, sliding farther down into her chair.

Kendra suddenly looked back up.

"Filthy little *Jew!*" she yelled, bounding out of bed as Cornelia shrieked and leapt from her chair. I pulled up into a ball as they ran around the room and jumped across the bed—Kendra in her rainbow-striped knicker-length nylon romper pelting Cornelia with slippers, throw pillows, and, repeatedly, a giant stuffed strawberry. Then Kendra caught Cornelia's ankle and she screamed and thrashed and kicked until the whole thing dissolved into tickles.

I have to say, I felt embarrassed to hear someone use the word "Jew" like that. It was shocking and it confused me. Later I'd come to understand the way the Löwenstein siblings talked, with their slippery little mouths . . . I thought at first it was a kind of self-loathing. Later I'd realize it was a throw-it-back-in-your-face thing to people who really did say things like "filthy Jew." (And later still I would learn what the root of it all was: what Clarice's mother called her daughter's fiancé when she announced her engagement.) But I was stunned when I first heard it, because I grew up in a household where if you said anything like that when you were a kid, if you were stupid enough to, for instance, try out the *n*-word, you would be slapped right across the mouth.

It was a bright winter day. I had no memory of coming up the stairs the night before, but in those days I often drank to the point of blacking out, so this was nothing new. I remember the morning light in Kendra's room so well, that first time, but I was to spend so much time in that house that I can't properly remember my first impression of it. Beautiful things would often hush me, so maybe the memory is buried with that silence.

I remember going down to the parlor floor alone that morning and pausing to look in the front room. The tall curtains were pulled against the light. And then I realized there was a man sitting in there, a very old man in a wheelchair. He must be blind, I thought.

"Kendra, that's you?" he said to me.

31

I cleared my throat.

"It's her friend, Chess."

"Open the drapes," he said to me.

So he was not blind? But just sitting there in the dark, no one to help him?

I crossed the room and opened the curtains.

"Turn me around," he said then.

I wheeled him around in my confident yet inept way and we both were at the window, looking out on Eleventh Street. He was scanning the street with great expectancy.

"What happened to my father?" he said.

"Your father?"

"My father was right here," he said, pointing his gnarled hand toward the window.

I felt shy about looking directly at him, but I did. His eyes were milky with cataracts, but he was able to see somewhat, because he was tilting his head around to find the sweet spot. He'd been a big man, I could tell, and still gave the impression of hardiness, of toughness, even hunched in a wheelchair. He had a singular appearance, with his bald head covered in liver spots and trimmed with a small, countable number of discrete white hairs, his large, waggly ears, his incongruous cupid's-bow mouth, his cloudy eyes and mashy prizefighter's nose. I found myself thinking of the Jewish Mafia, mug shots of Monk Eastman, Louis Lepke, people like that. He looked very, very old to me, and the idea of his father existing I chalked up to dementia. And yet he seemed lucid enough.

"Shit," he said, "not my father ... my *father*." He tilted his head around, looking at me as if I could give him the answer. I heard Kendra bounding down the stairs and I felt great relief.

"MORNING, ZEYDE!" she called out.

"I'm not deaf, you know," he said.

"Sure you're not, honey!" she said, kissing him on his head, while he, turning from her, resumed looking out the window.

"What was my father, there?" he said, more annoyed than confused.

He's looking for the car, she mouthed to me.

"They drove it upstate," Kendra explained. "Sidney and Clarice and Bert went upstate to the house, remember?"

"Upstate!" he said. "*That* they can have!"

Kendra looked at me with a twinkling little smile. She loved this guy, her grouchy old gramps, her *zeyde* (which I honestly thought was his name and which, in fact, I called him to his face all the time I was to know him, not understanding that it was Yiddish for "grandfather"; but he never took issue with it, so I think maybe he didn't mind). I would think years later that maybe her *zeyde* was the only person Kendra really loved, completely and without conditions. Maybe because he was powerless, nearly helpless? She could demand only so much of him, and so he would never fail her.

She clicked down the brake to his wheelchair—I saw that she had put on ridiculous, denim-trimmed platform sandals, a quilted satin bolero, and a kind of sarong picked out with beadwork—and announced in a cartoon-posh voice that we would be going into the "solarium," where, it turned out, Cornelia had laid out breakfast for four, with extremely formal place settings involving grapefruit spoons and napkin rings.

*

"Did you ever notice that Kendra dresses like a drag queen?" one of my wiseacre friends said soon after this, as the four of us—Trina, Audrey, Fang-Hua, and I—sat together in the dining hall, John Jay, over the remains of our dinner.

Memory is imperfect, but it was most likely Fang-Hua, who, as a self-punishing dancer, comp lit major, worshipper of the Frankfurt School, and hoity little reverse snob—her family had come over from mainland China when Fang was little, and her father had gone from being a teacher to being a mechanic—was extremely critical of other people. Which was something we had in common, and for similar reasons. Her criticality, however, most often manifested itself in judgments about people's weight and looks, whereas I was much more likely to brand a person stupid, shallow, sheeplike, but neither of us had exclusive rights to either course of criticism. What charming, well-adjusted eighteen-year-olds we were. Fang and I shared the idea, unspoken but understood, that much of life was about having your back up against the wall, better to fight My War. She and Trina both came from the greater D.C. area, and this being at the height of second-wave D.C. hardcore—a golden age!—they had a whole scene down there that they shared and that provided meaning and identity for them, something I was more than a little jealous of. The fourth in our group was Audrey, who came from a Nowheresville similar to the one I'd come from, a town where, as she once put it, *People still say "colored."* She was an artist and an introvert and without a doubt my closest friend during the first two years of college. When I first knew Audrey, she was a deep, contradictory, haunted person, a lover of Lucien Freud, the English band Crass, Harley-Davidsons, and the romance of her own family, which her brother Ciaran, well in his cups, once famously character-ized as The Walking Irish Tragedy. Audrey's father was a college profes-sor, and her mother taught piano at a Montessori school. To my mind, there was a safety net in her life (as there was in Trina's) that people like Fang and me didn't really have, even though Audrey would try to tear her net to shreds. Meanwhile, Kendra's safety net was that much bigger, that much stronger, and her will to destroy it, and herself, that much fiercer as well. But I'm getting ahead of myself. In the late '80s we were just teenagers, freshmen, with our tics and our mouths and our wants, coming together, hungry for experience and knowledge and sensation.

Kendra wasn't on meal plan, so you didn't see a lot of her on campus. What was her deal, anyway? Everyone wanted to know. There were all kinds of rumors about her. That she'd been a dancer as a child, a young prodigy at the School of American Ballet. That her mother was some big literary muckety-muck, although the name Löwenstein rang no bells with any of us. When Kendra was spotted around the neighbor-hood, it was almost never in class but in places like the Night Cafe, a dive bar on Amsterdam, where she was seen with some roving-handed older guy, snorting coke in the men's room. Stories like this freaked me out, because I wanted to see her as my friend, but hard-line me just couldn't get with this kind of behavior. I told Trina, Audrey, and Fang all about the adventures the weekend before—leaving out the part about Kendra stealing Knucklehead the Nonracist Skin's stash, and also the fact that the next day, not long after breakfast, she was already mad deep into what she called her "Saturday morning chill-out," which involved bunches of little pink Percocets. She'd asked me if I wanted some, and I was pretty frank in telling her that while I drank like a fish, pills and things you snort and any shit like that just weren't my cup of tea. This attitude was shared pretty much by Trina and Fang, children of the straight-edge scene, while Audrey, like Kendra, would generally gobble up anything in the name of having a transformative experience. Anyway, I remember Kendra sighing deeply when I told her this on that Saturday morning, as if I'd confirmed a guessed-about aspect, perhaps peasantish, of my personality. Not long after, however, we were bundled up and walking around the Village, and I felt happy as a clam to be with her.

It was a beautiful winter day. Her family had long been in the neighborhood, and as we walked she'd point out a building here or there and tell me something about its history: a narrow house on West Twelfth Street that had in fact been cut in half, the little gate that led to Patchin Place, where Djuna Barnes and e. e. cummings used to live, the apartment building named for Albert Pinkham Ryder, a painter of great appeal to the young and mystical. Toward Sixth Avenue was the tiny, triangular cemetery of Shearith Israel, the Spanish and Portuguese synagogue, and, on the avenue, the great Gothic stack-up of the Jefferson Market Library, beside which, Kendra told me, there used to be a ghastly, light-blocking women's prison, where she remembered seeing as a very little girl women hanging out the windows to throw down notes to their lovers on the street.

And of course there was what Kendra and her siblings called "the Blown-up House," which was an object of fascination for them. One can read about it all over the Internet now, but back then information about the Blown-up House had a kind of samizdat quality: it was where members of the Weather Underground accidentally detonated a bomb meant for, by some reports, the tunnel system under Columbia University. (What's funny was that not long after Kendra showed this house to me, two Columbia students in our year entered the realm of bubble-headed myth by stealing uranium-238 from somewhere in that same tunnel system.) In the window of the Blown-up House—which had a cornice and top row of windows in line with the other Greek Revivals on the block, but a protruding modernist treatment on the two floors below, as if the facade were a pivoting door that had been pushed in on one side only to jut out on the other—Kendra pointed out to me the bear. It was a Paddington Bear that, she told me, the owners would dress up according to the weather. The Weather Bear. It was wearing a wintry ensemble on that day. Its existence in that window seemed to her to underscore the comparative toothlessness of the times we lived in, the Reaganomic '80s.

At that point in my life, I just didn't know anyone who could do this, who knew secret histories, who could point to a place and tell you what it was witness to, what had happened there, what a building was "doing" and why this was so. I was always looking for signs, for secret gestures, in the city where I grew up, but it was a dull, conservative place, and things like this were rare. I looked nonetheless, and I do remember not long before I left for college walking under a construction shed in that city's paltry downtown and doing a double-take when I saw, on the plywood wall, a naïf painting of a woman with this written underneath: *Young Lesbian Girl Crying at the Funeral of Alice Neel.* I stopped and stared at it. It seemed amazing to me that anyone in that soul-crushing city would know anything about the existence of lesbians, let alone Alice Neel. It must have been some kind of temporary public art, and I remember I found myself looking around me, as if to find out who had done this and meet them. But I was alone.

After we walked around the Village that Saturday, Kendra and I got a slice at Stromboli's on University and sat in the window making obnoxious noises with our drinking straws and looking at the people passing by. Some of them were neighbors of the Löwensteins, and Kendra seemed to have stories about them all, culled from years of studying their habits with Harriet the Spy–like intensity. Such-and-such was a famous stage actor and a drunk, putatively straight but who wore a marabou-trimmed wrap around the house—she'd once seen him close the arm of it in his dishwasher and stay stuck there for a full hour. Such-and-such made what Kendra called "loud sex sounds" that echoed through the backyard canyons of their block. Such-and-such would stand at her kitchen sink washing her hands like Lady Macbeth and singing "The Surrey with the Fringe on Top."

It was starting to get dark—the early dusk of winter—and I had to get back uptown and get cracking, seeing as how I had a paper for my Latin class due on Monday that I'd barely started. Kendra walked me to Union Square, and it was there that she began a strange little pleading routine, as if we were lovers about to part. Did I have to go back already? We could make dinner and watch movies at her house. I was flattered that she was enjoying my company so much, and it was tempting to stay. But I really did have work to do; didn't she? Kendra waved this away, as if to suggest that school was the least of her concerns. I kept telling her I was sorry, I really did want to stay, and we did one of these complex multiple-good-bye back-and-forth dance routines at the subway entrance. When we finally said good-bye, we hugged and I ran down the steps to the subway, not looking back in case I lost my nerve. I touched my face and found there some of the extreme-white foundation makeup that Kendra used, I understood now, to hide her rosacea. And on the train I thought about how it seemed like she had tears in her eyes when we parted.

These things I did tell my friends in the dining hall some version of, jerk that I was. Mostly I was—and they were—annoyed by Kendra's lack of seriousness about school. Because if you messed up and flunked out, then what? Go back to your town of Bumblebee, Pennsyltucky, and get a job flipping burgers at the DQ? Go to the local community college in better-living-through-chemistry land so you can get a secretarial certificate and a typing gig? Similarly, when those dopey Columbia guys got busted for stealing the uranium-238 from the tunnel some weeks later, my friends and I had nothing but scorn for them. Does this life mean so little to you, our thinking was, that you would do something that meaninglessly stupid and screw it all up? Again, it seemed to us that these were the actions of seriously entitled kids who, if they fell, had a hundred strong arms to catch them.

And yet I felt myself growing protective of Kendra, who it seemed to me had a face made for tragedy.

It's funny; eventually I'd introduce Audrey to Kendra—something about their, how to say, ability to withhold judgment suggested that they'd get along—and the three of us would sometimes go together to Zooprax, the Barnard film society, to see great old things like *The Major and the Minor* and *Angels with Dirty Faces*. But I knew Fang and Trina would have no interest in the likes of Kendra at all. And in fact I was all too aware that Trina was looking at me in her canny way with her amber eyes as I told these stories. After we'd all finished smoking and put out our cigarettes, I'm ashamed to admit now, right in the remains of our dining-hall dinners (I can picture a Camel Filter plunged into the blameless side of a barely touched slice of sponge cake), we all wearily picked up our satchels and trudged off to our various places of work and/or study. Audrey headed to Havemayer, Fang to Avery, Trina to her dorm, and I to my job at Burgess-Carpenter, which was at that time the cool library within the hulking mass of Butler, cool not only for its wonderful holdings but because the guy who oversaw the work-study students was very understanding of angry young punk-rock kids and, as a bonus, played in a Yo La Tengo–ish band with his wife, whom I remember to be an extremely short person and an almost preternaturally awesome guitarist.

Anyway.

Trina lingered with me a moment—we of course had to pollute our lungs with another cigarette before parting—and I remember she said to me something like, *It's not that I don't think Kendra's nice and all, but maybe you should watch your back.*

4

It should probably be stated that once I was infatuated with a person, I displayed very little talent for watching my back.

Also, I'm probably making this sound like I was one cool customer, rolling with the punches, taking things as they came, etc., but in reality I was an extremely self-conscious, consistently second-guessing, routinely defective personage. I wanted to be all hard and bad and not caring, but really I was just about as tough emotionally as your cake-baking granny.

But neither was I one of those weepy, sentimental teenagers. I hadn't gone out for any high school theater group, I did not write lavish how-I-will-miss-you notes in friends' yearbooks, I did not believe in group hugs. I was suspicious whenever I saw lots of people all doing the same thing at the same time. At my all-girls Catholic high school, sometimes they'd make us assemble for whatever reason on the bleachers in the gymnasium—there was, for example, an annual faculty-student volleyball game, just the kind of thing to make you want to projectile vomit—and at the end of the day, Brother Zuppa-de-Zum would lead the prayer, *In the name of the Father, and of the Son . . .* And since the great banks of bleachers faced each other on either side of the gym, you would see two hundred girls all crossing themselves at the same time, like a synchronized stadium wave, and you would understand that you were on the other side, with the two hundred other girls, subsumed into this stadium wave yourself. And if you were like me, you preferred not to.

Anyway, after that conversation in the dining hall, strangely enough, Kendra began showing up on campus.

I was at my work-study job, doing the thing they called "shelf-reading" one day—which consisted of looking at the spine of each book on a given set of shelves to make sure the order of the call numbers was correct, and which was kind of a useless activity, since things in Burgess-Carpenter were in shockingly good order, which perhaps proves that angry punk-rock kids make conscientious book shelvers—when she appeared. Actually, by that point in the semester it had become clear to me that being sent off to shelf-read actually meant *Go disappear into that room for two hours, young person, and do whatever you like!* And so I would go, take Elsa Morante's *History* down from the shelf, make myself comfortable in a hidden corner of the floor, and read until my time was up. In this way I actually read that whole 555-page novel while in the employ of Columbia that semester. So I was off in a corner reading Morante when I looked up, and there stood Kendra.

"Do you want to go get a drink?" she asked me.

It was just about three in the afternoon.

"Strange to say, I'm actually working."

She tilted her head to the side and gave me a devilish eye.

"I totally have an urge for shake-and-bake right now," she said.

"Shake-and-bake?" I said with low seriousness, not wanting to appear ignorant about drug varieties.

She rolled her eyes at me.

"Chicken, honey! That shit with the beet coloring and modified food starch and all that crap—*mmm!*" she said in a pretend southern drawl. She stuck out her hand and pulled me to my feet, and that day I clocked out early.

The rest of that semester was all sewed up: it was go to class, go to work, hang out with Kendra, and study when I could. Sometimes she'd convince me to blow off the dining hall and we'd go to her dorm kitchen to make dinner, which invariably consisted of some junk-food thing she couldn't have at home because Clarice was such a *fascist WASP*. Weekends, when Kendra's parents and brother Bert were up at the country house, we'd hang out at Eleventh Street, ostensibly because Kendra had to watch Cornelia and Zeyde—her brother Jerry never appeared—but really because despite everything, Kendra loved being in that house, that world, and maybe understood how much I did too. It wasn't long into this scene when I came to understand that her mother, the Clarice she was always referring to, was Clarice Marr.

Clarice Marr!

I should mention that I grew up in a house full of books. My father was an equal-opportunity book buyer, a man with a BA, an EdM, and a JD who nonetheless believed that every book ever produced had some kind of wisdom to impart. Child of the Depression who carried that Depression on his back all his waking hours, he trawled library sales, flea markets, and discount stores, buying books for his kids, for himself, for his incarcerated students up at Hell's Acres (who were generally appreciative of Dr. Varani's kindnesses, except for the boy who set a copy of *Otto of the Silver Hand* on fire and threw it at my father's head). In our house we had incomplete runs of long-defunct encyclopedia sets, easy-eye editions of *Erewhon* and *The First Men in the Moon* that had something like five lines to the page, automotive manuals, Time Reading Program Special Editions of books by Agnes Newton Keith and John P. Marquand that smelled strongly of glue and whose spines would loudly and irreparably crack when you opened them, multiple copies of *Robert's Rules of Order*, enormous and contradictory histories of the Black Plague, the Great Game, and the Expedition of the Thousand, issues books from the '50s and '60s like *Why Johnny Can't Read, The Power Elite, Soul on Ice, The Hidden Persuaders*, big nostalgic scrapbooks with names like *I Remember Distinctly*, Fighting Forces Series paperbacks about the fish, plant, and reptile life of the Pacific, and cool-looking things that yielded little explanation when seven-year-old me tried to read them, such as *Pedagogy of the Oppressed, The Wretched of the Earth*, and *Extraordinary Popular Delusions and the Madness of Crowds*—that last was quite something, but I stuck with it for one whole afternoon round about 1976. My terminally furious, righteously indignant dad also had hundreds of law books and journals, self-improvement books that concentrated on positive thinking—ha!—and how to get ahead in the world. Besides all these, there was my mother's humble stock of art and architecture books, her large stock of devotional literature—she had a special interest in stigmatics, beheaded or disemboweled martyrs, and saints beset with any sort of skin affliction—and her much-read pamphlets on topics such as the coming of the Antichrist, Venerable Edel Quinn, and the Great Chastisement. I am actually not doing justice to the breadth of books that were packed double-deep and in no particular order in the bookshelves of our house. I remember, as an early teen, the friend of one of my brothers saying to me, *I always like coming to your house because there's always so much to read*—he was holding a copy of *One-Dimensional Man* in his hand, though I didn't know who Marcuse was at the time—and how I sniffed at him, offended, because I had been to his house, his palatial house in the north part of the city, which was equipped with a swimming pool, a laundry chute, multiple bathrooms, and an Anglo lawn jockey, and I thought he was making fun of our crummy little row house. But it turned out that he was sincere. Now I appreciate these things, but for many years of my life I saw only what I did not have.

What I did not have, and wanted so much.

At any rate, amid curios like *I Saw Red China* and library-sale paperback bargains by Frances Parkinson Keyes, I came across a book with a photograph of a very striking woman on the back of it. The book was a big '70s-looking thing with a title in the swoopy, chunky typography used on a lot of books by women in that era, and the writing inside didn't interest me so much as did the photo of the woman, who sat at a desk in an elegant room lined with bookcases. In her hand is a cigarette with an agonizingly long ash, which she holds beside her cheekbone. She looks directly into the camera with a thick, studied insouciance, and her arched eyebrows give an imperial cast to her face. Actually, the woman reminded me of no one so much as Tallulah Bankhead.

Clarice Marr. That particular book, *Waxen Minds, Marble Wills,* I was to find out much later, was her one crossover hit, and it had dated badly, not unlike the other issues books kicking around our house (*Famine 1975!*). It was the kind of book that was refuting another book about some very specific midcult moment that was perhaps refuting *another* book, but the linkages had been lost to history. When I finally read it, I found it mostly boiled down to an embarrassing defense of what could only be called female exceptionalism. But that came later, once I knew Clarice. And knowing her, let's just say, colored my judgment.

In college, Clarice Marr was just a name. She wrote essays, I knew, and I classed her with Susan Sontag in my mind, though somewhat down the ladder and minus the boots and the cool and the skunk stripe. Years later, when I was so much in her company, Clarice would always be going on about how *we're only allowed to have one female public intellectual at a time,* and because of the mere bad luck of her having started publishing later than Sontag, she had to walk forever in the woman's shadow. Maybe it was because of this that Clarice endlessly insisted on herself, lavishing superlatives on her own work, complimenting her reflection in the mirror, implying that any woman around her, insightful or lovely or intellectually nimble though she might be, was strictly Amateur Night.

One late hungover morning Kendra, Cornelia, and I had been playing hide-and-go-seek, with Zeyde temporarily left alone in the parlor, listening on his little orange transistor radio to the station named for Eugene V. Debs, WEVD, which at that time still had some Yiddish-language programming. Kendra had never really given me a tour of the house, and so I just followed her lead and went where she did, roaming up and down and all over its floors. That is, except for the master bedroom. Kendra never seemed to open that door.

Sometimes we'd go to her brother Bertrand's bedroom and snoop. It was an amazing room, a *Wunderkammer,* filled with very particular collectibles such as antique electric fans, bone-handled penknives, vintage hatboxes artfully stacked in order of descending size, and an entire wall of turn-of-the-century hand-tinted postcards of impossible places like Örebro, Sebastopol, and Île de Salagnon. Kendra didn't get along with Bertrand and especially hated the fact that he worked as their mother's secretary: *What a successful parasite,* she would hiss. She also hated the excruciatingly neat order he kept his sock drawer in, and she was always yanking it open and messing up what she called his *candy-ass gangster hose*—men's silk dinner socks, stored with rolls of colored tissue paper stuck into them—or leaving an old and curiously disgusting-looking jar of Nutella nestled in their midst. From Bertrand's room there were double doors leading to a kind of storage area and, on the other side of it, pocket doors that led to the master bedroom. Sometimes the doors were left slightly open and one could almost see in, but Kendra never entered that room.

That day playing hide-and-go-seek, as Cornelia counted *one Mississippi, two Mississippi* loudly up to one hundred, I soundlessly ran up the stairs until I found myself in Bertrand's room. I tried under the bed, but it was too low, and then I found myself in the storage passage, thinking I could close myself in the tall, narrow linen closet (I was about a hundred pounds at the time). Then I heard Cornelia speed up her counting, and I squeezed through the pocket doors into the master bedroom.

I stared. The curtains were half closed against the light, but even so I could see it was the most extravagant room in the house. Except for Kendra's rumpus room and sleeping quarters, the Marr-Löwenstein abode was in impeccable taste, but this room looked like the set of some naughty operetta.

An enormous bed filled the room, canopied and festooned with swags of stiff pink-and-silver stuff that trailed to the floor. The same fabric, gathered and ruched and overabundant, hung before the tall windows, which flanked a gilt-edged pier glass. A recamier in contrasting silk stood by one of the windows, and there was a rococo *coiffeuse*, a vanity, with another big mirror, this one framed in bunchy, curling garlands of carved and painted roses, with a low, tufted stool in a more sedate Directoire style before it. On the marble mantel of the fireplace sat a big silver loving cup stuffed full with dried hydrangeas, and over it hung a gloomy nightscape of a wood in the style of Ralph Albert Blakelock, which seemed out of place in the room, it being so dour and lonely. That was when my eyes landed on the photograph of Clarice Marr. I went around the bed, picked it up, and gazed at it. And as I held it in my hands, my mind did a kind of delayed, exhausted *Oh.*

Oh. Clarice. *That* Clarice.

And looking about this silken, tufted, overdone, feminine-in-the-worst-way room, all silvers and golds and pinks, I couldn't help but think that Kendra never came into it because she was disgusted by the idea of her mother having sex.

"You're supposed to *hide*, Francesca!" Cornelia, exasperated, said to my back.

I put the photograph in its heavy frame down again, and I turned to her. But she had seen me looking.

"Isn't it beautiful?" Cornelia breathed out.

"Yes," I said, and I surprised myself by the unexpected ardor in my voice.

There was some noise in the hallway. The door opened, and Kendra stuck her head in. She looked from me to Cornelia and back again.

"Let's get out of here," she said coldly.

Kendra liked nothing so much as the Saturday morning chill-out: to hole up in what she called the rumpus room, which looked out on the backyard, with cinnamon toast and picture books, mountains of pillows on the floor, favorite movies in the VCR, lolling around in pajamas late into the afternoon, having pizza for lunch. The only thing that kept this from being what a lucky ten-year-old did was Kendra's obligatory inclusion of Percocets, Vicodins, or at the very least codeine. Valium and such sedatives only made you "flat," Kendra explained to me, like any competent research chemist, and were no fun at all. You needed a good painkiller to "take the edge off." Conversely, amphetamines were only for nighttime. Back in the city where I grew up, which was a lickety-split exit off the popular Miami-to-Maine I-95 drug-trafficking corridor, I would think of anyone who knew as much about illicit psychopharmacology as a hopeless loser, but with Kendra it was something else entirely. We spent so much intense time together so quickly that in fact I became magically immune to Kendra's quirks and contradictions.

For example, my crew all liked to think that we were, as Fang-Hua would say, *punk as fuck,* but when I hung out at the house on Eleventh Street, it became clear that Kendra's heart really belonged to Tin Pan Alley. She liked show tunes. It would be hard to explain exactly how uncool this was at that time. The Löwensteins had a baby grand piano in the parlor—*the absolute ruin of a room,* Kendra would say with mock disdain, paraphrasing Elsie de Wolfe, which I of course didn't know back then—and one Sunday morning when it began to snow hard, she ordered Cornelia in from the kitchen downstairs (where she often could be found making freaky old desserts like war cake or cherries jubilee) and told her she wanted to sing. Cornelia had great piano-playing chops for an eleven-year-old, and she opened the lid and did some crazily good Fats Waller–style glissandos up and down the keyboard.

I went and wheeled in Zeyde from the solarium, pulled over a chair, and sat to listen.

Kendra, who had briefly disappeared, made her entrance. We all turned to look. She wore a glamorously tattered kimono and, tied around her hips, a fringed scarf. Dangling from her ears were big chandelier earrings, and on her head was a lamé toque with a mashed feather aigrette. In one gloved hand she held a long cigarette holder, a red Fantasia burning in it. She crossed the room, turned haughtily to her audience, and leaned against the piano in a seen-it-all-sucker posture. She turned to Cornelia, whose dangling feet in blue PRO-Keds barely reached the pedals, and gazed upon her for some moments with a weary Marlene Dietrich stare. Then she gave Cornelia the chin, signaling her to start.

Cornelia played an introduction that I didn't recognize, drew it out to a lugubrious length, then tipped her head somberly to Kendra, who began to sing with a laden heart:

> When the only sound in the empty street
> is the heavy tread of the heavy feet
> that belong to a lonesome cop . . .
> I open shop.
> When the moon so long has been gazing down
> on the wayward ways of this wayward town
> that her smile becomes a smirk,
> I go to work.

" 'Love for Sale'!" Zeyde said to me, turning. "It's a heartbreaker!"

Never mind that the idea of singing a song about a streetwalker to your eighty-seven-year-old grandfather was, to me, crazy obscene. But. No one in that house ever noticed any eccentricity in their own behavior.

In truth, Kendra had an amazing voice, big on charm and mimicry, mannered in a much earlier era's hyper-enunciated way, a bit like Gertrude Lawrence or one of those people who sound so odd to the ear now; but then she could drop her pitch and really belt it out. In the house were piles of sheet music with elaborately illustrated covers, some of it predating the Great War (I remember particularly a piano rag called "The Oceana Roll," with its drawing of a big ship billowing oddly ominous-looking black smoke against a border of jolly fish, smiling chairs, and dancing sailors—the *Titanic* hadn't yet sunk). After Kendra's little recital, which would be repeated numerous times on those winter Sundays, we'd all find ourselves around the piano: Kendra, me, Cornelia at the keys, even Zeyde, and we'd crowd together and sing standards in our quartet of barnyard voices. We'd sing "Georgia on My Mind" and "You're the Top," "Too Marvelous for Words" and "Lookie, Lookie, Here Comes Cookie," we'd sing train-travel songs like "Chattanooga Choo-Choo" and "On the Atchison, Topeka and the Santa Fe." We'd sing "Our Love Is Here to Stay" and gaze upon each other with big, sentimental eyes. Cornelia for whatever reason loved novelty songs like "Abercrombie Had a Zombie" and, amazing to relate, something called "Who Put the Benzedrine in Mrs. Murphy's Ovaltine?" ("Now she wants to swing the Highland Fling . . .") I have a terrible voice and an absolute tin ear, I can't carry a tune even if it's handed to me in a ziplock bag, but the delight I took in singing around the piano with the Löwenstein family was, I have to say, tremendous.

Needless to say, back uptown, I made no mention of these deeply uncool activities.

I was seeing my other friends, of course, doing my work for school, attending to my job in the library, but it felt to me like real life was lived on Eleventh Street, on the weekends.

Kendra and I could get very silly, and we both liked absurd things and ridiculous contrasts. She had a riotous appreciation for Emily Post's *Blue Book* and was in possession of a copy from the 1920s, which she loved to read aloud from, making us dissolve in glee.

"'At times a few words of explanation make the introduction of a stranger smoothly pleasant,'" she read with a didactic, lock-jawed delivery. "' 'Mr. Worldly! Miss Jenkins—her pen-name is Grace Gotham.' "

Or, "'Mr. Neighbor, I should like you to meet Mr. Dusting—he has just returned from Egypt, where he's been searching for buried Pharaohs.'"

"Mr. Vanderslice!" I would riff. "May I present Knuckles, doing five-to-ten at Dannemora!"

"Miss Vandergriff," she would add, "I should like you to meet Mr. Not in Your Backyard, who operates the squeegee at the base of the Lincoln Tunnel!"

"Mr. Vandersniff!" Cornelia would chime in. "May I present my sixth-grade homeroom teacher, who is a big fat fartbrain?"

Sunday nights would hit Kendra hard, and she would plead with me to stay over. I'd always say no, because I had plenty of work to catch up on after goofing off all weekend, but also because I had a terror of meeting the redoubtable Clarice. At these times Kendra quieted right down, high spirits gone, and fell to sulking. As the holidays got closer, she got gloomier and gloomier. Silly riffing turned to endless complaint about her family. Winter break loomed large for her, and not in a good way. Her family had a house in France, in Burgundy, *a drafty old barn of a place,* as she described it, with nothing around it and nothing to do, and traditionally the family packed themselves off there for the holidays. She was facing the prospect of winter break stuck in that *sweaty-walled dungeon,* with nothing but her *asphyxiating family* and *some dismal Charolais cattle* for company. Normally it wasn't so bad, because her brother Jerry would be there, but he was AWOL, in case I hadn't noticed. How could I, since I'd never met him? I wanted to say, but there was no interrupting Kendra on one of her gloomy jags. And so there was *nothing at all* to look forward to. How could I explain to her that the prospect of going to France was amazing to me? That the idea of staying in a house from the seventeenth century was like something out of a dream? I was eighteen years old, hungry for living, and I had been nowhere. Nowhere, that is, except New York City.

But like Kendra, I'd always hated holidays. They brought only disappointment. There just wasn't enough to go around. At Christmas as a kid, each year I'd make up my list of gifts and I'd magically think that, all precedents to the contrary, come Christmas morning these things would be mine. Instead, the gifts my dad bestowed on his children were mostly identical, anonymous, and universally, if accidentally, insulting.

Here was a guy who went in for novelty nail clippers, treats from the day-old bakery shop, tiny sewing kits for the girls, cheaply made flashlights for the boys. He liked anything that could be bought in bulk: three-packs of adhesive tape, penny candy, tube socks, hankies. I would understand the reasons why later in life, get that he was casting back to his own childhood and buying us "practical" things that he and his brothers and sisters wished they could've had, their dreams kept small by their circumstances. His own father had been taken by TB, that poverty disease, in the late 1920s, and my grandmom was left with nothing—no money, no English, no skills beyond cooking and cleaning, and too many kids to feed. I remember when I was a teenager my dad would sometimes pick me up from school and we'd be cruising home in his beater through the sad old section called Hilltop, me scowling out the window, and he'd point to what seemed like every third broken-down row house and say, *We lived there, and there, and there . . .* They moved whenever the rent was due. Anyway, with Kendra I could commiserate over hatred of the holidays quite sincerely, although I was loath to mention details such as my familiarity with bakery thrift shops.

And then she had a plan.

Why not spend winter break together? There at the house on Eleventh Street? They all knew that Zeyde didn't travel well, so the rest of her family could go off to Bourgogne while we stayed in New York to take care of him. And this'd also mean they wouldn't have to board Agnes Smedley. Wasn't this a great idea? And what kind of argument could Clarice have against it—especially since she and Zeyde weren't, let's just say, the closest of pals? What kind of argument could *I* have against it? It's not like I was homesick, Kendra told me, as if I needed reminding.

And it was true, I felt no joy at the prospect of seeing my sisters and brothers. We were in those days constantly at one another's throats, which is what having a recently dead, violent, and angry failure of a father can get you. But I knew my mother would be hurt, because I had a feeling I was her favorite child (not that she'd ever say such a thing), and I was her youngest, after all. Beyond this, I did need to pick up some secretarial temp work over winter break back in my grim home city if I wanted to have any kind of spending money, but I was too embarrassed to tell Kendra this. She must have sensed something along this line given my hesitation, though, because she was quick to add, *Don't worry—my dad'll leave us all kinds of cash.*

And for the first time in my life, the idea of Christmas seemed wonderful.

The city was all turned out for the holidays, and I found myself wanting only to walk the streets and look at the lights. One weekday when no one was around and I was feeling studied out, I took the bus over to the Met to see the Christmas tree, paying a dollar for admission. I'd taken some fruit from the dining hall for lunch, and I sat on a bench in the sculpture hall and ate an apple, an orange, and a banana while looking at the old Gothic facade of the original Calvert Vaux building. Afterward I took the bus down Fifth Avenue. This was the first time I saw the Cartier building all tied up in its red bow—I think I actually said *Wow* aloud, like any little yokel. It was so thrilling to see a building wrapped up in ribbon like an enormous present. New York to me was alive, electric, delicious with possibility.

I called my mother from the suite phone, reversing the charges, and told her that a friend (a girl, I insisted to my deeply Catholic mother), a girl named Kendra Löwenstein, had asked me to stay on in Manhattan for the holidays. My mother told me I shouldn't impose on someone for such a long time, it was too much. I told her it was quite all right, I'd be helping her look after her pop-pop, who was wheelchair-bound. *It's okay,* I added, lowering my voice and feeling cretinous, *they have money.*

"Is Kendra a Jewish girl?" my mother asked.

"Mom!" I cried out. "Why do you ask?"

"Because, honey, I want you to go to church."

"I'll go to church!" I said.

"I had a Jewish friend in college," she mused.

"Yeah, some of your best friends are Jews," I said.

"Oh, honey, I didn't mean anything like that. Only that Jewish families tend to—"

"Oh my *God,* I have no *idea* what you're going to *say* but do *not* finish that sentence."

"Say *gosh,* honey, say *gosssh,*" she said.

I felt the slow burn of insane Mom Annoyance rising in me. Any kind of broader ideas she'd had in her youth had been worn down on the daily wheel of poor people's Catholicness that was her life, until she seemed to me just as provincial as the ignorant people around her. This is what disappointment had done to her, I would understand later. But in those days I still blamed her for so much, and I only wanted her to shut up.

All I thought about, however, was the lovely Christmas and the month with Kendra in the house on Eleventh Street.

The semester was winding down, and I said good-bye to my friends. Trina and Fang were taking the train down to D.C., and Audrey got on the bus for Bumblebee. Other friends were going north to Cambridge or Providence; some were flying east to Asia or west to Cali or to those midwestern states that lived in our minds like Saul Steinberg's map of the USA as seen from Ninth Avenue. Kendra's family wasn't leaving for France until Christmas morning, but days ahead my bag was already packed. Most everyone had disappeared by then, and that evening I ate a quiet meal in the dining hall and then went back to my empty suite in the echoing dorm with its view down Claremont Avenue, where, I had been told, Diana Trilling still lived.

I must have dozed off, visions of sugarplums dancing in my head, because next thing I knew I awoke to the suite phone ringing off the hook. I jumped up and raced out to get it.

"Kendra!" I said.

"Hi, honey!" she said.

"I'm so excited!" I said.

"Me too!" she said. "Check it out—we've had some amazing news."

"Yeah?"

"Jerry came back!"

"Jerry came back!" I repeated, though I didn't understand what bearing this had on us.

"Jerry came back and he's going to France!" she said.

"He's going to France?" I said.

"Isn't it great?" she said. "So they're all thinking I should go to France!"

"They're thinking you should go to France . . ."

"Yes! What do you think?"

51

"What do I think?" I said.

There was a full-length mirror beside the telephone, and I turned and looked at myself in it.

"Uh?" I said.

"I'm thinking I want to go," she said flatly.

"You are?" I said.

"Yeah, I'm gonna go!" she said, now with glee.

It seemed to me that my heart had begun to beat inside my mouth.

"What about Zeyde?" I said. "Is he going with you? How can you leave Zeyde?"

"Oh," she said, "I have a Jewy aunt in Jersey who looks after him."

I stared at my face in the hallway mirror in disbelief.

"You do?" I said.

I stood staring at my face, aware that it was starting to screw itself up in an ugly, stupid way.

"You're not mad at me, are you?" she said to me.

I pressed my hand to my chest to make myself speak without emotion.

"I am not mad," I said.

"Cool! Chess, you're the coolest! We'll hang out when I'm back! It'll be cool, I'll have a ton of stories. I've gotta go—I've got so much crap to pack!"

I searched my face in the mirror, and thought of something.

"What about Agnes Smedley?" I asked with undue passion.

"Oh, that old whore!" Kendra said. "We're taking her with us!"

5

Even now I can remember the acrid taste of disappointment, so like the smell of iodine, that I was to carry around in my throat all that winter break.

I was too humiliated to go home. I could well imagine all the shit teasing—*Chess's snooty friend left her behind*—that my brothers and sisters would inflict on me. Most of them had either remained in or been slapped back to where we grew up, though Olivia got as far as Philly, so my ambitions to get out and move to New York were already seen as greedy and theatrical, if not downright alien. Actually, it was during this time that I ceased thinking of that place as home. As for the house itself, I just thought of it as the place my mother lived. It wasn't my house; there was nothing for me there.

But I was nowhere. I'd missed the deadline for permission to stay in the dorm over winter break, so I found myself in the Housing office, pleading my case. I was too embarrassed to explain what had really happened, so I concocted some needlessly complicated story involving a sick uncle in Brooklyn, just the sort of thing you'd never remember after you dreamed it up and yammered it out. The dining hall was closed, Housing reminded me sternly, but I was positively smooth in my assurance that I was completely equipped to cook for and feed myself from the dorm kitchen for the next four weeks. In reality, I had three subway tokens and $42 to my name.

Christmas found me eating Chinese food and going to the movies, like any nice Jewish girl.

Afterward I walked the hundred blocks back up to Barnard from Theatre 80 St. Marks to save the cost of a subway token. I had all the time in the world, after all. Strange to say, as I walked and thought of what had gone down, I fixated on the fact that the Löwensteins were taking Agnes Smedley, the fucking cat, with them but Kendra had never even thought of inviting me. I felt so hurt that the only way I could deal with it was to pretend I didn't hurt at all. It was nothing to me, being left behind, ruining the holiday and winter break. It was nothing. Everything was all the same, going or not going, staying in a chilly, empty dorm and eating ramen noodles alone or being with my friend in her magical house on Eleventh Street, our stocking feet up on the warm andirons of the fireplace.

I had plenty of time to think about Kendra in those days.

Well, here was something weird, I thought: how come she didn't seem to have any other friends? She mentioned names and told stories, but I never met these people, and weekends always found us alone, with only her nerdy little sister and wheelchair-bound grandfather about. And it wasn't as if she'd come from East Jabip. She'd grown up in Manhattan. What kind of a person, I wondered, has no friends? The kind of person who burns through friends . . . the kind of person who takes up and discards.

After that I pulled myself out of my funk, put on one of my roommate Jackie's snappy outfits, and got myself down to the gloom-shrouded Midtown area around Lexington Avenue where the temporary agencies clustered. Oh, this was the old New York all right, when I think about it now: shabby second-floor offices with broken clock radios fuzzily playing "Sussudio" and blinking *12:07 12:07 12:07* in the reception area, joyless recruiters in pilled cardigans eating pasta primavera out of plastic clamshells while they asked you what you like to do—which to me seemed a question wildly incompatible with a job interview. The ubiquitous typing test in those days began *Mark Twain said he could live for two months on a compliment* and then immediately broke down into slabs of advice from the corporate cracker barrel. I quickly grew to loathe that paragraph and, after taking seven of these tests, wanted to punch Mark Twain, whose fault it really wasn't, right in the teeth.

However, I'd taken typing in high school—because academics need to know how to type, not because I envisioned life as a secretary—and I generally clocked about sixty-five words per minute. So it was easy enough to find something, at the going rate of $8 an hour, which was at least better than what I would've made in my hometown of Barfonia. Anyway, I found myself installed in the plushy office of some pooh-bah at an entertainment conglomerate, opening the mail, typing up an occasional memo, and mostly sitting beside a big floral arrangement from Irene Hayes Wadley & Smythe and reading a succession of Marguerite Duras novels.

In this way my winter break passed. For a treat I'd go down to Theatre 80, get a chocolate bar, and see a double bill of revival flicks. But mostly I was by myself, a small fish in a pond the size of the universe.

One evening, back in my dorm room, while I was sitting on the airshaft windowsill, smoking and gazing up at all the empty windows surrounding me, there was a booming knock at the suite door. This was strange, because there was still a week to go before the semester began. I froze. I knew it was Kendra, and there was nothing I wanted to say to her. The banging persisted, however, and I stubbed out my cigarette, flicked it down the airshaft, barged out of the room, and ripped open the suite door. And there was Fang-Hua, holding a peace lily.

"Whoa there, Hulk Hogan," she cried out, rearing back.

"Fang!" I said. "You're here!" A huge rush of emotion came over me.

"I had to get out of that *hellhole*," she said, thrusting the plant into my hands. "I thought you might like this plant thing. It's just so *big*. My mother's busting my balls all day long! I thought I'd about kill my sister, she's such a fuckhead accounting major! The Chinese respect no privacy! You got any doughnuts?"

Still clutching the plant, I felt something in my head explode. And I found myself sobbing and sobbing all over Fang's skinny shoulder.

". . . well," she said, not without sympathy, once I had told her the full story, "I always did figure her for a jerk-off rich kid. I mean, girl has a fucking Kelly bag."

"Kendra has a Kelly bag?"

"I *think*."

"I actually don't know what that is," I told her.

"It's like a fucking mad expensive huge bag that Grace Kelly used to cover her pregnancy."

We were sprawled out on the floor of my dorm room by then, drinking beer, eating doughnuts, and listening to *Double Nickels on the Dime,* which was just about our favorite album at that time. Fang was leaning back against my roommate's bed, her hair a lustrous brown-black puddle against the white coverlet. She was a beautiful girl, slender and long-limbed, with an elegant, uneven face and a high-pitched, nasal voice. It was at first hilarious to me to hear such a person curse, as she did, like a sailor.

"What the fuck are you going to say to her when she comes back?" she asked me.

"Not sure," I said, not wanting to think about it.

"Tell her she's a jerk-off entitled rich kid with an ass the size of a lampshade."

"Oh geez, Fang," I said, rolling my eyes up to heaven.

I still had another week of temp work, which I was glad for, because that would score me another $320 if I was careful not to take more than a fifteen-minute lunch each day. Fang was similarly cash-strapped and, dressed in her one "acceptable" skirt and a sweater that looked like a giant pile of black concertina wire, went down to the gloom-cloud temp hell district to sign up with some agencies. At the end of my workday I found her in my room, sitting on the airshaft windowsill with the family-sized box of Stella D'oros I had bought earlier open beside her. She had taken off her crazy bunchy exasperated-thought-bubble sweater and thrown it on my bed, and she had eaten all the cookies.

"How'd it go?" I asked her.

"Well, at the first place I got a twenty on the typing test. The lady told me my clothing was *unusual.*" She shrugged. "I told her that her *face* was unusual, on a human that is. The second place was a little better, but I got a *sixteen* on the typing test, and the only work they had was in White Plains and involved the cataloguing of phlebotomy samples. The other places were pure crap, like there was an actual *sock* plugging up a crack in the window in the one, and the other had lots of morbidly obese people in the waiting room, all eating smelly food from what looked to be a big vat—it was *gross,* and weirdly inexplicable. But. So I went to the library, the Rose Reading Room, and took a nap."

"It's nice," I said, "in there."

"Yeah, I'm thinking I'm sort of constitutionally incapable of temping."

"It's a buck," I said.

"Right, it's a buck," she said. "But I was thinking, if you and I cleaned ourselves up, got like some girly dresses and high heels, we could probably score us some escort service work."

"Fang!" I shrieked, scandalized.

"No, I'm not saying put out any cooch, I'm just thinking dinner at the Four Seasons and some intelligent conversation, sympathetic cooing noises. Most men only want someone to *listen.*"

"Bleh, I'm totally going to hurl," I told her.

By the time the semester started and my other friends came back, Fang had spread the word about Kendra screwing me over for the holidays and Kendra was, to borrow some D.C. parlance, x'ed from our hardcore scene. My sense of hurt and humiliation had lessened by then, and while I was still angry, I almost wished I hadn't told anyone what had happened. Because they were all for cutting her flat, but I was curious to see her again.

But then Kendra did not appear.

6

I should back up and say that if I'd hated Christmas in the past, after that year I associated such disappointment with it that for a long time I looked down with smirking condescension on anyone sentimental enough to celebrate it. The residue of this would stay with me for years, and when I got the gig at Acme, I was appalled to realize that I was expected to attend the office holiday party.

Poor old Walt actually rubbed his hands together in anticipation while talking about it, which depressed me beyond belief. The party would be within the confines of Acme's office—Dee-Dee was big on economizing—and there was much debate over whether Team Acme would let us knock off at 3:15, 3:30, 3:45, or 4:00 to begin the festivities. In fact, talk of the holiday party became the major focus of activity in the office in the weeks leading up to it, all work activities be damned.

I watched with curiosity as Cissy went around the office hanging armfuls of glitter tinsel on the crooked boughs of misshapen Christmas trees and touching up the boardroom windows with spray-can snow, humming merrily to herself all the while. To understand just how nuts this was, it needs to be stressed that the office was a pigsty of Collyer brothers–like proportions. Lining the walls were battered file cabinets piled with odd assortments of debris that included heaps of dusty files, appendix-like plant cuttings in dirty jam jars, bobble-headed dolls, and, in one very creepy instance, the wrestling trophies of elderly Petey, who turned out to be the single long-term employee of the Acme Corporation and who spent his friendless days spying on and making trouble for everyone else. One tripped over the old space heaters, portafile boxes, and mountains of FedEx supplies left hither and thither all over the floor. Beside my very own workstation was an empty cubicle that had become the repository for any junk people wanted off their desks, and it was packed like some Keystone-Kops-in-a-tiny-car sketch with broken aluminum easels, trade journals, scrawled-over flip pads, piles of scrap paper, and an enormous, half-smashed point-of-purchase display unit for the See It and Say It phrasebook series. All the assorted crap that people had gleefully thrown into this workstation enclosure was literally spilling out onto the common floor, and if I got up from my desk too quickly and turned too sharp a left, I would invariably wipe out on the slick surface of a GSA *MarkeTips* magazine from 1996 that had slid down from the top of the heap. Imagine, then, Cissy and her chuckling-with-private-holiday-joy self going around this place and "decorating" it.

On the day of the party, I hunkered down, the grouchy curve of my back telling anyone who came by that I had serious work to do. However, Dee-Dee was in high spirits, buzzing around in his intrusive, coked-up way. On his fifth or so buzz by my desk I turned and acknowledged him. I was to come to the party! There'd be free food! Free booze! Free cheesecake! And I'd get to meet his wife, Tootsie. *Oh, thanks,* I said, keeping my face as neutral as a rapper's.

Have I mentioned that Acme also had a translation wing?

There were three of them, and they clustered tightly together like a circle of Conestoga wagons. Besides an acid-casualty former Peace Corps guy who specialized in Modern Standard Arabic and a polyglot Bolivian woman with a French given name and the quiet manners of a diplomat, there was a third person, a young man. He had a lavishly ironic way of talking, and I initially took him to be Japanese, given the nature of his groovy styling—skinny hipster jeans, brightly colored Converse All Stars, gigantic Dolce & Gabbana eyeglasses, zip hoodies with cryptic sayings in nouveau Blackletter script on them. Once I learned his name was Qi-Shi, I realized he must be Chinese, which turned out to be correct; he was in fact from Hong Kong. Qi-Shi was not quiet by any means, and on one of the first days I was there stayed after hours to write an erotic love poem in French to one of his boyfriends, calling out naughty words over his workstation divider to Françoise by way of checking his work. His manner of being loud was at least immensely literate, and yet at first I was so rattled by the whole Acme scene it didn't much rise over the general cacophony.

Anyway, somehow I got dragged into the party, which began with an incoherent cokehead speech from Dee-Dee, during which the dispatch girls furtively slapped and pinched one another while guzzling Dixie cups of room-temperature Freixenet. Then it was time to race over to the buffet table. I hadn't planned on eating anything—it was hard not to think of Persephone and the pomegranate seeds—but I put some grub on a plate and sat back down. I realized I had no idea what to say to anyone beyond offering mutual condolences that we were all stuck working there, and so sat staring wanly down at a broccoli floret. That was when Qi-Shi turned his head my way and gave me a sweet little wink.

Later, as the booze continued to flow, everyone settled into random groups throughout the office. I found myself standing in a small circle of people, Qi-Shi, Françoise, and a nervous young IT guy named Jacob among them, who, although somewhat loosened up by booze, were having a carefully coded conversation that appeared to be about what a cheapskate Dee-Dee was, what a creep Petey was, and what a witch Cissy was, but one could not be entirely sure. Qi-Shi told a story about the holiday party the year before, which was held in a bar, a bar that switched from open to cash after each employee used up her or his two-unit allotment of well-only drink tickets, and how in spite of this he had gotten so drunk that he threw up in a urinal. Then Dee-Dee popped out from nowhere and strode among his troops, apoplectically hollering, *Cheesecake! Time for cheesecake! We got a cheesecake! Free cheesecake! Frances, Qi-Shi, cheesecake—get in!* Once he had passed, Qi-Shi drained his glass and said, "Well, kids, I guess it's time to eat our bonus."

At this point I was able to slip away and return to my proposal. After all, I was being paid by the hour. And I was counting down those hours until I could finally finish the thing and be free.

Later, for our Christmas, Fitz and I baked a tray of manicotti, opened a bottle of wine from the motherland, and watched the snow fall on the rooftops of the slumbering East Village. Like myself, Fitz came from a big family, but we'd learned over the years that to see any of them on either side en masse for the holidays meant, invariably, tears by dinnertime. And so our favorite thing to do was to block out the noisy world and spend Christmas by ourselves. Although it still strikes me, come the holidays, how quiet our life has become.

*

At any rate, back in college, after the second semester started, Kendra stayed AWOL. She didn't call, and after a while my curiosity got the better of me and I found myself at her suite, knocking on the door. An annoyed upperclassman wearing pajamas decorated with little drawings of sushi answered and told me she hadn't seen Kendra since before Christmas. She also told me that Kendra had stiffed her for the phone bill, so if I saw her, tell her she had to cough up $400 posthaste, all right? It was obvious the girl didn't like Kendra one bit or, by extension, any smart-assed little freshman who might be her friend. I left the building.

Of course I could call down to Eleventh Street, but there was no way I was going to do that.

I was taking the maximum course load that semester, eighteen credits, and working my job at Burgess-Carpenter, and soon enough I had little time to think about Kendra. Trina, Audrey, Fang, and I hung out together as we had before, but the initial elation of living large in New York City had somewhat passed. There was work to do. And so instead of going down to the East Village for fun, we stayed uptown, around campus, seeing films at Zooprax or going for midnight burgers at Tom's. At any rate, life "went on."

Zooprax, the Barnard film society, was a wonderful thing, and over the years I'd be exposed to untold riches through its film series: Jean Vigo, Maya Deren, Robert Bresson, Agnès Varda, Satyajit Ray, Akira Kurosawa, Chantal Ackerman, wonderful old Hollywood movies like *Dinner at Eight* and *Grand Hotel* or corny musical comedies like *One Touch of Venus*. I'd see *Blood of a Poet, Scorpio Rising, Entr'acte, À Nous la Liberté,* and so many other great things there, and all of this for, as I remember it, a single buck.

Except for horror movies or something strictly avant-garde, it generally took endless persuading to get Fang to go to the movies, and Trina was also somewhat less inclined, but Audrey and I went all the time. Not only did Audrey love movies like I did, but she was a procrastinator par excellence, and really any excuse or errand at all, no matter how outwardly boring, would put her right off her schoolwork. You could say, *I need to go down to the Economy Foam and Futon Center to buy some industrial soundproofing material* and she would say, *Cool, I will help you pick it out.* But somehow this particular Tuesday night I couldn't even get Audrey to come out, and so I found myself at Zooprax alone, watching Ginger Rogers and Katharine Hepburn in *Stage Door.* Not a lot of other people were there, and it was only when the lights came up that I realized someone was sitting directly behind me. Whoever this jerk was, they began kicking my chair. I turned around: it was Kendra.

"Hi, honey!" she said.

I was set on getting right out of there.

Instead, she plunked herself down beside me. She had with her an enormous satchel, some sort of European GI-issue thing, bulging and overstuffed, and an overnight case covered in floral decoupage. She wore a shaggy blue pile coat, huge Cossack boots, scarves of clashing patterns wrapped around both her neck and her wrists, and a kind of futuristic bonnet, square like a box, fastened beneath her chin. She looked like a stylish bag lady, or Baroness Elsa von Freytag-Loringhoven fresh from her cold-water flat in Paris. Actually, what she looked like was just plain crazy.

"What is *up* with you?" I said.

" 'The calla lilies are in bloom again,' " she said.

"Seriously, Kendra?"

I went to get past her, but she caught me by the arm.

"Look, I need you, and I knew if I called you'd give me shit. I saw the Zooprax flyer and I *knew* you'd be here. Chess, I have so much to tell you. France was a fucking ruse. To get me into rehab. Can you believe it? *There was no trip to Burgundy.* They all ganged up on me. Bertrand, fucking Clarice. My fucking dad. Cornelia. Even Jerry. I couldn't believe it. Fucking two months in motherfucking New Hampshire, making potholders and watching the snow fall. So I ran away," she said.

"You ran away from *rehab*?" I said. "Are you kidding?"

"No," she said, her eyes filling with tears.

Well, Jesus. They had reassigned her dorm room by then, she told me, and she had no place to go. She couldn't possibly go to Eleventh Street—she was bound to kill Clarice, or burn the goddamn house down. So it was natural enough for me to say why didn't she just stay with me for a while? She protested, but I insisted it'd be fine. Jackie was remarkably generous when it came to people crashing, and there was even an air mattress we could borrow.

Finally she relented. We walked down Broadway together, I with her big rucksack over my shoulder, Kendra holding her absurd overnight case and taking dainty, sylphlike steps. I was so outraged by what her family had done that I didn't even think to be angry with her.

Kendra produced one of those big $9.99 bottles of Alexis vodka out of her knapsack, and we stayed up in the suite kitchen for many hours that night, smoking, drinking, and talking. We were chasing a trail of meaning, and feeling that we were getting closer to it the more we drank. There was a profound sadness in Kendra, a kind of precocious exhaustion, and there was something like that in me too, which manifested itself in my need for final proof and "answers." I walked around angry at my dead father, angry at the failure of his life, angry at the way he took out that failure on his children . . . Thinking on it now, a lot of my behavior back then was about throwing my grievances out at the world, while the real issue was with someone who was dead. But you cannot get a hearing with a pile of dust. Kendra's anger at her mother was different. It was about having her *soul crushed*. She was *supposed to be a ballet dancer,* did she ever tell me that? She was the best in the room at the School of American Ballet. Mr. B. himself had loved her. *Loved* her. But this could only be a source of sorrow now. Once Kendra dropped out she ceased to exist for Clarice. *Poof, you are invisible—you have disappointed me once and for all.* Kendra could never just be who she was, she could never compete with such a towering ego, such a narcissist. She was always walking in the shadow of Clarice, who was the smart one, the slim one, the beautiful one who was powerful, a star, and who was always reminding her of this. Kendra was an ugly duckling beside her, fat, inept, *wrong.* At this Kendra raked a hand through her hair, which she had dyed a deep and glossless black, as if to mirror her mood. And if she was hooked on painkillers and amphetamines, guess where she'd learned *that*?

Had I been more sober, I would have found some holes in what she was telling me, especially when she talked about things that had gone down with Clarice over the holidays that didn't fit in with the rehab story. But.

We were still sitting up in the kitchen as the sun rose. We crashed for a few hours, and then I had to get my butt to Latin class. Kendra woke up with me long enough to tell me she was broke, and since I still had some of the money I'd earned over winter break—I'd spent about two-thirds of it, mostly on schoolbooks—I gave it to her. I told her I'd steal us some sandwiches from the dining hall for lunch and be back around one. I left feeling furious at Kendra's bitch of a mother, Clarice, my heart suffused with the noble feeling that I was helping a much-wronged, innocent fugitive.

When I got back, holding my stack of turkey sandwiches wrapped in paper napkins, the first thing I saw was a note on my door. And I knew she was gone.

Sorry, Chess, had to go . . . thanks for being my friend.

It was signed with a drawing of a unicorn winking, and the whole thing was as banal as it was uninformative. I stood there, the note in my hand, with a blank, dry feeling of sucker abandonment in my body.

That night one of my suitemates, a senior named Ainslie, called all of us into the kitchen.

She was a decent enough person, this Ainslie. Self-involved in that Barnard way familiar to many of us, but no kind of complainer. She was visibly upset. Her shower kit, she told us, which she'd happened to leave on the drying rack in the suite bathroom, had disappeared. Now, she knew none of us had taken it, but maybe it had been moved accidentally . . . ? Thing was, inside it were all her prescription drugs.

I put my hands over my face, then sat there smacking my head, over and over again.

7

It is kind of astonishing, the many ways in which a person can disappoint you.

I felt miserable about what had happened, and it was my responsibility because I'd brought Kendra over, but I just did not believe in ratting on people. You just do not rat on a person. Ainslie, bless her, took the time to hear me out—picture a poised, plump girl with a sweater that matches her lipstick, haircut by Bergdorf's and tiny Fendi-shod foot impatiently tapping—but told me that if I didn't call Clarice Marr and put things to rights, she'd have to take "other steps," and go to the Barnard powers that be. Which would mean putting Kendra's ass publicly on the line and perhaps—Fendi foot tinily tapping—getting that ass expelled. And so I found myself calling down to Eleventh Street, my heart in my mouth.

Funny thing was, no one ever picked up.

I finally left a message, saying that Kendra had been here, some things had gone down, I was worried about her. I pictured the house standing empty, its heavy curtains pulled against the light.

And here is how I remember her. Clarice. First seeing Clarice. It was the next morning, and I was coming in from my fencing class. I remember I was of course wearing the sloppiest clothes possible: plaid pajama bottoms, a puffy pair of faux-snakeskin British Knights scored at the Goodwill for $3, and a Misfits T-shirt that had been worn down to the state of fine tissue. Over this I'd thrown my favorite coat, a Joan Blondell number with a zany sort of shawl collar so big it pretty well stood up by itself. It was a shame I wasn't also wearing cymbals on my knees.

A young man and a tall and erect older woman were in the lobby, which was basically an unpleasant, impromptu place with a stained couch. The young man had one foot on the coffee table and was checking his watch, while the woman stood cradling her coat at her hip as if it were a pile of fox furs. They both seemed offended by the unexpected shabbiness of the surroundings—Barnard was the second most expensive school in the country at that time—and they reminded me of nothing so much as a couple of toffs on the cover of a P. G. Wodehouse novel, waiting for the steamer to Le Havre, nostrils quivering with disdain.

Instantly I knew who they were. And I felt a troubling mixture of hatred and covetousness toward them. Also instantly I knew I'd get nowhere by being combative with such people. So I went up, stuck out my hand, and said, "Ms. Marr?"

The woman turned to me and began to look me up and down. Slowly. Very, very slowly, as if she were sizing up a beggar and wondering, Leprosy or no? Then she peered into my face with the most withering of looks. I recoiled. But in a moment I flashed back to the conscientious high school friend, the one who talks to your parents about the parish bake sale even as he's wearing a spiked dog collar, and I smiled at her. I said my name, pronouncing it very Italianly to show I wasn't some cultureless gavone. She softened a bit at this, taking my hand, and introduced me to her son Bertrand. He had a florid face and the high color of a Pre-Raphaelite painting and seemed to me dreadfully self-important. I thrilled to the memory of Kendra putting the gross old jar of Nutella in his sock drawer.

We rode up in the elevator together in silence.

They followed me down the long hallway of my suite and into the kitchen, which was piled with great bales of newspapers, Rolling Rock bottles, and heaps of pizza boxes and Chinese food containers. There was a paper napkin on the table on which someone had written *Fichte go fuck yerself,* and this I swiftly dispatched into the trash bin. They refused my offered cup of tea, and Clarice cautiously took a seat, first examining the table for contaminants before she placed her lightly folded hands upon it. Bertrand seemed to be looking for a piece of wall to lean against, but visibly rejected them all as dirty—as repulsive, in fact, judging by the ripple of contempt that passed through his person. Instead he stuffed his hands into his pockets and stood rocking back and forth on his feet.

This will sound strange, but I remember it suddenly struck me that Clarice wanted to be hip. I mean, odd to say, I sensed that she cared what I—an eighteen-year-old wearing a *Mommy, Can I Go Out and Kill Tonight?* T-shirt—thought of her.

"Where's Kendrick?" she said to me quietly.

"Where's Kendrick?" I repeated. "Well, she came and went, like I said. Out of nowhere she showed up on Tuesday—she told me she ran away from rehab, and she was back but they gave her dorm room away. So she stayed over. Then she disappeared the next day. She left me a note. Then my suitemate Ainslie told us something of hers had disappeared. Her prescription drugs."

"Did you take them?" Bertrand asked me.

"Wait—what?" I said.

"Did you take the drugs from Ainslie?" he spat at me.

"What do you *think,* jerkhead?" I spat back at him.

"It *is* a stupid question, Bertrand," Clarice said, waving him away.

"Not really," he said.

"Bertrand, shut up or leave the room," she said.

Amazingly, Bertrand left the room, slamming the door behind him.

"Now what is all this about?" Clarice said to me.

I studied her. She wasn't her picture—that had been taken years before, anyway. She was impeccably groomed, her dark blond hair "lifted" very cunningly with flattering golden streaks. Her face was oddly downy, and on the side of her cheeks by her ears I could see a thick swirl of fair hair, suggesting some sluggish evolutionary tendency. Otherwise her makeup was immaculate, definitive, like that of an actress, especially her eyebrows over her uncanny ice-blue eyes. She wasn't precisely a beautiful woman. There was too much hardness in her. I could imagine how that glamorous mouth would falter in anger, turn down and wither at the corners. I could imagine her yelling and even hitting. Somehow, beneath all the grooming and sophistication, I smelled something tentative, something unschooled that was trying to read me to find clues: what was the correct behavior in such an awkward situation?

"What are you asking? I told you," I said to her, "someone took my suitemate's prescription drugs and it wasn't any of us."

"How do you know it was Kendrick?"

"Look, she's my friend. Do you think I enjoy doing this?"

"I'm sure it was Kendrick," she decided, waving her hand in dismissal. She pushed angrily back from the table, fanned her hand over her face. "Why would she do this?" she said.

It was rhetorical, but I decided to answer it. I wanted to wound this woman.

"Well," I said, in a voice dripping with sarcasm, "maybe because you put her in rehab instead of taking her to France? I mean, *damn.*"

She dropped her hand and looked at me. A sour smile came to her lips.

"Oh," she said, "she conned you. You really don't know our Kendrick. Little Miss Suffering. She's a wily girl. She went to Bourgogne all right, and had a fine old time. Do you think she wanted to do anything when we got back? The girl is lazy, foremost. She's a lazy little cow. So we get her sob story about her addictions, oh, my, my, my, so *sad,* and she wants to extend her vacation. She wanted another vacation really. So we send her up to Old Briar, which is a very nice place, and not cheap, and what does she do? She gets *bored* after a week and walks away. And in the meantime we get her straight-D report card. Oh, no, I should say—she did get a high mark in her *bowling* class."

I felt my eyes filling up.

"I don't believe you," I said.

"She's not an honest girl," Clarice said.

"I just don't believe it," I said.

She had softened now, made her face kind. But it was the kindness of a woman talking to someone she pitied.

"She lied to you, honey," she said.

Honey. She said it the same way Kendra said it, long and drawling. I got up from the table and went to leave the room, but I remembered stupid Bertrand in the hallway. Instead I went to the window and pretended to look out at the viewless airshaft view. But I was seeing nothing anyway.

"Did she take money from you?" Clarice said gently, behind me.

And I said no.

So it is an awful feeling, even years later. Being used. I understood nothing at that age. I was used to more straightforward cruelty, not subterfuge. I was used to angry Italians, yelling and violence. This was all too baroque for me. I remember thinking, This is the way rich people play, even though part of me wanted to disavow that sort of difference, wanted to disavow difference in the name of friendship. Or in the name of not wanting to be treated as something lesser.

Before she and Bertrand left, Clarice knocked on Ainslie's door and gave her some restitution money. Three hundred dollars, Ainslie would reveal later, thrilled and instantly sailing down to Saks to get a pair of Gucci flats she'd had her eye on. I could have screamed out loud, because $300 was just about what I had given Kendra, and now I had nothing at all. Nothing at all, that is, until my next work-study check for $87.93 came in.

I think I must have pulled in a lot after that, shut down, become super-diligent in my studies. I felt burned and I shunned company, even of the friends I cared about and could trust. But what I did more than anything was banish Kendra from my thoughts.

I remember it was a cold winter.

Always it would be late at night, it seemed to me, and I'd be walking home up a wind-battered Broadway as trash blew by me. Maybe I was coming from the library, but it seems like I was always walking too far for that, so who knew? New York was a lot dirtier then, New York in the '80s, much of which was really just a hangover from New York in the '70s. It was crack-cocaine city, with prostitutes on nearly every corner of Broadway north from Seventy-Second Street until, for whatever reason, they vanished at the bend at 105th, by the Titanic Memorial. It seems incredible to me now, but sometimes just to get out of Columbialand I'd ride the subway for hours, doing my course reading this way. (I remember reading a book about a lesbian nun in Renaissance Florence in this manner, furious that I had to pause when the train dead-ended at New Lots Avenue.) Empty crack vials would go rolling the length of the train cars. There were a lot of crazies. People kept eye contact to a minimum.

More people read on the train in those days, actually, instead of being all plugged in and oblivious. You would see people reading James Baldwin, Renata Adler, Semiotext(e) books, *Things Fall Apart*, thick new novels in hardback. You read and you kept one eye out, you know, just in case.

When early spring arrived, I guess I started to come out of my exile. Seeing buds on trees seemed to jazz up everyone, and Riverside Park became the place to go. April found Audrey, Trina, Fang, and me down there in the park, sitting on the wall and eating big Toblerone bars while smoking cigarettes. This seemed European to us, smoking and eating at the same time. I remember these things as if we were static beings before a constantly rolling screen, as if we had sat there for weeks, the four of us, on the wall in Riverside Park.

In time, talk turned to what everybody would be doing that summer.

I had no desire to go home, but neither did I have the money or savvy to make other plans. Another group of friends, women I was less close to but mostly liked, talked about us all going out to the Hamptons, renting a place together, and waitressing by the sea. This sounded great (though I hadn't a clue what these "Hamptons" were—I thought it was someone's last name), but I had no idea how to realize it. In this particular group, I have to say, were some very entitled girls—I cringe now to think of the way we, Jews and non-Jews alike, threw around "JAP" as if it were okay to say—and part of me felt somehow touched to be included at all. I mean, these girls were not punk rock, quite the contrary, so in a way I was their funny mascot, the person with crazy hair who would do and say outrageous things and then get suddenly shy and artistically sensitive. Later we would grow apart, but back in freshman year I think the group's draw for me was their utterly flawless upper-middle-class lack of alienation. They just did things. There was no angst or questioning. So when they were like, *Hey, let's summer in the Hamptons,* they were talking about an easy reality, while for me it was almost like saying, *Hey, let's go to Galaxy NGC 1300, it's only sixty-one million light-years away.*

So most of that clique went to the Hamptons that summer. Audrey went back to Bumblebee, Trina and Fang went down to D.C., and I had no choice but to go back to Suck City and temp.

I remember my mother picked me up from the train station in her Ford hatchback with its antiabortion sticker on the bumper. She was so glad to see me. She asked me nonstop questions, and she genuinely wanted to know about my life, about my new friends, about what I was reading and the art I was seeing. Maybe she wanted to remind me that she had interests and talents, that she knew things too. Maybe that she had been young once, with a future ahead of her. I knew the story, but it just seemed so abstract from the woman who was my mother, the pious, disappointed lady whose vinyl purses and endless patience made me so pissed off and miserable.

Yes, I knew the story. She'd immigrated when she was a little girl and had gone to high school "with the Quakers," as she would always say, the only Italian in college-prep courses among the many Boones and Howells and Smiths. She'd gone to the University of Pennsylvania on a violin scholarship, taken life drawing at the Academy, and had an actual career back in the day as what they used to call a "commercial artist," working for an architect in Philadelphia. She drew with flair, had a great line, and she was chic, popular, WASP-looking. As a child I'd tunnel deep in her closet to find her fur, a full-length cape coat from those cool, clear days of the 1950s, now covered in an old sheet. I'd rub my face against its arms and plunge my hands into its pockets, where I knew there was a crumpled but fascinating-looking silver certificate dollar bill from 1947. There were other things in that closet: a golden chain-mail evening purse still in its fancy pale-pink box, a bundle of filmy tissue paper printed with cursive French that yielded a darkly glittering garnet brooch, a glossy black Wanamaker's box that contained an impossibly snow-white stole, light as a confection. Gifts from men, I knew; they seemed dangerous. This was of course before my mother married my father, quickly realized the mistake she'd made, and, as I saw it, signed away any agency she had in this world. By the time I was a little girl she had perfected her hiding and was able to pass as a mild neighborhood church lady, handy with "creative" projects such as making colorful posters for the parish Christmas bazaar. Yes, she'd really hooked her wagon to a star.

But there were the photographs, photographs of my mother, Rachele, before she was my mother. Beautiful, elegant, young. Laughing.

Of her five children I was the youngest, so everyone else was out of the house by then and doing their own thing—my brothers, Horatio and Sandy, and my sisters, Olivia and Stanze. Except it turned out that Horatio, who was by then nearly thirty, had had another manic break, so he was there, padding around the house with the plaid bathrobe of his boyhood tied up under his armpits. He and I would sit and eat cereal at the dining room table together, hiding our faces behind a big box of cornflakes. He barely spoke to me, or to my mother for that matter, but he didn't seem to mind my company so much, which was a change from his attitude toward me during childhood. I think we each recognized in the other just how down we were to be home again.

The most salient memory I have of that summer was that there was a rerun of a PBS miniseries about Lillie Langtry on at the time, and through some tacit understanding Horatio and I would find each other in front of the TV at the unlikely hour of 5:30 each morning to watch it together. I also remember that in this series Oscar Wilde was presented as a heterosexual man, deeply smitten by Lillie's charms—pining and sighing and languishing, a Jersey lily in his hand—and Horatio and I were both richly amused by the inaccuracy of such a representation. Anyway, he and I would watch this show together, deeply engrossed, and then exactly fifty-two minutes later, turn off the television, sighing our own sighs. It was time for me to get ready for work, and it was time for Horatio to go back to bed. My mother would be dressed by then, sitting at the dining table with a cup of tea before her, *The Pocket Treasury of Novenas to Our Lady* in her hand. She'd be eager for the time we'd have in the car together that morning, the half hour it took to drive me to my temp gig at a blank suburban office park on the way to another blank suburban office park where she'd worked for some years, after reentering the job market in middle age. She was still a commercial artist, but by then it was called a "graphic designer," and she made a poverty wage, $5.45 an hour, as a permanent freelancer working for one of the richest corporations in the world.

She was grateful for the work.

In the evenings it was easy enough for some high school friends to pick me up, and we'd get some cheap eats, tool along the strip-mall highway that cut through the north of the city, hang with the decaying group of street punks who frequented a certain Dunkin' Donuts parking lot, or go to the one art-house theater to see *Eating Raoul* for the nineteenth time. Those of us who were in college knew this was nowhere, and those of us stuck there seemed bitter and sarcastic or else were quick to point out the changes our absence had caused us to miss. *Check it out—there's a new Happy Harry's on State Street.* Each night I'd get dropped off at my mother's house and find her sitting up waiting for me, dozing on the couch with the radio for company. She would kiss me good night, able to go to bed *now that you're finally home, Chess.* Never mind my argument that she didn't need to stay up, she didn't know the hours I kept at school, so what's so different here? But she never could hear it. And then the next morning Horatio and I would be back in front of the TV at 5:30 again to watch Lillie Langtry, anticipating the fresh installment with a kind of insane hunger.

I couldn't wait to get back to New York that September. And when the weather turned unseasonably cool in late August, my bags were already packed.

8

I don't remember fixating much on Kendra at the beginning of sophomore year. She hadn't come back to Barnard after all, and when it was clear she'd dropped out I did some initial conjecturing—I'd heard a rumor that she was living in a squat in the East Village—and then I let it go.

That first semester, actually, although I was constantly busy I was also miserably depressed. I was spending most of my time with Audrey, drinking, smoking, pitching pennies into the empty airshaft, and feeling trapped by the city. Audrey was doing increasingly erratic things, like ripping color-plate pages of crucifixion scenes out of expensive library art books and walking around with an eight-by-ten-inch framed picture of Saint Thérèse of Lisieux in her book bag. Having to ask the newsstand lady to break a buck for bus fare would send her into a tailspin of nervousness. She could spend hours dissecting a line from a Joy Division song or *The Cloud of Unknowing*, exercises that inevitably reduced her to tears of exhaustion. Hindsight being twenty-twenty and all that jazz, I realize that her mind was starting to unravel at that time, and loving her as I did, part of me was attempting to follow her down that path.

Maybe it had something to do with Audrey's increasingly mystical religiosity, but agnostic though I was, I found myself wanting to go to church. Columbia had an excellent Catholic ministry, I remember, with a cool, smart, scholarly chaplain. I hadn't grown up with cool priests. The ones of my childhood were the worst sort, more interested in the roof fund than in compassion, bullies who would suck up to the more moneyed people in the parish and work my mother, who was forever volunteering for everything, like a slave. Meanwhile the Italian priests of my high school, transplanted long ago from Emilia Romagna or Lazio, were harsh and haunted, scarred by the fascist Second World War. My high school Italian teacher, Father Mario, had hair-raising stories about Rome after the Germans came in, things like pulling weeds out of the cracks in the pavement in order to have something to eat, and in his class we'd watch films like *Roma città aperta,* all of us screaming and crying when Anna Magnani gets shot down in the street. So yeah, there was not a lot of sweet tending of the soul going on until I got to college, by which time I was pretty well soured on the Catholic faith. But something was moving me toward church that sophomore year, and every once in a while I would find myself at Columbia's church, St. Paul's, for the Sunday five-o'clock.

It might not need to be said that in my eyes the Columbia students who went to Catholic mass were among the most excruciatingly uncool of just about all the Columbia students. They were even more nerdy than the Orthodox Jewish students—who at least, to me, had the charm of exoticism on their side. The Catholic mass students wore Sears Toughskins, buttoned their top buttons, and appeared to be pre-ironic. They smiled and asked questions. They were mad friendly! But I had no use for this at the time, walking around as I was with my big fat hating-everything Louis-Ferdinand Céline head on. So instead of going to St. Paul's on campus, I cast around for a church where things were dark and dour and Gothic, where I could sit in a corner and cry my brains out.

One Sunday morning shortly before the end of the fall semester, I woke up too early, as if shaken out of sleep by a pair of rough hands. My whole suite was still sleeping. Indeed, the entire dormitory building seemed to be, but my feet were itching to walk, so I dressed quickly and got myself out the door.

It was a cold December morning, brisk and clear. I walked down Broadway and went to Columbia Hot Bagels, where I got an everything bagel and held it warmly in my hands as I walked south, tearing off great sections of it and chewing all the while. Few people were out, and there was a magic descended over the neighborhood. Things seemed dear to me, and deeply, singularly New York. I gazed at the stacks of the Sunday *Times* on the metal racks in front of the bodegas, peered in the window of the Judaica store, stopped in front of an old barbershop seemingly preserved intact from the '40s. I must have walked thirty blocks in this way, looking at everything around me. At some point, for no reason that I can remember, I turned and walked east, and toward the end of the block there was a church. It was large and broadly striped, Byzantine, almost like a synagogue. And yet it was Catholic.

I bounded up the stairs and slipped inside the doors and through the vestibule. A mass was going on, though sparsely attended. I slinked up a side aisle and into a pew. I unzipped my coat, pulled off my scarf, briefly knelt, and then sat back, letting my eyes close.

But I had an odd feeling. I can't explain it, but I was almost expecting someone to touch me. As I sat, the feeling grew until I found myself with one hand curled around the nape of my neck. There were certain social niceties that my mother—a woman whose elaborate system of manners was kept bizarrely intact even while raising her puling children in what was basically a slum—had instilled in me, and one of them was that, other than during the kiss of peace, you should never turn around in church.

Minutes seemed to blossom into hours as I sat there with a sickening dread, waiting for the inevitable. I heard nothing, saw nothing, though I must have been gazing up at the dome of the church, because I can picture it yet. And then the next thing I knew I was standing and the priest was saying, *Let us offer each other the sign of Christ's peace . . .* And I turned to see, several rows behind me, Kendra.

My heart began to thud in my chest.

She was swaddled in layers of black garments, voluminous, shapeless things, with a shawl covering her head. Her hair poking out from the shawl was bleached white. With her ghostly foundation makeup she looked drained of all color, a tabula rasa. Matching this was a soulful, contrite look on her face—contrived, like the rest of her.

Immediately I was done—down the aisle and out the door.

On the steps outside the church she caught me by the hood. I whirled around.

"Tell me everything you know about the Catholic religion!" she yelled at me.

"What?" I said.

"I need to become a Catholic!" she yelled again. She was all up in my face, her shawl fallen down. Her eyes were red and fierce, and she was on some manic new high. I twisted around and pulled out of her grasp and then I was pounding down the street. But she was right beside me.

"Kendra, you know, fuck you and your fucking daily mania and pretend enthusiasms! What's the new lie, huh?" Suddenly it was my turn to yell in her face. *What's the new lie?*" I yelled, bearing down on her.

She backed away and yanked up her shawl, clasping it at her chin and angling herself away from me as if to fend off a blow. Instantly I was wretched. Though in the midst of this—so completely art-directed did my ridiculous and dramatic friend make herself—a certain Annunciation painting flashed in my mind, of a scowling Virgin Mary recoiling at the strange news.

"Kendra," I said quietly, "I need you to fuck the fuck off."

I turned and kept walking.

"Chess," she said, "I've turned over a new leaf."

"Do I care?" I said.

"I thought Catholics were supposed to care," she said.

"I'm lapsed," I said. "I'm not a fucking Catholic!"

"You can change your spots so easily?" she said.

"Bah," I said. "You always do!"

"I need you to sponsor me for my conversion," she said.

"What?"

"You heard me!"

I stopped and turned to her.

"Kendra, the help you need can't come from me," I said. And then I kept walking.

She had stopped but in a moment caught up to me again.

"Clarice kicked me out," she said.

"Why don't I believe you? Why do I find it hard to believe you about anything anymore?"

"Oh, man, you've *gotta* believe me," she said, in an awful, almost babyish voice I hadn't heard before. She stopped but I kept walking. I kept walking! What was she, expecting me to save her?

"Chess!" she called down the street after me. But I did not turn around.

*

When I got back to my dorm, my head still fizzing with anger, I found Audrey sitting in my suite kitchen. It was barely ten in the morning. We'd said good night only about six hours before, when we'd finished drinking two six-packs together, and she wasn't the light sleeper I was. She was still dressed for outdoors, in her long midnight-blue winter coat, a strange garment that seemed to swallow her up in its enormous pilgrim collar, and she sat hunched over, fiercely sucking on a cigarette and staring violently down at a fixed spot on the table as if it offended her.

"Hey, what's going on?" I said, falling into a chair across from her and pulling off my watch cap. I looked at her special spot on the table.

She looked up.

"*Duh,*" she spat.

"Aud, what is it?" I said. What was the matter with everyone? I was still reeling from Kendra and I just needed her to be regular right now.

"Give me your shoes," she said.

"Why would you want my shoes?"

"You know why," she said, her voice dripping with contempt.

I looked down at my feet. I was wearing my favorite boots, Carolina engineer boots that were three sizes too big for her. There was no precedent for this request. I shrugged, pushed back from the table, gave a big show of yanking off my boots, and put them on the table in front of her.

"Here you go," I said.

"You understand *nothing,*" she spat.

I reached out to take her hand across the table, but she snatched it away. What with the Kendra morning and this new weirdness—Audrey had been growing strange, but not angry like this—I felt my eyes filling up.

"I *don't* understand," I said.

"Duh, Chess, you pretend to be so smart." She pushed back from the table and raked a hand through her lusterless red hair. I could feel her mind racing as she snapped her head from side to side, trying to shake something away. She was a tiny person and sat shaking her head like this in her huge, dwarfing coat.

"Audrey?" I begged her. "Tell me what's going on."

She looked at me intently.

"WPA," she finally answered.

"WPA?" I repeated, lost.

"Duh!" she barked. She shook her head at my stupidity and then pronounced each letter slowly, as if this would explain it: *Double-you. Peeeee. Aaaaay.* She glared at me, needing me to understand this piece of important information.

"Works Progress Administration?" I finally said.

"Don't be a fool," she said.

"Jesus, Audrey," I said as she got up from the table. She was banging out the door as I struggled into my boots and raced after her. I hit the hall just as the elevator door closed on her. I banged on the button and then started racing down the stairs. I got to the reception desk just as I saw her pass through the barely open front door, a floating nun in a skimming habit.

"Audrey!" I yelled as I chased her down Amsterdam Avenue.

I caught up with her at the corner, and she whirled around and looked at me as if she were just seeing me for the first time. She started pounding her fist on her heart and yelling: "I am *here,* I am *here,* I am *here.*"

"Of course you are. Of course!" I said.

"Something's wrong, oh God, something's wrong," she said to me, and collapsed crying in my arms.

*

So okay, it was clear that some serious shit was going down and Audrey needed to be pretty closely watched until she could be safely deposited in Pennsy with her family for winter break, at which time—I really believed this was all it would take—she could get some much-needed rest and come back well again.

Amazingly, she had muddled through most of her classes. In the week and a half left of the semester, she took two incompletes and, using a charcoal stick and a twenty-two-by-thirty-inch newsprint pad, wrote a paper on Max Weber. She brought it over for me to type—I had a Brother typewriter with a tiny read-out screen that allowed you to check fourteen characters' worth of work before the text appeared on the page (a fascinating piece of "technology" about as sophisticated as one of those collapsible umbrella hats)—and when I saw the state of Audrey's paper, I thought I would tear my fucking hair out. I was already buried in finishing my own work. The joke of all this was that when I sat down and read Audrey's paper, I was astonished to see that it was much more lucid, filigree-free, and representative of a subtle, agile mind than anything I'd ever managed to write in my life.

Well.

Winter break was almost upon us. Audrey had taken to camping out in my dorm room, and broke as we were, we were living pretty much on cigarettes, $2.99 six-packs of Knickerbocker beer, doughnuts, twenty-five-cent bags of plantain chips, and ramen noodles. She seemed all right—I kept an eye on her—but just before she was to get on the bus to Pennsy, a kind of stupor came over her. She could barely bring herself to get out of her pajamas or sit upright, never mind leave the building. The thought of her taking herself alone to Port Authority, which still felt like a place to get stabbed in the eyeball at that point in time, seemed just plain wrong. Worse than this, she couldn't bear to be alone. When I would come back to the dorm from any trip at all, I'd find her right by the door, shaking with panic.

We mapped out a plan that I would take the bus with her out to her family in Pennsylvania Dutch country, deposit her there, spend Christmas with them, and then get on a train from Harrisburg to Barfonia to see my family. Actually I was secretly thrilled at the thought of spending the holiday with a family other than mine and being spared the pained and uncomprehending eyes of my mother, if only for a few days.

It's funny, I remember how Audrey's mood seemed to improve in stages as the landscape changed. Small relief came once we were out of the city, grew larger as we passed the urban doom-clusters of New Jersey, and when we finally hit the open highways she was sitting up and smiling like a kid at a party. It had snowed and then frozen over, and the fields all around us were covered in a heavy, untouched frosting of whiteness that sparkled in the sun. It seemed to me that nothing could ever look so clean and brilliant in the city, which felt like a hooded, blackened, corralled place in contrast. But as we pulled into the bus station in her little town, Audrey's mood changed again, and an extremely shaky nervousness overtook her.

"Oh, shit," she muttered to me as we got off the bus, "there's Edwina." This would be her eldest sister.

I looked up to see a tall woman some yards away from us, unsmilingly standing her ground. You couldn't help but stare at her. She exuded a terrible seriousness—she was so straight-backed and inelastic—and a kind of gloomy elegance. She should have been dressed in a bonnet and habit like Mother Seton, but instead she was wearing an Ike jacket and leather motorcycle jeans. In fact, what she looked like was a taller, darker, and altogether more severe edition of Audrey. Both she and Audrey had narrow, aristocratic faces with pointed chins and tiny mouths: preoccupied Van Eyck faces, seemingly unknown to pleasure. They were like the frowning angels from the Ghent altarpiece.

As we approached, Edwina looked at Audrey with cold eyes and then gave her a stiff hug. Then she smiled at me and greeted me as if I were the truly welcome figure.

"Come on, Chess," she said, ripping my bag out of my hands while Audrey, much smaller and daintier than me, stumbled along under a huge load like an ant with a Shredded Wheat biscuit.

It's a strange thing to be let into someone else's family and see what passes for normal among them.

The Devane family, a.k.a. The Walking Irish Tragedy, makes more sense to me now that I've come to understand something of life's creeping disappointments than it did back then, when I was a hard-line little asshole clutching my Minor Threat records. The parents were originally from New England—father Harvard '52, mother a hat-and-gloves girl who grew up on Beacon Hill—but their ship had run aground in one of the least intellectually fecund places in the country round about 1961, when Professor D had landed at a small college in central PA. It was supposed to be a stepping-stone to bigger things, but something wicked had intervened. Maybe the environment had overtaken him. I have to say, I found Professor D a prickly, intimidating figure, with his Central Casting tweeds and pipe, perpetual air of amused disdain, and casual schadenfreude ("Oh, Dr. Franzel fell into a vat of polymer. Tough luck for *him*"). Whenever I used a "big word" around him, Professor D would unplug his pipe from his mouth, raise his eyebrows, and say, "Oh, pardon my French!" His kids all revered him, particularly Audrey, Edwina, and their middle sister, Maud, who fell all over themselves to get his approval. Mrs. D was a much more interesting figure to me, with her raspy, cigarette-cured voice, finishing-school speech patterns, and hairdo that tipped up at the ends like that of a '50s sitcom star. She had a kind of utter über-mom ease in the world and was what they used to call a "good conversationalist."

Though they'd been there for at least twenty-five years, the parents looked on their surroundings with a sad condescension. It was as if the arrangement were merely provisional and better things were on the way. Meanwhile their five kids had grown up in this landscape and seemed trapped between two worlds. There was the high-culture fairy-tale version that existed within the walls of the Devanes' Craftsman bungalow—which, again, seemed to me like something out of a television show, with its sunken living room, slate flooring, and Mid-century Modern furniture—and the underfed reality of the town all around them, with its crumbling downtown, scrimpy auto-body shops, and Bible-thumping utility-shed churches. Driving down the main artery, you saw neon crosses everywhere. Audrey's brother Ciaran, the eldest but one, was a haunted med student who wrote poetry in the style of Yeats and who would tell you all about cardiothoracic harvesting trips, his great brown eyes shining with an almost paralyzing compassion. Maud, the roiling middle sister, had a BA from Amherst but worked as a bartender at a dicey local. She chain-smoked Sweet Afton cigarettes and had excruciating funds of knowledge about Gaeilge orthography, Bloomsday, and the sport of camogie. The girl talked about the death of Bobby Sands as if it had just happened yesterday, and I was not surprised to learn that she'd once knocked a patron out cold when he ordered a drink called an Irish car bomb. There was the eldest brother, not present, a sort of blessed supertramp called Niall, whose name was always mentioned in a reverent tone, and who had disappeared into the cloud forests of Amazonas before finishing his dissertation on microtonal composer Harry Partch. Edwina, who was, by contrast, extremely present, spoke like a punishing librarian, constantly correcting everyone's already near-impeccable grammar; but she also seemed the most troubled—a hyper-meticulous, lonely person in space, and probably a real barrel of monkeys to the trembling youth she tutored in French. Everyone drank too much. Taken unawares at any given moment, the family, with the exception of Mrs. D, could all be caught frowning with intense and probably tragic thought.

Mrs. D was especially glad to see Aud, and greeted me kindly when we stepped in. I'd been on the phone with her a few times, explaining Audrey's situation, and I was expecting a quiet reception. Instead the house was full—with uncles, aunts, faculty members, and a group of what I must have misheard to be botanical statisticians—and next thing I knew the Jameson's was brought out and a tumbler clapped into my hand. I was going on about three hours' sleep, and what with all the unexpected people and the music blaring—Professor D was a great Louis Armstrong fan, particularly of the Hot Five era—after talking variously with Mrs. D, Ciaran, Maud, and Edwina, I quickly became dull and overwhelmed. Worse than this, I have the weak liquor stomach of (just to quote Henry James here) *a mere vague Italian,* and so next thing I knew I was in the guest bathroom yakking up the hors d'oeuvres.

I looked up from the toilet bowl to see an unearthly pale and beautiful little girl standing next to me, regarding me with interest. She had the tiny, precise features of the Devane family and was dressed in a pillowcase and Christmas garlands. This would be Eugénie, I realized, Edwina's interestingly acquired five-year-old daughter. To hear Audrey tell Edwina's version of the story, Eugénie had come mail-order from France, like some excellent baking dish.

"Ugh, so sorry," I said to her. I wiped my mouth on some toilet paper and sat back on my haunches. "What are you, dressed so nice like that?" I asked her.

"I'm a fancy ghost," she said gravely.

"That's pretty cool," I told her.

"I need to show you my animals," she said.

I was barely able to flush and clean up before she had grabbed my hand and was dragging me down the basement steps. At the foot of the stairs I stopped. Spread out all around us was a miniature wonderland of plastic and stuffed animals and dinosaurs and shoebox buildings and silk flowers and trees. Eugénie pulled me down and began telling me about each of them in exhaustive, genius-surreal descriptive detail: *This is Mr. Potts, he's a dromedary, not a camel, which is called the Bacitracin camel, which is an antibiotic, and that's two humps, and you can tell because he has one hump—hello, Mr. Potts!—he's Arabianic . . .* We met Mrs. Boodles and Friendly and Uncle Wag and Zilly and many dozens of others this way—it seemed as if no one in the history of the world had ever listened to Eugénie at all and she'd saved this up for the first hearing person who happened to show an interest—and at some point I must have gone clean asleep, because the next thing I knew I was on a pull-out sofabed with Audrey (how had I got there?) and Mrs. D, already with lit cigarette in hand, was waking us up for Christmas mass.

Everyone but the missus was in a grumpy-assed mood as we drank our glasses of water—too late for coffee if we wanted the Eucharist!—crunched across the lawn through the snow, piled into the 1967 Chrysler Newport Town & Country, and drove down the long, skinny highway to church. Something had gone down at the party the night before, and Edwina, Audrey, Maud, and Ciaran were bickering in a hiss-hiss secret sibling way. The windows were rolled tight and everyone but Eugénie and me was puffing away—pipes for the men, cigs for the ladies—and the car was filling up with smoke like some *Guinness Book of World Records* endurance stunt. I was close to death.

Eugénie and I were rolling around in the back. The bickering subsided, and in a moment Audrey turned to us, a little smile on her face. As if just remembering something, she said, "I've got a surprise for you."

"What's that?" I said, mad nauseous and in no mood for silliness. Eugénie was tucked up by my side, most of her head in the pocket of my parka to avoid the cigarette smoke.

"Someone's meeting us at St. E's," she said.

"Mr. Potts?" I said.

"Mr. Potts!" Eugénie screamed with joy from inside my parka.

"You'll see," Audrey said, smiling.

We pulled into the parking lot of St. E's, and as soon as Professor D cut the engine, all the Devanes sprung from the car as if popped from a pneumatic tube. I slowly rolled out and got to my feet. Eugénie ran ahead to a stunningly dressed woman leaning against a big white old-model Mercedes in front of the church. The woman was like a vision, all in white: white fur coat and white patent boots and glamorous white turban. I sighed, cursed with the inevitable.

The woman, of course, was Kendra.

*

Needless to say, it was a little unnerving to see her in this context.

Audrey introduced Kendra to her family, who all gathered around her smiling and shaking hands, as if meeting a dignitary, but who obviously had all been let in on the surprise. I hung back, jealous, and stared at her with a look of great sarcasm affixed to my face, disgusted that she could have so seamlessly invited herself into someone else's Christmas. As we filed into the church Kendra fell in next to me and we had our own hiss-hiss back-and-forth argument:

Me: *Why are you here?*
Kendra: *Why are you so mean?*
Me: *Why are you so phony?*
Kendra: *That's not very Christian.*
Me: *Screw you, Tinker Bell.*

I plopped to my knees in the pew and laced my hands in front of my face, pretending to pray and fighting down the urge to slug Kendra. The organist was laying it on thick, and the church, an ugly '70s thing styled on a Quonset hut, shook with the strains of "Angels We Have Heard on High." Through the lattice of my fingers I watched the people filing into the pews ahead of us, all so cow-country conservative. Almost everyone who passed in front of us did a full turn and stared at Kendra, some with their big cow mouths fully open. This pissed me off and made me feel protective of her. I stole a look her way and watched her as she prayed, eyes closed, a weary angel look on her face.

85

What if she really was serious, I thought, and here I was mocking her intentions?

We stood for the procession, and as soon as the choir leader raised her hands, Kendra began belting out the hymn. However, Edwina was also a belter and the two of them kept upping the ante, Edwina pitching higher and higher until everyone around us was standing on their tippy-toes and singing into the ionosphere. By now I had fully closed my froggy mouth and leaned forward and turned my head to catch Audrey's eye. She looked back at me, and for the first time in months I fancied I knew what she was thinking—nothing complicated, just something like *I want to run out of here, over the hills, and into the land of the cigarette trees.*

During the mass Kendra followed the book very closely and was perfect in her responses. It was as if, driven by a real spiritual thirst, she'd made a study of the mass, all the exterior things, as a way into the spirit. What if she's sincere? I thought again, hearing the loving caress she made of every word as the rest of us mumbled our responses. Whenever the moment came for an amen, the whole congregation said it the flat, standard Catholic way: *Ay-men.* Kendra's voice alone sounded it the "fine" Protestant way: *Ah-men!*

With a flutter of eyelids.

This is just another snow job, I thought.

*

Back at The Walking Irish Tragedy homestead for dinner I sat at the farthest end of the table from Kendra and watched with a deep, spongy cynicism as she entertained the Devane family and extended clan with her glittering, "outrageous" stories of Life in New York City. I'd been looking forward to a nice home-cooked meal and being kind of like the guest of honor, but clearly someone more worthy was here now. I increasingly retreated until I had demoted myself to the kids' table, with Eugénie and some wriggling cousins imported from Massachusetts, where I sat mostly smoking instead of eating. And it was all I could do not to stub out my Camel Filter in the pumpkin pie.

I wondered about that elusive thing called charm.

At some point I realized that Audrey kept getting up from the table and disappearing, and at about the third time I rose and followed her. I walked soundlessly behind her as she went into the living room and over to the Christmas tree and touched a homemade clothespin-person ornament in a little cutaway coat meant to represent Éamon de Valera. She did this three times. Then she went to the front window and surveyed the yard, moving her head slowly in a 180-degree sweep; when a car finally passed by, she was free to move. She went into the library, took down a copy of *The Great Cat Massacre,* removed a bookmark in it, replaced the book, took down a copy of Ciano's *Diaries,* and put the bookmark in that instead. Then she stood at the library window and surveyed the side yard for some minutes before going into the kitchen, taking the lid off a Kromex brushed-aluminum flour container, one in a series of flour-sugar-coffee-tea, and peering deeply into it. Once certain about the flour, she returned to the dinner table. And in another seven or so minutes, she rose and did the whole circuit again, this time moving the bookmark from Ciano's *Diaries* to a paperback copy of Admiral Byrd's *Alone.*

"Hey there," I said to Audrey at the Kromex station, "what do you say we go for a walk?"

We'd dropped our coats in the mudroom, so it was easy to steal away without anyone seeing us. Outside was wood smoke and frozen snow and quiet, resting prewar stone bungalows, tall fir trees and sleeping hedges. Not a soul was out. We both immediately lit a smoke, looking at each other as we put flame to cigarette, Audrey with her dour, delicate Van Eyck angel face. And then we began walking down the middle of the street, stark and unfamiliar as we were in our boots and long dark church clothes. That unexpected childhood good mood seemed to overtake Audrey again, and she began kicking up her heels as she walked. I started to walk like her, kicking up my heels and throwing my head back to look at the cloudless blue sky, and then she hooked her arm through mine and we were spinning each other around in the street. We went spinning and spinning, and it was fun and great and heedless. It was as if we had escaped from everything, we knew we had this moment of stolen time and it was ours and couldn't be rescinded. There were almost no words from her, and this would increasingly be the case, but in these times Audrey was my best friend in the world.

We'd been out walking for not half an hour when we heard the screech of a car taking the corner too quickly behind us. I turned to see the big white Mercedes, with Kendra at the wheel.

She pulled up beside us and abruptly hit the brakes, then threw open the passenger door at us with an angry jerk.

"Why'd you leave me like that?" she yelled.

"You seemed just fine," I said.

"Fuck you, Chess, I'm talking to Audrey."

"Fuck you, Kendra, *I'm* talking to Audrey."

"Fuck you, snot brain!" she shouted.

I stared at her until I felt my face getting all loony-looking and then I kept walking. Clearly she had mistaken me for her little sister. Behind me there was silence, until I heard Audrey, momentarily undecided, start walking again. She caught up to me, and then so did Kendra, cruising in her big white car, the passenger door still open. I stopped and turned to her.

She just sat there staring at me, her face shadowed, her mouth screwed up into a failed rosebud.

"Come on, girls," she said at last. "I'm lonely."

*

The winter night had come on early out in the strange wilds of south-central PA, and we cruised the hills and flats and thin blank highways. Towns had names like Mount Zion, Palmyra, Shiloh, Deodate. Give to God, God-given? Out in the in-between spaces there was no light but the moon, sometimes bright, sometimes obscured behind scudding winter clouds. Kendra produced an enormous spliff, and though I didn't like pot so much we all passed it around and smoked it and a kind of textbook mellow came over us all. Any anger left me completely. We were surrounded by night paintings: Pinkham Ryder, Blakelock. The land was silver, strange, and shimmering, and the feeling was that here we were, the three of us all together as one, protected in the dark and security of the enormous old car.

It was outside a town in Berks or maybe Lancaster County, Pennsylvania Dutch country, that we pulled over and gobbled up magic mushrooms.

I'd had these before and was sure they had no effect on me at all. As far as I was concerned, they just tasted like dirt and chewed up to the tooth like my childhood memory of chicken hearts. Things were good and fine. Then I was aware that the time in the car and the time outside the car had lost their sync. I was communicating this to Kendra while Audrey was splayed out happily in the back, her head lolling against the back of the seat. By now we were really cruising, but the inside of the car was very slow, and Kendra had jammed in an unlabeled eight-track tape, which was the only available music option and which turned out to be a Perry Como Christmas album. I can't explain it, but Perry Como was seeming deeply sinister to me just then. We were cresting a hill on the long, skinny road when all of a sudden there was a kind of *bump-bump* and we flew up a little and I knew we had hit something—run it over.

"Holy fucking *shit*," Kendra said.

She swerved wildly to the right and we jumped out of the car and attempted to race through the occluding, puddinglike air. And there it was, an opossum in the middle of the road.

"Is he dead?" Audrey asked.

Kendra turned and gave her a look. The opossum was in two fully separate pieces.

We all stood staring at him.

"The poor little guy," Audrey said at last. She started struggling out of her coat.

"Oh no, no, no, Aud, please don't do that, Aud," I said as she attempted to throw her good winter coat over the little guy.

"I doubt he's cold," Kendra told her.

A debate ensued. Should we bury him? After all, we had ended his life. Isn't burying the dead a corporal work of mercy? We turned all this over for some time.

In the end we simply cleared him off the road, which Audrey was all too happy to do, except that when she approached him with her beatific face and thin white hands we thought she might pick him up and hug him. So it was up to me to gingerly nudge and roll the opossum parts to the side of the road, where I more or less assembled him so he was somewhat intact-looking. There we prayed over him a little bit and I wiped the guts off my shoes, and then, suddenly propelled forward by a force stronger than me, I puked all over the little guy.

"Mr. Potts!" I said, between hurls. "I'm so sorry!"

But the puking did not end there, and I leaned on the cow fence and kept my head down until I puked out all of Christmas Day: turkey, ham, green beans, dinner rolls, pumpkin pie, fruitcake.

I had the knowledge that we were way fucked up, but we all got back into the car and we kept cruising. I felt like hell. We passed a big sign and Kendra began chanting: "Roadside America, Roadside America!"

"Roadside America, Roadside America!" Audrey picked it up.

"Roadside America, Roadside America!" they were both chanting.

"Fucking A, Roadside America!" Kendra yelled out.

I was dimly aware of this thing, Roadside America, some kind of big diorama or something, but specific knowledge of anything at all seemed very distant from me at that moment. Kendra took a quick turn that threw Aud and me against one side of the car, and for an awful moment I thought I was about to decorate the inside of the wind-shield with new Christmas upchuck.

We rolled across the parking lot, and then Kendra cut the engine abruptly. She and Audrey leapt from the car. I sat with my head down for some moments before I could make my body move.

I found them over at the other end of the parking lot, staring up at a huge Amish couple perched on a kind of dais. They must have been fiberglass or papier-mâché, and both of them were smiling madly. The male half of the couple had one ineptly articulated hand raised in greet-ing and a pitchfork clutched in the other. The woman was bent forward as if she were praying, and maybe because of this her smile took on a sad, grave aspect. She must have been holding something at some point, because her hands were close together, describing something circular in shape, perhaps a lost Amish baby. They were like some denial-ridden mother and father in couples grief counseling.

Behind us stood a long, rangy building with a kind of frontier-style stepped facade with ROADSIDE AMERICA MINIATURE VILLAGE across the top. In a moment Kendra had gone back across the parking lot and was up at the building, yanking on the door.

"It's *closed*," she called out.

"It's three in the morning," I yelled back.

She backed away from the locked door and stood staring at the facade. The affront to her seemed immense. Why should Roadside America be closed at three in the morning? What is this *bullshit conspiracy*? I had trailed her over to the front of the building, Audrey following, and now Audrey appeared to have keyed in to Kendra's disappointment and began quietly sobbing. Kendra turned to us, white and commanding against the dark night.

"Let's break in," she said.

Even in my pretty well completely incoherent state, I thought this was a bad idea. I actually stood there thinking, Why is it that I'm always the one who doesn't want to do something dumb? Why can't I just get with the dumb flow, hotwire that dumb car, steal that dumb item of small electronics, skip out on that dumb restaurant tab and go prancing gaily down the avenue?

But the Amish couple had caught Kendra's interest again. She began walking back across the parking lot toward them. Meanwhile Audrey had strayed in the opposite direction and I saw her plop down on the cold ground in front of an outdoor soda machine. I watched as she slowly extracted her cigarettes from her coat pocket, took one out, and meticulously ripped off its filter and threw it to the side. She found her matches, and it took her something like nine licks of the match on the striking panel to get a flame. As I watched her I began to well up with sadness.

On the other side of the parking lot, Kendra had somehow climbed up on the dais and was desperately clinging to the breast of the enormous Amish woman.

Roadside America seemed like the loneliest place on the planet at that moment, with the cold empty parking lot, the long dark Christmas night, and each of us lost in our own imploding head.

9

A few days after Christmas—Christmas 2008, this would be—I found myself trudging back to Acme, which I had taken to calling Nadir, after another lunchtime visit to St. Michael's. I was walking very slowly, drawing out the moments before I had to go upstairs and close the coffin lid on myself.

In the building lobby I greeted Mr. Shah, the sad man from Gujarat. He had arms like weeping willows and distracted eyes and gave me his usual sympathetic grimace. Then he got up from his chair and passed behind a panel that framed the space behind his desk and began singing. He did this a lot. As he sang his usual chanting, tragic song, which I imagined to be about death and loss, I stood waiting for the elevator with my hands over my face.

Upstairs, I plunked myself down at my desk and stared at the latest page of the proposal, which read like a list of canned soup ingredients.

An IM popped up.

Hi! Smiles?

It was from Qi-Shi.

Sad, I wrote back.

His workstation was only three away from mine, so I rolled my chair out and looked his way. He'd poked his head out from his workstation too, and greeted me with kind eyes behind his gigantic groover glasses. Today he had on something that could be classified as hair jewelry.

In a moment he came over for our Afternoon Visit.

"I'm liking the headband—very eighties," I said. "Olivia Newton-John, aerobics, 'Physical.'"

"Oh, I knew you'd get it," he said, twinkling. "I miss the eighties! I mean I missed the eighties. They were probably pretty cool, right?"

"Oh, you must remember them. What were you, like, four in 1989?"

He had this cute habit of gingerly dragging his bangs across his forehead with his hand.

"Six!" he said.

"I'm just old enough to be your mom," I said.

"That is *so* fucked up," he said, beaming. Qi-Shi had a nervous, sweet way about him. After the holiday party we'd kept finding ways to talk until we'd evolved a daily Afternoon Visit, which was absolutely the only thing I looked forward to in my Nadir workday. Qi-Shi was a delight, a polymath with a mind both visual and verbal, a Fox with deep stores of Hedgehog. He was interested in everything and genuinely thrilled about all sorts of topics, such as Japanese Notan, the Slow Food movement, fisting, German noun declensions, and the travails of Egon Schiele's long-suffering mistress, Wally. What he was doing in this dump was a mystery.

"Here, I brought you something," I told him, reaching into my bag for a book. It was Cookie Mueller's *Walking Through Clear Water in a Pool Painted Black*. "There's a really great part where she's in Germany for, like, a film opening and she's really messed up and she has to get out of a hotel in a hurry and jumps out a window and climbs over this stuff and the next day she finds out she accidentally scaled the Berlin Wall."

"Cool!" he said, beaming. "I finally just saw the John Waters movie where Divine eats the dog shit, and of course we had to skip back and watch it nine times."

"He was *lovely*," I said.

"He *was* lovely," Qi-Shi agreed. "And so brave!"

I have to say, when Qi-Shi and I were having our Afternoon Visit it was the only time in the history of the Nadir company when the office was actually quiet. I mean, crazily quiet. There was something about our easy exchange of what I guess seemed like arcane enthusiasms that appeared to actually frighten people, as if we were using code to hatch a plot to murder them. Thus the hush over the office: how could they crack this code and foil our plan?

Qi-Shi had somehow managed to hang on at Nadir for a year without losing his mind, and because of this he was a treasure trove of gossip about employees past and present. We were working late one evening when he came over and said to me, "Wait, can I show you something?" He led me to a dusty plastic palm tree outside Dee-Dee's office and dolorously pointed to its pot. I crouched down. Inside it were many small slips of paper. I selected one. It read: *Rosie Sanchez 12/23/08.* Rosie had been the accounting person until Dee-Dee, Cissy, and Petey had, for no apparent reason, called her into Dee-Dee's office, shut the door, and told her they didn't like the beads in her hair, she was missing too much work, and they didn't care if she was a single mother whose son had whooping cough, she should clean out her desk and vacate the premises immediately. Nikki had stood outside Dee-Dee's door and applied her L'Oréal Paris Infallible Plumping Lip Gloss for twenty minutes so she could get all the details about Rosie's firing and instantly disseminate them around the office. Despite all our differences, this had created a bond among us, and we had nothing but sympathy for Rosie and contempt for the Dee-Dee/Cissy/Petey triad of evil.

I looked up at Qi-Shi.

"You're kidding," I said.

"Yup. I mean, nope. No kidding. Each time Dee-Dee fires somebody, he writes their name on a piece of paper and adds it to the palm tree."

"A thoughtful feng shui gesture," I said, shaking my head.

"You know that feng shui is like goofy white people's stuff, right?"

He crouched on the other side of the palm tree and we rummaged around in the fired people. There might have been a hundred.

"Dee-Dee always says a perfect day for him is to fire somebody, beat down a sucker in small claims court, then go for dinner at Sizzler in the Cross County Mall."

"I feel like someone should kill him," I said.

"People have tried," Qi-Shi said. He adjusted his enormous groover glasses thoughtfully and found a slip. "Check it out. This was one of the old accounting guys: *Rick Johnson 3/11/08.* He was a Scientologist, crazy fucking bonkers, and he told me one day Dee-Dee was a

Suppressive Person—an SP. Someone who gets in the way of the true spread of the Scientology moment. Like, Rick also told me Hitler was an SP, right? Though how he reconciled that on the historical timeline is beyond me. When Rick got axed he went to choke Dee-Dee, but old Deed gave him the slip and next thing you knew Rick was in the lav ripping the sink off the wall. Then he just bashed it and bashed it until, did you ever see that documentary where Werner Herzog talks about Klaus Kinski getting locked in the bathroom and he pulverized the tub, the sink, the toilet until they were a powder so fine you could sift them through a tennis racket—*jah?* That's what Scientology Rick did. Smashed the sink to baby powder. They had to threaten him with a staple gun and carry him out."

We were crouching there by the palm tree.

"Sweetie, you've got to get out of here," I said to him.

"Oh, you too, Frances!" he said very sympathetically.

That night I took the elevator down from Acme lost in thought.

Out on the street, even though it was the supposedly quiet week between Christmas and New Year's, the Garment District evening rush hour was in full cry. Usually I could push through this like a cowcatcher, but this evening somehow I felt so dejected I didn't have the heart to push back. As I was buffeted by the throngs of ticked-off fashionistas pouring down Seventh Avenue, I remembered a friend of mine from Turkey once telling me how she'd have to walk the streets of Istanbul to get to her lycée during a military coup in the 1980s and how it wasn't uncommon to pass dead bodies lying in the street. There were so many bodies that people would just cover them up with newspaper. I felt like if you died in the Garment District during rush hour, people wouldn't even take the time to cover you with newspaper. They'd just trample your body until it was reduced to bits, and then they'd look at those various bits—intestines, pinkies, hanks of hair, pieces of bone—long enough to kick them into the storm drain, cursing you for being in their way.

On the subway home I went back to thinking about Qi-Shi, the kid who was interested in everything. I was thinking I used to be like that, excited by all kinds of stuff, the World of Ideas my oyster. Until a certain family beat it out of me. Snobbed it out of me. Showed me the error of my foolish, trusting ways.

*

The day after Christmas—in the eighties, this would be—Kendra and I drove back east together. We'd gobbled up a few handfuls of aspirin, said good-bye to Aud, but done an Irish exit on the rest of The Walking Irish Tragedy. Not good manners, but it was just too much. Neither of us was in much of a people-loving mood, but I had softened toward Kendra, and when she lit up a spliff in the car and passed it to me, I took it, mostly in the spirit of solidarity. Together we got quietly baked as we rolled east through the blindingly white Pennsy hills, driving into the sun. I remember we talked about religion and how fucked-up the religious landscape was in those parts. Here was a place where religions, punitive and damning, we said, are founded, angry-god religions. Kendra wondered aloud how angry the Catholic God was and I said the Catholic God was never so much angry as disappointed in you, which was really much worse. I found myself telling her about my dad, which was something I just never did, unless I could make a joke out of it.

I found myself telling her how I was always made to feel like I was extraneous, like I was a fifth wheel. Like I had to apologize for taking up space. Like I had no business living. So I always had to jump higher, run and fetch, make myself useful. The worst thing to my father, my terminally furious father, was a person who was useless. He would say things to us kids like *Don't just stand around with your hands in your pockets. Make yourself useful. What are you, useless?* There was no room for dreaming, there was no room for error.

And I was telling her about how my father had been a failed public-interest lawyer. Never passed the bar, even though he took it six times in several states. Which was the main reason that he was always so furious, probably. After he died and my mother and I were trying to throw stuff out, a previously unknown event in our house, I'd found taped in one of his seven copies of *Robert's Rules of Order* a newspaper clipping, no doubt meant to be inspirational, about a Kennedy relative who had failed the bar something like eleven times before finally passing it. But as luck would have it for my dad, he died before anything good happened. Fucking died at sixty-two, still studying for the bar exam.

Somehow I went on to tell Kendra about how I had actually saved one of his shoes, one of my dead father's shoes, a budget-priced wing-tip of great lawyerly pretensions, and how even at that moment it was stowed in a dresser drawer in my Barnard dorm, and how every once in a while I would take out that wingtip, hold it in my hands, and smell it. And how it mostly just smelled like Kmart.

I even told Kendra what a violent motherfucker my father had been, and how he had broken the dining room table with my sister Olivia one day, never mind throwing my brother Sandy down the basement stairs, dragging my sister Stanze up the stairs by her hair, and contributing to my brother Horatio's many nervous breakdowns by forever giving him sucker-punches to the head and referring to him as the Pussy. Or as *My son—that bitch.*

All along Kendra had been listening to me, asking helpful questions, making sympathetic sounds, but now she stopped replying. There was utter silence as we drove through the Pennsylvania hills. I swallowed hard. I realized I had gone too far, shared too much. What a dope I was, telling this silver-spoon girl about my cheap little problems. How stupid! Why didn't I realize that rich people's problems are much more interesting? Much more noteworthy and tragic?

I cleared my throat, looking straight ahead of me.

"We were poor, my father was violent," I said, "but at least my mother didn't collect Hummel figurines."

I looked at Kendra out of the corner of my eye. She was pulling over into a strip mall.

She stopped the car and turned to me. She hadn't put on any makeup, and her unprotected face with its rosacea blotches looked sad in the harsh white light. Sad but real. A rolling sensation overtook me, and I felt like this was the first time we had really looked at each other. It was as if our many masks had finally dropped. And then she reached forward and took my face in her hands.

"Chess," she said, "I love you."

And then, she kissed me deeply on the mouth.

I wonder where we were. I wonder if we were in one of those tiny Pennsylvania towns with the strange names. There is Panic, there is Desire. I wonder exactly where we were.

After that we somehow got out of the car and went to get a falafel.

It is hard to explain exactly how exotic it was to find a falafel shop in a place like that. The young man who came out to wait on us wrote down our order on the ticket exactly like a dot and a dash. Kendra and I both leaned forward and stared at it. That must be Arabic, I remember thinking, glad to have this other thing to wonder about.

We ate our falafels looking out on the nearly empty parking lot. Every once in a while we would look at each other, searching, and then look away. Once we were done we simultaneously wiped our mouths with our wax-paper wrappers.

"That was the fucking best falafel I've ever had," she said.

"Fucking delicious."

"Fucking outstanding, private."

"Fucking tremendous, sergeant."

"Fucking fuck-off brilliant."

She ended up dropping me off outside Philly. There was a SEPTA line I could take that would put me in downtown Barfonia, where I could walk or take the bus to my mother's house. Kendra wanted to drive me to my mother's door, but I couldn't bear the thought of her seeing that house. I think she understood this, because she pushed and pushed but then just let it go.

We stood on the platform of the small suburban station, somewhere east of the Schuylkill, saying an awkward good-bye. It was as if neither of us could make it end, and we were both dancing about forward and backward and side to side, looking around us as if to find an answer. A kind of giddiness overtook us both, and we launched in with our *Etiquette* schtick—"Mr. Vanderslice, won't you please avail yourself of the crack pipe?" "Mr. Vanderwhipple, perhaps you would lend me your shiv?"—and when some guy walked by blaring the new Kool Moe Dee album on a big boom box, we both spontaneously busted out in a purposely ridiculous white girl's bump.

And then the train came.

In the air was a real kind of beauty, previously unknown. And yet I was glad to leave. We hugged good-bye, barely looking at each other.

Once I got on the train I looked out the window for Kendra, but she was already gone.

*

I couldn't say how I loved her. Or even if I loved her. This would not matter for some time, however, because it would be years before I saw Kendra again.

10

It's probably no surprise to hear that Audrey also didn't come back to school after that semester.

Our friendship became phone calls, endless, excruciating phone calls, during which Audrey would fall silent for minutes at a time but never want to hang up. This was, needless to say, before cell phones, and even before Columbia installed a fancy new campus-wide phone system with voicemail. The infamous Little Mermaid chain message on it would crash the entire Columbia phone network in 1990, a moment that was later captured in an episode of *This American Life,* which was nice and all but somehow killed the subversive beauty of the thing in my memory. At any rate, there was no voicemail in those days, so if the suite phone rang someone would have to answer it, and if it kept on ringing for fifteen times or more you could bet it was Audrey. Sometimes I would stand by the ringing phone with a towel clamped down on it rather than pick it up and get trapped on a two-hour misery call with Aud. Mostly I just hoped she would snap out of it and get well again. I was a simpleton in those days and thought a person could will herself back into sanity. On top of all this, I was sick of walking around feeling bad all the time, worrying every last feeling, making the world into an endlessly problematized landscape.

So it was just Trina, Fang-Hua, and I back in school, and for a number of reasons, one being that Trina and I were both Latin minors, she and I got very tight. By junior year we were onto Catullus and we worshipped him, his suffering at the hands of the woman he called Lesbia, his rancor, his changeability, his melancholy soul. We made endless jokes about people having goats living in their armpits and loved recounting how our bashful professor almost expired from shame as he blushed through his translation of Catullus 16: *I'll, um . . . fuck you up the ass, um, and in the mouth, fellator Aurelius and, um . . . catamite Furius.* We had glee in our hearts. Trina had a way of making everything fun, like Mary Poppins—a cooler, cuter, and more groovily dressed kind of Mary Poppins—but I also began to see that she had a real kindness about her. Senior year we got assigned the same dorm, 600 West 116th Street, right there on the corner of Broadway over the Chock Full o'Nuts, Trina one floor up from me. The underclasswomen in Trina's suite, besides the bonus of their all being into punk rock, were much more fun—and much more tolerant of my many stupidities and rudenesses—than the ones in mine, so I spent a lot of time up there. The D.C. vibe hung heavy over that suite: the two juniors, Sarai and Zany Mina, were, like Trina, D.C. scenesters, while the sophomore was a quiet, conscientious, nonracist skinhead from Chittendon County, Vermont, who had taken the whole straightedge thing to heart (no smoking, no drinking, no sex) and whom, because of her wholesome, clean-living ways and general niceness, we all called Baby Skin. Fugazi tapes were always being played in that suite, and everyone sure knew the correct pronunciation of the surname McKaye. To top it off, Sarai had a computer, a beautiful new Macintosh SE, and she was a very generous person, so I was always haunting the halls of their suite writing my dithery-assed papers and eating up their vegan snack foods. Sometimes Trina, Zany Mina, and I would fall into the gin rummy pit and plant ourselves at the kitchen table until the wee hours, drinking hot toddies, smacking each other on the forearms, and smoking like burning buildings. This would often end with Zany Mina, deck in hand, throwing herself across the table and flipping the cards into the air fifty-two-pickup style.

Zany Mina was a certified kook, nine feet tall and gorgeous like a model but the biggest spaz in the universe. She specialized in dancing in people's faces. I'd knock on the door of the suite and hear the dim strains of Ignition playing in the background, and Mina would rip the door open, stick her big gorgeous face in mine, and hold it very steady while punching out her arms and kicking out her feet in every direction. It was a lot like Snoopy's happy dance. Then Z.M. would grab me around the neck and dance me down the hallway.

"I've discovered the source of Mina's crazy exhausting energy," Trina announced one morning as we sat in our nine o'clock Apuleius class clutching coffees, big black circles under our eyes.

"Crystal meth?"

"She sleeps for sixteen hours at a stretch. And then she's up for eight. Bed for sixteen, up for eight. She's got the cat-sleep ratio absolutely down. Next thing you know she'll be prowling around the bookshelves about to knock a trophy on your head."

The other thing that happened with us all was that Fang met a guy.

Of course, it was really not fair to be so utterly in one another's business as we all were, especially when it came to a person's choice of love interest, but we hated this guy. He was a sort of minor jerk-off celebrity on the Columbia campus. He kept his hair in a carefully tousled, cascading fashion, and was never seen on campus without his tweed blazer, sunglasses, and copy of *Of Grammatology* glued under his arm, his tender lip curled in disgust over anyone not lucky enough to be him. Worst of all, he was one of the biggest ass men around. I remember sitting on the Low Library steps smoking a cig with a woman named Karina, who was out of the L.A. scene, which seemed to be the exact opposite of the D.C. scene to my mind in that people out west actually did and had things like drugs and sex, when Decon Head happened to pass by on College Walk. I watched as Karina followed him coolly with her kohl-lidded eyes. Something made him turn our way, and Karina looked to the side and flicked her cigarette butt down the steps.

"See that guy?" she said, once his tweed back was in sight.

"Decon Head?"

"I did the deed with him last night," she said.

It would be hard to convey the just-come-in-on-the-turnip-truck alarm that the casualness of her words gave me.

"And you . . . um, don't say hi to each other?"

"It's not like that," she said, a world of West Coast cool about her.

I took it at face value, this attitude of hers, not really understanding in those days how people could pretend when it came to things like their hearts. I was not made that way. I knew myself to be completely transparent. There was too much at stake, there were too many ways to be hurt. Girls I'd grown up with back in Barfonia were mothers at fifteen, had to drop out of high school—and as far as I could tell, that was it with their lives. You would see them at the mall, pushing strollers and looking at frilly prom dresses in the window of Merry Go Round. Then there were other girls I knew, more sophisticated ones, who'd had two and three abortions by the time they were nineteen. They said it was no big deal, but they trailed this sadness after them. I hated that women could be hurt in this way while men could walk away. I was confused by the idea of random hookups, confused by the concept of a "flirtatious" blow job, by phrases like "walk of shame," and by all the trivializing. I knew if I met someone and fell in love I would give myself completely, my heart and my body . . . and maybe because of this I was forever guarding my heart, holding it close. I just didn't understand an attraction to a person who was known to be a player.

Anyway, Fang revealed the big news to Trina and me late one night as we sat in Tom's over our cheeseburger-special plates, which, if I had any insight at all into the ways of a bulimic, I would have realized ninety-pound Fang would only be throwing up an hour later. Had I clued in to this, I also might have understood the appeal of her choice of men.

"Decon Head?" I said. "You're going out with Decon Head?"

"Please don't call him that," Fang said, suddenly demure.

"*Decon Head?*" I was incredulous, and of course drunk.

"It might be time for you to turn that shit down," Trina said to me.

"I just can't believe it," I said, shaking my head. "He's such an asshole poseur."

"It's definitely time for you to turn that shit down," Trina said to me.

Fang did the thing she always did when she was on the defensive, which was to twine herself up into a human Twizzler.

"You don't know him at all," she said.

"Do I need to?" I said.

"Once you actually meet him, you'll see he's really great," she said.

"For a talking monkey," I said. And then took a big bite of my cheeseburger.

Trina had stopped eating and was fixing me with a look.

"Chess, what is that repetitive jackass disorder you have again?" she said.

True, I was always tactless, always blurting, hurting people's feelings; and then I would retreat and be nearly immobilized with shyness. It was like I had to dare myself forward, and any reflection on this made me think better of it, pull back, and shut down.

At any rate, as graduation approached we were all bursting at the seams. We just needed to be on the other side—needed to have "real life" begin. We all shared a certain kind of young elegiac tendency that was almost crippling. Everything was so new that lived life felt incredibly full: you accrued experience with such intensity, examined it so lavishly, felt feelings so deeply that it made for a twenty-one-year-old self nearly immobilized with world-weariness. The only way over this was through it—and what we needed was to burst out and start a new phase.

Of course, I had a real dearth of any actual plans. There were probably all sorts of job fairs and career seminars and things like this, but they had nothing to do with *me*. I preferred not to. I was an old pro at temping, so I figured I'd just do that for a bit until I (a) finished my monograph about Simone Martini's Blessed Agostino Novello altarpiece and its influence on alternative comics, (b) was randomly discovered by some nice person who would pay me just for being smart, or (c) wrote the Great American Novel. Twenty years' wisdom tells me a positive outcome would have been much more likely if I had pinned a dartboard to my chest and stood in the middle of Times Square.

Trina was always a lot more clued in than I, and she was the one who got us going to Career Services, where they had fat three-ring binders full of job listings, their pages sent in via exotic fax machine from publishers, entertainment conglomerates, and sundry other concerns all over Manhattan. Those pages had the air of possibility about them. I'd read them for their dollar value and think, for example, Twenty-five bucks an hour for Romanian translation? Sure, I can figure out how to do that. Trina was far more together, and it was she who showed me the page, one afternoon just before graduation, that told the Barnard community that Clarice Marr was looking for an assistant.

"Isn't this Kendra's scary mom?" is what she said.

I leaned over and looked at the page. It wasn't on fax paper but instead on something I would become all too familiar with, Clarice's stationery, which had her name, in fancy interlocking cursive, at the top of it. We stared at the page together.

"Doesn't that look like the Cosmetics Plus logo?" Trina said.

"I think I'm going to call her," I said.

"But you said she's awful."

"She is." I was staring at the phone number, which I realized was still engraved in my mind.

"You want to work for a freak like that?"

"I think I just want to ask her about Kendra," I said.

I wasn't sure what I wanted, actually.

Rumors had flown around campus. Kendra had gone off to London to work in Vivienne Westwood's shop. Or she had gone off to art school. Or off to bale hay at a Catholic Worker farm in Wisconsin, or was it California? Whatever it was, she had left New York City behind.

That evening I held the Clarice job notice in my hands and stared at it for a long time. I was the only person still there in the suite, and maybe because of this I was feeling beset by that left-at-school, Ghost of Christmas Past kind of thing. I remember sitting on the hall floor, which was covered in black-and-white vinyl tile, and staring down the length of it, through the open kitchen door and out the window, which looked out on the streetlights of Broadway.

I finally picked up the phone and called down to Eleventh Street. Amazingly, Clarice answered.

"Ms. Marr?" I said, involuntarily standing up. "Hello, this is Francesca Varani. Chess. A friend of Kendra's."

There was a pause—a pause so long that I thought I maybe should just quietly put the phone down again and slink away. Then I heard smoke slowly being exhaled. I thought of the Clarice Marr of the old glamour photograph, the insane-makingly long ash at the end of her cigarette. Here was a woman who liked to keep people waiting.

"I remember you," she said finally.

"I saw your job posting," I said, "and it made me think of Kendra. How is she?"

"When can you come in for an interview?" she said.

"I'm actually just calling to ask about Kendra."

"You're not interested in the job?"

"Um, well—how's Kendra?"

"I wouldn't know," she said.

"I heard she went to a Catholic Worker house—?"

She laughed a rich, theatrical laugh much like Kendra's.

"You girls have some comediennes up there. What a thing to be known for. *What a false scent.* Well, she was there. That lasted maybe a week—a long time ago. I could have filled you in at some point perhaps last year, but she's a big girl now, twenty-two, and frankly, I've lost interest. The last I heard she was in Morocco."

"Morocco?" I said.

"In Tangiers, visiting Paul Bowles."

"Paul Bowles!" I said.

"Do you like his writing?" she asked me. It seemed strange that she might want my opinion about anything.

"Not so much," I said. "Too solitary. Too . . . chilly. Jane's more my cup of tea."

I could hear her exhaling again.

"Jane Bowles is your cup of tea, eh?"

"Genuinely strange," I said, "sui generis."

There was another long pause.

"Why don't you come in for a talk, Francesca?" she said.

I turned to the full-length mirror. My posture was already much straighter.

"I suppose I could," I said.

"It's been terrible," she said. "Bertrand was my secretary for *years.* But the poor boy just got tired—he went off to live in London and work as a *florist.* Do I blame him? Yes, I blame him. I've had no luck since then. Terrible, terrible girls. Lazy, unreliable girls. And the ridiculous part is that this is a great job for the right person—the right conscientious type of girl. You'd live here, in his room. Or in her room, frankly."

Or in her room.

In her room, frankly.

"Come down here," she said when I didn't reply.

"When?" I said.

"How's tomorrow?"

"Tomorrow's graduation."

"Oh my dear, you'll want to go to that," she said. "A lifetime of memories." She said this with no irony whatsoever.

At that moment I knew I was going to ditch graduation. No one in my family was coming anyway. And my thought was also this: how redoubtable could this woman be if she said something like "a lifetime of memories"? My own mother, her mind reprogrammed with one million Catholic banalities, would nonetheless never say anything so insipid.

"Actually, tomorrow's fine," I said.

After we set the time, I put down the phone feeling expectant—and flushed with a kind of greed.

*

The next afternoon I sat in the parlor on Eleventh Street maintaining eye contact with Ms. Marr. *Clarice,* she insisted.

I'd gone to only a few job interviews at that point in my life. One had been with a writer who was blind and who regularly advertised at Barnard for an assistant. He sort of shot to hell the (okay, foolish) idea of blind people being nonjudgmental. I had no decent work-type shoes at the time, so I'd borrowed a pair from Trina—she was a full size smaller than me, but she'd managed to find ones with long, witchy points that I could cram my feet into if I taped up my small toes with Band-Aids. Trina of course thought it hilarious that I was borrowing a pair of shoes to go have an interview with a blind man. Anyway, the interview itself was no great shakes—the man lived in a big, bland-fancy apartment with a much younger wife who at some point came into the room with a hush-before-the-great-man sort of attitude and gently deposited a baby on his shoulder. The guy wasn't much of an interviewer, and I wasn't much of an interviewee, so I seized on this opportunity to look at the baby and announce, "What a little doll." He raised his eyebrows and said, very slowly, "No—she is a little *baby.*" Then he leaned back with satisfaction, glad to have set the record straight. I remember thinking, *This bore is a writer?* Not long after, he excused me and I went back up to Barnard wondering what I did wrong. Later I told this story to my brother Sandy.

"Wow, Chess," he said, incredulous, "I guess you don't read *Spy* magazine." They'd done an exposé on this very writer about how he endlessly advertised for assistants so that he could have young women to size up, sniff, and insult. Of one of them he famously asked, *Are you menstruating?*

It was heartening to realize that I must not have been sufficiently smelly.

At any rate, as soon as Clarice opened the door of the house on Eleventh Street and looked at me that morning, I knew something. How to explain this? I knew the job was mine. And that if I took it I'd have to jump through hoops to prove myself to her.

She showed me into the parlor. Unlike on the weekends, the curtains were open and the room was flooded with afternoon light. I realized I had to put myself in the false position of pretending I'd barely been there before, and managed some "surprised" comments on the beauty of the room. Clarice, I knew, would be one of those people who liked to hear her taste complimented.

The house on Eleventh Street, I'd come to realize, was an entirely different place during the week than on the weekend. During the week the stress fell on the front of the house, the public face that overlooked the street. The back, which looked out on the garden, had been Kendra's domain, the realm of dreaming. But now it was all business, and we were in Clarice lockdown. She was dressed extremely formally, in a Chanel suit—a real one, as far as I could tell—of taupe bouclé trimmed in black. She had on high heels and her hair was in a complicated upsweep.

"Do you like 'Francesca' or 'Chess'?" she asked me once we'd sat down. She had indicated the low, notoriously-uncomfortable-unless-you-were-sprawling daybed for me to sit on, while she took the most generous and comfortable chair in the room. Later I would learn that this particular kind of chair was known as a *bergère à la reine*. Clarice was the queen.

"Chess," I said.

"I think I'll call you Francesca," she said.

"If you must," I said.

"Francesca, what languages do you speak?" she asked.

"I can translate Latin. And Italian. Sort of slowly."

I could tell she thought this was a ridiculous answer.

"Can you at least read French?" she said.

"Not so much . . . but . . . enough to babble through the scene when Hans Castorp talks to the girl with the Kirghiz eyes."

She sat staring very weirdly into my own eyes.

"Well, what a very literary response," she said.

"I like to read," I said, wretched with obviousness.

"What was your major?"

"Art history."

"Preposterous," she said.

"I like—"

"You like to look at art, eh?" she said.

"Yes," I said.

She pushed a pack of cigarettes out of the nearly flat pocket of her jacket and lit up.

"How's your grammar?" she said, blowing smoke at me and then turning away.

"It's pretty well, I guess."

She turned back to me, horrified.

"Sorry," I said. "I'm nervous."

I stood up.

"It was nice to have a chat," I said.

"What are you doing?" she asked me.

I shrugged.

"Clearly I'm not your gal," I said.

"Not the case at all, not at all," she said. Then she reached out, grabbed me by the forearm with the grip of a man, and pulled me back down.

I stared at her. Her face, I realized, was different from what I'd remembered. It occurred to me that she must have had some "work" done. Oh, she was a vain woman. Something about her was not really human, suggesting that she made no concessions to anyone who might be. I felt foolish, unsophisticated, beside her. She was like a movie actress, playing herself in her life. It was alien—but it was glamorous, and I realized that some of the charge I'd got from Kendra came from this very quality. But Clarice was a cold fish. I wanted to study her but not be studied by her.

And yet I couldn't leave. It was as if there was something we knew about each other, some understanding we could just about smell in each other—some familiar embarrassment. She was fronting, just as I always was.

"The job pays three hundred dollars a week," she said, "and you'll live here. No friends will stay over, of course. You'll be on call as I need you during the week, at any hour. The time on the weekend is your own, unless something particular comes up. Lunch together, unless I have a date, and dinner occasionally. Breakfast is your own, unless something comes up. If things work out, I'll put you on the family insurance after three months."

She stood up then, so I did too. I opened my mouth to speak, and a gust of silence blew out.

"Why don't you go get your things?" she said.

*

Trina and I had talked about getting a place together in the "forgotten" neighborhood of Williamsburg. It was then the land of struggling Dominican and Puerto Rican families, old-school Gs, Southside crack houses, Satmar Hasidim, suspicious Poles, and a handful of mostly white artists and hip spots such as the art collectives Brand Name Damages and Minor Injury, bars like the Ship's Mast, Brooklyn Nights, Teddy's, and the old-man Greenpoint Tavern, warehouse clubs that would pop up and then be abruptly gone, and the old reliable thrift shop Domsey's, where you could find a black eyelet dress preserved intact from 1954 for a cool five bucks. In fact the plan was for Trina, me, and a friend of Trina's from D.C., Starr, who had just finished at NYU, to get a place together. I thought Starr was bullshit because she had combat-"style" boots made by Joan & David, was something of a cokehead, and was the first person I knew who ran together *Oh my God* as one word. Actually, the woman could've been Hannah Arendt and I still would've been critical of her—because my level of insecurity, I realize only now, was such that any friend outside our circle carried the risk of pulling Trina away from me. But. Trina thought the Clarice gig sketchy at best and tried to talk me out of taking it. Most of all, she was skeptical about the living situation.

"I don't know, Chess, but the words 'house slave' come to mind," she said.

I was, however, adamant. And I told her that anyway, it would be easier to find a two-bedroom than a three-bedroom, so she and Starr would have better luck without me. The more Trina argued against it—Trina, whose nickname was the Philadelphia Lawyer—the more I knew the job was *supposed* to be mine. It felt to me almost like the course of my life depended on it.

Trina's parents had come up for graduation, along with her brother Matthew, and that night they took us to dinner at the Yale Club. Her family was the coolest family in the world to me. Trina's mother, Jannicke, was beautiful, blond to the max but with a severe, Kierkegaardian turn of mind, and she had a lot of amazing, atypical, and to me decidedly unmomlike pursuits such as smoking a clay pipe and collecting daguerreotypes of dead Victorian people. The Judge was a creature of myth. On the surface, and certainly in photographs, he had the militarily serene eyes of a pitiless son of a biscuit. A massive Irish American guy, a bomb defuser in Vietnam and an airborne Ranger, he was without fear and seemingly immune to pain—you could well picture him calmly cutting off his gangrenous toe with a tactical knife—but he was a lover of life, thrilled to laugh and be silly and, mostly, see his people happy. He loved his family like nothing I'd ever seen before, and no matter the incendiary things a person like me might have said about the GOP over the years while eating at his table, he never took offense. Once you were in, you were in, and I thought of this as very Irish in the best way: you never peach on a fellow. Trina's brother, Matthew, was terribly handsome but shy about it and always told stories about things like going down the side of an Alp on his face, his snowboard a plow behind him.

I remember that night at the Yale Club so well, even now. To quote Ben Gazzara for a moment here, *The booze we consumed.* The champagne flowed and we all told funny stories and our table was just roaring. The Moriarty family all had crazy infectious laughs. Everyone was looking at us, but not because we were arguing or being awful, not because we were weird or embarrassing—which would be the reason that people always chose to stare at my family—but because we were beautiful. Happy and laughing, but beautiful. I wondered later if the people looking at us, smiling at us, thought that I was part of this family, the odd dark-haired daughter among the blondes and redheads. The thought was thrilling to me. Thrilling in the way that some half-remembered Shirley Temple movie, where she's whisked away from a life of drudgery by the appearance of her real father, had been to me as a child.

That evening really was a kind of farewell, I realize now. To the life of college, to the 1980s, to being a kid. And I wonder if I admitted to myself then that if Trina's was the family I wish I had, my hope was that maybe Kendra's would be the one I would be taken in by—the family that would make manifest some version of my dream life.

Part II

II

When Trina saw I was dead set on working for Kendra's mother she gave in, and she and Fang helped me cart all my stuff down to the house on Eleventh Street.

It was only June but already freakishly hot, and we were all crazy sweat machines schlepping my trunk and boxes down on the 1 train, through the long alligator alley to the L, and then over to Eleventh Street. Once in front of the house, the whole thing seemed newly unreal. How could I be moving into Kendra's house without her? I was glad it was the weekend and Cornelia the one there to greet us.

"Francesca!" she yelled out when she opened the door, smashing herself into me. Puberty had hit in the years since I'd last seen her, and overlaid on her stony little Austrian-businessman self something bubbly, gushy, extravagant. I introduced her to Trina and Fang-Hua and she was immediately captivated and touching them all over.

"Oh my God, I love that you're so *pretty*! I like your hair, isn't it just so pretty and so *nice*? Asian hair is just the *best* hair *ever*. I like your Docs, they're the coolest, can I try them on? Oh, I love that you're all so *totally sloppy* but you're all like so *totally pretty* too!"

We were up the stairs and down the hall and she was beckoning us into Kendra's room. I felt a shyness come on.

"Cornelia, I think I'd rather stay in Bertrand's old room," I said.

"Mum wants you here," she announced.

Fang and Trina had gone into the room and were gently picking up Kendra's things, studying them. The room looked a lot like it had the first time I'd been there, almost four years before. There was the metallic wallpaper with its psychedelic print, the preteen-dream bed set with its dainty vanity mirror covered in band stickers—Kraut, Bad Brains, False Prophets, Undead—and the piles of pillows and stacks of books and *stuff* of Kendra, her feather boas and European unguents and glitter makeup. The same light came through the French doors that led to the terrace. And yet the animating spirit was gone.

"I'd feel like a ghost," Fang said. She picked up a hat—the toque with its broken aigrette—popped it on her head, and turned to us, framing her face with blossomlike hands.

"Mr. DeMille," Trina said to her, "I'm ready for my Thorazine."

Fang took off the hat and hung it back up.

"We already took anything valuable," Cornelia announced. "So Mum said to throw out whatever you don't want."

Trina gave me a look. WTF? When she was home in D.C. and cutting her hair in the earlier punk-rock-dreadlocked days of her existence, her mother would take knotty bits out of the wastepaper basket, tie them in ribbons, and place them in Trina's baby book.

"No foolish sentimentalism in these parts," she said flatly.

I looked around at the wallpaper, the book piles, the big strawberry-shaped pillow.

"I don't think I'll touch a thing," I said.

*

Because, as they'd later say in television commercials, that's just not the way I roll. I mean, I may have been given to eating other people's food out of their refrigerators, rummaging through their bathroom cabinets, and distractedly leaving balled-up tissues on most available flat surfaces of their apartments, but in many ways I conduct myself like a person who leaves no footprints. I remember I felt a huge amount of gratitude in being allowed to be in that house at all. I felt as if I'd been chosen for something, and because of this I had a debt to repay. I was there to serve.

Time moves slowly at that age, and I remember the texture of those summer workdays very clearly. I've always been a terrible riser, but

I'd be up early, dressed, and down in the kitchen drinking coffee with Cornelia by eight. We were both mad coffeeheads and mostly didn't eat breakfast unless there was a bread product about, like some special cakey thing from Balducci's, and then we'd stuff our faces with it. Cornelia was addicted to the worst sort of news radio, like 1010 WINS, where reporters were always shouting at you live from a tragic house fire in Queens, and this we'd listen to over our coffee, trading back and forth our versions of the more amazing outer-borough accents. We especially loved the financial guy who sounded like deepest Brooklyn circa 1942 and who'd sign off with words paraphrased, bizarrely enough, from "To the Virgins, to Make Much of Time":

Gather those rosebuds!

Then Cornelia would be out the door to one of her pursuits: piano lessons, a volunteer gig at the Episcopal church, or a "play date" (the first time I'd hear the silly phrase) with solitary girls of similarly specific enthusiasms—an oboe recital, ikebana class, or unicycle-riding jaunt around Washington Square. Cornelia was one fascinating little weirdo. I liked her fine, but she could go from nice to brat in seconds, and she liked to direct her frustration at me. One morning when we were doing our 1010 WINS voices, she suddenly turned to me and said, "You have an accent."

"I do?" I asked. No one had ever told me this.

"Yes, you have a hint of a kind of bizarre maybe like Philadelphia accent? Or I suppose it would be like a mid-Atlantic accent. Some Catholic-ethnic thing."

"I don't know that I do," I said.

"Sure you do—say the word 'O-R-A-N-G-E.'"

I swallowed, never expecting to be called out on something like my language skills.

"Orange," I said.

"See, you said '*ar*-ange.'"

"Okay, well, Cornelia, how do *you* say it?"

"*Or*-ange. How one should."

117

Times like this I would feel an insane anger flash up in me, instantaneous and worse than poison. But just as quickly I'd swallow it, make light of it.

"Ah . . . let's call the whole thing off," I said.

Once Cornelia was gone, I'd go upstairs to Clarice's office and make sure things were just the way she liked them. Every item on her desk, I have to say, is burned into my memory as if each were actually enormous and standing with its companions on a wide, flat, Stonehenge-like plain. There was her blue Wedgwood table lighter; her fountain pen in its majolica cup; her Indian silver ashtray; her black rotary telephone with ALGONQUIN 4-8629 on its sepia label; her Lalique crystal bowl full of parrot tulips or peonies; her twin French lamps with their garlanded bucrania; her leather blotter with its butcher-paper inserts that I had to measure, cut, and lay in fresh each morning. Similarly, every morning I had to take care of the flowers: trim them on the bias, change the water in the big crystal bowl, crush an aspirin on a section of the previous week's *New York Observer,* then fold it and pour the crushed bits into the water, all the while holding my mouth in a tight clamp of concentration lest I nick, chip, or, God forbid, drop the Lalique.

When everything was ready I'd sit on the little low lady-in-waiting tabouret with a book (I was reading, and loving, a succession of Mary McCarthy books all that summer) and wait for Clarice to show herself. I might wait twenty minutes or an hour, but whenever Clarice finally did appear—always impeccably dressed and with a full face of makeup—her entrance had the practiced fervor of a diva taking the stage: "I am *overjoyed* at this beautiful morning."

She would beam, and, thrilled that she seemed to be beaming at me, sitting there in my absurd pretend-grown-up clothes—a '60s-era polyester minidress with matching hairband, a reclaimed men's suit in metallic sharkskin, the odd plaid faille midi worn with a "romantic" jabot-collared blouse—I would beam back at her.

The mornings were dedicated to her correspondence. She would walk around the room, smoking and dictating letters while I sat bolt upright on my toadstool and scribbled in a little steno pad. In those early days I didn't understand Clarice's completely irony-free ways, her allergy to the unserious, and sometimes the timbres of her voice would sound so plummy that I was sure she was making a joke, knocking someone else's pretensions. I'd raise a goofy eyebrow and try to catch her eye, but any look she gave me acknowledged nothing at all. It was as if she were looking through me at some elegant, far shore. I quickly learned to drop my hint-making ways and tried to cultivate a thorough and complementary seriousness.

I couldn't get enough of looking at her, and she must have known this about me. Sometimes she'd break off in midsentence and stand at one of the tall, north-facing windows to show me her profile while she peered out at the trees on Eleventh Street. Surrounded by her things, all so fine and French, and with her dramatic, artificial looks, she seemed to be posing for Cecil Beaton.

Lunch with Clarice was an exercise in what it was to be a WASP. Oddly, it seemed to grow in complexity over the course of the week, like the *New York Times* crossword puzzle. Straight on through Thursdays it was some retro thing prepared by Cornelia. Mondays we'd have a version of the Chock Full o'Nuts "Classic," that is, date-nut bread with cream cheese, which was laid out on Spode plates in the enormous refrigerator with a side of thinly sliced celery. Despite the Spode, this always felt like punishment. Tuesdays' club sandwiches on white bread (which I hadn't grown up eating and which, because of this, fascinated me) were slightly better, while Wednesday was usually potage parmentier or some other soup of complex preparation yet bland result. Thursday would be some horrible "salad" dolloped into parfait cups, one of which involved grapes, canned mandarin oranges, shredded carrot, miniature marshmallows, and—I wish I were kidding—mayonnaise. Disgusting! This was pretty much the only thing I couldn't make myself choke down, try as I did. This was, however, noticed by Clarice, and we saw a moratorium on creamy salads by the end of June.

In contrast to the rest of the week, the Friday luncheon was like a gift. It consisted of a complicated three-course meal, cooked and served by a long-suffering, 98-percent-silent lady from Puebla named Dolores (whom Clarice called, almost to her face, "the little catering woman"), using Clarice's hardback Julia Child with the little fleurs-de-lis on its cover. Dolores was absolutely top-notch as a chef, and as gloomy as a mile-wide storm cloud. I've never liked being served, so I was constantly hopping up in the course of our luncheon, diving for the water pitcher or an extra plate, so much so that once, in my enthusiasm, I knocked Dolores down and almost gave her a skull fracture. (Bizarrely, after that she was much friendlier to me.) Better than the food even was that guests usually came on Fridays. These guests might be Clarice's editor, her agent Hat Lady, or sometimes, most thrilling of all, other writers. When Clarice let slip that a writer was coming, what with me being so into fiction and knowing by then who all was rumored to live in the neighborhood, I held my breath for the appearance of Grace Paley, Donald Barthelme, or maybe even Thomas Pynchon, whom I somehow pictured stealing down the street in batwing cape and Freddy Krueger mask.

Instead, the writers who did come to lunch were never novelists. They were belletrists: essayists, journalists. And for whatever reason, they were almost exclusively elderly. Their books seemed mostly to have come out during a small window of opportunity from 1952 to 1957, to respectable acclaim and thin sales. I'd never heard of a single one of them, but I loved meeting any kind of writer and I was nothing if not enthusiastic. One in particular wasn't elderly at all but a preening young man with the made-up-sounding name of Broyer Weatherhill, who was so naked in his ambition that he was like some joke figure out of Evelyn Waugh. But more about him later.

To get back to the daily routine, after lunch I usually typed up all the morning correspondence, as well as any "pages" Clarice may have worked on the evening before. The first time such pages were entrusted to me, I couldn't wait to race up the stairs to the typing study to be the first person to see this precious Claricean output. And can I tell you? The pages were nothing. They were as bland as morning oatmeal. It was a shocking thing to see, like your first-grade teacher naked in high heels. Years later I would meet a writer who described his fledgling work as so blank that it was uncritiqueable short of saying that it consisted of marks on a page—and Clarice's early pages were like this, a seemingly unfertile humus seeded with the skimpiest of letters.

But I didn't understand her methods. I'd type up those pages—and she instructed me to format my typing in a narrow column down the center of each page, with two-inch margins on either side—and the

pages would come back the next day festooned with all sorts of emendations and additions written very neatly in the wide margins. I'd type
these up, give them over, and the next day, same thing: more additions,
more emendations. Thus the work was tended and nurtured and cul-
tivated day by day until it grew into shapely, many-leaved maturity. I
admired Clarice's diligence, and I could recognize the worth of her
writing, even as I realized (with no little letdown) that what she chose
to write about—always overspecific but from a too-distant standpoint,
as if she didn't want to dirty her hands—was of no real interest to me.
Try as I might to get with the house brand, her concerns weren't mine:
how globalism has destroyed regional poetry; why modern classical
music has failed us; could Peter Martins even be considered a chore-
ographer? Many of the essays in fact shared the same subtext, which,
simply put, was this: standards were really slipping. She used the old
Noted with Pleasure "we" a lot: *While we may go to the woods to find*
peace . . . She was resolutely apolitical. Worst of all, I found her writing
style dowdy. It was an odd match for the sharpness of her person, the
chicness of her eye—her lavish charisma.

Which might have been exactly the point.

She was amazingly prolific, and lots of important people clearly
liked her work, however, because these essays would get published
in journals, reprinted in anthologies, and subsequently collected into
her own books. Like Edmund Wilson, her approach to writing was "no
waste."

And so each day, after typing everything up, I'd run back downstairs
and give Clarice her ever-evolving pages. By that point she'd be making
her phone calls, sitting in her chair half turned to the window, a cigarette burning in her silver ashtray, her formidable manicured fingers
drumming the desktop in an impatient tattoo—those fingers telling me
to get in and out but quick. And so I'd wordlessly lay the papers on her
desk and steal away.

After that, I was free to leave the house.

And once I hit the sidewalk I could finally breathe again. True, I was
on a short tether—this was the errand portion of my day—but just to
be outside was amazing. Don't get me wrong: in those early days I loved
my job, I loved having such responsibility placed on me, I loved being

Gal Friday to a person whose books, even if they weren't my cup of tea, I could reach out and touch in a bookstore. Actual *books* written by someone I *knew.* It was as if that luster rubbed off on me: I was an emissary of that world. I clearly had value, because such value was an extension of Clarice's.

And yet I was quickly becoming aware that the person I had to be in front of Clarice was a buttoned-up, laconic, and in fact dully inaccurate version of me. On the street I was myself again, and often, as soon as I turned the corner off Eleventh Street, I'd make the world's craziest face, opening my mouth wide as a satchel and squeezing my eyes shut. On particularly stressful days I'd stab my hands in the air and go *wah-wah-wah* in short, bleating blasts.

At any rate, my afternoon errands might take me to places like the stationer's, the elegant hardware store on University Place, the picture framer's over on Third Avenue, the Jefferson Market Library. Sometimes I'd go to the garden by the library and try to imagine the women's prison that Kendra had told me about all those years ago, which had once stood there. I'd think about her, wondering where she was (Morocco?) and what she'd make of all this. I could still hear her calling her brother Bertrand a *successful parasite* back in the day when he worked for their mother. And since I could imagine Kendra's disdain all too easily, I'd quickly push those thoughts away.

Sometimes my errands for Clarice would take me out of the neighborhood entirely. She was a great giver of books, the rarer the better, and so I'd be sent to any number of specialty bookshops in search of these gifts, an envelope of clean fifties tucked inside my pocket. Maybe I'd go to New York Bound up in Rockefeller Center for a first edition of *Gangs of New York,* or to the Complete Traveller for a WPA Guide to Nebraska (!) or a Baedeker of Lower Egypt, or over to the Diamond District, where the Gotham Book Mart was—and where Trina had just got a job—for a 1940s-vintage New Directions hardback, say, *Three Lives* or *Nightwood,* with a perfect jacket by the great Alvin Lustig. Or I'd go up to the Argosy on Fifty-Ninth Street for the 1930 edition of the last word in deco bookmaking, *The Savoy Cocktail Book.* These errands stay in my mind with a singular sweetness. Wrapped up in this was the excitement of exploring the city, out on my own and earning my bread;

the beauty and charge of the summer afternoon, and being surrounded by books, which I loved most of all.

I'd signed on to make dinner once a week. "Something *robusto*," Clarice had told me—just assuming I'd been born with a wooden spoon in my hand—and so, back in the neighborhood, I'd often end up at Balducci's. I had a kind of fetish for how much I loved Balducci's, which I remember back then, in its old incarnation, as dark and dramatic, still a little bit '70s but lovely, painted all over a deep forest green, with amazing cheeses, fruit that looked like jewels, and marbled meat stamped in purple and unsettling in its bounty, all of it twined around with faux grapevines. Everything looked like a gift there. And I probably didn't put this together at the time, but I think I loved the specific nature of the Italian Americanness that played in that store. There wasn't anything cheap about it. The feeling was graceful, hardworking, rightfully proud of itself: *This we know how to do.* I have always liked people who take pride in their craft, whatever that craft is.

Most nights dinner was just Cornelia and I, but often on a day I cooked, Clarice would join us. And every blue moon Sidney, the elusive Mr. Löwenstein, would materialize.

It was frankly a disappointment to finally meet him. The first time I was told that he was in town and would be coming up to say hello, he walked into Clarice's office with such self-effacement that I actually craned my neck to look behind him to await the real Mr. Löwenstein. How can I put it? This man . . . there was no moment about him. He was nearly a head shorter than Clarice, rounded and shoulderless and with a slight walrusy aspect, an effect that was offset by a child's too-pretty green eyes. He was a mild person, tending toward kind, and seemed so in thrall to Clarice it was embarrassing. I fought down the image of Erich von Stroheim as the butler to aging bitch-goddess Gloria Swanson in *Sunset Boulevard.*

At the first dinner together I made the mistake of asking Sidney what he did for a living. All movement at the table stopped dead.

"I'm in the fur business," he said at last, not looking up from his plate.

"Oh," I said helpfully.

Clarice and Cornelia quietly continued eating, their icy silence communicating to me the terribleness of my huge piece of gaucherie.

123

Sidney traveled all the time, to places like Denmark and Finland, which was a good thing because these dinners *à quatre* were pretty stiff and performative, as if we were being watched by an outside party. More often, however, Clarice was out of the house for dinner, at an event or one of the clubby restaurants where she loved being seen— La Caravelle, Le Grenouille, La Côte Basque, Lutèce; things generally had to be French, and expensive. If she told me what time she'd be in, that meant I was to be ready for her and we'd have some after-ten work session. If not, that meant I could fly out into the night. And so I'd usually be right on the horn with Trina or Fang.

Trina had found a place in Williamsburg on the cut between Southside and North, Grand Street, while Fang had moved in with Decon Head in his apartment up by the old CU, much to our distress. Since there was only one phone line in the Marr-Löwenstein house and no call waiting, I had to keep my phone calls quick and infrequent. Whenever the phone rang I was always pouncing on it lest it be one of my friends and, God forbid, Clarice had to answer it. Thus I was up and down the four flights of stairs in that house many, many times a day, panting like a son of a bitch. On the weekends, however, the phone could ring all it wanted to, because Clarice would be at the country house up near Hyde Park, miles and miles away.

Usually she'd go alone, or with Sidney on the rare occasions when he was in town. Always, however, at exactly the moment Clarice's old Volvo turned the corner off the block on Friday afternoon, from the other direction, timed like a break-in caper, a dark-blue Toyota would roll into view. This would be Sidney's sister Anne—Kendra's "Jewy aunt" from days of yore—bringing Zeyde to stay the weekend, to be watched over by Cornelia and me.

When I saw him again, I realized Zeyde was in deep decline. Evidence suggested that once Kendra went AWOL the task of caring for him fell completely to Anne, who seemed permanently exhausted and very much needing these weekend reprieves. She was a modest, momish lady, shy about her girth, and her eternal long skirts and long sleeves suggested that she practiced a much more conservative Judaism than anything her father or her brother might. She was in her late forties when I first met her, and spryly youthful in that way that big but agile

124

women can sometimes be. She was not book-smart at all, but she had a quick wit and a compassionate way about her.

She really was the polar opposite of Clarice, the least glamorous or public-faced person one could think of. On the rare occasions when I saw the two of them in a room together, it was clear that each was the other's least favorite person, maybe in the entire world. Clarice's glittering eyes would travel Anne's body, going from sexless mom haircut to wide-stripe I'm-so-big-I've-just-given-up shirt to skirt that pitched to the ground in front and in back revealed thick ankles and sneaker-clad feet, pulled up as it was by the bulk of her huge bottom. Sometimes Anne wore appliqué sweatshirts with bears on them. Clearly to Clarice she was the last word in the Suburban Horrendous.

So anyway, on the weekends it was just Cornelia, me, and Zeyde in the house. During Saturday afternoons we'd take him for brunch at one of the wheelchair-accessible diners on Sixth Avenue, and then we might wheel on over to Washington Square Park so that he could watch the chess players. From there I might leave him with Cornelia and go off briefly to buy stuff for our dinner, or just to snatch a little time alone. But never too much time. And when I'd come back, I'd always feel a smile on my lips as soon as I saw the two of them sitting together, both so stolid, heads bowed, Cornelia reading *Battle Cry of Freedom* or *The Silver Palate Cookbook* and Zeyde napping or dreaming or enjoying the sun on his ancient head. I would have a leap of something like joy in my chest when I saw them: I was here to protect these people.

Zeyde phased in and out much more than before, but sometimes he'd have incredible spates of lucidity. At these times he might go into a story from the past, tell a joke, or ask me to read from his favorite author, Anthony Trollope. Anthony Trollope! I loved this fact so much it could almost bring tears to my eyes. The stories from the past would sometimes make him go straight to Yiddish, which fascinated me and made me think of my Abruzzese grandfather, who'd spoken Italian, *dialetto guardiese*, and Portuguese but had no use for English, which he once termed *distaccata*. "Detached." This I took to mean that it could not express what he needed to say.

It was from Zeyde that I first heard a version of the herring joke: "So a rabbi asks his student, What is green, hangs on the wall, and whistles?

And the student says, I don't know. And the rabbi says, A herring. The student replies, You might be able to paint a herring green and hang it on the wall, but definitely you can't make it whistle. And Mr. Rabbi says, So it doesn't whistle!"

Cornelia would scream with glee at this, but I, always scratching around after causality, couldn't make any sense of it at all. I mean, Catholics just didn't have jokes like this. It was only once I'd hit about thirty and realized that life ran on all kinds of random tracks and you had to roll with it or stand by sniffing and blinking about "unfairness" that I could finally appreciate the thing.

After dinner, if I wasn't reading *The Way We Live Now* to Zeyde, we'd wheel him into the piano room and Cornelia would play for us. This wasn't like it had been in the past, however. Without Kendra, none of us seemed to know how to begin to sing. It was one day late in that summer when Zeyde, after dinner, turned his milky old eyes to me and said, "Kendra, honey, why don't you sing for us?"

I looked at him and then looked to Cornelia, who just shook her head.

"Oh, sorry, sorry, sorry," he said in a moment, tenting his hand over his eyes, squeezing his temples, trying to draw the right memory out of himself again.

Fond of Cornelia and Zeyde as I was, Saturday nights round about eight my foot would start to tap and all I could think about was getting over to the East Village to meet up with Trina and Fang. We had a standing order to convene at the Holiday at nine p.m. Back then this was our clubhouse, the Holiday Cocktail Lounge, and I remember in each booth in the back they had little shanty-style wall-sconce lights with tiny pull chains. In my enthusiasm I'd often go early, and when Trina showed up and slid into the duct-taped maroon vinyl booth, she'd reach over and turn on the light. I was so glad to see her, always, that I thought of this as a kind of THE DOCTOR IS IN sign. We loved the Holiday, with its eternal Christmas lights, crummy wood paneling, dented pressed-metal ashtrays, so-so jukebox, and complete lack of, I guess you might say, pandering.

The bartender was an old Ukrainian guy who scared the bejesus out of us. One could readily imagine him eating boiled shoe leather in the forests of Galicia during World War II or killing a man with his fingers. Beside him we felt young, sheltered, and frivolous—which I guess we were. He was always decent enough to the three of us, I remember, because he never yelled at us or threw us out (which you'd see happening frequently enough), but in all the endless bar-well V&Ts or bottles of Bud we drank there I don't remember one buyback. Which was fine, actually, because the prices there were strictly 1972. Under the ledge around the bar, they had those press hooks like you see in older churches where men could clip their fedoras. There was also a tall, depressed-as-fuck barback I remember, with a Fu Manchu mustache, who would go around collecting your beer bottles, take them into a back room, and smash the crap out of them.

The Holiday, Mona's, Joe's, Sophie's, the International, the Old Homestead, Bar 81, sometimes Max Fish, less so the Blue & Gold and Blanche's and the stupidly named Downtown Beirut, every once in a while the Horseshoe Bar or the Mars Bar (where we once saw a guy, in a misguided attempt to prove his punk-rock bona fides, smash and smash and smash another guy's face against the floor), the Wah Wah Hut, No-Tell Motel—we were all over them. Anything that was too slick or themey confused us, so we'd never set foot in, let's say, Korova Milk Bar, which had a kind of silly cheap-futuristic vibe. We were out to make our own thing, our own meaning.

Friends, this was an exciting time. Fang had gotten a paid internship with a slick design magazine and Trina, like I said, was working at Gotham Book Mart, which was in those days one of the maybe ten best places in the world. Gregory Corso, all big and wrecky, might come streaming inside dressed in a huge rumpled raincoat, or maybe a gaunt and saddened Arthur Miller would show up, and definitely Ginsberg, in a surprising cloud of modesty, like a shy, avuncular sunflower. Once Trina answered the phone and there was some strange old lady putting on an impossibly exaggerated Katharine Hepburn voice. Trina was about to hang up on her when she looked up at the stacks of Katharine Hepburn's new autobiography that had been set aside for signing and realized, *Oh.* The owner treated anyone nonfamous, especially his young employees, like dirt, but one of the buyers there was a cool middle-aged surfer-looking cat, and he was forever giving Trina her weight in remainders, titles they had too many of, or other things that caught her fancy. A free book to us in those days was like a bar of gold, and Trina would bring out her score, having snagged books for me and Fang as well. We were over the moon with delight.

Emblematic of these times, the wide-open world ahead of us, was one night that hot June when we were at Holiday, just before last call. Holiday closed early, at one a.m., and the three of us had put all our money on the table and were trying to arrange it in such a way to make it equal more than $4.73, when an older guy came over to us and said, "Do you girls need any money?"

Trina squinted at him like a cowboy.

"Never that badly," she said.

"No, no, ladies, I don't mean anything by it—I just like to do people a good turn." He smiled at us, surprisingly uncreepily, and I registered him as looking like my childhood best friend's uncle Yahtzee, who managed a Cumberland Farms franchise. Then the guy dropped a $50 bill on the table, told us we were all very cute, and walked out the door.

We sat looking at the $50 on the table. Then we looked up at the door, then back down at the $50. In a moment Fang was on her feet. We watched as she looked up St. Mark's Place and then down St. Mark's Place and then came back in.

"Fuck it, girls," she said, "let's get plastered."

We couldn't get enough of talking and drinking and laughing and loving the night—New York City, glittering Manhattan, the East Village back when it still scared most white people away. When the Holiday closed for the evening we'd roll east, and then up Avenue B because Mona's had the best jukebox, then down Avenue A, maybe to 2A or this one sort of heavy-metal place that had a good pool table. Trina was absolutely crackerjack at things like shooting pool and bowling, whereas I, nothing if not enthusiastic, was the one most likely to sink the wrong ball or throw the iridescent purple Brunswick into the next lane. After that maybe we'd go down to Houston for a late-night bagel or back up Second Avenue for pierogi at Veselka, which still at that time had a tiny little john area accessed via short yellow saloon-style doors, the passage through which provided something of a laff riot if one was three sheets to the wind and desperately in need of a pee. I never knew when to quit, which meant I was always the sloppiest drunk and the one insisting we stay out till four a.m., when Trina would be saying some equivalent of *There's still tomorrow* and Fang, elbow propped on a tabletop, would be falling asleep into her hand. But I never wanted these nights to end.

Gather those rosebuds!

By late July, though, Fang was coming out less and less, and when she did, she was filled with complaint about the long trip down from Columbialand. Actually she was filled with complaint about everything. Her drink was too strong or too weak; her magazine job was increasingly monotonous; her guy, Decon Head, had an annoying propensity for disappearing to the Hungarian Pastry Shop, manly chessboard tucked under his arm, while she did their laundry.

"Why are *you* doing *his* laundry?" Trina asked, incensed.

"Because I don't like the way he does laundry," Fang said.

"What's there to like and not like?" I asked.

"He mixes everything together so my whites turn pink."

"Couldn't you maybe teach him?" Trina said.

"He's not interested."

"Girls, is anyone actually *interested* in laundry? Why's it fair that it always lands on you?"

"It just does," she said.

"And Jesus, Fang—when do you ever wear *white*?"

Fang took a long sip of her drink.

"I'm bored by this topic," she announced.

Fang was also heavy into one of my least favorite habits of hers: the Astonishing Contrary Paraphrase. She'd be talking about something that annoyed her, some Murphy's Law thing, and I'd say in sympathy, for example, "Yeah, it's like when you're waiting for the bus and debating having a cigarette and as soon as you light one, the bus comes," and she'd say, "No, actually, it's like you're waiting for the bus and you light a cigarette and *then* the bus comes." With this, she'd look at me as if I were the biggest moron in the world. And I'd think, Girl should really stop reading that Žižek.

Actually what I'd really be wondering was why she always seemed to have such a nonresponse to the smallest suggestion of empathy.

One night when it was just Fang and me, I suggested we meet up for sushi at Sapporo in the East Village. Fang sounded fine on the phone, but when she turned up I instantly saw she was in a bad mood. She gave me a stiff hug and spilled herself into a chair.

"What's the matter?" I said.

"Nothing," she said, immediately hiding her face behind the menu.

"What do you mean, nothing?"

"Nothing." She turned to the side and flipped her long hair in her characteristic way, so that it instantly flooded down again to wash her bird-wing shoulders.

"Really, what is it, Fang?"

"Nothing. *Nichts—méi shénme.*" She redoubled her studying of the menu.

"You want a Sapporo?" I asked her.

"I guess."

And because it was summer and Friday and golden with light, I started talking. I talked about how great the week had been and the view out the terrace to the backyard hydrangeas all lazy with summer; about my transect walks of what I called "our neighborhood" for Clarice's Jane Jacobs essay—a topic that *did* interest me; about Clarice's way of saying "rother" rather than "rather" and "dour" like "door," about how she—

"Clarice, Clarice, Clarice—do you know how sick I am of Clarice?"

I sat up in my chair.

"Geez, sorry," I said.

"All you talk about is Clarice."

"Geez, um, I'm sorry," I said.

"What are you, in love with her?"

"That's supposed to be funny?"

Our food had come and we both shut our mouths until the server, a lanky guy with a rocker-boy haircut, went away again.

"Wow, retro boy could be one of the Plastics," I said, sliding my chopsticks out of their paper wrapper and trying to defuse the situation.

"Jesus, Chess—fucking don't rub your chopsticks together. Don't you know that's an insult?"

"What? Why?" I said. I'd only recently learned how to eat sushi, and I thought I was slick.

"It's like telling them they have shoddy stuff that you have to repair," she said.

"But Cornelia showed me," I said.

"Yeah, *Cornelia* would know," she spat.

"Geez, should we even stay and eat?"

But she was already tucking into the food, putting a huge piece of sushi into her little mouth like someone angling a couch through a doorway. She looked down at the plate, chewing away and ignoring me. What was bugging her so badly? I tried to ask her again, and opened and closed my mouth several times. I gave up, too easily, and picked up a piece of sushi.

We said very little. Dinner was a joyless chewing exercise that went on forever. Fang was simmering. When the cute waiter finally came to take our plates, he gave Fang a long, tender look. Once his back was turned, Fang leaned in my face and hissed, "Did you know the Japanese race was started when a bunch of thugs kidnapped a Chinese princess and raped her?"

"Jesus Christ, Fang, can we get the fuck out of here?"

Out on the street, we pounded down the avenue until I finally had to turn to her.

"Would you talk to me?"

Her eyes were open wide and she was staring down wretchedly at the ground as she walked, her mouth all contorted. She didn't say anything.

"You're looking like some grieving Mary out of Mantegna," I said.

"Why do you have to make everything into a *joke*?" she said.

"I don't know," I said, "I don't know. The opposite's worse."

"The opposite's reality," she said.

"Since when has either of us been so fond of reality?" I said.

"Well, it's not like *you* have to live in reality. You have your shit all taken care of."

"What is *up* with you?" I said.

But she'd stopped walking and just stood on the sidewalk staring at the ground.

"This is just crap," she said. "This is all just total crap." She put her hands over her face and in a moment she was dry-crying, hiccup-crying . . .

I wanted to get her off the street to someplace sheltered, but all I

131

could do was wrap my arm around her skinny shoulders. Some stupid guy walking by turned to pointedly ogle us and I flipped him the bird—*Mind your own fucking business.*

"Come on, Fangy, let's move it on down," I said.

She let herself be maneuvered down the street and we ended up in the sliver of park by the subway, a place where people went to puke or shoot up. We sat down on a bench. I pulled out my cigarettes and offered her my pack, and she shook her head, not unkindly, and took out her own.

"Since when do you smoke lights?" I said. I hated it when my friends changed things on me.

She shrugged. She had regained her cool, tough, yé-yé girl exterior.

"Is it about . . . is it about, um . . . ?" I knew all this had to be about Decon Head, but I so totally thought of him as Decon Head that I was completely blanking on his actual name.

"Yes, it's Clark," she said.

"What's going on?"

"I think I need out," she said.

"Tell me," I said.

She turned to the side and put her feet up on the bench, pulling herself into a little ball.

"I don't even know where to start. It's like he doesn't know how to share. Sometimes he comes home and I don't even know he's there until I go to the kitchen and find him crouching inside the refrigerator door cramming cheese singles into his mouth. This is just not normal behavior, right? He actually snapped at me for leaving a *bookmark* in his copy of *Truth and Method.* He said it might crease the pages. Like crease his ass, right? That's just really weird OCD kind of fucked-up behavior, right? And he's greedy. He's greedy! This one time we were at Dynasty and he ordered moo goo gai pan and I guess I said something about the way it looked when they put it on the table and he said, *Okay, too bad, you're not getting any.* I thought he was kidding and then when I reached out to get some he actually *slapped my hand away.* Not like a funny kind of thing either. And it got me that he'd been just looking for an excuse not to share his moo goo gai pan. He's greedy, and he's cheap. And his parents are like filthy rich motherfuckers."

"Of course they are," I said bitterly.

"And you'd think this would be like suggesting that he wants to be by himself, right, wouldn't you? We got into a huge fight last week and I went to get the fuck out of there and he grabbed my shoes off the floor and held them way up in the air above my head. He's like, *Where you going, where you going, little Fang? You can't go out without your shoes.*"

"Jesus Christ, Fang," I said.

"I know, right?"

"Don't you have another pair of shoes?"

"Like, well, yeah, but they're all in storage. I have my work shoes and those plastic shower things you buy in the grocery store that your Chinese grandpop has."

"I want to slap Clark's head off," I said.

"Oh, he's not so bad," she said.

"Fang, he's a sociopath. That behavior is abusive, is what it is."

"Yeah, I guess," she said.

"I'm serious. You've got to get out of there."

She straightened up, slid her feet to the ground, and stretched. Then she looked at me.

"Whatever, it feels better now. I guess it's what they say. *It feels good to talk about it.*"

"But no, don't you see? It's only going to escalate."

"Yes, but whatever. Where would I go, Chess? Hmm? Back down to D.C. to ask can I have my old job at Olsson's back? I'm going to move in with my fucking family?"

"Why are you acting like that's your only option? There's a million apartments or shares or whatever you can find here—did you even look?"

"Did *you* even look? No, you didn't—you got hooked right up. Job, apartment, lifestyle, welcome to swanky town. Climb that *social ladder.*"

"Please don't be quoting Marginal Man at me, okay? What the fuck, Fang? It's a job. I work and I get paid for it. What's so wrong about that?"

"What's wrong with that? What's *wrong*? What's wrong is I see you *changing.* I see you *modifying* yourself to fit into some kind of new shape, modifying yourself to please that bitch."

"Look, that's not true. How can that be true? I don't think it's true.

133

Look, what if it's true? I mean, I have so much to learn anyway. Can't you cut me some slack here and not be so eternally hard-line? I mean, Jesus, Fang, maybe I have a million things to learn. Maybe I *need* modifying."

She didn't answer but busied herself with lighting a cigarette. I fumbled for my pack, tried to shake one out, and realized it was empty. I sat staring at my empty pack until Fang reached over and handed me her lit cigarette.

"It's my last one too," she said quietly. "We can share."

I said nothing, but took it and nodded. Across the tiny square, we watched as a short punk-rock kid, *TSOL* painted on the back of his jacket, went up to the wall of the bunkerlike building in the middle of the park and unzipped.

"Hey. *Hey!*" Fang yelled at him. "Yeah, *you,* BAD TASTE IN MUSIC BOY. Take your goddamned potty break somewhere else, you little WRETCH. Can't you see we're having a CONVERSATION?"

Fang turned gently back to me.

"Thing is, Chess," she said, "you always seemed okay to me. You know? *You always seemed okay to me.*"

*

So right here might be a good place to reiterate some things about me. First off, while I did nothing but pretend otherwise, even after four years at Barnard, next to the sophistication of the Löwenstein family I was really as green as Kermit the Frog. I was the wide-eyed peasant who'd hitched herself a ride to the big city on the hay baler. I'd come from such a closed-off background that when I entered college I thought if your family had a microwave or VCR you were well on your way to being "rich."

That said, I was also a quick study. If I found something to my liking, I could immediately assimilate whatever it was—ways of thinking, talking, acting, even eating—and pretend that I'd done it all my life. Some of this behavior was almost universally convincing, some 50 percent successful, some as transparent as weak tea. Despite my fancy speech to Fang, it took a while for me to fully realize what a hideous little provincial I still was, and I had the Löwenstein family to thank for that. I mean, I must have been some real weak tea to Clarice. Kendra—I like to think she was fond of me in spite of this tendency of mine, or maybe even a bit *because* of it. I think maybe she was moved by—how to say this?—the evidence of my striving. Theirs was the club I longed to join.

Just to digress a bit further for a moment here. Recently I remembered this guy who worked at the Barnard bookstore. He had deeply pockmarked skin and wore Aloha shirts, but I remember realizing one day that I found him curiously attractive. Later I was talking with a group of women, and one of them—I think it was Karina, the L.A. scenester who, among other fantastically cool things, had attended John Doe and Exene Cervenka's nuptials back in the day—mentioned the Barnard bookstore guy and how she found him "curiously attractive." She used the very same words that I'd used in my mind. And it turned out that *all* the women in this group found the bookstore guy curiously attractive, which says something either about tenderness and vulnerability or maybe about the kind of women I knew in those days. But just to get to the point here, sometime after that I was in the bookstore buying *The Book of the City of Ladies* when Curiously Attractive Bookstore Guy happened to be working. One of his coworkers was going out to get coffees, and at the door he turned around to ask Curiously Attractive if he wanted anything else. Curiously Attractive was up on a ladder, I remember, and he called out to the guy, *Yeah, get some water. And don't get any of that domestic crap—get some Evian!*

I stood there clutching my Christine de Pizan, and I was fascinated. I was amazed by such a fine level of taste. I mean, in every sense. He could tell the difference between domestic and imported bottled water? Or did he only *think* he could? Or did he only want others to *believe* he could? I bring this all up as a way of saying that *this* was the thing the Löwenstein family had: if not a rarified, excruciating, impossible taste, then the ability to make other people think that such a thing existed. And to have those people eat their hearts out over not being invited to the club.

Needless to say, after my upbringing by an outraged-by-the-injustices-of-the-world father and an offer-it-up Catholic mother, to me this ability was (guffaw-inducing understatement) a surprise. But after working my butt off for Clarice for a few long months and showing myself to be diligent, dependable, and doggishly loyal, it seemed like the door to the club was being ever so slightly held open for me.

Looking back on that summer, really this was my education in a certain kind of New York City–ness, a certain strain of upper-middle-class Manhattanness that traded in knowing all about particular institutions, attitudes, preferences. The New York City Ballet, family-run butchers where you took a ticket to buy a chop, the Municipal Arts Society, the watch repair place in the tunnels beneath Grand Central, taciturn sweater-menders who'd emigrated from the Balkans with only a golden *zlatka* in their pocket, tiny shops that sold antique scrimshaw buttons—the Löwensteins knew all about such things. They knew all the old-school types and—yelp!—what ethnicities did what trades best. They liked superlatives, exclusivity, and it wasn't necessarily the most expensive of something, it was the most singular, rare, or ineffable. There was an itinerant *arrotino* who cruised the streets of the Village in his heap of a jalopy, ringing a bell so that you knew to bring out your knives to be sharpened on his medieval-seeming razor strop, and the Löwensteins would never consider taking their knives anywhere else. There was one right way to do something, and anything else was heresy.

On her own, Clarice made herself even more rarefied. Because she was without what I thought of (bear with me here) as the warmth and the humor of the Jewish side, her brand was mandarin, bespoke, exclusionary. Chilly. Quickly that summer I learned the simple rule that anything old was pretty much good, while anything new was pretty much bad. But the list of Clarice's specific dislikes, written on ticker tape and laid flat on the ground, would easily encircle the globe. She did not like the "tacky" light-wrapped trees of Tavern on the Green; the tendency of Hollywood movie directors to rely on close-ups; the use of "less" to mean "fewer than" in grocery store signage; the word "signage"; any woman who carried a knockoff handbag; any woman who was at all overweight, unless elderly; any woman who was taller than she was, regardless of age; any woman who wore the color pink, even for Breast Cancer Awareness Day; working-class Chinese people ("They sit down in the subway with their sixteen bags and they just *expand*"); Chinese cuisine; Mexican cuisine; Indian cuisine; the entire borough of Queens; the entire landmass of Staten Island but for Sailors' Snug Harbor; anyone who ate anything at all while walking down the

136

street or gave evidence of chewing gum by moving their jaw in a repetitive fashion; architecture after 1945; architectural restoration work that sought to tip a postmodern hand to separate itself from a building's original vintage; children who made any kind of noise at all in enclosed public spaces. She cursed Marcel Carné for his sentimentalism, hated the sight of young men in baggy "thug" pants, and with a certain smiling pride would tell anyone who listened that she had never used an ATM. She was overly fond of the word "dreadful."

Clarice also didn't waste time being concerned with other people's feelings. My realization of just to what degree this was true came one evening late that summer. Jovanna, the cleaning lady, had made the mistake of buying not the brand of dishwashing detergent Clarice liked but instead a bottle of Joy. Lemon Fresh Joy, innocuously enough. I remember it was one evening when I'd cooked dinner—I'd pulled out all the stops and made my Abruzzese grandmom's scrippelle 'mbusse as an appetizer, which is nerve-racking, because you have to make like a million little crepes on top of whatever else the dinner is. But it must have gone okay because Clarice, in an uncharacteristic show of goodwill, had helped carry the plates into the kitchen. Once at the sink, however, she did a kind of theatrical double-take and pointed.

"What is this?" she asked me.

Cornelia and I both snapped to attention.

"The Joy?" I asked.

"The Joy," Cornelia said.

"Did *you* buy this?" Clarice nearly spat at me.

"Um . . . no. I know you like the eco stuff," I managed to say.

And then she did that thing that I would grow to hate, which was to stare at a person who was awaiting a response for way too long without saying a word. Her face would betray nothing, leaving you to sweat and squirm.

"Of course you didn't buy it," she said at last, "because you *see* things. You *observe* things. You are *careful*. But some people are not." She picked up the bottle of Joy and carried it over to the step can, holding it well away from her person. She put her Ferragamo foot down on the pedal, flipped up the lid, and dropped the bottle into the trash.

"Joy," she said. "Disgusting."

And she was so angry and I was so hardwired to think I was a fraud that I thought, My God, *did* I buy the Joy? *Did* I buy the Joy?

But of course I hadn't bought the Joy.

"That Jovanna's always breaking something," Clarice said.

"She's been fine lately," Cornelia said quietly.

"No, Cornelia, she hasn't," Clarice said. "And you'd think she'd be *grateful* to clean such a beautiful house."

With this, Clarice turned on her heel and walked out of the kitchen.

Cornelia and I stood there, staring after her.

I turned to Cornelia. She turned and looked at me. I was about to mouth the words, *You'd think she'd be grateful to clean such a beautiful house,* but then I saw her make her face blank. *Zotz!* Totally blank. She stared back at me with her strange different-colored eyes. She was telling me that she wasn't going to sell her mother out. And that she wouldn't side with the hired help.

She was nothing like Kendra.

"Look, I'll do the dishes," she said, by way of apology.

I stared at her.

"With what?" I said.

Cornelia shrugged. Well, she was used to her mother. Perhaps she had different expectations. Or perhaps she had none at all? She went over and fished the Joy out of the garbage, and I pushed out through the back door to the garden, just to be out of that house for one blessed second before the evening work shift began. As the door closed behind me I heard Cornelia begin singing in her loud, space-alien voice:

Freude, schöner Götterfunken, Tochter aus Elysium . . .

*

Jovanna, who had worked for the Löwensteins for three years, was fired the next day.

Help was cheap, right? Interchangeable.

The summer was waning. I developed some kind of terrible ache in my heart, almost physically pinpointable, something to do with unsure contingencies and the feeling of time passing. When September came, it seemed strange not to be going back to school. It was like I was wait-

138

ing for someone to call and find me: *Where are you?* they would ask. *We were looking for you.*

I still kept Kendra's room exactly as I'd found it, my own things only lightly overlaying hers, my presence there temporary, provisional. Sometimes I'd pick up a book of hers and read around in it at random (the Bhagavad Gita, Trinh T. Minh-ha's *Woman, Native, Other,* an Everyman history of France that was stamped on its first page CLIFFORD ODETS NEW YORK CITY). Sometimes I'd take an old dress of Kendra's out of her closet and try it on, swooshing the skirt from side to side as I looked at myself in the mirror. And sometimes I wondered if I should just leave.

I remember I went to the San Gennaro Festival by myself, one long melancholy weeknight when everyone else had other things to do. I got a sausage-and-peppers sandwich, one with a hot link from Faicco's, and I stood on the wall and watched all the Gs pass by. At some point I realized that someone had set up camp next to me. I turned my head to see a neighborhood G, not exactly old but nothing like young, who had brought out one of those walking sticks with a padded circle on it that you could fold out into a little stool.

He was sitting there with his porkpie hat, his stogie, his immaculately kept rayon shirt with some kind of bowling embroidery on it, watching the parade of humanity along with me. He could have been my Uncle Pasquale, who was in the faucet supply business.

"Nice," he said to me, meaning the night, meaning the people, meaning most of all me, somehow I knew, arched over my sandwich, with its slick neon oil running down my fingers.

"Nice, yeah," I agreed.

We chatted comfortably about the weather and the liquefaction of the blood. He had multiple scientific explanations for it but said that he understood how it was important for a person to believe in miracles if you needed miracles to believe in. He wanted to know if I was *Napoletan'* and I told him no and what I was, *Abruzzes'* and *Marchegiana.* I always liked to say it. And the fondest window opened up. We stared across to pictures of the land, remembered nostalgia, keening grandmothers and dead grandfathers, their eyes to the sea . . .

When I had finished eating and was cleaning up, he said to me, "You want your palm read?"

"You read palms?" I said.

"Sure I do," he said.

"It's a little messy."

He gave the shrug, *boh*, I don't know, only if you want to, and I wiped down my hands with a bunch of little two-fold napkins and gave him my left hand, palm up.

He took it in his own hands, which were huge and pillowy Charlie Brown mitts, and stared at it for some time.

"You an actress?" he asked.

"Oh! No," I said, somehow flattered.

"You're something creative," he said.

"In theory."

"It's clear you are."

"I guess so," I said. "Though right now I just—"

He gave a start and pulled my hand away from his face, holding it out in front of him.

"What?" I said.

He didn't say anything, just sat there studying my hand.

In a moment he curled my fingers together, patted them gently, and gave me back my hand.

"You'll be fine, *piccola*," he said to me. "You'll be just fine."

And then he stood, folded up his seat, and disappeared down Mulberry Street.

12

One morning that October I sat in Clarice's study with my book, waiting for her to come down.

I'd gone through all the Mary McCarthy I could find by then, and I was trying to read her last novel, *Cannibals and Missionaries*. I had a smelly copy from the dollar cart outside the Strand, but that wasn't the problem. It was that the prose felt so arched-eyebrow and yet so creaky and straining, as if trying to simulate the dash of the young Mary. Later I'd come to see how completely one could age out of being the Clever Girl.

Outside it was raining hard, one of those thunderstorms that makes morning feel like night, and I realized I was really just watching the clock. Clarice was never this late. Should I go check on her? In the summer Cornelia would've been the one to do this, but she'd been sent off to a fancy school in Vermont where she was learning how to churn butter, speak Chinese, and play the doumbek. What gave me pause was that the night before I'd heard what sounded like an argument between Clarice and Sidney echo up from the living room as I lay in Kendra's bed. That had been followed by a door slam, rendered with the sharp fidelity of a Foley artist, and then silence.

Just before noon I knocked on her bedroom door.

"Oh, come in, Francesca," I heard her weary voice say.

I went inside. She was in her bed, her festooned throne, propped up in a ruffled and beribboned bed jacket against a thousand pillows. She had a glass in one hand, a cigarette in the other, and a crystal ashtray on her belly. All around her was a flotsam of papers and books, packets of cigarettes, tissues, a jar of face cream, a ripped-open gold-foil package of sugar wafers, and a bottle of Laphroaig. The silver loving cup from the mantel, empty of its dried hydrangeas, lay beside her.

She hadn't put on her eyebrows or her lipstick, and her big face, set off by a scarf in Schiaparelli pink, looked to me like something uncooked.

"Come over here," she said. "Don't be so shocked and Catholic."

I dragged the tufted vanity seat over to her bed, cutting a groove in the rug, and sat by her.

"Are you sick?" I asked her.

"Am I *sick*?" she said.

"I mean, are you unwell?" I said.

"You kids are so boring with your *sensitivity*," she said.

She was . . . drunk!

"You're not yourself," I said helpfully.

"Gimme that," she said, flicking her finger at the bottle of Laphroaig.

"You sure that's a good idea?"

"Shut the fuck up," she said, "and give it to me."

Well.

Years later I would wonder what course my relationship with Clarice would have taken had I grabbed that bottle, poured it down the sink, and told her to get her fucking head together. Sometimes I wonder it still. But I was someone with no experience of alcoholic parents or abrasive mothers. The same three bottles of anisette, Centerbe, and Galliano sat in the family liquor cabinet from about 1962 well through the 1980s, and my own mother was like a soft little lamb.

So what I did for Clarice was to shut up and give her the bottle.

"Oh, you know I don't mean a thing by it," she said, pouring herself a fresh glass.

I sat on the stupid tufted vanity stool determined never to say another word to her again.

"You kids—you're all so *susceptible*," she said.

All? I wondered.

She took a belt of whisky. She'd slipped down enough in her frilly bed that the angle of the glass was wrong, and I watched as little rivulets trickled down her frown grooves to come together at the high ruffle of her bed jacket. Who owns a bed jacket anyway?

"Take this," she said, thrusting her glass at me.

I took the glass without touching her hand.

"I have four terrible children," she said.

I said nothing.

"I have four terrible, terrible children," she said.

I looked down at my hands.

"Actually," she said, "I have two terrible children and two *wonderful* children. It's true. My Bertrand, oh, always a wonderful boy. Such a, *such a* good boy. Such a fastidious little boy, never liked his food to touch. Loved his flowers. One day I found him doing sit-ups in the bathtub. Such a perfect little faggot! And oh, our Cornelia, little Sister Parish with her tea cart! Cornelia with her fat little waddle and her fat little do-gooder ass! Gimme that back."

I picked up her glass and held it out to her.

"*Thank* you, dear. And then we have of course our Kendrick. Kendrick the fuckup! What was so bad? I always wanted to know. What was so bad? She was a *perfect* little girl. You must have seen her. She was an angel. Best in her class at the School of American Ballet. Doubrovska *loved* her. She *loved* my girl. My girl could have been Wendy Whelan. And what does she do? What does she do? She eats her way into the history books and scotches *that* plan pretty neatly. A heroic eater, this girl of mine, as if she could win a medal in a contest. And when she's sick of that and she's ruined her chances, she goes and starts snorting things up her fucking nose. Thirteen years old, she's running around with a bunch of perverts. Oh poor baby, she thinks no one loves her! And then she has to run away and live with those *animals* in Alphabet City, those lunatics who have things *written* on their *faces* . . . but then she has her brother Gerhardt to thank for that—

"My Jerry," she said, "my, my, my, my Jerry."

Suddenly she seized my hand and squeezed it tightly. Her own hand was like a nutcracker, and it was all I could do not to cry out. And then it was as if I felt something snap inside her. Her head dropped forward and it had a terrible reach, as if it were barely attached, as if she were folding up like some wretched construction, a collection of ruffles and rancor and sad old bones.

And I realized that this woman before me was just some grieving old lady, alone in her castle.

"Here," she said, raising her head. She swam her hand through the papers on her bed until she found what she was looking for and handed it to me. I roved all over it with my eyes. What was it? It was a hand-bill, advertising a concert of early music, Taverner, Byrd, someone called John Browne. It looked like it had been crushed into a ball and smoothed out again several times over.

And then I saw his name: *Gerhardt Marr-Löwenstein, Tenor.*

"And here my boy hasn't been home to see his mother in almost two years," she said.

The concert was on the Lower East Side, and it was that evening.

"Are you going to go see him?" I asked her.

"No," she said, her voice at the very end of its weariness. "You are."

She rolled onto her side, away from me.

"Pick these things up," she said over her shoulder. "Get this shitty loving cup off my bed. Ha! Sidney's anniversary gift. He'll be in Denmark forever now. Oh, forget it, just get out of here."

And she flicked me out of her room.

*

Despite everything, I confess that the strongest emotion I felt for Clarice at that moment was an enormous rush of gratitude.

She wanted me to meet Jerry!

I must be in fact a special person to her, I realized.

The rest of that afternoon I made myself useful, running errands, typing up anything I could find, dusting every inch of Clarice's study. All the time I expected her to show herself, but as I went about my labors, running up and down the stairs, she never appeared.

Toward evening I was as beset by thrilling expectation as any young debutante. What would I wear? I tried on and threw off everything I owned until I'd heaped a mountain on the bed. I finally found the perfect thing, a tea gown from the '40s with rhinestone buttons and a thin velvet belt—very Gene Tierney. I stuffed some old nylons into a pair of Kendra's heels and stepped into them.

When I finally came down, I found Clarice sitting at the dining room table.

The only light came from the next room, but she sat excruciatingly erect, herself once again. Her hands with their polished thick nails were folded on the table in front of her, and one of those padded kinds of envelopes, stuffed full of something, sat beside them. She was very pointedly waiting for me. All trace of that morning's sloppiness—and softness—had vanished.

"Why so fancy?" she asked me.

I deflated instantly.

"Well, I'm going to the concert," I said.

"I *did* ask you to do that, after all?" she said.

"What do you mean?" I didn't understand.

"Did I say anything strange?" she asked me.

"What do you mean, strange?"

"What did I *say* to you, Francesca?"

"You told me Gerhardt would be singing at the concert and that I should go. That you wanted me to meet him."

"I said that?"

"In so many words."

"Did I say anything else?"

I looked at her, aware that I should not move my eyes up or down. Or blink, or swallow.

"Not really."

She searched my face.

She had no memory of that morning at all. Nothing.

"Well," she said, "here's what I want you to messenger to him."

And she shoved the package across the glossy table at me. Then she got up and left the room.

*

I walked to Eldridge Street choking on my bile.

The sidewalks were still wet from the rain, and as I wobbled in my borrowed heels I seemed to step into every last city-scum puddle, all the while turning over in my mind the full measure of my stupidity, my vanity, my presumption. I was ridiculous, absurd. I was pathetic. Foolish. Naive.

And then I was incensed, furious. I was *furious*. How dare that woman do this to me? How dare that phony wretch? I wanted to punch her in her fucking uncooked old-lady face.

And then I was just sad.

The streets were empty as I walked down the Bowery with the stupid package in my arms. I just wanted to get this over with.

The concert was in a community center, in what turned out to be a huge turn-of-the-century building, maybe once a school. In the foyer, an old fellow wearing a beret and reading the *Workers Vanguard* waved me up the stairs. Inside, with its heavy wood wainscoting, high ceilings, and smell of strong, cheap disinfectant, the place felt like another era. There was the feeling of many years of a specific history—English lessons, striving, civic responsibility. Girls with huge floppy hair ribbons and homemade sailor dresses, immigrant newsboys with button shoes.

Upstairs, I looked down a long, dark hallway. At the far end sat a severe-looking gal at a folding table, leaning over a metal box and counting money in the faint light. As I got closer I saw she had a punk-rock Bettie Page dyed-black-hair-with-bangs thing going on: serious eyeliner, red lips, vamp dress, lots of rack; a hard, manufactured style. She looked up at me and we instantly slit down our eyes at each other, doing that dog-sniffing-dog, are-you-cooler-than me? thing. From the door behind her, music leaked out.

"You're real late, so be quiet," she said with a proprietary air as I handed over my money.

*

I stood inside the auditorium door, letting my eyes adjust to the light.

I could just barely see the stage, but it appeared to be crowded with singers. None of them seemed a likely Jerry. I clutched the bulging package to slow my beating heart and tried to listen. As my ears began to prick up, I could tell the piece was in Latin, but I couldn't make sense of it. I stood straining to take it in.

The music began to be overlaid with multiplying amens and I realized it was slowly, so slowly, ending. When the clapping started, I slunk to the first empty seat and looked about me.

Almost every seat was taken, mostly by older people with gray or white hair. These were the kind of New Yorkers you'd still see downtown in those days, wry and smart elderly folks with canes and library hardbacks and Bella Abzug hats, people who drank in culture but didn't have a lot of cash. I stared at the program, and the lady sitting next to me leaned over and stabbed her finger at it, as if critiquing my lateness: John Browne's *Stabat Mater* was about to begin. It was the last piece.

I'd missed almost everything, lost in my daydreaming.

The singers on the stage moved and regrouped, and when I lifted my eyes again, I saw him.

And then the voices began.

I am a musical ignoramus, I understand nothing of theory, and so I must step out of the way here. There are some things that can't be learned. I am thinking of that Bible verse about faith: the evidence of things not seen. I closed my eyes and the voices that started so sparely began to double and echo, and then they swam up and soared. None of the words meant anything at all to me, nothing at all, but the sound was beautiful, the somber complexities weaving together, unweaving, massing. Stilling. And then I heard the voices come back to the incipit, *Stabat Mater,* and it was like a burst of color blossomed out into the air above me. And some hard-secreted thing in my heart sprang up with it, sprang up and came loose, and I felt a flush of insane grief as tears filled my eyes and then went burning down my face.

I understand that thing now, now that I am older, when you have so much sadness inside you and you can't find a way to let it out and then something, or someone, gives you a way to put your burden down.

I had turned to the side, to the darkness, to calm my face. Now I looked back to the stage. This young man called Gerhardt was looking directly at me. We locked together and his gaze was shocking, almost shaming, in its frankness. We stared at each other as he sang, and it was as if together we kept hovering in the air between us this thing, this unnamable grief.

It was a communication we would almost never be able to reach with words in the life we would have together.

He was slender, tall, with dark auburn hair and Kendra's pale skin. The cruelly pale skin. He was narrow, trim in his clothing. He looked sickly almost, nearly transparent. Something about him suggested a person in the ministerial profession. His eyes were a strange pale green and turned up at the corners. Kirghiz eyes. There was a quietness, but also an arrogance, about him. There was precocity, a precocity past the right age for the word, and an anger over its passing. Maybe he was a bit of a show-off? Like Kendra, like Cornelia, like Bertrand, there was the chilling poise. But there was also a terrible formality about him. This was beyond the formality of a child who had grown up performing. It was as if his own private self had been stolen from him.

*

I sat watching him take his bows with the other singers. He wasn't looking at me, but I was aware that we were communicating across space.

I drank him in.

The doors to the auditorium were open by now and people were gathering their things, talking with the singers, taking their leave. How would I approach him? A handful of people encircled him and were shaking his hand.

And yet it seemed as if he were waiting to talk to me. I felt a childhood shyness in my limbs, a churchy embarrassment. I got myself out of my seat and stood a little away, as if enjoying the random middle air. As soon as the others left, he looked at me.

He looked at me, reader, as if I were an angel.

I clutched the package to my chest.

"Are you Jerry?" I said.

He tilted his head to the side.

"I am," he said, curious.

"I'm a friend of Kendra's. I mean, I was a friend. I'm supposed to give this package to you. I mean, it's from your mother. I work for your mother. Your mother asked me to give you this."

In the course of my little speech, I watched his interest warm and then drain and then turn into anger.

"Oh, Clarice is *giving* me something?"

"I don't know—she just asked me to bring it to you." I held it out as if it were dirty.

He snatched the package from my hands and immediately yanked it open to show me what was inside.

It was a massive, massive wad of greenbacks.

"I don't want her money," he yelled out grandly.

"I didn't know what it was," I said.

All at once he took the package by either side and ripped it in half. Bills and packing fluff exploded into the air. He slapped the mess of it to the floor with a violent flourish.

"I do not accept this," he announced.

And with this he marched out of the auditorium.

I stood frozen, staring at the money scattered all over the floor amid the settling cloud of confetti. My face was burning. *Don't look up,* I told myself. *God, don't look up.* Silence was all around me, which made it that much worse. I didn't know what to do. If I touched the money, I was implicated. I was dirty. But if I left it . . . ? My heart was pounding, but I also felt an expansion, that terrible thing when people raise their voices in anger and something in me clicks back to childhood and I think, Now we're really living.

In a moment people began speaking again.

"He's like that," a woman's voice at my elbow suddenly said.

I turned to see the Bettie Page girl from outside.

"Like what?" I said, my voice stupidly cracking.

"Like he knows someone else will pick it up for him."

She got down on the floor in her tight vamp dress and stilettos and began to gather up the bills. I felt a visceral repulsion watching her on her hands and knees. I knew I should join and help her, but I just couldn't get down on my knees.

"Dude," she said, briefly looking up at me, "don't worry. We can totally use the cash."

And she went back to her task, completely unfazed.

13

I wonder if I knew the word "enmeshment" back then. Or knew what it actually meant.

What I knew was that Clarice would be waiting for me back on Eleventh Street, but all I wanted to do now was run away. I dragged my feet as I walked, stopping at some hard-luck pizza place on Chrystie Street where I ate a slice and watched a roach slowly crawl up the white-tiled wall. I sat chewing the straw of my seltzer.

I thought of Trina over in Williamsburg, Fang stuck in her own unhappiness up in Morningside Heights. I thought of other friends, Bronx up and Battery down, with couches or futons or even extra rooms. I could crash with any of them for days or weeks or even months. But in the end I'd have to go.

And I had nowhere to go, of course, but back to Eleventh Street.

What was strange was that when I went in, Clarice *was* waiting for me, but her mood had changed again. She was stretched out in an uncharacteristically languid drape across the scroll-head daybed in the front parlor, one foot tucked beneath her, an arm thrown behind her head, a photo album I'd never seen open on her lap. Embarrassingly, I realized that her pose reminded me of a Giorgione: the Dresden Venus. Except in that case Venus was naked.

"How was the concert?" she said, smiling her luxurious smile.

It would take me years to learn how not to ape other people's behavior, how not to copy their tone and reflect back at them their own uncontested view of reality.

"Wonderful," I said, smiling.

She indicated one of the low fauteuils, and I pulled it over and sat with her.

"Did you give him the package?" she asked.

"I did," I said.

"Did he open it in front of you?"

"He did," I said.

"Well?"

"He threw it on the floor and stomped out like Mozart," I said.

She threw her head back and laughed and laughed.

"Such grand gestures!" she said approvingly.

"But his girlfriend picked it all up."

"His girlfriend! His *girl*friend. What did she look like?"

Clarice sat up and leaned forward with curiosity. I was instantly warm on the subject.

"Like, va-va-voom," I said, tracing curves in the air with my hands. "Like retro fifties. Red nails, red lipstick, serious eyeliner. The chick who stands outside the sock hop with a scarf around her neck, waiting to split your lip."

"Oh, that's not a girlfriend—that's just the circus girl who lives at *the squat* with him. A disgusting word, 'squat.'"

"Circus girl?"

Clarice waved this away.

"One of those idiotic Coney Island things. Neo-vaudeville. They like to play dress-up, hang from wires. As if this is something new! Fortunately your education has saved you from such tendencies."

And with this she clapped her hands, and it was time to go to bed.

*

The next day was Saturday, and when I went downstairs I found a note from Clarice saying she'd left for the country house.

It was the first time she'd gone since Cornelia had been carted off to boarding school. And because without Cornelia there Zeyde hadn't been coming over on the weekends, I realized that I'd be alone in the house for the first weekend ever.

How strange an idea this was. Looking up from the note, I immediately stiffened, as if a surveillance camera were trained on me. With dainty movements I made my coffee and, once it was ready, sat with it at the breakfast table with excruciatingly correct posture. When I finished, I immediately washed my cup and saucer, dried them, put them away, and walked quietly into the parlor, where, very carefully, I eased myself onto Clarice's *bergère à la reine.* I looked about me, gently smiling.

I realized I was reminding myself of spaz-faced Joan Fontaine creeping around Manderley.

And then I saw that Clarice had left the photo album out on the side table. It was a fancy thing, covered in leather, into which was embossed the name Gerhardt.

Jerry.

I opened to the first page, and there he was.

A newborn. A pale baby on a light blanket in a dark wood. I studied the photograph. It was black-and-white, "artistic," distanced. The baby looked away from the camera, almost as if he'd been abandoned—it was the kind of thing Roland Barthes could write a whole chapter about, dwelling on the *punctum,* the thing that made it strange. I turned the page and there was Jerry again, a toddler in overalls, lurching across the very room in which I now sat, the waist-down body of Clarice having just sent him across the rug, the crouching figure of Sidney (thankfully) there to catch him. There he was again, perhaps five years old, mouth contorted, tiny tie askew, reaching up with some hideous puppet as if to demand a hearing while the cocktail dress that is his mother turns her back on him. So many of the images were like this, with the photographer taking a worried child's-eye view of the world and, in the process, cutting off Clarice's head.

I sensed something odd and looked up. Jerry stood in the doorway.

"*Jesus!*" I shouted, leaping up.

"Sorry," he said. "I thought you'd have heard me."

"No," I said. For some reason I was clutching the album to my chest.

He stepped into the room, trailing his coat behind him.

"What are you looking at?" he asked me.

"Your mother left it out," I said. I held out the book like a supplicant.

He looked at me. He wore a shirt as white as his skin, ripped black jeans, combat boots. An absurdly long and badly knitted scarf fell blackly to his knees. In the bright light of day he looked seriously ill, like an invalid unused to the open air. His dark auburn hair was matted and greasy, and he smiled an unhappy smile, something so thin and tight-lipped that it suggested smiling was a form of punishing himself. Or that he was just barely suffering the fool in front of him. His all-over thinness and singularity suggested that he was self-engendered, had nothing to spare. And yet his pale green eyes sought something.

"She was looking at it?" he asked.

"I think she misses you," I said.

"Too bad about that," he said coldly.

You are all so solitary, I thought to myself.

He opened his mouth to say something else but suddenly thought better of it.

"She's gone upstate, if you're wondering," I said.

"I wasn't," he said.

I said nothing at all, and quietly put the book down on the table.

"I'm really just here to get something," he said.

"Well," I said, making to turn my back, "I'd imagine you know where it is."

"I'm not supposed to be here unattended," he said.

"You *what*?"

"I think you heard me."

"Why?"

"Clarice is afraid I'll steal something."

"But she just gave you all that money!"

"If she gives it, that's one thing—"

"Jesus, this is your house," I said.

"This has never been my house," he said.

He cast around the room with his gaze, throwing contempt every-where. When it seemed he'd finally exhausted himself, his eyes came to rest on me.

"Where are you from?" he asked me, almost violently.

"Nowhere," I said.

*

He had come, it turned out, to get his flute.

His old bedroom was at the very top of the house, on the low-ceilinged floor that had a series of rooms that had started life as maids' quarters: oddly shaped, diced-up pockets, among them the windowless typing study where I did my work for Clarice. I had by then scoured all these rooms, picking up in my hands anything there was to be touched, but I'd never gone into Jerry's room. I'd only as much as opened the door, stood at the threshold, and peered inside.

It was neat as a pin and bare as a monk's cell. It spoke of rigor and starvation. Somehow, perhaps because it was whitewashed and received intense early-morning light, it put me in mind of a certain kind of Nordic desolation, of Knut Hamsun walking around Christiania wretched with hunger. Inside was a narrow bed covered in a rough, woven navy-blue fabric, a nickel lamp sitting atop an old orange crate, a five-drawer highboy of pale wood. And that was about it. There was a thin shelf affixed to one wall with small items on it. The only other object, and the one thing that seemed to indicate anything other than utility and deprivation, was a famous poster that I knew to be by Cassandre, of the enormous hull of an ocean liner: *L'Atlantique*. Bold, graphic, almost filmically stirring, the image trumpeted the idea of escape.

Jerry was standing in the middle of his room. He turned to me.

"You can come in," he said.

"No thanks," I said, gesturing down the hall. "I actually have some work."

"Please come in," he said, bowing formally.

I laughed and stepped inside.

"Will you sit?" he asked.

There was no place to sit but the bed. Slowly I sank down on it and crossed my ankles, upright and Catholically demure.

He dropped to his knees before me. He ducked and I reeled back. My hand flew to my mouth and I stifled a scream. In a moment he reappeared from under the bed, a flute case in his hands.

"Do you play?" he said.

"Do I play?"

"The flute."

"I know."

"So you play."

"When I was little I did. I can play 'Twinkle, Twinkle, Little Star.' And it would be terrible."

He slowly blinked his eyes.

"Please play it for me, then."

I opened the case, and it was odd how familiar it felt to put a flute together, especially the moment of turning the last piece slightly clockwise to accommodate the short pinkie, even though I hadn't done this since I was ten years old.

"I'm terrible. I had a scary Austrian teacher who was always telling me how bad I was. My older brother Sandy had the musical talent. It's like that thing in big families where you get to have only one of each. You know? Everything gets apportioned. I was the verbal one." And true to form I was chattering away, unfortunately like an idiot.

But he nodded.

"Yes. Bertrand is the presentable one. The suck-up. Kendra is the wild girl, the flake. And the scapegoat. Cornelia is the civic-responsibility child. An okay kid but kind of a prig. She'll turn out essentially boring if she's not careful," he said.

"So what are you?" I asked him.

He smiled, and this time his thin smile broke, revealing an extremely sharp set of canines.

"I'm the murderer," he said.

And with this he took the flute out of my hands and played a strange wandering song that, had I known anything at all, I would have recognized as Debussy's "Syrinx."

*

He was an electric presence, an animal trapped in a room.

There was something black-and-white about him, in every sense: his clothing, his likes and dislikes, his sense of morality. You were either for him or against. Later I would see the woodcuts of Frans Masereel and think to myself, That's how Jerry must see the world—as a series of struggles, anguishes, epiphanies, all played out on a bold stage. Color in such a world would be a distracting mitigation. His own green eyes and auburn hair—the accidental prettiness of his looks—he seemed to

155

want only to downplay, if not ruin. When he wasn't smiling his painful nonsmile, he kept his mouth in a sideways snarl of contempt. It seemed almost cartoonish to me.

And yet all through his flute playing he kept his eyes fixed on me, and just as when he sang, a strange ardor passed between us.

When he was finished it was as if it had never been.

"That was beautiful," I said.

He shrugged this off as if it were offensive.

"I would love to be able to play like that," I said.

He was on his knees again, taking the flute apart, pulling an ancient cloth through the pieces with the thin threaded rod.

"She taught us to be trained monkeys," he said.

"But you have so much talent," I said.

He looked up at me for a moment, and then back down at what he was doing.

"I'd rather have had a childhood," he said.

I was standing by now, and I backed myself up against his window. I turned away. On the narrow shelf I saw a tiny figure of a metal rabbit, a handful of acorns, a piece of pyrite, a Big Little Book, *Popeye Sees the Sea* . . .

"I was thinking of making some French toast," I said.

"Okay," he said. He was fitting the pieces of the flute back into the case now.

"No, I mean, would you like some?" I asked him.

He looked up.

"For real?" he said. Color rushed to his face.

"Of course," I said. I was bewildered. "What a question!" I put my hands together and waggled them at him like an old grandma. "You so skinny! You gotta eat!"

And with this I saw that he could smile for real.

*

Of course I had to go and blow it.

I knew squatters, and it seemed like all of them took as a given this idea that you pulled together, stone-soup style, and when you made food everyone contributed and everyone ate. These folks were handy

156

and could do things like rehang doors, make a dress with a bedsheet and a glue gun, and wire electricity from sidewalk Con Ed boxes. And yet when we got to the kitchen Jerry just pulled out a stool, sat on it, and watched me work. He watched with such intensity that it was all I could do not to fuck things up. Of course I started chattering away. Had he ever read *The Varieties of Religious Experience*? I was reading it off and on, and it was kind of uncanny how the experiences of mystics throughout the ages were very often almost identical to those of '60s hippies taking hallucinogens and experiencing oneness with the universe. Really pretty uncanny. What was this urge for oneness with the universe, anyway? Did it suggest a fear of the abyss—I mean, was it that everyone's afraid to be alone? I was thinking of that term *horror vacui*, actually I sort of backed into it through visual arts, I was an art history major, Clarice actually laughed aloud when I told her, suggesting this was all so much basket-weaving, what a thing to formally *study*, but did he know this idea that people fear blank space and have to fill it with doodling and bric-a-brac, though obviously he didn't have such a fear, his room being as spartan as it was, I was the opposite, I liked a lot of tiny detail, I was curious about everything and I still did this thing that whenever I went into a dive bar with an old small-tile wall I'd look for a loose tile and pry it out and stick it into my pocket as a souvenir. Things like this, I said, seemed important to me, although I wasn't really sure why. I guessed I did have a fear of empty space, I said, and sort of was confused when people were . . . too quiet.

I was frying up the French toast by now, and looked over at Jerry, perched on his kitchen stool in his watchful silence.

"I think most people talk too much," he said.

"There's that," I said. "There is that."

I imagined myself flipping the French toast up so violently that it would never come down again.

"But you are . . . interesting," he said.

I turned and stared at him.

"Well, thank God for *that*," I said.

Like his mother, Jerry had no ear at all for sarcasm, and so he actually nodded in reply.

I'd already set the table, and in a moment we sat to eat. I served him a few pieces and he slathered them with butter and drowned them in maple syrup and tucked into them as if it were the first food he'd had in weeks. Not to say he was sloppy. He was elegant, elaborate, and European, moving hands and knife and fork around with complex orchestration.

In a moment he stopped dead to gaze at me.

"This is delicious," he announced.

"I'm glad," I said.

"What makes it French?" he asked in a moment.

"I have no idea," I said, and I did something strange, made dancing scales in the air with my fingers and then opened them wide to send the music into the room.

"*Vous êtes belle,*" he said.

"What?" I said.

"No one's made me breakfast in years," he said.

I looked down and moved my French toast around my plate. *What made it French?* I didn't understand what he wanted from me. Sympathy?

"Do you ever hear from Kendra?" I found myself asking him.

"Not for a while," he said. "Maybe six months."

"Where is she?"

"Málaga."

"Málaga?"

"Spain."

"Spain!" I said.

He sat blotting his mouth with the cloth napkin with precise, womanish gestures.

"Have you been?" he asked me.

"To Málaga?"

"To Spain."

"Spain?" I said.

I should lie, I thought. Tell him I've been everywhere, no one has ever been so worldly, so elegant, so lucky . . .

"I've been nowhere," I said at last.

"Your parents never took you to Europe?"

"No."

I looked down at my plate. I am not at all interesting to him, I thought, and I have failed.

I looked up to see him staring at my plate.

"Would you like this?" I asked, though it seemed rude to offer him something I'd been eating.

He hesitated.

"I'm sorry, I know I was eating it, so maybe that seems odd to you," I said miserably.

"No no no, not at all, I just want to be sure you're not going to eat it."

"I guess I wasn't very hungry," I said.

"I would very much like it, then," he said. He reached over and stabbed the toast with his fork and flew it to his side of the table and dexterously folded it into his mouth.

"How did you learn to make this?" he said, chewing. "It's really excellent."

"Are you making fun of me?"

He stopped and tilted his head at me.

"What do you mean?"

"I mean, seriously, you've never made French toast?"

He was blotting his mouth again, and then he knotted his napkin and threw it down.

"Clarice didn't let me in the kitchen. She thought it wasn't manly. She thought I'd grow up to be homosexual. Because Bert is of course as gay as a daffodil. He can make all sorts of things like marrons glacés. She said she didn't want two fags in the household. 'Fags'—her word. So when I'm in the kitchen I always feel like I'll ruin something. Once when I was eleven I tried to help with the dishes and I overstacked the wooden thing and it broke and I smashed a whole set of Spode or whatever it was she loved so much and Clarice burst out crying." He said this with a kind of hypnotized wonder.

"That's a shame," I said.

He looked at me with disgust.

"Yes," he said, deeply back in his bitterness.

"No, I mean it's a shame that she made you feel so bad. Who cares about the damn dishes? It's mean to do that to a kid. You didn't do it on purpose."

"I *didn't* do it on purpose," he said. It was as if I'd just presented him with a revelation. "She didn't understand that. She accused me of *sabo-*

taging her." He cast his gaze around the surface of the table, as if to find something there to testify for him.

"I'm sorry that happened," I said.

"The thing is," he said, looking up at me, "that was the only time I ever saw her cry."

I dropped back into my chair. What kind of a mother is this? I put my hands over my eyes, and when I pulled them away, Jerry had recovered himself.

He was looking at me so coldly I couldn't even speak.

"If you find Kendra's address, I'd like to write her," I said finally.

"She probably wouldn't want to hear from you," he said.

"What? Why?"

"Because you work for Clarice," he spat.

"Excuse me?"

"She'll think you're *in* with her. Siding with her. That you took this job to *insinuate* yourself with her. To get in with her."

I stood up.

"I took the job because I need the *money*," I said.

"Sure," he said.

"So what do you live on?" I said to him. "What do you live on, Jerry? Why do I feel like you've never had a job in your life?"

He stood now too. We squared off, and we were circling like prize-fighters. He looked furious but had no words for it.

But here I had the trump on him, because I grew up in a screaming family.

"Why'd you let that *girlfriend* of yours get down on her knees to pick up *your* money?" I was nearly spitting at him. "Why, so you can register your contempt but still benefit from the cash? So you get to have your—your—your fucking *cake* and eat it too?"

He opened his mouth to fulminate against me but instantly snapped it shut again. He swiped his hand in the air. He advanced toward me and then thought better and suddenly pushed out through the kitchen doors so violently they slapped against the wall and then just flapped and flapped and flapped.

And then I heard the front door slam, and he was gone.

160

14

"Stupid girl," Clarice said to me when I told her that Jerry had come for his flute. "That was a sterling silver Muramatsu. It cost eight thousand dollars."

All I could say was, "What?"

I didn't know things could cost that much. I mean, my flute, back in the day, had been a student Gemeinhardt that seemed mad expensive at $200 used. When I gave it up because of my utter lack of skill, my mother was all long faces at me for weeks, as much as for my dearth of stick-to-itiveness as for the amount of money she had wasted on my fickle musical ambitions.

I was so hurt by Clarice's words and felt such a wretch that all I could do was hang my head.

"But how would you know?" she said. "No one ever told you the boy wasn't to be trusted." She touched her hands to her cheeks as if to express a sudden idea. It struck me as rehearsed—an actress summoning up a housewife's eureka moment.

"You'll just have to go and get it back," she said.

"I what?" I said.

"Just pay him a visit."

"Do you even know where he *is*?"

"I'm sure Cornelia has the address," she said.

"I feel very awkward about this," I said.

"There's no reason to," she said with a sunny finality that made my heart sink.

And so a week after Jerry's visit, despite my many protestations, despite the sense that I was on a fool's errand—despite, stronger than these, my still being so furious with Jerry for thinking I was some double agent that I only wanted to slap his smug face—I found myself way east on Fifth Street, yelling up at a squat from the middle of the street.

The building was a battle-weary old tenement with mountains of rubble piled up against it. Instead of a door, a sort of reinforced wood pallet covered its entrance. Its first-floor windows were cinder-blocked up and all the other windows were dark above them, most of them broken and taped up with plastic. There was of course no frivolous nicety such as a doorbell.

I am no kind of outdoor yeller unless angry or surprised by a truck backing into me, but I tried a few weak little exclamations of *Jerry!* My words barely rose in the air before evaporating into the slumbering dusk. Still I stood gazing up at the dark windows. No one stuck a head out.

In fact I knew this block well, because the bar Sophie's was at the far end, a few doors in from a bunkerlike Con Ed station, in front of which no end of lost souls could be found, in even the coldest weather, doing the heroin nod. Earlier that summer I'd been at Sophie's with Trina when, because of the hot dry air, my rigid-as-a-Pringle contact lens suddenly popped out of my eye and flew behind the bar. Of course I had only one pair of contact lenses, which I took great poor-person's care of, so when the bartender saw us freaking out and leaning over to look at the filthy floor behind the bar, he came on up and said, "Contact lens?" I said yes. He swooped down, disappearing from view entirely, and in less than a minute stood and handed me my contact lens. I gushed my thanks at him, popped my contact lens in my mouth to "clean" it, and stuck it back in my eye.

At any rate, it would be hard to express just how hopeless and utterly uncool I felt sounding my feeble yawp in front of an East Village squat with the specific goal of repo-ing an $8,000 Japanese flute. There was a bunch of assorted junk in the rubble piled up against the building, so in a moment I pulled out a cinder block, dragged it to the curb, perched myself on its upended side, and lit a cigarette. I needed a plan. What was my plan? There was some meager light from the streetlamp, so I took out my copy of *The Varieties of Religious Experience*, which I'd slid into the back of my jeans—I always liked to keep my hands free—and began reading. I was on what would turn out to be its densest chapter, "Philosophy."

"What the fuck are you doing?" a voice said.

I looked up to see the head of Hard Bettie Page Girl sticking out from a second-floor window. I stood up and swallowed.

"I need to see Jerry," I warbled, drowning in uncoolness. "I'm supposed to get his flute."

She only stared down at me.

"He's in bed," she said at last.

I gestured to my nonexistent watch.

"This early?" I said.

She leaned there, staring at me. There was something going on, some assessment. In a moment I felt I could read something in her face and was surprised to realize what it might be: defeat.

"Wait," she said. Her head disappeared.

It took forever. I lit another cigarette, paced the length of the building, lit another. Finally I heard almost like a battering noise and turned to see the pallet shudder, shudder, buckle and then a person pop out. A person just barely, more like a Dr. Seuss creature.

It was Jerry, wrapped up to his neck in a zigzag afghan. He stood there a moment as if to let us both register the weirdness of this, and then he erupted in a fit of hacking. The tail of his afghan must have been snagged in the door, because he turned to yank it free, but the effort pitched him forward. His hand with the flute case in it swung out and his feet cycled on the rubble and all at once spilled him down the hill. Then he stood before me, breathless, blanket stripped from him, and neatly wiped his nose with the back of his hand.

"I seem to have a cold," he said, setting the flute case on the ground.

He looked insane. He erupted in another fit of coughing and covered his mouth with his hands, then pressed his fingers into his ears, dulling some pain. His face was swollen, distended, and his eyes were bloodshot and purpled as if he'd been punched. His hands and face were riddled all over with tiny welts. He wore his coat, but I saw that he was literally shivering in the cold.

"You're really sick," I said.

"I've got to get back," he said, picking up the flute case again and handing it to me.

I set it back down.

"Please, you're much too sick to be fucking around like this," I said.

"Oh, I'm fucking around, am I?"

"Do you guys even have heat?"

He showed his canines in his wretched unhappy smile.

"We're having some technical difficulties this week," he said.

Something in me fell away then.

"You look like you're dying," I said.

I had my arms out—I don't know. He went to turn but instead swayed before me. *"Please,"* I said, and his knees buckled . . . and then the tall, dissolving entity of him collapsed into my arms.

"Jerry," I said, "Jerry."

"You are soft," he said, his face buried in my neck. "I like that you are soft."

*

I got him in a cab back to Eleventh Street. Clarice was at a dinner party.

He leaned heavily on me, wheezing as I got him up the stairs. We went slowly, feet going together step by step. Once we cleared the first staircase he pointed up, meaning keep going to where his solitary bedroom was. We kept on, and it was as if we were on that staircase for hours.

He collapsed on his bed, shivering. I went to take his coat off and get him under the covers but he resisted me, hugging his dirty coarse coat around himself. I ran to get blankets from the hall. This was all like steps you do in extremis, like building a fire with your two last matches. I covered him with blankets, but he was still shivering so badly the bed shook. He was wheezing and went through a horrible hacking bout, painful to watch, like some scrap of lung was going to fly out of his mouth. Then something clicked off, his eyes closed, and he began to speak.

"Laudo," he said. "Laudas. Laudat. Laudamus, laudatis, laudant. Laudabam, laudabus. Laudabus? Lauda-*bas*. Laudabat. Laudabamus, laudabatis, laudabant."

164

He was delirious, and conjugating Latin verbs.

I dropped to my knees and began petting his head.

"That was very good, very good, first conjugation. Present and imperfect, Jesus Christ, you can do the rest later, okay, what the fuck, let's let that go, okay?"

"I'm so cold," he said. "I'm so very cold."

He was burning to my touch, shaking. I ran my hands on him up and down over the bedclothes, up and down, building friction, trying to warm him. In a moment I knew what to do. I climbed on top of him and lay down flat on his body. He was lean and taut and stretched beneath me. I lay on him, forcing my weight on him, kindling him.

"That is good, thank you, thank you, that is so good," he murmured.

And I don't know how long it was but he fell into a noisy, racked sleep.

Oh, thank God, I thought. Thank God, thank God.

I lay there as strong and still as a sentry, forcing my heat down into him. This might have been hours. From the hallway there was a noise at last.

"I wish I had a camera," Clarice's deeply smirking voice said.

*

And so it turned out that Jerry had a bad case of bronchitis, Jerry had an intense allergic reaction to black mold that brought back his childhood asthma, and Jerry had fleas. Fleas?

"My poor boy! It's as if he's won the Triple Crown," I would hear Clarice saying over the phone for days afterward. She told everyone with huge, hushed concern how the doctor had warned that Jerry was too weak to get out of bed, let alone go anywhere; but it seemed to me she was simply thrilled to have him home with her.

She made calls now all through what were supposed to be our work sessions, and I heard her tell the story of Jerry so often that it lost the weight of meaning. And slowly it morphed into *her* story, her daring venture into the wilds of the East Village to rescue her prodigal son. It was all so strange. I would put aside my pen and notebook, hop up from my stool, and go around the room pulling down random books, waiting for her to finish. I'd stare at her with searching eyes, willing her to look up at me and explain herself. But she never did, and I might as well not have been there at all.

Sidney flew back from Denmark to be with his son, and whatever break he'd had with Clarice was mended. Clarice told me we'd have a temporary moratorium on work sessions, but for some reason she brought in Dolores to tend to the young master, even though I was there, walking the five stories of the house, wringing my increasingly idle hands. It got so that it felt like a treat to be given any task at all, any tiny errand, from going around the corner for a loaf of bread to taking the knives out to the *arrotino* in his old jalopy. He was an ancient man and seemingly deaf, never answering me even if I tendered some stiff Italian at him, but unlike Clarice in her current state, he never seemed to mind my presence.

What was going on? On the upside, since I was released from work duties, I was free to go eat lunch with Trina and ponder the situation. I'd meet her up at Gotham and we'd sit in the big bay window of its second-floor gallery with our tuna sandwiches, looking out over the bustle of the Diamond District. We'd take out from Berger's, where if you got a coffee and the counterman asked *Sugar?* and you said *No*, he'd smile and say, *Sweet enough as you are,* which caused me no end of existential torment, so much so that I began getting sugar in my coffee even though I didn't like it.

Trina cleared things up for me.

"Duh," she announced. "You were the bait."

"I don't get it."

I felt thick as a tree.

"Look, she wanted Jerry home. So what does she do? She knows Kendra liked you, she's no dummy, so she sends you to Kendra's fucked-up Irish twin, who thinks you're quite the groover—"

"Oh I don't know that he likes me like that," I said, smiling into my tuna in spite of myself.

"No, really. She used you to reel in the prodigal son. Who's now helpfully down for the count with his, what the hell, mold-and-flea disease. Defenseless. And so *perfect* for her to coddle, fatten up—reprogram—and crush the radical right out of him. Dude'll end up like Winston

Smith, under the spreading chestnut tree—the 'indispensable, healing change.' "

"Like she's got some huge agenda," I said.

"She sounds so manipulative she *must* have one. They're all so manipulative—I can't believe you don't see it."

"Jerry's been through some bad shit," I said.

"Oh, boo-hoo, the Sorrows of Young Jerry! Name me one person in New York who hasn't been through what they think is some kind of bad shit. Whether or not they really have been." She paused to waggle my arm gently, which is what she did when she thought she might be harshing too much and she didn't want me to feel bad.

"You're a soft touch, Chess," she said, not unkindly.

"I need to get out of there," I said. But I didn't really feel that way. Somehow I felt as if life had directed me to the Marr-Löwenstein family. They contained something for me. I just had to figure out what it was.

But this was nothing I could explain to anyone, not even Trina.

After we finished eating, Trina and I would ball up our paper bags and take turns soccer-bumping them into the wastepaper basket on the other side of the gallery. I'm sure the grumpy owner hated the stinky tuna bags gathering up there day after day, but he was so mean, what did he expect? The gallery often had Edward Gorey drawings on display, and it was also the meeting place for the James Joyce Society—and since I, for one, never did see any of the Joyce Society convening there, they somehow melded in my mind with the Gorey characters so that I pictured them as all having shaggy raccoon coats, Edwardian bowlers, and, hidden behind their backs, big, dripping axes.

Before Trina went back to work, we'd smoke a cig in front of Gotham and say our good-byes, sentimental or insistently oh-I-forgot-to-tell-you even though we'd be seeing each other the next day. Then I'd roll down Forty-Seventh Street, where you'd see all kinds of intriguing characters in those days. There were unsmiling men in cheap suits and puckered loafers with, legend had it, bags full of diamonds in their pockets. There were rosy-cheeked Hasidim wearing the full Orthodox Cleveland in the summer heat, and hotshot Israelis with velour jogging suits and thick gold chains around their necks who reminded me of the hip-swiveling Guido relatives of my '70s childhood. From Forty-

Seventh Street I'd go down to the library or up to a museum, anything to prolong the time before I'd have to go back to Eleventh Street and feel unneeded.

I never saw Jerry. He was kept quarantined on the top floor, and I was given to understand that I had no reason to go up there.

It went like this for a while, until Clarice called me into her study early one morning.

She was writing when I went in and didn't look up. I stood before her, waiting for her to acknowledge me. She didn't, but instead began talking to her paper as I stood there.

"Do you like it here?" she asked the paper.

I leaned forward and tried to look at the paper.

"You, silly girl," she said, looking at me. Her eyes were hard and gleaming.

"Of course," I said.

"I'm afraid Jerry's going to leave again when he's well," she said.

"Well, he's an adult," I said.

She looked through me, abstracted.

"He really is no such thing," she said.

"I don't know what you mean," I said.

"He has a learning disability," she said. "He can barely read."

"Oh please—you're kidding."

"It's true, or he would stay and be my secretary," she said.

I stared hard at her and then had to look away.

Don't you understand how much he hates you? I thought.

And then: So I am nothing?

"How is he?" I asked.

"He's asking for you," she said.

I somehow felt a bright jolt at these words.

"Oh?" I said, swallowing.

"He's grateful to you for helping him."

"It was the only thing to do," I said.

She went back to looking at her paper.

"False modesty is so unbecoming," she said.

I stood blinking, looking at the top of her head.

"I wasn't being false," I said at last. Or was I?

168

She was writing again now, and began humming to herself.

"No matter," she said in a singsong voice. As I stood there I felt all kinds of sureties washing away. What did she want from me?

"Clarice," I said, "what would you like me to do?"

She slowly put her pen down and flooded her big face at me.

"Just be your own sweet self," she said, an insipid edge to her voice. "But not *too* sweet. We'll start work again when the time is right. Meantime, go see Jerry."

"I don't understand," I said miserably.

"Oh, you'll figure it out," she said, raising her hand to wave me out of the room.

It has occurred to me over the years that if I'd had a mother I could talk to, a mother I could have gone to for guidance, I probably would have saved myself a lot of grief. I was blessed with no such mother. My mother was a confused woman. She understood my sisters and brothers and me when we were babies, but when we reached the age of reason we could only baffle her. For all her learning, she had been raised not to question any man in her life, and she was incapable of protecting her own children while her husband knocked the shit out of them in the name of "discipline." She just stood there screaming and crying and wringing her hands. And then when we grew up and got the fuck out of that house, she felt deeply hurt, as if it were some cruel trick we were perpetrating against her—a conspiracy passed down from oldest to youngest child. How heartbreaking that we become adults and inhabit our own grown-up bodies and make our own choices.

Anyway.

Was Clarice suggesting I seduce her son? Make him cocoa? I didn't know. I knew if I told Trina about it, she'd tell me, *Run—don't walk—the hell out of there.* Fang was in an increasingly miserable way, always complaining about the many narcissisms of Decon Head, and whenever I saw her seemed barely to come out of her brooding.

When I knocked on Jerry's bedroom door that morning, he called for me to come in. He lay flat in his bed, staring at the ceiling, arms straight down at his sides atop the bedclothes.

"How are you?" I asked him.

"Okay, I guess."

He didn't look at me but continued staring up at the ceiling. I pulled over a chair that had been brought into the room, a stiff ladder-back chair, and sat by him. His face was calmer and clearer than I'd ever seen it, but he looked completely exhausted, almost lifeless.

"I'm not being rude, it's just that everything spins when I move my head," he said. "Something to do with the fluid in my inner ear."

"Vertigo," I said.

"Yes, it actually is called vertigo."

I smoothed my skirt.

"Are you out of your mind with boredom?" I asked him.

"I am," he said.

I looked up at the ceiling where he was looking, then turned my head to the window.

"The light's beautiful in here. There's like a snatch of sky you can see, framed in the window at this angle. Such a clean, flat light. It reminds me of a painting by Købke, just a corner of sky and Lutheran sort of steeples. An impossible view in a way. There's a loneliness about it."

"Cupcake?" he said.

I swallowed a sigh.

"Købke," I said, "like with a Søren slash through the *o*. I'm sure I'm saying it wrong."

"I wish I had a cupcake," he said.

"I could get you a cupcake," I said.

"No," he said, "I couldn't taste it anyway. I guess I'm just thinking of the sweetness. I want the sweetness."

I leaned forward and looked at him, because liquid was leaking out from his eyes. He was so still and emotionally flat that it took me a moment to register this as tears.

"I'm sorry, I don't know why this is happening," he said. "I never cry."

"Maybe you need to cry," I said softly.

Why are you so shattered? Why are you all so shattered?

"We're not supposed to cry," he said.

"Screw that nonsense," I said. Impulsively, I took his hand.

He turned his head, just a fraction, to look at me. The tears stopped as suddenly as they'd started.

170

"Are you doing that because you're paid, or because you're kind?" he said.

"I feel sad for you," I said. I went to take my hand away, but he held it fast. He was suddenly full of all the strength in the world and pulled me to him. The medal around my neck swung out and he caught it in his free hand.

"Do you wear this because you're religious?"

"My mother gave it to me." I pulled it out of his hand and dropped it beneath my shirt.

"But are you religious?"

"I'm lapsed. I'm very, very lapsed."

"They didn't raise us with anything. They didn't give us any of that. Clarice always says the sight of a cross makes her want to vomit."

I pulled free from his grasp.

"A lot of bad has been done in the name of religion," I said, "but faith is something else. Faith comforts people. Whatever kind it is. When I was little we'd go to this old church up in Philly sometimes and I'd see these Puerto Rican women holding on to the feet of statues and just crying and crying. It was so heartfelt, it was so naked, it fascinated me. My father would see them and say how they made themselves ridiculous. But I always thought if it comforts people, why is this so bad?"

"Because it is bad. It controls people."

"Yeah, well, I went to Catholic school for twelve years and hated every minute of it, so you don't have to tell me. What I'm saying is why not take the good you find in it? Leave the rest. So, what, you're supposed to tell those women crying on Jesus's feet to go home and stop being so foolishly controlled? Isn't that just as bad? Isn't that worse? I think your family has the worst fascist streak I've ever seen in my life."

Oddly, this made him smile.

"I see why Kendra liked you so much."

"What? Why?"

"You're feisty," he said. "But you're also sweet."

"Oh, please—don't make fun of me."

I got up to leave.

"No, no, no," he called out. I turned. He had raised himself on his elbow. He smiled at me, and his smile was like a wolf's.

"You can't leave, Francesca," he said. "You're paid to be with me."

I stared at him.

"Get the fuck back here right now," he said.

"*What?*"

I squeezed my hands into fists.

"You are *not* doing this to me," I said. "Tell me you are *not* doing this to me."

He beckoned me back to him, his eyes shining.

"Look, look, I'll be nice to you," he said, patting his bed. "I promise."

Slowly I went back and sat in the chair, the two of us staring at each other. The smirk on his face changed into something else. It changed and changed again like the light in September.

He collapsed back in his bed.

"I'm sorry. Oh, God. I am so sorry. You can go."

I cleared my throat.

"It's fine," I said.

"It is?" he said flatly.

"You're not well."

"Am I ever?" he said.

At this we both somehow gave a laugh.

"I could read to you," I said.

"You want to read your William James to me?"

"I could read you *One Fish Two Fish.*"

He blinked at me, seeming not to know what this was.

"Do you know any poems by heart?" he said.

"I do. I know lots of poems. Mostly old ones." I smoothed my skirt. " 'Loveliest of Trees.' 'Dover Beach.' 'Dust of Snow.' 'Break, Break, Break.' I know lots of 'The Wreck of the Deutschland,' don't ask me how. 'Whoso List to Hunt.' 'Who Has Seen the Wind?' Huge passages from 'Goblin Market.' Countée Cullen, 'And Yet Do I Marvel.' Some *Fleurs du Mal,* which I will only butcher. Delmore Schwartz, somehow. John Donne. Anne Bradstreet, the one about sending her book out into the world. All kinds of things, come to think of it, most of it way old. 'Lullaby,' I think it's called, but the meter's so jerky it always trips me up . . ." I trailed off.

"What's 'Lullaby'?" he asked.

172

"Oh, it's, uh, W. H. Auden." I realized the first lines would be hard to say to him.

He settled back into his bed, stared straight up at the ceiling.

"I think I'd like to hear that one."

"I don't know that I remember it all," I said.

"Please proceed," he said, and closed his eyes.

I sat looking at him, saying nothing at all. I looked off, cleared my throat, and began.

" 'Lay your sleeping head, my love, human on my faithless arm.' "

I paused and looked at him. He lay there with his eyes closed like a child. I let my eyes close then as well, and as he lay there on his bed and I sat in my stiff chair, both pairs of eyes closed to the sun, I recited the entire poem to him, my voice growing sonorous and saddened as I spoke.

When it was over, we both opened our eyes, but neither of us said a word.

"It's a beautiful thing," I said at last, surprised by the emotion welling in my throat.

He rose on his arm once again.

"It is," he said, running his fingers forcibly over his lips and looking deeply into my eyes. "It is."

I realized he was the hungriest boy in the world, then.

I leapt up from the chair and clapped my hands together.

"Let's play Botticelli!" I said.

*

And so in this way we worked out a routine together. I'd go to him in the morning and I'd recite a poem to him—sometimes I would read one, but he seemed to like it better the other way, as if he wanted to know just what was in my head—and then we'd talk for a while, talk about things that were sufficiently distanced from us, never emotions or faith or family or pain. He was never cruel to me the way he had been. I think he realized that he risked playing king of the hill over me, his captive audience. His captive.

He'd grown up without a TV, so any sort of stupid pop-culture touch-stones that my college friends could riff on for hours were lost to him.

173

He made me embarrassed that so much of this crap was in my head: *I'm the sole survivor. Golden flaky tender cakey outside. When I bite into a York Peppermint Patty* . . . Instead we played endless rounds of Botticelli. We loved to stump each other: I stumped him over Frances Farmer, Nella Larsen, and Eleonora Duse. He stumped me over Rabindranath Tagore, Osip Mandelstam, and David Ben-Gurion.

Always I watched him like the weather. Like a gathering storm.

"What is that nonsense about you having a learning disability?" I asked him one day.

"Clarice told you that?"

"Yes, as if to say you're dyslexic."

He looked away.

I've embarrassed him, I thought.

"Not so much that. I have a . . . it's a visual processing thing."

"I don't know what that is."

He moved himself around in his bed, unfolded and folded the pillow behind his neck, rolled his shoulders around, trying to make himself comfortable.

"It means that when I read things I take it in differently. I can read perfectly, I can see perfectly, that's not the issue, it's just that things take a different path in my head so they come in strangely. Like a randomized bunch of stuff, a kitchen drawer with all the stuff that won't go somewhere else. It can be exhausting, just reading one page. Even now. It was awful when I was little and we'd have to read aloud and I just couldn't do it. I would sit there and shut my eyes and go silent. I would think, Everyone else can do this. Everyone else can see the pattern but it's not a pattern at all."

"I think that probably just means you're creative."

"No, it's a thing, it really is a thing that they've told me I have. I went to a million doctors when I was little, it took them forever to find out. I would hear Clarice talking, saying that I was retarded. It was a relief when they put a name to it. Because I realized it wasn't my fault."

"Jesus, of course not."

"She always needs things to be someone's fault."

"I think she should lighten the fuck up," I said.

"Yes, exactly—lighten the fuck up, Clarice," he said. This struck him

174

as incredibly funny and he began to laugh. "Lighten the fuck up, Clarice!" he said again, choking up with laughter. He laughed until he blew himself out into a coughing fit. I pressed tissues into his hands and he expelled all kinds of goo, swabbing his mouth and drawing a line of mucus away to his hands, unembarrassed. He wiped his mouth more neatly, looked at me. "It's just that no one besides Kendra ever said anything like that. I've just never heard it in someone else's voice. It sounds so, I don't know, funny and cute." He let his head fall back onto his pillow.

"I'm exhausted," he said, smiling.

*

As he started to feel better and could sit up for more than a few minutes, I'd sit at the foot of his bed and we'd play games. It started with checkers, then Chinese checkers. I found a deck of cards and taught him Crazy Eights and Go Fish and War. We could play for hours, but there was a degree of labor in this, a thing with the letters and numbers; I wondered how such forms looked to him. Neither of us cared who won. It was like we signed that over somewhere, and it was about the moment of play only. I memorized his hands, so long and articulate, knobby and raw, cut and healed over in a hundred little ways as if he'd been a short-order cook and not a musician at all.

I racked my brain for other things to play and found some old pick-up sticks, in a Lucite box from about 1978 at the stationer's on Sixth Avenue. We spilled them out on the floor and sprawled there, taking turns at selecting the color we were and making nothing move. This was the sort of thing that fascinated Jerry: that such a game existed, and that I knew what it was. Did most people know about things like this? His rearing had been so singular and specific that it sometimes seemed like the most banal scraps of knowledge were the things that intrigued him about me the most.

We played dominoes, built houses of dominoes, built houses of cards. I taught him how to play jacks, and sometimes we just sat against the wall and bounced a dime-store bag's worth of tiny balls all over the room, seeing how many we could keep in play at once. I taught him a modified version of this Spaldeen handball game I played as a kid:

Namesies, Clapsies, Rollsies, High as the Sky, Deep as the Sea, Touch My Knee, Touch My Toe, Touch My Heel, and Away We Go.

"Namesies—what the heck is Namesies?" he said.

"I don't know. It might have been 'Mainsies,' but we all butchered everything in my neighborhood."

"In your neighborhood," he said, smiling at me so unguardedly I had to turn away.

I brought in a stack of scrap paper and bought one of those big boxes of crayons that were such magic to me as a kid. We both liked the metallics, especially copper and bronze. We sat and drew for hours that day, hiding our drawings and then trading them at the end, like I had done with my sisters and brothers when we were kids.

When he showed me his pictures, I gasped out loud. They were extraordinary. They were alive and huge and cosmic, filling every last inch of the page, crazy abstractions and fantastic starbursts and spirals and mad crazy colors. His mind was bursting with creativity.

"These are amazing."

"Yours are much better," he said.

"Mine *suck*," I said, most sincerely.

"Yours are so precise and linear."

"And completely tight-assed. This is why I didn't go to art school. Jerry, you don't really get how great these are. You could sell these for, like, cash money. This is a *thing* you're doing—look, this is something I know about. You've got the insistence of a real artist, a singularity, a need. What do you say we clean you up and get you in a cab and take these over to Sonnabend?" I was doing my funny-girl shtick, but I also meant every word of it.

"Oh, it's fun, but it's kind of like garbage," he said.

I was shaking my head, baffled by his lack of enthusiasm, by how he devalued his work.

"May I keep these?" he asked.

"*My* drawings?"

"May I?"

"Sure, but that's the real trash," I said.

He looked at them, smiling. It made no sense to me.

"Why do you always draw houses?" he asked.

176

"I don't know that I always draw houses," I said.

"I think you do," he said. He fanned out my pictures and pointed from one to the next, showing me the house in each.

"I had no idea," I said.

I studied them.

"'Tired and unhappy, you think of houses,'" I said.

He looked up sharply.

"You are tired and unhappy?" he asked.

"No. No no no—it's a Delmore Schwartz poem," I said.

"Because I'm not unhappy at all," he said.

I showed him how to cut out paper snowflakes and together we made hundreds of them, a million tiny paper scraps littering his bed like a snowfall. I stood on the chair and taped them up all over his bedroom ceiling as he lay in his bed, looking up at me with his somber green eyes.

"I like this a lot," he would say. *I like this a lot*—as if too much enthusiasm would risk ruining a thing, cause it to disappear.

I lived and breathed him, ate and slept him. Looking back at it so many years later, it was a perfect moment, some breach in space that allowed only us to inhabit it, some momentary stalling of the clock that gave us something like this: a childhood together.

And then Thanksgiving came.

15

In the days leading up to the holiday, Jerry became well enough to leave his room. I'd help him down the stairs, bundle him against the weather, tuck him into a chair in the bright and cold solarium that looked out over the garden, and read to him.

What did he want to hear? At first he told me to pick out something I liked. But make it a story, he said, nothing "from the world." Thus I tried favorite book after favorite book with him—and each one of these he waved away after a few minutes. On one hand things were too old or too florid, but on the other he wasn't interested in anything remotely experimental. He wondered at my penchant for what he called *fussy books*. When I picked up Walter Abish's *How German Is It* and read to him its opening piece—"What are the first words a visitor from France can expect to hear upon his arrival at a German airport? Bonjour? Or, Guten Tag? Or, Ihren Pass bitte?"—he held his hands up in the air and nearly shouted.

"You *like* this?"

"Oh, it's brilliant. It kills on many levels."

"What does that mean, 'it kills on many levels'? I don't like a book that's so much smarter than I am."

Finally I started reading him the story of Cosimo, who pushes away his plate of snails one day when he's twelve—"Never had we seen such disobedience"—climbs a holm oak, and stays there for the rest of his life. *The Baron in the Trees*. Jerry listened deeply, his eyes flashing as he looked out into the backyard garden. But I knew he was seeing a different landscape. That day I read until my voice was hoarse.

The next morning we were back in the sunroom early to finish the book. Jerry really did want to see "what happens." It was crisp and bright outside, one of those autumn mornings of exceptional clarity. I can still see it now. And I remember how silent he was as I read the final passage, as Calvino's narrator writes his last words with a thread of ink that "splutters and bursts into a last senseless cluster of words, ideas, dreams, and so ends."

I closed the book and looked at him.

"It's over," he said at last. "I can't believe it's over."

He held out his hand and I gave him the book. He sat rubbing its cover with his hand, as if he were petting it.

"I'm just so sorry it's finished," he said.

"There are others," I said softly.

"But this is the only book that is *this*," he said.

Thanksgiving was just days away now, and Dolores brought in her sister Marta and daughter Yolanda to help with the cooking and baking. We would have, as Clarice said, quite a table for the holiday, meaning not only the menu but who would be there, and Dolores, Marta, and Yolanda would serve the dinner. Clarice had even bought them matching black frocks, cut a bit in the style of Edwardian maidservant mufti. This sat especially badly with me, because by then I'd met Yolanda, a thoroughly hip kid in an oversize MC Lyte T-shirt, paint-splatter-look leggings, and enormous gold shrimp earrings, and I could see that for her this whole *Upstairs, Downstairs* routine was a source of humiliation. She covered up this fact by relentless eye-rolling and constant use of the word "Duh!" Which is just what I'd have done if I'd been in her shoes.

Since Clarice was always telling me what elegant cursive I had, I was the one who sat with her to make the place cards, a nerve-racking job that involved writing with a glass dip pen and sepia ink on special paper bought in Florence. Cornelia would be coming down from boarding school for the holiday, but Bertrand had no plans to come in from London anytime soon, and there was of course no need to ask about

179

Kendra. Sidney's sister Anne, brother-in-law Mitchell, young niece Shoshanna, and father would be there—and this was how I learned that Zeyde's name was actually Isadore—as would other extended Löwenstein cousins from the New Jersey hinterlands.

I wrote no names of anyone from Clarice's side of the family, a fact that I puzzled over. Instead, as if to fill the gap, Clarice would be opening her table to a throng of widowers, childless divorcées, and, as she put it, *unattached young people.*

"The young people will keep things lively," she told me, as if I didn't actually count among the members of this special tribe.

The house was humming with activity all that week. Rented tables were set up, stacks of napkins ironed, piles of chestnuts shelled, pumpkin and mincemeat and apple pies with crisscross crusts made, a thirty-pound turkey from Balducci's delivered to the door.

The night before, I was sitting with Jerry in the solarium. I had found us a copy of Calvino's *Italian Folktales,* but after I read him a few, they ceased to hold his interest. He thought them too short and most so *méchant*—he said this in French—and the endings too pat or moralistic. Someone was always getting killed or eaten, he said. To which I replied, "Yes, they are folktales."

"I guess I don't like folktales, then," he said. We were both looking out the window into the trees. Lights had gone on in many of the buildings across the backyard canyon, and we could see various people in their apartments moving about their lives, making their own pies or vacuuming their rugs or taking down special glasses from high cupboards or some, alone, sitting in the blue light of a television screen.

"Do you think any people across the way are watching us?" he said at last.

"Probably. Someone in the dark, some lonely soul. Some bored kid."

"Kendra and I used to do that when we were little," he said.

"She told me. The Shakespearian actor who closed the arm of his wrap in the dishwasher."

"Oh, she made that up. She makes up all kinds of things. What's absurd is that some of the things that really happened were actually much stranger than her stories."

"Such as?" I asked.

"Terrible things." He shook his head, gestured. "We were here one day, just the two of us. I was probably twelve. Kendra was at the barre there, that used to be there, and I was practicing my flute. And a woman went down right there. Right down from that window. A jumper. It was so sudden and the sound it made was so strange, like a big comforter hitting the ground. The sound *she* made. I mean, it was muffled, not like a bang but a thud. She was an old lady, a widow. Her husband died and she was left alone."

"Horrible that you saw that," I said, turning to look at him.

"No one believed us when we told them we saw it. They thought we'd made it up."

"Maybe it was too scary for them to think of you seeing it. Young as you were." I studied his profile.

"I always felt like everything is cursed here."

"In this house? I'm just not feeling such a thing."

He turned and looked at me.

"It's different with you here," he said.

Now I was the one to turn and look out the window.

"Different how?" I said.

"Different good," he said.

"That's good," I said. Some kind of nervous laugh came out of me.

"That's banal," I said then.

"I just think it would be good if maybe it would be able to stay like that," he said.

"Well, I haven't been fired yet," I said.

"No, I mean—because I'll have to leave here. I'm getting better and then I'll have to leave and find somewhere to go."

"You'll go back to the squat?"

He didn't reply for a while.

"I think I'm done there," he said at last.

"So where will you go?" I asked.

He turned away and now we were both looking straight ahead, out the window.

"I'm thinking. I'm thinking. But. Somewhere that maybe you'll come with me."

"What?" I said.

Because I couldn't possibly have heard him right.

He opened his mouth to say something, but he seemed to suddenly freeze with the night.

The double doors burst open and Cornelia flew into the room.

"JERRY!" she screamed, landing on his neck.

And the rest of the night it was Cornelia showing us the traditional dances of Zaire, Cornelia playing us beats on her doumbek, Cornelia saying in terrible-sounding Mandarin, *These are my shoes, How is your uncle, Where is my drinking glass,* Cornelia talking a mile a minute and jumping and spinning and laughing, and me wondering if I'd hallucinated everything that came before.

*

Thanksgiving morning I was up early. I had to talk to Jerry alone before the day began.

I dressed in any old clothes and stepped out into the hallway, closing the bedroom door softly behind me. I looked up and Clarice was standing there on the landing. Some crazy noise leapt out of my throat.

"You startled me," I managed to say.

How long had she been there, waiting?

"We'll need your help in the kitchen," she said. She had her hand on the banister going up to the next floor, where Jerry's room was, as if she were barring the way. She came forward, sweeping me thither, and marched me down the stairs to the kitchen.

Dolores and Marta already had things humming, pots on all six burners, every counter covered. The menu was impossibly elaborate—fancy versions of all the usual Thanksgiving things but also roast duck and a sweetbreads plate and vegan dishes and multiple sauces and the mac-and-cheese option for the young Löwenstein cousins. I was thrown right into it, directed by Dolores, peeling and chopping and mixing. Dinner would be early—at two o'clock—and there was still so much to do. At some point Cornelia materialized by my side, mashing and pureeing and, in a moment, running to the back door to violently shake out a contraption that she insisted was a nineteenth-century French precursor to the salad spinner, an absurd wire armature shaped like a chicken.

"Where's Yolanda?" I thought to ask at some point, and Dolores, looking down at her able fingers moving over her own work, only shook her head in an angry-sad way.

"Yolanda no' here today," Marta offered.

I had a blip of an idea in my head, but we were all too busy gunning for me to take the time to examine it.

Too early we could hear the doorbell start to ring.

"*Ai!*" Dolores and Marta and Cornelia all yelled together.

I was at the sink when Clarice came in through the swinging doors. She was beautifully put together in a new Chanel, and I could see that her hairdresser must have come by that morning and "lifted" her hair. The maids' uniforms hung from her arm.

"Here, Dolores, Marta," she said, holding out the uniforms to them. They took them.

"And Francesca," she said, "you'll take this."

And she held out Yolanda's uniform to me.

"I've gotta go get changed," Cornelia yelled, diving through the doors and blasting out of the kitchen.

I stared at the black polyester uniform in Clarice's outstretched hand. What?

Dolores and Marta, usually so industrious, were suddenly still as statues.

"Take it," Clarice said, thrusting the uniform at me again.

"That's too big for me," I said.

"The belt ties like a bow in the back and you can make it snug."

All I could do was stare.

I wanted to say, *Why are you doing this to me?* But I felt embarrassed saying this in front of Dolores and Marta. Because why should Dolores and Marta have to wear stupid demeaning uniforms? Why was I special?

Miserably, I took the uniform out of Clarice's hand. I couldn't look at her, but I had no doubt she was smiling.

I was out of the kitchen and up both staircases and I ran into Kendra's room and slammed the door. The dress was balled under my arm, and I whipped it out and threw it against the wall. I stomped around the room, banging my fist into my palm. I wanted to jet away, explode into a million particles.

183

In a minute I grabbed the dress and looked at it in my outstretched arms. I went to the mirror and held it up in front of me.

It was marginally less ugly than it had first appeared.

But it was not the stupid ugly dress, it was the fact of it. It was the fact that Clarice was laying down this thing on me.

All at once I had the dress by the either side of the neck and I yanked it and yanked it until I heard the fabric give—and I ripped it full down the front. I threw it on the floor.

"Well, I can't wear it now," I said to the room.

*

When I went downstairs, it was in my own dress.

The house had filled up and people stood in tight groups, wineglasses in hand. Was I imagining a kind of heaviness in the air? Bach played, just slightly too loudly. To fit everyone in, the doors between the sitting and dining rooms had been thrown open, and a series of tables stretched in one long line from the front of the house to the back, like a single, endless banquet board, somehow medieval in feeling. Everything was colorful and festive, but I saw it all at a remove. It had nothing to do with me.

Then I saw Zeyde in his wheelchair, left by the windows that looked out to Eleventh Street. His weak old head leaned to one side, and his eyes were half closed. I wondered what he was dreaming of.

I leaned down beside him and softly greeted him. His eyes opened wide.

"'Cesca!" he said. He grasped my hands and squeezed them and then, in a moment, deanimated entirely. His hands slipped away and his eyes closed, and his head drifted gently back down, like a baby chick nodding in sleep. I realized he would be gone from this world soon.

I searched the crowd, wanting only to get this moment over with, and it was at the far end of the room that I saw Clarice. She was talking with two nearly identical blondes, both sleekly groomed and dressed in Calvin Klein taupe. Her head turned my way like a homing device. She instantly assimilated what I'd done, and in a moment she was coming toward me.

"What happened to the dress?" she asked in an awful smiling-to-cover-extreme-anger way.

"It didn't work out," I answered, smiling back at her.

She did that thing that I hated, studied my face while saying nothing, roving her eyes over me for too long a time. But I thought I could read in her a new factor being contemplated: some intimation of a previously hidden, not-so-Catholic recalcitrance.

"Well, please help Dolores and Marta," she said, and turned on her heel.

I passed Sidney's sister, Anne, briefly greeted her and her husband, Mitchell, and was introduced to their daughter, Shoshanna, a skinny, all-elbows girl eating herself alive with self-consciousness. I could only imagine the condescension her cousin Cornelia probably showered on her. Anne was never happy to be in Clarice's house, and I felt her trailing me with a sad face as I made my way toward the stairs to the kitchen. Cornelia saw me and immediately cut her eyes away.

Everything seemed to be passing in underwater-like slow motion. I saw the preening young writer from Clarice's Friday luncheons, Broyer Weatherhill, not yet thirty and too formally dressed, with comb marks cut through his gelled hair. He was talking to the Calvin Klein blondes while scanning the crowd, ever the player looking for an angle. He raised his eyebrows to greet me and I nodded. The blondes swung out like bookends, took me in with a competitive girl sniff, and then tossed their collective head and turned from me.

And somehow I knew then that my place had disappeared from the table. I was not going to be eating up here with these folks at all.

I looked, but found Jerry nowhere.

Anyway: I was there to serve.

*

After the last dessert plate had been cleared from the table, I sat at the kitchen counter downstairs with Dolores and Marta, staring at the plate they had fixed for me. Turkey, stuffing, homemade cranberry sauce, haricots verts, some colorful squash thing, all lovingly arranged. They had even accented it with a garnish, a needless, pretty flourish: a parsley sprig and a tiny fan of spiced apple slices. I pictured myself picking up the plate, calmly carrying it to the door, and Frisbeeing it across the backyard canyon.

"*Come, come, tienes que comer,*" they said to me, pointing to the food.

Instead I sat tracing the last few hours over in my head. Everything came back to me in miserable little flashes. I saw myself carrying an enormous gravy boat around the table, a foolish thing the size of a soup tureen, and Anne giving me a confused, disbelieving look as she picked up the ladle to serve herself, mouthing the words, *Why don't you sit?* Cornelia squirming in her seat, waving me away. And then, as if seeing it through the pinhole of a silent movie camera, I replayed in my head the sight of one of the Calvin Klein girls dropping the ladle back in too forcefully, calling herself *butterfingers* as gravy exploded across my chest.

That's why you should wear the uniform, the disembodied voice of Clarice said from across the table.

But the worst and the strangest was Jerry. He presented himself after everyone was seated and noisily took a chair at the far end of the table. In a kind of fog I saw that he was in his pajamas, with his ugly woolen scarf twined around his neck. When I came to him, he wordlessly took the ladle, helped himself, and returned it to the dish. And then he turned to me with a face like stone.

He said nothing, spoke up for me not at all, but simply sat there like a princeling and let himself be served.

I stared into the plate in front of me, and my head was so thick with misery that I saw nothing. In a moment there was an odd sensation and I realized that Marta had picked up my hand from my lap and was trying to shape it around my fork.

Dolores climbed down from her seat at the counter and went to get some pie. Marta tipped her head in the opposite direction, toward the swinging doors, and with this she was indicating the upstairs world, the kingdom of white people, and Clarice in her ass-whipping surety. Marta had a determined look on her face and, quietly lest Dolores hear her, whispered to me, "Don' let the beech win."

"But how?" I said.

"I see everything. That boy is in love with you."

I shook my head and slid from the stool. I went outside to smoke a cigarette.

By now I had discovered that there was a spot where I could sit, on what was left of an old brick border swollen out over time by the roots of a mimosa tree, and be invisible to all the windows of the house. I had to be up against the stockade fence, right where an old yellow gravel path abruptly dead-ended, and if I moved even inches to the right I would be seen. But if I was still and steady, I would be invisible. I sat there and lit my cigarette.

I was thinking.

I was thinking that I didn't understand these people, the game-playing, the quiet cruelty. No one was screaming in anyone's face, which to my mind would have been a lot more honest. I wondered about my own course of learning their ways, and about the fact that I could smile back in matched falseness to false Clarice.

This was nothing I could have done in the past. And this was no way I wanted to be.

Jerry I couldn't even think of, it all felt so false now and so painful.

I needed to get out of there. I needed a plan.

I mashed out my cigarette on the ledge beside me, pinched and rolled out the last bit of tobacco, and scraped the filter along the brick ledge. I thought of a thousand cigarettes I had smoked and mashed in my hometown while I played the waiting game that was like drip, drip, drip, water torture until I could finally escape and find someplace real, someplace where I could *be*.

I'd tried to clean off my dress, my Bergdorf's-via-Domsey's-in-Brooklyn good black dress, and looked down to see brown food that I'd somehow missed caked along the length of my serving arm. Disgusting. I pulled at the sleeve, folding it together to scrape it against itself and "clean" it. I thought of my mother and her thousand depressing econo-mies, darning ancient socks and hanging paper towels up to dry and taking a Magic Marker to the shiny elbows of her good black blazer . . . and she did this all so regularly, as if this were the stuff of actual liv-ing and not a meaningless biding of time, with minutes adding up to hours and hours adding up to days and days to weeks and weeks to years and those to decades until you are, at last, dead in the ground.

Night had come early and I found myself looking up at the sky. I heard the back door open and close again. I froze. The footfalls were not slow or hesitant but somehow encumbered, and then the person was in front of me.

Of course it was Jerry. He stood on the dead-end path, in line with the trees that hid us from the windows.

"Ha, funny, this is just where I used to sneak cigarettes in high school," he said.

Do I care? I thought. I said nothing.

He held out his hand, as if to ask for a cigarette.

"You're too ill for that," I said.

"Just one?"

"None at all," I said.

"Just a *little* one," he said, smiling.

"I'm glad you can smile," I said.

He had an instant lingering familiarity, a lack of formalness about him now, which was humiliating. This would be where he revealed his game and laughed at me for my believing ways.

I felt myself welling up but would not, would not.

"You have something to say to me," he said, smirking.

"I have nothing at all to say to you."

"You do and you're dying to say it."

I turned away, then turned back to him.

"Why did you *do* that? Why did you *act* like that? Like you barely know me, let alone—uh!"

"Let alone?"

"Nothing."

"Let alone what?" he said with his canine smile.

I went to get away but he blocked my path.

"Let alone *what*?"

"Please let me go," I said.

He held his place in front of me, bearing down on me.

"Cornelia told me the whole tragic tale. The uniform—she was tied in a thousand knots. Oh, it offended her sense of order. How terrible, terrible! But the only shame that I see is on Clarice. My fucking mother with her delusions of grandeur and her pathetic need for payback. She embarrasses only herself. But she's complicated, my mother, and you don't know the half of it. So—maybe I wanted to see what you'd do. Maybe I needed to see how you would conduct yourself."

"How I would *conduct* myself?"

"Yes, exactly. And the thing is, you were *perfect*. You were so somber and quiet, and the way you lowered your eyes—"

"Jerry, do you know how horrible you sound? What are you, directing a movie? You act like this isn't real! Don't you understand? People don't act like this. People with *compassion* don't."

He held his eyes on my face, searching.

"I don't know—that was never a word we used. Compassion. So I don't know, I don't know. Look, it's like this. You're so filled with life. You love things. I wonder about it, I do. It makes you seem far away from me. And I realized I wanted to see you sad."

"You wanted to see me *sad*?"

"Because then you would be closer to me."

"No, Jerry—this is my *life*. What's this game? How can I trust you? You're more like your mother than you know. Get out of my way."

"Please," he said, "I don't understand."

"You're all aliens and none of you see this *at all* except Kendra. She's the only honest one out of you and that's why she's gone."

Still he didn't move. I watched as he drew his hands to his face and rubbed at it as if he would rub it away.

"You must forgive me," he said. "I never know how to *be*. You could show me, I guess I think you could show me. I think we could be happy together. It's never happened in my life and I don't know how to name it. But you see, I've been so happy with you, so happy . . ." And he stuck his hands out before him and stood like this, out in the cold in his scarf and pajamas.

I felt a warmth in my chest, a painful, inevitable warmth. He was fettered, pierced by a hundred arrows, comprehending nothing. And yet he was beautiful to me. Beautiful. I sometimes wonder if I'm cursed by my love of beauty, if for me that is how the infection comes in, my life course of distraction and infection: it comes in through my eyes.

I put my hands out to him, unable to speak. And he took my hands, gathered them to his lips, and kissed them.

We walked this thing through the November streets that night, wrapped in old canvas coats from the garden shed, shaking with cold, smoking. Talking, or trying to. He had decided on me, chosen me, he told me. But please, what does that mean, I asked him, for my half of the equation, my half of this story of his? So the man chooses, and the woman must be flattered and give in to him? But more than flattered I was, because it was that night that I admitted to myself that I'd loved this boy from the moment I first saw him.

But I wasn't about to tell him this.

We went to the Hudson, to the West Side piers and the crumbling docks. That landscape is gone now, cleaned up entirely, obliterated. But there was mystery back then, when things still could be hidden—there was the frisson of danger, the feeling of peril that I realize now thrilled me so much in my youth.

"Are you cold?" he asked me, both of us shivering. I shook my head. He pulled off his scarf and gently twined it around my neck while I stood, still and somber.

What do I do with this strange kindness?

We stood there unspeaking at the water's edge, the wind coming in hard off the Hudson. I wouldn't let myself give in. I needed to think, but I couldn't think at all with him beside me.

We leaned against the rotted railing and looked silently out across the water.

It was late when we finally came in from the piers, stiff with cold and sadness.

All of Greenwich Village seemed a ghost town with its dark storefronts, and the unusualness of this gave the city a kind of science-fiction desolation. Something in it seemed to stir us both, tell us we were two people together in a long night. We'd been walking silently and not looking at each other for some time, and all at once Jerry reached out, grabbed my hand, and plunged it into his coat pocket. I felt an almost gleeful tingling rise up inside of me.

Maybe this could be possible . . . ?

We passed a diner lit up like *Nighthawks,* almost garish amid all the dark, and both of us turned to look in.

And this is how I remember it. The order of events. The mink, draped from the shoulder, hanging straight to the floor. The blond head, the lifted hair. The profile: pitiless, yet somehow bored. Her jeweled arm on the counter in front of her. Before it, a cup of coffee, and me thinking to myself, That coffee must be very cold by now. And beside her, the young writer Broyer Weatherhill. Broyer—wait, what? Start again, I don't understand. And at that moment of confusion, watching Broyer lean forward to kiss Clarice on her lying mouth.

16

The next morning Jerry would be gone.

It must have been that Jerry pulled me away from the window, from that public kiss beneath its theatrical spotlights. And then we were walking, the wrong way, headed downtown.

Neither of us said a word. It was as if we still had to process it. I kept seeing it over and over again in my mind: the mink, the hair, the cup of coffee, the Broyer ... the kiss. Devastating in its implications. Everything would be gone, it seemed to say, and I saw the Marr-Löwenstein dynasty come crashing down: the five stories of the house on Eleventh Street pancaking one atop another, bringing down plaster ceiling medallions, pendant lamps, Napoleonic bedsteads, brocaded fauteuils, recamiers, poufs, and *coiffeuses* and Her Majesty's *bergère à la reine,* smashing stacks of Spode and Clarice's writing talismans, hurling twenty thousand books from their cases, crushing to a fine flat plate the silver loving cup that stood on Clarice's mantel. All that would remain, miraculously, would be the tiny, desolate Blakelock nightscape that hung over the fireplace, and maybe this had been Clarice's way of telling her husband that despite all the riches he had showered upon her, she really had felt desperately alone all along.

"I don't understand," Jerry said at last. "I don't understand at all. Broyer Weatherhill is *such* an asshole."

It seemed strange to me that he was fixating on Broyer and not the fact of the affair.

"Has she ever—?" But the way Jerry looked at me stilled my tongue.

"If you want to know, actually, she has. She has, she has. Last time five years ago, maybe six. It was with another younger man. In France. A man who made cheese and wore a leather string around his neck. Why are you *smiling*?"

"I'm sorry, it just sounds so ludicrous, 'made cheese.'"

"Well, it was awful. Sidney threatened to kill himself."

"That's awful."

"It was. It was awful. Bertrand hates him and said, *Go ahead.* I think Bertrand hates him because he's not pretty. Or maybe Bertrand hates him because Sidney's not his father. So Kendra used to say. She had all sorts of theories . . . she used to conjecture for hours, and she decided Sidney had been Clarice's way out of some affair, maybe with a married man? Kendra always had a head for imagining. But it's just impossible for me to picture Clarice young and vulnerable. Because, you know, my mother is a ghost. She has no past."

"I don't understand," I said.

"She never talks about her childhood. I can't even tell you where she grew up. There are no relatives on that side, nothing. She would tell us the same three or four stories that were supposed to satisfy us when we asked. One was that her mother's name was Mabel and that she was a silent film actress. Or perhaps she was named for a silent film actress? Another was that when my father asked for Clarice's hand in marriage, Mabel called him a 'filthy Jew.'"

I swallowed and looked away.

We had stopped by now, and in his uncanny way Jerry stepped to the side and immediately opened a random apartment building door and pulled me inside. The hall was dimly lit by a Depression-era fixture, the frosted kind shaped like a hanging bowl, and looking up, I could see a collection of old dead bugs in it, silhouettes and shadows.

"I can't tell you when I realized Clarice never loved my father," he said to me.

"Maybe he should leave her," I said.

He leaned back against the wall.

"He would never leave her. Life without her would kill him. It would kill Sidney dead. He loves her so much it's mystifying. None of us can understand it. And it's like this love of his is a recessive gene, because the rest of us . . . well, you see us," he said.

"I see you how?" I said.

"We're cold," he said.

I said nothing.

"Do you want to be?" I said at last. "I don't think you want to be."

"Tell me," he said, looking at me.

"If you're saying you can't love—that's wrong, you do. All of you love."

A shade passed across his face in the dimly lit hall.

"How do you know?" he said.

I shook my head.

"Come with me now," he said.

"What?" I said.

"Please, tonight, come with me. We won't go back."

"Where would we go?"

"I'll find a way," he said.

"What do you mean? Everything is *there*. Everything I own is there."

"We'll get you other things," he said.

I put my hands over my eyes.

"You forget we barely know each other. I barely know *you*."

"I think you know me better than anyone else in my life."

I shook my head violently, denying this, even though I somehow imagined it was true.

"Please," I said. "You have no idea about my life. I have nothing to fall back on. I have a mother who's a widow who lives in a row house on my father's schoolteacher pension. I have a student loan I'll have to repay. A *student loan,* do you know what that is? You don't understand—"

But worse than any of this was my fear that his caring for me was based on the slim moments we'd had together and that it could be revoked in a second. I thought of Kendra, notes left on doors, promises made, the way she would grab my hand and squeeze it like I meant more to her than anyone else in the world, and then . . . the inevitable disappearance.

"I want to understand," he said. "I want to."

"If you are serious," I said, "it will take time."

194

"I think I can do this," he said. "I think *we* can."

He came to me. He smelled like sharp citrus and the wind off the Hudson but with the stench of sickness still rising from his chest . . . and then his mouth was on mine in a kiss so awkward, so maladroit, so lipless and ravening that I can feel it on my lips even now. Even now, so many years later, the sadness of that time pulling me back into the past.

"Things will happen, but tell me you might wait," he said.

"I might," I said. "I might."

*

The next day I was not surprised that he was gone, but I was surprised by the enormity of my grief over his leaving.

I woke up to find a note right on the pillow beside me. He had come into my room at night, and I'd heard nothing at all.

The note read:

FRANCESCA,
    I AM SOREY. I AM ANGREY WITH HER AND I HAVE
TO ~~LIEVE~~ LEAVE. SAY NOTING. TO HER OR TO SIDNEY.
PLESE WAIT I WILL BE BACK. PLESE BELIEVE ME. SHE IS
SPITEFULL.
    I L— YOU.
    GERHARDT

I sat on the bed and read this over and over for a long time.

At last I folded it up and slid it between the mattress and box spring. In a moment I took it out again, unfolded it, smoothed it flat, and closed it in a book. I cleaned myself up and went downstairs, heavy with dread.

Clarice was already in her office, seated at her desk. Sidney stood beside her, one hand in the pocket of his trousers, the other around a cigar cocked at an awkward angle, as if he were holding it for someone else. He looked pale and worried, and said good morning to me in an artificially loud voice. Clarice studied me long and hard, saying nothing at all.

"Of course he's gone," she said at last.

"Jerry," I said.

"How did you know?"

"Who else would you mean?" I said.

Clarice gave Sidney a look, and he left the room.

"Did he leave you a note?" she asked me.

"Why would he do that?" I said.

She cut her eyes away, looked back at me.

She has no idea I know about her, I thought, none at all.

"Well, he left *me* a note," she said. She held it in her hand.

"May I see it?" I said.

"I'll read it to you," she said. " 'Clarice. I am going now. Don't look for me. I suppose I should thank you but I will not. Tell Dad I love him. Be nice to Francesca. Watch yourself. Gerhardt.' Now. Why would he write such a strange collection of words?"

"I have no idea," I said.

She looked so mean and so angry with me that I stared at her in order to burn her image into my mind. Lest I ever made the mistake of feeling sorry for her again.

" 'Watch yourself,' what could that mean?" she said.

"I really have no idea. I'm sorry."

"Do you know where he went?"

"My guess would be back to the squat."

"Well, he can rot there with those animals. I don't miss him at all! But who told you, I want to know, who told you to make him fall in love with you?"

"I'm sure you're mistaken," I said.

With this there was a change in her face. Oh, I had studied this woman for what felt like years. Some certainty fell away. And then I saw her rooting around in her mind for clues—what is counterfactual, what is known? What was she to *do* with me? Was I an impediment to getting Jerry back, or once again the bait? Why did he leave, what did he know? I had shown myself to be a deeply un-Catholic game-player, a figure of suspicion. Maybe she had suspected me all along? But if so, she was mistaken. Because I'd come in like a good little dog and only learned my duplicitous behavior so recently, and from the best: her.

*

Strange to say, in no time at all the routine at the house on Eleventh Street went back to something like normal.

At least on the surface. Clarice and I both knew we were only waiting for Jerry to return. And then what would happen?

I had to get out of there, but I had developed an almost crippling phobia about the outside world. I read the want ads on the sly, but where in the past I'd see anything from baby wrangler to genome researcher and think, Sure, I can do that, now even the most basic office jobs made me shudder with the knowledge of my incompetence. Must type fifty words a minute—what? Of course, I typed sixty-five words a minute. But somehow I called into question everything I thought I knew. It was as if so much deep interaction with the Marr-Löwensteins had changed the shape of my brain, distorted it and devalued it.

I just had to do something—find any job, find any apartment, and get out of there.

And then I would start to imagine Jerry coming back and finding me gone. Clarice would say, *Oh, I don't know what became of that girl. She was so unreliable.* She would speak these words after burning in her ashtray a note from me she'd promised to give her prodigal son.

And then we would be lost to each other.

I had become an island. It was impossible to leave the house now—Clarice was on me for typing, for dictation, for cooking and even cleaning at every turn. My workday swelled to fourteen hours but I put my shoulder to the wheel, thinking of these as my labors of Psyche, that I would prove my worth by separating out the heap of wheat and barley and millet, but Venus remained unmoved. I needed to check in with my friends for sanity, check in with Trina, but I couldn't even get ten minutes on the phone. Clarice in her new mania watched me at every turn.

And Sidney was home all the time now, conducting his fur business by telephone and fax. Had he understood Jerry's words to Clarice, *Watch yourself*? He was there at every moment. We three ate every meal together. It was as if I were the mouse being watched by the cat being watched by the dog. No one could make a move.

Sometimes the whole thing made me giddy in a just-this-side-of-crazy way, but more often I just felt wretched.

But most of all what I wanted was to drop the game-playing and say to Clarice, *What did you mean by throwing us together if not to have us fall in love? What is all your playacting and pretense? Why not end your marriage?* Because it was clear to me, if not to Sidney, that she was miserable. Her mouth grew harder by the day.

Maybe what I really wanted to ask her was this: *Why don't you love me?* Love me like a daughter, and that would fix everything.

17

One day late in that endless winter I was alone in the backyard of the house on Eleventh Street, wrapped in my heavy coat, smoking a cigarette and listening to music. It was early evening, the sky slowly going pink. The yard was covered in that weary snow, sooty on top, demoralized . . . but as my mind roved around, I looked at the ground and my eyes seized on something unlikely: peeking up through the snow was a purple crocus.

So spring would come after all.

Though the harshness of that autumn had relaxed, somehow, even when I was alone in that house, I clung to my self-policing ways. The one thing I'd allow myself was to play music. Down by the kitchen was Kendra's old rumpus room, with its '60s hi-fi and hundreds of record albums in old wooden soda crates, their spines scratched to a soft fringe by the long-passed Agnes Smedley. I'd go through them until I found something I'd never heard of, put it on, and listen. Sometimes I'd crack the window so I could hear the music outside and then go to the garden and smoke a cigarette. This was the closest I'd get to a holiday.

Earlier, months before all the surveillance had slackened, I'd managed to sneak off at the first opportunity and make my way over to the squat on East Fifth. I didn't know the actual name of Hard Bettie Page, and I knew Jerry wasn't there. But something told me she was still around and would know something about his vanishing.

Well, I was a fool. I stood on the sidewalk for an hour staring up at the dark windows before I finally dragged myself back down the street.

What'd I been expecting? I happened to look into Sophie's and there, on a payphone in the window, was Hard Bettie Page herself. Our eyes met and I stopped abruptly, almost making a cartoon skid sound with my boots. She kept talking on the phone while looking at me, and since I couldn't hear her through the glass I imagined all sorts of unsavory exchanges. She made movements like she was about to hang up and then she half turned away, but I distinctly saw her red lips mouth the words *Love you too, Mom*.

She spilled out of the bar and sort of clicked her heels together, half Dorothy from Kansas, half Stasi hatchet girl. We were wearing identical motorcycle jackets.

"Hey," we said at the same time.

"Nice jacket," she said, after a beat.

"Good taste," I said, gesturing back at her with my chin.

I took out my cigarettes, offered them to her. She took one, put it behind her ear, took another, and I lit us both up.

We stood smoking and looking at each other.

"I'm Chess," I said at last, sticking out my hand.

"Chrissy," she said, shaking my hand.

"You keeping warm?" I asked.

"Why, do you have a generator in your pocket?"

I cocked my head at her, having grown deaf to sarcasm.

"We're fine," she said. "We're dealing."

I nodded, kept nodding, nodded too long.

"You know he's gone," she said at last.

"Gone?"

"He came back to get some of his shit. Then he took off. Said he's going to see his sister."

"Kendra? Cornelia? Not Cornelia."

"The spacey chick with the habit and the Manic Panic hair," she said.

"Kendra," I said.

Kendra. Morocco? I hated that this girl knew more about Jerry than I did.

"Did he say where?" I asked.

"Nope," she said.

"Did he say when he'd be back?"

"Nope."

We both sucked on our cigarettes, coolly studied the pavement.

"But he told me to tell you something," she said.

"He did? What was it?"

She looked up the street, down the street, and then at me.

"I forget," she said, smiling.

I'd packed a bag of groceries for this stupid chick and her stupid friends, and for a moment I thought I'd just take it down the corner and give it to the crackhead couple by the Con Ed station. They could go up to that special place past the park, jam it through a hole in the wall, and trade it for some rock to smoke. Instead I flicked my cigarette into the street and handed her the bag.

"What's this?" she said.

"Food from where I work. Stuff they won't miss." And then I was walking away.

"Hey!" she called out.

I stopped and turned, wondering what her final insult would be.

"What he said was, have faith. He said to tell you to have faith."

She stood in the middle of the street, probably freezing in her unzipped MC jacket and leather mini and fishnets, and held her look on me. None of this made any kind of sense. And then she turned on the heel of her Trash and Vaudeville thigh-high boots and vamped down the street, crossing her feet one in front of the other in an exaggerated runway walk. I watched her big ass rolling back and forth and I thought, What? I'd never heard Jerry use the word "faith."

Months had passed since he'd left, and there had been nothing: no letter, no phone call. Nothing. The memory of my weeks with Jerry spun and turned and mutated, and in time they acquired an impossible, roseate glow about them. The words we spoke to each other sounded in my head in stark, formal cadences, something like the way I remembered sentences from *The Princess of Cleves*. This was just nothing I could explain to anyone.

When Christmas came, Clarice and Sidney flew to London to see Bertrand, leaving me to watch the house. Cornelia was working out her own issues, and called me from Vermont on Christmas Eve to complain about what *selfish bourgeois* her parents were and to ask me to make a donation to her local chapter of Food Not Bombs. And then she got on a plane for London.

Of course I'd shown Jerry's note to Trina at the first opportunity. She'd taken it in her hands, read it carefully, and then looked up at me and said, "Are we on *Candid Camera*?"

"Seriously," I said, "he has a learning disability."

"Seriously," she said, "that family has a freak-show disability."

She was all over me to get out of there and get back to who I was again. I loved her and I knew she was right, but it was as if I were magnetized to the house on Eleventh Street. I was deep into magical thinking and was constantly buying Jerry gifts, fancy chocolates and Caran d'Ache colored pencils and a beautiful cashmere scarf that took away most of my paycheck, as if these things would make him come back to me.

I was smoking my cigarette in the backyard thinking about all this, looking at the purple crocus in the snow and listening to the record playing. It was a piece for solo piano, some orientalist thing, a Frenchman imagining the Middle East, and on the album cover was a drawing of buildings with Moroccan arches—a watercolor, a fantasy, something indistinct, pale and shimmering in the distance.

"Oh, I'm so sorry," a voice behind me said. "I thought you heard me."

I turned to see a young man standing at the iron gate that led out to Eleventh Street.

The first thing I noticed was his kind, wide-open face. He was tall and long-limbed, with unruly hair, and had on big schoolboy glasses that appeared to be held together with tape. He might have been twenty-nine, thirty, and he wore a dark coat and a rag-wool scarf that looked eaten up by moths. I had no idea who he was, and yet he struck me as instantly familiar.

"I work with Freddie," he said when I hadn't responded.

"Who's Freddie?"

"Freddie Knives, the *arrotino*. I guess you're new. Is Bert or Dolly here? Dolores, I mean? Or Mrs. Marr?"

"Bertrand's been gone since last summer. How is it I don't know you?" I said, studying him.

"You tell me—how is it? Bad, good?" he said, instantly absurd.

"I mean, I've seen Freddie lots of times," I explained.

"Well, I work with him off and on. Whenever his sciatica is acting up. He *learns me* stuff," he said, talking in quotes and touching his hair as if to flatten it down.

"You're a knife grinder?"

"Oh, I do all kinds of things. In the high season I work in animation, but the season's been low for some time now. I paint houses. I hang art in grim corporate hallways. I milk the cow, shave the pig. Slap the creep. Not really. But. I do the Police in different voices."

I stood looking at him, and I felt a strange sensation overtaking me. I realized what it was: I was smiling.

All these months I had made my face a mask.

"I know that line, it's from a Dickens novel," I said. "The dust-heap one. *Our Mutual Friend,* what a hodgepodge! The 'Veneerings,' not so subtle. I remember our prof glossing that line, the *Police Gazette* he meant, the kid did funny voices when he was reading it aloud."

"That was the working title for 'The Waste Land,' if you can believe it. I was just reading that. Terrible idea, right? Not as bad as *Trimalchio in West Egg,* though."

"Oh, that was going to be the name for *The Great Gatsby*!" Somehow it felt wonderful to talk about things that I knew.

By now I had slid the lock from the gate and let him in.

"Are you a writer?" I asked him.

"Geez, do I look that bad? Kidding, sorry. I, um, I'm actually an artist, a printmaker. I do some cut-up poetry, but people generally hate it. You can't really perform it or folks throw shit at you. I have this friend Ricardo, he read some tricky Brion Gysin kind of stuff at Nuyorican, and someone clocked him in the head with a Nerf football. But then he wrote a poem about it."

He was holding something bundled in tea towels, and this he presented to me in mock solemnity.

"Madam," he said, bowing.

I took the bundle in my arms.

"Heavens, Rhett, there must be some *mistake,*" I said in a silly voice.

"It's actually Bert's pruning shears. Freddie forgot all about them— he's sort of phasing out, the poor old sock, welling up to 'Una furtiva lagrima.' I found these under a crate of Moxie empties."

I wound up.

"I guess he, uh, used to have a lot of moxie, right?"

"Oh, groan! Fair play to you, kiddo. Wow—I have no idea why I just called you 'kiddo,' I'm so sorry! Too much time alone in the truck and I turn into Uncle Fergus from County Cork."

And then he just stood there, looking at me, until he tilted his head to the side.

"Persian Hours," he said.

"Persian . . . ?" I said.

"Persian Hours," he said. "Charles Koechlin, I think, is the composer. Is that what you're listening to?"

"Oh! It is. Yes. Such a strange thing," I said.

We stood looking at each other.

"I should get back," I said, suddenly embarrassed. His gaze was so open. I wasn't used to this sort of thing at all.

He wanted to know what my name was, and I told him. Then he put out his hand and I took it. His eyes were blue: gentle, intelligent.

"I'm Fitz," he said, smiling.

The phone was ringing. I gestured at it, and he shooed me forth with a mock-professor face.

"See you again!" he said as I darted inside. I ran down the hall and grabbed the phone.

It was Sidney's sister, Anne. I couldn't tell what she was saying.

"Anne, I'm sorry—what happened?"

It was as if she couldn't catch her breath.

"He's gone. My father. He's gone. I just never thought it would come to this." And she was off in a rush of tears as Mitchell took the phone.

Yes, old Zeyde. *I'm so sorry,* I said. *How did he . . . ?* Gently, in his sleep. *Oh, yes, how old was he?* Ninety-one almost to the day. *He had a long life,* I said. *Yes,* Mitchell said, *yes.* He'd been born at the dawn of a new century, Mitchell said, as if to indicate that such an era of discovery was gone.

*

The next day I was dispatched to get Kendra's old Mercedes out of a garage way west in the fifties, over by the old McKim, Mead, and White power station, Clarice making sure to tell me how they wasted *sixty fucking dollars a month* on the parking space. It was strange to me how angry she was, and it wasn't until Cornelia got home that I understood both her anger and the need for the car: old Isadore, cool old Zeyde, had had a lifelong hatred for his daughter-in-law and had forbidden her to ride in the family limousine to his final resting place.

"I can ride in the limo, but she can't," Cornelia told me. "She's so mad. God, she's so mad!" It was clear that this pleased Cornelia no end, but in case I hadn't got this, she danced a little jig around the room. I'd thought her crunchy Vermont school would have made her sweeter somehow, but now she seemed harder to me. Less gushy, more difficult. Angrier.

"Aren't you sad about Zeyde?" I asked her.

"I am but I'm not. He was soooo old. Kendra was always his favorite anyway."

"I miss her," I said. "I miss Jerry." I hadn't meant to say anything like this at all.

Cornelia threw a look my way, not a kind one. Then she came over and interlaced her hands with mine, holding them up in the air.

"Push," she said.

"What?"

"Just push my hands," she said. "It's a game."

She was pushing, so my only option was to push back.

"You've got to try harder than that," she said.

"I don't like this game."

"You've got to really push, Francesca!" she said.

"Why are you doing this?" I said.

She arched herself forward and leaned into my face, her odd-colored eyes flashing.

"You're in love with my brother, aren't you?"

I tried to pull away.

"Aren't you?" she said.

"I feel sad," I told her.

"You give up. You give up just like *that*. But you've got to fight."

I yanked my hands free from hers.

"Cornelia, you don't know a thing about me. I grew up fighting. I don't like fighting."

"You've got to fight if you want him."

"Oh, come on, how corny is that!" I said.

"You don't understand. My mother has this thing about Jerry. She won't let him go. She *ruined* him. She did something to him as a kid."

"Do you know how tired I am of people saying—"

"I know Clarice is fucking that guy with the hair," she said.

"Oh, God," I said. "I'm so sorry you know that."

I turned and caught sight of myself in Kendra's mirror. It was as if I were vanishing. But when I turned back to Cornelia, she was the one gone slack, as if she'd lost the spirit of fight herself. There was no real hardness in her. There was only the inability to self-comfort, the family coldness. This orphaned quality they all had.

Which somehow only made me want to save them all the more.

"Not that I even care," she said, leaving the room as her voice was breaking.

The next morning a late-season frost hit. I remember thinking it would kill all the crocuses.

It was left up to me to pilot Clarice in the old Mercedes out to the funeral parlor in Brooklyn. I was grateful that a couple from the neighborhood, the Horowitzes, had been pressed on us for the ride, because it meant that Clarice had to be on her best behavior. She sat on the passenger's side upright as a schoolgirl, an enormous purse on her lap, while the Horowitzes sat in back. Mrs. Horowitz appeared to be turned out for a wedding in a satiny car coat and crazy lady's single-flower hat, while Mr. Horowitz told all sorts of squirm-inducing jokes—"Oedipus shmedipus, as long as he loves his mother"—all the way out. Once we got to Ocean Parkway, he started a running commentary.

"Jew, Jew, Italian. Jew. Italian, Italian, Jew," he said, indicating the houses streaming past the window. No one else in the car paid him any mind.

"I'm sorry, do you know these people?" I finally had to ask.

"No, dear. You can tell because the Italians go in for the white wrought iron and the Jews like the black."

After the funeral the Horowitzes cabbed it back to Manhattan, meaning that it would be just Clarice and me on the long drive to the grave.

And as soon as Clarice got back into the big old Mercedes it was as if all control fled her. She flopped herself down on the seat like a pile of laundry. The first thing I noticed was the smell: booze. She reached into her huge bag, pulled out a big bottle of Laphroaig, and took a belt right out of it.

"Clarice, Jesus! Put that away."

"Francesca, Jesus! Shut up and drive," she snapped.

"At least get down so they can't see you." I reached over, but she slapped at my hand.

"Propriety," she shrieked, "oh, propriety!" She was already gone—drunk and not caring.

A young guy in a yarmulke was waving us out of the parking lot, and I put my lights on and pulled out of the space, following a big Lincoln in front of me. Clarice lolled around on the seat and I barked at her to put on her seatbelt. I had no idea how to get to the cemetery in Queens, so it was one eye on the car in front of me, one eye on Clarice all the way there, in an unending processional.

Clarice was dead quiet until suddenly she was not.

"Old Izzy never liked me," she announced.

Don't pick this up, I told myself.

"Old Izzy thought I was a gold digger," she said.

"Let it go," I heard myself saying, "please, Clarice."

"But I gave Sidney beautiful children. *Beautiful children.* Which is more than he would've got with Naomi. Blah blah blah, Naomi the psychologist. As if I care! You should've seen that broad's nose. She was Barnard. I wouldn't have gone there for all the tea in China. Too many Jews."

I swallowed. I weighed all possible responses, forward and backward and backward and forward again. She was so drunk that she'd never remember any of this.

"Time to shut your Nazi mouth now," I said, slowly and brightly.

Amazingly, she did. She slid so far down in her seat it was as if she'd melted into a teenager. Her head flopped against the door, and in no time she was talking to herself in a quiet singsong.

I drove on, twenty miles an hour, saying in my head, *Jew, Jew, Italian, Jew.*

We passed through a blighted neighborhood somewhere on the

Brooklyn-Queens border. A huge sigh came up out of me. This seemed to ignite something in Clarice.

"You know, you really ran a racket on me," she said.

I pasted a benign smile on my face.

"How's that?" I said.

"Oh you, false advertising. Coming into my house as you did."

I turned to see her attempting to glare at me. Her lipstick was comically smeared. She tried to lean toward me, but she was so sunken in her seat that the lap belt had her pinned across her chest, like a lunatic in a straitjacket.

"You see," she said, "I thought you were lesbian."

I turned back to the road just in time to screech to a stop at a red light. The Lincoln sailed away through the intersection.

I thought you were lesbian.

Just like that, with no article in front of it, as if it were a nationality. As if I hailed from the island of Lesbos.

"So nothing with Jerry should have mattered," she said.

Far up ahead, the Lincoln pulled over to wait.

Clarice sank to the side until her head rested against the door.

"You were supposed to distract him, not make him fall in love with you. You're a little snake. You're all snakes. You can all go to hell."

And then she was out again.

I drove on in silence, turning all of this over in my head.

Oh, I had lots of time to think to myself on that drive. This was it. Yes, I would go now. I was surprised by the mildness I felt over this decision. If Jerry was supposed to be in my life, he would find me. We would find each other. I had read enough Epictetus to believe in something like fate. All I knew was that I couldn't stand one more minute in this woman's company.

I followed the Lincoln as it turned into the cemetery.

It was such a strange place that now I feel like I must have dreamed it. It was crumbling and overgrown, and though it dated back to the nineteenth century, there was none of the pleasant greensward aspect of a grand Victorian cemetery. Through the windshield I could see tombstones with Magen Davids and Cohen hands and twinned lions and menorahs on them, tilting sideways out of the earth. Big pieces of them were broken off and you could see where nameplates had been pried free and stolen for the metal. Whole rows of headstones lay flat behind their pediments, as if they had been kicked to the ground, and brambles and winter-dead weeds covered everything. It hurt my heart, what had been done to this place.

The path we drove in on must have ended abruptly, because all of a sudden the Lincoln in front of us just stopped. I hit the brakes of the big old Mercedes and we lurched sickly forward, almost kissing its bumper. Clarice jolted suddenly awake.

She thrust her enormous handbag at me.

"Here—fix my face," she said. All traces of drunkenness were gone, *poof!* She unbuckled herself, stuck out her huge face at me, and closed her eyes. I had one confused second when it seemed as if she wanted me to kiss her. In a moment I pulled out a bunch of tissues and began to clean up the face of this woman I had come to hate.

Out of the car, in the frozen air, Clarice became the dutifully grieving daughter-in-law once again. I'd never met anyone who could turn it on and off so quickly. She was like an actress pinching her own hand to bring tears to her eyes. She was the least human person I'd ever known.

I watched her walk ahead of me to the graveside, and let myself fall back into the crowd.

And then, out of nowhere, I felt a familiar hand on my arm.

"Come back with us and sit shiva," Kendra said.

18

Good luck getting a straight answer out of this girl.

She had dyed her hair a dark, ruddy pink, and she lay on a rose-pink coverlet in Zeyde's old room, a clutch purse in deepest pink thrown down as a pillow for her cheek. Her terminal red lipstick was gone, and the new color, an orangey red, clashed with her hair. There was a luxuriousness about her, and the sensation of the delight she took in feeling herself watched—but there was also her old familiar indolence, her sense of being tragically stuck on this earth: *Is that all there is?* I'd forgotten about Kendra's particular style of self-made drama. You miss a person, and then you see that person and you miss her in a different way.

"Ain't it great to be in Joisey?" she said. "We've got that TGI Friday's right down the way. And the craft store, where you can buy everything you need to make a birdhouse. Plenty of culture."

"Last I heard you were in Spain. And before that Morocco, hanging out with Paul Bowles."

"Ha! That made it over?"

"What's he like?"

"It's complicated," she said. She let this go into a big yawn, and lazily flew her hand to her mouth. She had carried in a two-liter bottle of Diet Coke and set it on the floor in front of her: she told me she was sober now.

"For how long?"

"I don't know—five months?" She was weaving her hand in the air.

"That's great," I said, though I didn't know enough not to feel confused when anyone I knew gave up drinking—although drinking was maybe the least of Kendra's addictions. "You in AA?"

" 'Easy does it,' " she said.

"I guess," I said.

"I'm actually in NA. Narcotics Anonymous."

"Oh," I said. I felt out of my league.

She was weaving her hand in the air, moving it in arabesques.

"When did you come back?" I asked her.

"Oh, I don't know. I was in Paris for a while. I was in, like, Belgium, and then Amsterdam. I mean, it's complicated. I did that courier thing on a ship, like carpets? Eventually it was enough."

"But what finally brought you home?" I asked her.

"I don't know," she said.

Everything felt baffling, borrowed. Unreal. Zeyde's room was a time capsule from another era, with an old Telechron clock, a tombstone-back chair against the wall, a deco bedroom set with exaggeratedly curved edges and a big round mirror gone silver around the frame. On the dresser was a massive lamp made up of a crystal globe with a prowling panther staring at it, a red nightlight in his mouth. All this time I was standing at the dresser clicking the switch of the lamp, which lit the globe and then the panther, then both, then neither, then the globe, then the panther, then both, then . . .

"You don't *know*?" I said.

"I guess I got bored," she said, as if all this were just another extension of that boredom.

I let my hand drop from the lamp.

"Kendra. I mean. The last time I see you is what, three years ago? At a train station in like Passyunck or whatever. And then you *disappear*. And then you're back and it's too complicated for you to say anything about it? Or, I don't know, maybe you might wonder how I'm doing?"

She smiled, her cheek against her handbag.

"How you doin'?" she said in a Bronx accent.

"Jesus Christ," I said.

"Jesus Christ is our lord and savior!" she said merrily.

"What is the *matter* with all of you?"

She slowly lifted herself up, slid her feet to the floor. She stretched, slow and slack, uncurling her fists in the air, and then she let her hands drop.

"I just want to know what you're doing sleeping in my bedroom," she said.

"What?" I said.

"You heard me, Chess. Why are you sleeping in my bedroom?"

"Kendra, please! Your mother asked me to sleep there."

"What are you doing in that house *at all*?" she said.

I cast around Zeyde's room.

"I called your mom when she put out that ad for an assistant last year because I wanted to ask about you, and it was weird, but I somehow ended up taking that job."

"You 'somehow ended up' taking the job?"

"Is it so unlikely?"

Now she wasn't languid at all. She was incensed. She picked up her heavy purse by the corner and slapped it back down on the bed.

"I just don't know how you could *ever* think it was okay to work for my fucking mother."

"I don't know," I said. I threw my hands in the air. What could I say? "It's complicated."

"Now there's a phrase that doesn't suit you."

I kicked off across the floor. I looked around the room and fell into the chair against the wall.

She sat staring at me until all I could do was look down.

"I'm sorry," I said at last.

"You betrayed me," she said.

"I never meant it to be like that," I said miserably.

"Everyone betrays me. Everyone. It starts out good and then the whole thing falls to shit."

"Kendra, you know I didn't mean to do that," I said.

"I don't know anything," she said.

"Please. You're my friend, but you've been away so long. I don't hear from you at all. How am I supposed to guess your feelings about something? This is a friendship, like this?"

"But we have a bond," she said.

"Of course we do," I said. "Of course."

At this she dropped her gaze and shook her head at the floor.

"Well, if it means anything at all to you, I was planning to quit soon anyway," I said.

She looked up at me.

"You were?"

"I think I came to the end of the line with Clarice." I didn't know how much to say to her, what to explain. "It's time for me to go," I said.

"That's great," she said. Suddenly she leapt up to the mirror. She snapped open her purse, whipped out her lipstick, drew an orange-red circle on her mouth. She dabbed the curves of her cupid's bow, rubbed her lips together. She drew an envelope from her purse and blotted a kiss on it.

"Thoroughly Carnelian," she declared, turning to me. "Do you like it?"

"I guess," I said.

She dropped the lipstick into her bag and snapped it closed. "Let's go tell her," she said.

"Tell who what?" I said.

"Duh, stoop! Let's go tell Clarice that you quit."

"What? Now?"

"No time like the present."

"But wait, how tactless would it be to announce my resignation at Zeyde's shiva?"

"Not tactless at all," she said.

"It's completely tactless," I said.

She stopped entirely, looked in the mirror, and then turned back to me.

"You're not sincere!" she shouted. "You're not sincere about any of this, about my feelings or how you've hurt me or anything!"

"Jesus, Kendra, please."

"You're lying and you lie like all the others."

"Kendra—"

Suddenly she swung her heavy purse and slapped it to my chest.

"Fucker," she said. "Motherfucker." I caught her purse in my hands as she turned away and clutched the dresser. I watched as she slithered down the front of it until she was sprawled on the floor, a mass of sobs.

Oh, I realized, *Oh.*

She is crazy.

Not quirky-crazy. Just crazy.

They are all crazy.

"Look, I'll do it," I said. "I promise I'll do it tomorrow."

"Good," she said between sobs. "Good."

*

Of course I was overlooking the fact that grief does strange things to people.

This was much clearer to me the next day, after I'd slept off the strangeness of the funeral, Clarice's uncensored spewing at me, and Kendra's suddenly materializing out of nowhere.

Everyone had stayed over at Anne and Mitchell's big house in Teaneck, with Kendra and me camping out on the floor in Zeyde's old room; somehow it seemed wrong to both of us to sleep in the bed that he had just died in. She woke me up way too early the next morning, insisting that we go to the local pancake house and get waffles à la mode. She was in high spirits and it was as if yesterday hadn't happened at all.

I'd forgotten about Kendra's food enthusiasms, and of course this was really just an example of what a later friend of mine would term Junkie Replacement Syndrome—this friend feeling okay to say the word "junkie" with unique viciousness because she herself had been a needle addict for many years. That morning I surprised myself by realizing that I was glad to see Kendra, sloppy, confusing, histrionic behavior and all. There was something about her that made things feel special, like she was sharing something amazing with you and you were thrilled to be chosen.

Out at the pancake house, she told me that families sit shiva for seven days.

"Why seven?" I wanted to know.

"I have no idea—I really don't know any of this crap. I'm just doing it to honor the spirit of Zeyde. I'm *such* a bad Jew. Like I feel like we probably should be tearing our clothes instead of eating waffles for whatever reason, except who cares? Actually Zeyde was totally secular, so he'd find this all *hilarious*."

"I feel like Catholics like to make things divisible by three. So like a novena is nine days. But I mean, who does nine of anything? You're more likely to do a week of something. It's as if they have to make sure they corner the market on sacrifice."

Kendra looked at me as she ate, and I found myself yammering on about all sorts of things, like the kick I was on then with Michel de Certeau's *The Possession at Loudon,* Kateri Tekakwitha, female-specific religious manias, the cult of Bona Dea, women so often taking refuge in delusions because they are otherwise powerless, etc., as the ice cream waffle mess melted in front of me.

"I forgot what it's like to talk to interesting people," she said.

"You forgot just now?"

"Duh, I mean, no, I was with so many losers and doing all this shit and it was like no one was talking about *ideas.* It's really not junk that makes junkies losers but all the planning around getting the cash to score. Like Burroughs said, the Job. He was fine, because he didn't have to worry about that."

"He had the cash."

"The Burroughs adding machine, baby," she said. She took a sip of her coffee. And then she looked away and back at me, as if to mark the importance of what she was about to disclose.

"I mean, I had the cash too," she said.

"What do you mean?"

"My parents fund everything."

"They knew where you *were*?"

"Of course! Sidney and I are regular pals, we see each other all the time. All that flying to Europe to go to those gross mink farms. And Clarice basically pays me to stay away."

"*What?*"

"Dude, where have you been? She buys me off. Although she'd like it better if I'd just OD and die. But die abroad, so it's less embarrassing. Less of a chance of having it hit the New York papers: 'Clarice Marr's Troubled Daughter . . . ,' 'Embraced Punk-Rock Lifestyle . . .' So at some point I realized the biggest fuck-you would be to get clean and show up in her face. You know? And what a delight it was to see her just about

215

pee herself at the cemetery yesterday. But what I forgot about was how quickly she always recovers. She really is the consummate actress."

"My fucking head is spinning," I said.

"Look, don't give notice today," she said. "That way you can still get paid while you're here. 'Cause you have to stay with me for six more days now or I'll lose my mind! Anyway, Sidney and I already worked it out. He sent Clarice back in a cab last night, and he's probably on the phone with Ms. Bitch now telling her not to expect you. *Kendra needs her friend.* I've got heaps of clothes you can wear, and if everything's too big you can just *belt* that shit. So you're all sorted out." With this, she gave me the corny, exaggerated wink that I remembered so well.

I couldn't respond. What? So now she didn't want me to resign? What if *I* wanted to? I played with the waffle in front of me, moving it around my plate.

"Are you mad at me?" she asked.

I sighed.

"It's like at some point I realized being mad at you is like being mad at dust or the moon or the color yellow."

She lit up into her million-dollar smile.

"Oh, Chess—I knew you'd understand!" she said.

*

Okay, so who knew what to truly make of this family, these machinations, this constantly roiling collection of relationships at all? Somehow I was still a sucker for Kendra's peculiar charm. And if she told me I understood her, it was as if with those words she made it true—and thus she made me necessary.

We had the old Mercedes, and Kendra and I tooled all over the Jersey hinterlands in it, smoking a million cigarettes, breezing through wooded byways, stopping at every diner we saw and drinking coffee until our hands shook. At first all she wanted to do was tell me stories about Zeyde, what a street kid he'd been, such a tough ass, how he had complained that her dad was a sissy—it was the old F. Scott Fitzgerald thing, he thought the rich were soft but he wanted his children to be like them—and how she'd always been Zeyde's favorite. Always, always his favorite. He was like a spotlight on her when she was a child, the person who taught her she was special: he was the glow she basked in.

In a way he ruined me, she said, *because I thought all my life would be like that.*

From there we would talk about everything, but we always seemed to turn eventually toward religion, or faith, which we could jaw about till the cows came home. The pretense of our sitting shiva was dropped: she said Zeyde was free already, and she pictured him piloting himself toward heaven in a contraption like a balsa-wood gilder—just big enough to hold his essence, since the things of the body had no meaning anymore. Not that she was sure that Jews believed in souls or heaven or anything. As for the seven days of shiva, Anne, Mitchell, and Shoshanna seemed to be the only constant attendees. I was fascinated by Judaism and was forever asking young Shoshanna all sorts of questions, which was probably everything you're not supposed to do, but the practice of religion in that house seemed like a complicated, multiform affair. I was used to Catholic "universality," there being only one acceptable version, and that there were all kinds of Judaism I found, in a word, pretty cool. It seemed to adhere to the reverse prejudice I had about Jewish people in those days: they were, as a group, so much smarter than the average goy and thus could more readily embrace complexity. Anyway, shy young Shoshanna was flattered to be asked anything at all and, at every meal we had together, blinked at Kendra and me as if we were movie stars.

The week flew by, and even before the end of it Kendra was throwing out all sorts of ideas about us getting a place together in the East Village. We could get jobs as waitresses or strippers or canvassers for that Ralph Nader activist group, or any old thing! She knew a girl who got paid to roller-skate around a dance club with big Lene Lovitch streamers in her hair shouting *Yi-yi-yi-yi!* while serving shots of tequila—maybe we could get a gig like that? I just had to give notice to Clarice and we'd be free.

All this time, despite my love for Kendra, always in my mind was Jerry. Kendra was in so many ways the opposite of him that somehow she ended up recalling him at every turn. Where she was voluble he was reticent. She wanted to be liked, and he refused to pander. He hid his wounds, while she flaunted hers. She *did*, but he stood back. They both had the family theatricality, but while hers was needy, his was disdainful: *How dare you think you will watch me . . . although watch me you must.*

It occurred to me that I didn't know him at all, really.

One night toward the end of our time out there, we were driving up the Palisades Parkway and I was seized by the desire to stop and look at Manhattan. Kendra pulled over to a lookout, and we climbed up on the back of the car and lit cigarettes. I gazed across the water at nighttime Manhattan dressed in all her lights, and as I looked, I felt that alluring champagne fizz of the city. Excitement about the future was like something tingling through my limbs.

And yet it seemed like Kendra's mood was beginning to sink.

"Big city of dreams," she said dismissively.

She put her hands up, framing the cluster of lights around Midtown between them.

"One look and you hear *Rhapsody in Blue,* right?" she said.

"I think of Berenice Abbott. Lewis Hine. Those paintings by Joseph Stella."

"So you think of an image even though here you are looking at the real thing?" she said.

"It's already an abstraction. Or maybe you see a representation first and it's taught you how to look at the real thing."

"Expectations will always take the piss out of reality."

"I don't actually feel that way," I said.

"Yet," she said. "You don't feel that way *yet.*"

"You really feel like that?"

She shrugged. Even she sometimes couldn't tell when she was posing. Across the water, something hovered in the distance. A light was turned off or on again and somehow the picture changed. But the source was untraceable, just one moment lost among millions.

"Do you miss him?" she asked me at last.

"Do I miss who?" I asked her.

She spoke, still looking at the city, not turning.

"Jerry."

I swallowed.

"Yes," I said.

A huge sigh escaped her, and she sank down into herself. I felt this keenly, felt the disappointment my words gave her, but now I knew I'd finally ask the question I'd wanted to ask all along but had not—because it was too much like looking past her, beyond her.

"Where is he?"

She violently flicked her half-smoked cigarette into the road.

"How the fuck should I know?" she said.

"I only thought—"

"You only *didn't think* at all," she said.

"Oh, come on, Kendra! Don't be like this. All I *do* is think." I flicked away my own cigarette and slid off the car. I watched her gathering her powers into herself, summoning up a great chill to blast at me, there from her perch on the big Mercedes. But it was pretty late in the game for her to pull her freeze-out routine. Suddenly I was giving her goofy little smacks all over her knees and boots and saying, "Oh, come on, don't be mad, come on!"

She slid from the car and maybe I put my hands up—because all at once we were on each other, grappling and grunting and shoving and then she got her hands around my neck. I was choking and she almost had me flat but I dropped my weight and twisted free. We spun out from each other. Then we were facing off again. I couldn't catch my breath and I stuck my hand out in front of me like a catcher's mitt.

"Punch my hand," I said.

"What?"

"Punch my fucking hand!"

"What the fuck?"

"*Come on, punch it!*" I yelled at her.

She flapped her own hand at me in dismissal. But then she changed her mind and wound up. And she punched so hard that my whole arm flipped back.

"Wa-*oww*-oh!" came out of me as my arm lit up like Christmas. I grabbed my shoulder and hugged it. I saw the ground shimmer in front of me, and it was all I could do not to whimper.

"I think I hurt you," she said at last.

She said it in a tiny voice, apologetic. But she couldn't hide the fact that she was smiling.

*

We drove into the city late the next afternoon and pulled up in front of the house on Eleventh Street. Sidney had flown out the day before, on a buying trip to Latvia.

Clarice was outside to greet us.

She was coatless in the cold air, dressed in her most elegant black Chanel and a pair of ice-pick high heels. As soon as we stepped up to the curb she spread her arms wide and wordlessly pulled us into her embrace.

She'd never done such a thing before, and I stood stiffly as she gave a yank and pinned me, smashing my face to her clavicle. I twitched and squirmed and fought to turn my head to Kendra.

But then the sight of her . . .

Kendra was swooning against her mother, eyes closed, as needy and desirous as a little baby. Even as Clarice fought to keep me clamped to her bosom—nothing kind or warm in any of this—she was pulling Kendra off her with her other arm. This was all happening in seconds and I yanked myself free. The stickiness I felt all over my body was repulsive.

But worse by far was Kendra's helplessness as she clung to her mother.

Just then Clarice opened her eyes at me, and it was as if she had turned into robot Maria from *Metropolis,* startling in her inhumanness.

In a moment she did get Kendra off her, thrusting her away like a sack of potatoes. I watched as Kendra staggered back, wobbling on her feet. The fizzle of humiliation in the air was so strong it was almost sexual. We both watched as Clarice pulled on a pair of new leather gloves and stepped out into the street with her arm raised. A cab sailed magically into view.

"I'm off to Chanterelle," she said. She turned to Kendra and fixed her with a look as if to dispel any notion that she'd been there to welcome her daughter home.

And with a slam of the cab door she was gone.

*

So it will be hard to explain what happened in the days that followed.

I watched as Kendra caved in. It was as if in that orbit, with the pull of her mother and the things of her childhood, all the refusenik notions that she held in her mind disappeared.

Once inside the house, Kendra walked through the rooms picking up things and examining them, caressing bookcases and patting pillows and running her hand over the backs of chairs.

"I've been gone so long," she kept saying. She had a look on her face I'd never seen before, something regretful, almost contrite.

"May I see my room?" she asked me.

"Why are you *asking*?" I said.

We went upstairs to her room, but she halted at her door. She took a long look inside. I'd barely changed a thing, and immediately I began gathering up my stuff while she walked the room, stopping at anything foreign: a stack of books, a sweater thrown over a chair. She looked at these things as if they were exotic mushrooms that had sprouted in a familiar wood.

"I'll stay in Cornelia's room until we're ready to go," I said, my arms full. She nodded. She was looking at a dress that I had for whatever reason hung on the closet door: it was the dress she'd been wearing when I first saw her. She took it by the shoulder, ran her hand down its arm until she held it by the cuff, and flounced it back and forth, like someone coaxing a partner to dance.

She turned and looked at me. Tears were in her eyes.

"How is it I got so old?" she said.

She was twenty-three.

"You just need some sleep," I said. "Why don't you take a nap before dinner?"

She went and flopped down on the bed.

"I'm so tired," she said.

I spilled the stuff in my arms to the floor and went and yanked her boots off. I rolled her under the covers and tucked her in, folding the sheet over so that the scratchy blanket wouldn't touch her neck. Then I took my sleeve and wiped her face, and the whitest foundation smeared itself on the black of my sweatshirt. All through this she was inert, blinking at me, dazed and almost paralyzed.

"Thank you." She rolled over and put her face to the wall.

She slept through dinner, slept the night, then slept the next day through—I'd gone back to work with Clarice, not sure what the plan was yet—and then, after sitting up for some soup, she went right back to bed. When she still hadn't come down the next morning, I took her some coffee and a slice of challah and sat down gently on the edge of the bed. She rolled over and opened her eyes.

"Are you okay?" I asked.

"Did she ask about me?" she said.

"Of course. She keeps asking. She's just surprised that you're still in bed."

What Clarice had actually said was, *That cow isn't up yet?*

"She doesn't want to see me," she said. It was as if the light had gone out of her face.

"I'm sure she does," I said. "I can go get her."

"Look at you," she said. I had on an "outfit," proper work clothes, and she was used to seeing me in jeans and combats. "You look so pretty," she said, touching my skirt. "You're slender and you have good posture."

"Oh boy, you definitely need to get up," I said.

She rolled onto her back and looked up at the ceiling, and in a moment she was sobbing.

"Oh, Kendra," I said. "Here, drink this coffee. It's good. It's, um, fair trade." I suddenly felt self-conscious, but I got her to sit up and I handed her the coffee. She took a sip.

"Good, right?" I said.

She nodded at me like a little girl.

She ate in silence, and when she was finished she handed me her plate. She had crumbs on her mouth, and I touched my own in a mirror to hers; but instead of wiping them away herself, she offered her face to me. I gently wiped her mouth with the napkin.

"Thank you," she said. She turned over and almost immediately fell back asleep.

When I got myself downstairs again, Clarice was at the window, smoking a cigarette.

"Is she up?" she asked.

I shook my head.

"Boredom will get her up eventually," she said.

"I think she's depressed," I said.

"Story of her life."

"Clarice, her grandfather just died. Why don't you go talk to her?"

"Because I don't care to," she said. She blew smoke into the air. "Please save your do-gooder speeches, Francesca."

"I really think she's very sick!" I said.

"So sad," she said. "So very sad. Poor little rich girl, ate too many sugarplums."

"Clarice—"

"Will you be telling me to shut my Nazi mouth now?"

A crazy sound escaped me.

"Don't worry," she said. She waved it away. "I thought it was funny."

She sat down at her desk and stubbed out her cigarette as I stood blinking.

"Step it up, Francesca," she said. "We've got a lot of work to do."

It was as if we had a new understanding now, contemptible though it might be: she had seen me see too much, and this put us in some creepy way on the same side. We were the tough ones. Her children were a bunch of weaklings. They were the rococo phase, headed for extinction. Somehow, in the eternal *ronde* I was dancing with this family, Clarice now saw us as united, as if she thought the shifting allegiances would actually end with her.

Four hours later she was off to Le Cirque for lunch and I was leaning over Kendra, rolling and punching her like bread dough.

"Oh God, Kendra, come on, you've gotta get up," I pleaded.

She turned over and rubbed the sleep from her eyes. I had brought in a plate of sandwiches and set it on the nightstand, and this immediately caught her attention.

"What's on the plate?"

"Sandwiches. Caciocavallo from Balducci's."

"Would you hand me one?"

"Only if you promise me you'll get up. Promise me—oh, *please,* promise me."

223

"Fuck you, Reginald De Koven," she said.

"Fuck *you*, Oblomov," I said.

"Fuck you . . . Dionne Warwick. Burt fucking Bacharach," she said.

"Fuck you, Alice James," I said.

"Well, clearly you win that round," she said.

She pulled herself up and I handed her a sandwich.

"Why's it on whole wheat?" she wanted to know. "I hate whole wheat. It's so *healthy*."

We both sat eating. I knew by now that the best route with her was the roundabout one, so I waited for her to say something.

"God, I could totally smoke a doobie right now," she finally said.

"Take the edge off," I said in my Sarcastic Punk-Rock Voice. No way was I going to let her get near any kind of controlled substance. "Look, why don't we find you an NA meeting?" I said.

"Because I don't feel like sitting in a church basement eating windmill cookies with a bunch of judgmental ex-hopheads."

"I'll totally go with you if you want."

"Shut up, Fifi," she said in a silly voice.

"Shut up, Kiki," I said, in the same silly voice.

But then she became somber again. We sat eating our sandwiches, neither of us speaking.

"I miss my Zeyde," she said at last.

"I bet you do," I said. "I bet you do."

I looked at the curtains, which Kendra had pulled against the light days ago and not opened since. Maybe this was how she had to mourn. Maybe I had upset the order of things. Except all of this didn't seem to be healing her . . . only weakening her, drowning her in sadness.

"So how do we get you out of bed?" I said at last.

"Usually I get the opposite question," she said.

Kendra had eaten the middle of her sandwich and left the dark crusts, and these she began tossing around her room, raising her hand and slowly throwing them, like a priest sprinkling holy water. She wilted back into her bed and pulled the covers up to her throat.

"Why does she hate me so much?" she said.

"Shhh, she doesn't hate you," I said. "It's just a game she's playing."

"Fucking hate this game."

"So do I," I said.

I leaned over and petted her head, trying to soothe her.

"That feels nice," she said, letting her eyes close for a moment.

"Kendra, why don't we just go?" I said.

"Where?"

"I don't know. Probably Williamsburg. Trina and Starr just moved again and they got something Northside off Roebling, six-fifty split two ways. And Southside is *so* cheap. I mean, it's Williamsburg, so everyone will be making art out of their tampons, but the rent'll be hard to beat."

"What would we do for work?" she said.

"Oh, I can always get any old office job for a while. Something not so all-consuming. I should be doing my own work by now anyway."

"But what would *I* do?"

"What do you mean? You had so many ideas," I said.

"Yeah, I think I'd rather hook than strip."

"Don't be a dope. You're smart and you could find something. You could work at a bookstore or whatever until you find something you want to do."

"Until I find something I want to do. Oh, Chess, you really are a young soul."

"What? What's the deal?" I said.

"There's *nothing* I want to do. There's never been anything I wanted to do. I didn't even want to dance, back when I was good even."

"Look, you're depressed. You've *gotta* get out of bed. Let's go for a walk. We can get a slice at Two Boots! We can get a coffee and go to record stores on St. Mark's. Come on, Kendra, *please.*"

She was looking at me with a sad smile on her face.

"You're neat as a pin, Chess. You'll always be fine."

"What do you mean? Why are you talking like this?"

"My mother loves you. You're the perfect fit."

"Are you kidding? She hates me and she thinks I'm a sham and a fool and totally wet behind the ears. She loves to laugh richly at my moronic ways and she hates that I don't even speak French. She thinks I'm a total bumpkin and that I've got my fare back to the hill village sewn into my underpants. She doesn't even *trust* me."

"Listen to me," she said. "I know her a teensy bit better."

"Kendra, you're driving me crazy."

For some reason she smiled at this. Then she reached out and touched my arm.

"Hey," she said, "I looked at *Wisconsin Death Trip*."

Inside that book was where I had put Jerry's letter.

"It's the real deal," she said. "You should go with him. He's better than I am."

"Don't say that. There's no 'better.' What the fuck number did your mother do on you all?"

"Oh, Bert's fine, and Cornelia will be fine too. I think in the long run even Jerry will be okay. I never will. I'm just not made that way."

"Man, I'm totally sick of your melodrama," I said.

"I know, right? I'm totally sick of it too. Sick, sick, sick! I wish it would go away." She yawned a huge yawn, slid herself down in her pillows. "Look, I promise I'll get out of this bed tomorrow. See? Promise. I just need to think for a while, okay? I'll see you tomorrow." She snuggled herself under the blankets, then took out her hand and pointed to her own cheek.

"Plant one," she said. And I leaned over, and kissed her.

*

I was up early the next morning, almost with the sun. I was so relieved. Finally we'd be getting on with our lives. I knocked lightly on Kendra's door and then went in with my little tray of coffee and buttered muffins. It was no surprise that Kendra didn't stir at all, and I put the things down on her nightstand and sat gently on her bed.

"Kendra," I said, and I touched her shoulder.

She was so still.

"Kendra?" The girl really could sleep, was a champion narcoleptic.

And then I realized. She was too still.

KENDRA, I screamed, and I grabbed her and she was loose in my arms, slack as a ragdoll, and I shook her and shook her. I was shaking and then I was slapping her awake, trying to slap her awake, and then I pulled her out of bed and we were both on the floor and a hollow prescription bottle rolled to the floor and I was screaming and screaming for help, screaming her name, screaming her name and *she was so still* as I cradled her and rocked her in my arms, but her flesh was warm, her flesh was still warm.

19

She did not die.

A young doctor with a ponytail was telling us that benzodiazepine overdoses are rarely lethal unless you mix the pills with something else—alcohol, other depressants, opiates, et cetera, et cetera. She told us they had given Kendra something called Narcan, a charcoal that would stop the absorption, and she told us something else about an antagonist, but I didn't understand what that meant. I was trying to listen but not really taking it in, and I could guess that she was an intern because she was peppy and talked in a way that suggested she was more proud of her knowledge than she was concerned about her patient. It was all the same to her. She might as well have been telling us about a new recycling program. She really did say *et cetera, et cetera,* which struck me in a doctor as imprecise, and she pronounced it like "eck cetera." When she said it again I turned to Clarice, but she was already fixing me with a look: *This girl might be a doctor, but she's obviously not very bright.* The young doctor was wearing a butterfly necklace, which seemed to me needlessly infantile. I wanted to take her by her face and push her to the floor.

I got myself over to the wall and was leaning on it. I felt like I could bend it back, put my hand through it as if through soft marshmallow.

Somehow knowing Kendra was in the clear was when it all really hit me, and suddenly I felt myself shaking all over. I felt my teeth chattering, and I put my hands to my jaw to hold my face together. It was like I was falling. Someone put me in a chair and that was when I guess I was given something. I remembered that feeling like when they're putting you out under gas and you're told to count down and it's like, Wow, this feels stupid, but then suddenly you're gone.

I woke up and someone had put a coat over me. It was a puffy down coat and I was trying to remember where I'd seen it. Whose was it? I was groggy and felt so cold even with the coat. There were no windows where I was but it felt like it was dark outside, the middle of the night.

I could hear voices, women's voices.

I got up to follow the voices, pulling back a curtain, which made an abrupt metal-on-metal *slt!* An orderly sat at an almost-empty nurses' station, his face lit by a computer screen. He flicked his eyes to me, not unkindly, and then looked away again. St. Vincent's felt like a dark wilderness of night and machine beeps and fitful sleep.

I followed the voices down the hall. There were two women. One I recognized as Clarice. I realized the other woman was Anne. It was Anne's coat that I held in my hands.

They were arguing.

I stood at the dark end of the hall, watching them.

". . . just doesn't make sense—she's in your house all that time and you don't go *see* her? And it's been how long, how many years? How's such a thing possible? You don't go to her *once* in—"

"You have no idea of the commitments I have."

"You think you're impressing me? You're not impressing me. You're not—"

"Anne, you flatter yourself if you think I'm interested in impressing you."

Anne caught her breath at the sharpness of this.

"If that had been *my* daughter, *my* child, and her reaction to her *zeyde*'s death was like that, you can bet I'd *make* some time to—"

"I'm sure little Shulamith is very lucky."

"Shoshanna! My daughter's name is Shoshanna!" Anne yelled. "My daughter, your *niece*."

I watched as Clarice stepped back, as if to warm up, and then stepped forward again.

"And what a *lovely* name to saddle that child with," she said.

Anne did not speak for a moment.

"You don't like us," she said quietly. "You don't like any of us."

"'Us' meaning whom, Anne? 'Us' meaning whom?"

"They're your own flesh and blood and you're no kind of mother to them. You're no kind of mother to your children."

"My children! Poor little Kendrick, my twenty-three-year-old child!"

"She needs you and you turn away from her—"

"She turned away from *me* a long time ago."

"Who is the mother here? Just who is the mother, Clarice? Are you competing with your own daughter? Is that why you do the things you do? Don't think I don't know. We all know. You're a disgrace. You're a *disgusting* woman—yes, disgusting for all your fancy B.S. and your airs and your—your shit manners! Your lousy, shit manners!" It was as if it were physically hurting Anne to curse. "You think you're such a lady, but you've got no kind of class. You hear me? No kind of class! You should clear out and leave my brother alone. He'd be a lot better off without you. You're going to bring him home the AIDS with this, you hear me? You loose, disgusting woman!"

"I don't have to listen to this," Clarice growled.

But, strangely, she didn't make a move.

How long did those two women square off in that corridor, burning at each other?

And I realized something then. Clarice *wanted* to leave Sidney. She wanted to leave them all. *She wanted to start over.* She wanted to be young again, and have every possibility open before her.

Her family meant nothing to her.

A squeaky sound came from the far end of the hall. They both turned. A nurse came out of the shadows in a gaily colored smock top and white clogs. She had skinny braids and a kind way about her, and she must have just started her shift, because she smiled at the two women. Both Clarice and Anne hung their heads in shame.

With this, I melted back around the corner.

*

Sidney had come in from Latvia at the news, and the moment Kendra was well enough to leave the hospital, she was bundled into the car and driven up to the rehab at Old Briar. It all happened so quickly that I wasn't even given a chance to say good-bye.

Clarice was not invited on the trip.

She was in a foul mood and made a point of telling me that Kendra had been back up at Old Briar half a dozen times since that episode freshman year. "The girl treats it like sleep-away camp," she said as I sat dully before her, in theory taking dictation but in reality staring into my cup of coffee. All I felt was blank, unresponsive, even as endless complaint came out of Clarice's mouth. Kendra would have to stay for a three-month minimum this time, Clarice told me, *and you can't even imagine the price of such a thing.* She went on and on about the *expense* of her daughter, the *absurdity* of her daughter, her lack of *imagination*—and the appropriateness of the *DSM* definition of insanity, which should really be called *stupidity.*

She treated the whole thing like it was some meaningless piece of theater. She didn't seem to care about Kendra's heart, mind, flesh, anything, just the *expense* of her. I responded by saying nothing. That was my new tack: let her run her mouth all she wanted, and say nothing in response.

After Sidney took Kendra to the rehab, there was one night of yelling and then he went back to Europe. Yes, he was punishing her. This left only Clarice and me in the house, in the enormous, empty, but increasingly claustrophobic house. As if waking up from a dream, I realized I had no idea what was happening with my friends. Where was Trina? Where was Fang? It seemed like ages since I'd seen either of them.

And Trina had gone rushing forward without me.

She'd always been beset by legions of groover boys looking to chat her up, but suddenly, all out of the blue, something changed and she actually started *going out* with a guy. It would be hard to express the amount of dismay this caused me. I mean, I wanted to be happy for her, but it was all I could do not to beat around the room in a tantrum. He could have been a saint, the nicest guy in the world, but I was filled with criticism—my friend was being taken away from me. Simon was a photographer and a musician and he had a cool old Chevy, and they went out to Coney to take Holga photos, down through Jersey to the Princeton Record Exchange, out to Montauk to capture the waning light. Trina began inviting me to go on all sorts of trips with them, but I begged off—they didn't need me tagging along. She'd been sympathetic but appalled at what Kendra had tried to do, and thought the whole Marr-Löwenstein family was an infection I kept willfully ignoring. She'd been telling me for ages that I needed to get away from them, and I'd just kept on ignoring her and making excuses, so it was no wonder that she stopped saying it now. What surprised me was that I missed it. I missed the lectures, I missed the reminding.

One awful evening Fang called, and I was so relieved to hear her voice that I immediately let out a stream of woe. What was I doing with my life? Why was I so stuck, how could I get anywhere, why was I so stalled out? I went on and on like this before I became aware that she was completely silent, saying nothing at all—simmering and about to boil.

"What is it?" I finally said to her.

"I broke up with Clark," she said.

"That's great!" I said.

"Fuck you, Chess," she said. "Why are you such an asshole?"

And then she started to cry.

"I'm so sorry," I said. "I'm just . . . I'm happy you got away from him."

"Do you understand a *thing*? God, Chess. Now I have no place to live and I have all my stuff in a fucking garbage bag. I schlepped it to work this morning and stowed it in the supply room at, like, six a.m. so no one would see me and here it is eight at night and I'm too embarrassed to leave until everyone's—"

"Look, Fang, I'll come help you—"

"Trina and Simon are coming," she said icily.

"Oh," I said. I stared at the yellow kitchen wall. *Oh.* Everything was going on without me.

"I wish you'd told me," I said at last.

"Well, I'm telling you now, aren't I? And how much would you care anyway, because you're *all taken care of* and you don't have to worry about a place to live or the Con Ed bill or buying your own food or sub-way tokens or anything and you're so obsessed with that scene I never see you anyway so why should you care about me?"

"Oh, Fang, you know I care about you!"

"I just never see it. I never fucking see it."

"I am so sorry," I said.

"Yeah, just keep saying that," she said.

I realized just how much I had underestimated her.

I'd never really updated my sense of her since we met as freshmen. In some way I'd seen Fang as a funny novelty, reading her Jürgen Habermas in the original German but becoming mad hostile if you asked her what the literal translation for "chow fun" was: *How the fuck should I know? You know how many dialects there are in China?* I was thinking of something Trina had clued me in on, the way I always seemed quick to harsh on Fang . . . I hadn't even seen this, but it made me remember certain things. I thought of one time in college when we were making some typically lazy dinner, soup from a can and grilled cheese, and I'd said, *Hey, I've got some Parmesan, that might be good,* and I'd taken it out and handed it to Fang and she put it on her grilled cheese. And I'd said, *What the heck are you doing?* She'd given a terrible start at this, as if she'd been zapped by an electrical shock. I hadn't even known how much I'd embarrassed her. Later I would realize so much: she had the shame of the immigrant, and there was the deepest insecurity in her—fear of missteps, fear of exposure, fear of criticism about her class background. To cover this she put on a tough face, sought to be uncriticizable, the smartest girl in the room. And in my own lack of worldliness, my own insecurity over my own missteps, *I* became the one directing criticism her way: the friend who should have been supporting her was instead poking around to find the gaps in her armor.

While someone like Kendra I was quick to coddle, quick to protect.

At any rate, we made up in some kind of half-assed fashion and attempted to hang out together. She was still working at the design magazine and had found a long-term sublet in Hell's Kitchen, an old floor-through of a Sam Fuller film noir grimness, a place where the aging chorine would get murdered, and sometimes I'd go up there to see her. These evenings always started out all right, but if we made the mistake of going out to a bar, things quickly got stupid. We'd be sitting in some place on Ninth Avenue, Rudy's or Holland Bar, neither any place to pick a fight in those days, and the more beer Fang drank, the more full of vitriol she became, hating any man who looked our way. If one of these unlucky guys had the temerity to come up to our table, she'd train a brief eye on him and say something so vile and wither-

232

ing that the cockiest operator would wilt away as if squeezed with the Spock nerve pinch. At some point she declared she'd be celibate: guys were self-impressed fools anyway, needy bastards or preening jerks who liked to dance in front of mirrors. It became so that, to Fang, only anything highly practical or highly theoretical was good, while anything too searching or dreamy—such as reading a poem or looking at the sky over Manhattan or feeling a huge and unspecific sadness—was a total waste of her time. She found me undisciplined, repining; she suggested that I had *lost my edge*. In contrast, I watched her grow harder by the moment.

I told myself this was all temporary and all of these things would eventually come to rights.

The moment of quitting my job with Clarice rolled forward without me. In my deepest giddiness, I saw a future where I was an old lady, Clarice a very old lady, the two of us still together in her cobwebbed study. I would be sitting on the decayed lady-in-waiting tabouret holding a pen in my arthritic hand, while she'd be wearing a Chanel suit so stiff with age it would crumble to the touch like Miss Havisham's wedding cake. She would light her one millionth cigarette—her face now indistinguishable from W. H. Auden's after her many years of alcohol and tobacco abuse—and then she'd set her Wedgwood lighter back down on her desk, turn to me, and say, *I am overjoyed at this beautiful morning!*

I wondered, would Kendra come back? Would Jerry come back ever? And at my lowest I wondered, Did he even care about me?

Instead, my long-deferred student loan repayment book came in the mail and I flipped through its endless pages of statement tickets, each with a due date in its right-hand corner. Flipping and flipping in that widening gyre, I watched as the dates cycled through into the next millennium—the falcon clearly could not hear the falconer. Barnard had given me huge amounts of grant money, but still it was one pricey place, and to make up the difference I'd taken out loans, signing my name on the dotted line as if it were just another occasion to practice the Palmer method. I was a young, bright dope, and the idea of this money was meaningless until I actually had to pay it back.

And in these long days of the still-clinging winter, I finally under-

233

stood something: *Oh, this is what grown-ups do.* They work for a living. They work and they work. I made some calculations and I realized I'd have to make almost twice as much as I did in order to afford an apartment on my own and be able to keep up my loan payments, eat, have clothes to wear, and do things I liked to do such as buy books and go out to bars or shows at CBGB. All of this somehow came to me as a surprise.

One afternoon when Clarice was out for lunch, I was in the kitchen eating a bowl of soup when I heard a familiar sound: the buzzer of the old *arrotino* jalopy trolling the street. I threw down my spoon, ran the length of the hallway, and flung open the front door. Standing in front of me was Fitz, his hand raised in the air.

"Hello!" I said.

I was over the moon to see him.

"Hello!" he said.

We stood blinking at each other. He was wearing the same threadbare coat and moth-eaten rag-wool scarf but seemed to have made some attempt to make his crazy hair sit flat. The attempt was not successful.

"What brings you here?" I said.

"A delicate matter."

Out of his pocket he wrested something: a coil of curling index cards bound with a million rubber bands. He started taking off the rubber bands to find the right card.

"I see you have some state-of-the-art bookkeeping techniques there," I said.

"Freddie Knives, Lotus 1-2-3 whiz," he said.

It was taking him a long time to get the rubber bands off the cards.

"I am *not* OCD, I swear to you," he said.

"I like to keep a hair thingie on my wrist."

"You're not going to say 'scrunchie,' are you? Please don't say 'scrunchie.'"

"'Onesie' is much worse."

"'Onesie' is obscene!" he shouted.

"'Doozy' is okay somehow," I said.

"'Doozy' is nice," he said.

"'Nice' is nice," I said.

"Aha!" he said, holding up the card. "Thirty-two dollars. Cash or check?"

"I'll raid the cookie jar," I said. "Come in!"

But he made no move.

"Seriously, come in," I said.

He checked back and forth.

"Just . . . is the dragon lady home? Is she going to run down the stairs and get all Lifetime Reading Plan on my ass?"

"What?"

"She loves to tell me how bright I am and what a waste of brain I represent. She's really down on me because I never finished college. And I haven't read *The Closing of the American Mind*."

"You never finished *college*?"

"Sheesh, rub it in!"

But he came inside, and followed me down the hallway and into the kitchen. The room glowed with late winter light.

"Wow, it's nice and warm in here," he said.

"Don't you have heat in that truck?"

"That the truck runs at all is a miracle. It's like some *Twenty-One Balloons* contraption with an elf and a bellows."

"You know," I said, "I just made a pot of soup. All vegetarian. Would you join me?"

He hesitated.

"Oh, why not?" he said.

I got busy putting out a setting for him, but he hung back, suddenly very shy.

"Maybe, I don't know, take your coat off?" I said.

"I didn't really think I was going to be taking my coat off in public today."

"Oh, so now I'm public?" I said.

He untwined his scarf, laid it on the butcher-block counter. It was tattered like a doily. He unbuttoned his coat slowly but held it closed.

"Okay, I'm taking the plunge," he said. All at once he pulled off his coat and slapped it to the floor.

He was wearing many, many, many layers of shirts, the topmost one a huge electric-blue sweatshirt that said *NASCAR*.

"Wow," I said. "Wow. I'm, um. Wow."

"So they turned off the heat in our building over there on Avenue C last month and we went on rent strike, but we've got the stove, so basically we just boil water and bake apple crisp all day, and one of my roommates goes to FIT, and she brought home this ragbag of stuff, most of which is like tubular body stockings and useless little knitted things that apparently are called capelets. Capelets and Montagues. This was the only thing that fit me." He regarded himself in the crazy sweatshirt. "I was hoping I could rock the irony? But I don't even say things like 'rock the irony,' so who am I kidding? I just feel bad for the obese twelve-year-old who must've owned this."

"You have no heat in your building?"

"Oh, we're fine. I mean, we're not, but we are, and it can't go on forever. I mean, spring's around the corner. I just get myself through it by thinking, What would Knut Hamsun do? I mean, the young distressed Knut Hamsun with the bundle of candlesticks, not the old fascist Knut Hamsun who wrote that stunningly ponderous *Growth of the Soil.*"

"I love *Hunger!*" I said.

"Yeah, yeah, but his others, not so much, it's a shame. *Pan,* wow, unreadable. *Mysteries—*"

"Oh, I love *Mysteries,*" I said. "Don't say anything bad about it!"

We sat with our big bowls of soup in front of us. He was so present and quick and funny, and a listener. It was as if I knew him from another place. He was way into theory-head stuff like Foucault but said things like "parrhesia" and "Geez Louise!" in almost the same breath. He asked me all kinds of questions and I asked him about his art; at first he was shy, as if he didn't think it would interest me, but then he talked about how he did everything from woodblock printing to lithography to complicated techniques that I sort of understood—mezzotint, aquatint, methods of intaglio printing. He talked about the artists he loved, the force of Käthe Kollwitz, the sureness of the black space in Félix Vallotton's *Intimités,* ghoulish James Ensor etchings like *Christ's Entry into Brussels,* but then all the beautiful old things, Dürer, Rembrandt; Goya was *devastating,* he could not look enough at Japanese ukiyo-e artists like Hiroshige, Hokusai. He talked about how Max Beckmann was one of his favorites and about how much he *loved, loved* Frans Masereel. He took classes with an artist named Bob Blackburn, who did the most finessed work in the world, genius work, and in fact there was a show coming up that maybe I would like to . . .

I saw the clock and sprang out of my chair.

"Jesus," I said, "Clarice'll be back any minute!"

Fitz hopped up just as quickly.

"How'd you do that?" he said.

"Do what?"

"Make hours feel seconds," he said.

Impossible not to smile at this boy.

He was pulling his coat on, and picked up his scarf, turning away as if to hide the full extent of its shabbiness from me. I thought of something.

"Wait, wait," I said. "I'll be right back." I ran out of the room and up two flights to the bedroom, grabbed the thing out of its box, and ran back down.

"Here," I said, coming back into the kitchen. I handed it to him.

"What's this?" he said.

"It's a scarf, silly."

"I have a scarf."

"What you have there is a sight gag," I said.

He held it out in front of him and then touched it to his cheek.

"It's so soft," he said.

"It's cashmere," I said.

"I can't accept this," he said.

"Why not?"

"It's so *nice*."

"Well, you're nice," I said.

"You're *too* nice," he said.

"I'm actually kind of a jerk," I said.

"No—but I'm a crazy moron," he said.

"I'm a freaking b-word."

"I'm an outrageous asshole."

"I'm a hideous shrew."

"I'm a pathetic mass of human sewage," he said.

"Wow, you *are* a crazy moron," I said.

Upstairs, the front door slammed and Clarice's heels began marching across the ceiling.

"Go!" I whispered to Fitz. I shooed him down the hallway and he tossed the scarf to me and I tossed it back to him and we batted it to and fro between us all the way down the hall as he ran backward to the door with absurd, exaggerated slowness, smiling at me all the way.

*

The routine with Clarice shifted again.

I was now warned away from answering the phone at all, and if my friends *had to* call, they were to do so only within the window of seven and eight in the evening. I could also now only make calls after eleven p.m. If the phone *rang* after eleven, however, I was by no means to answer it. Along with this, as if to contradict these directives, Clarice began spending more and more time out but gave strict orders that I was to stay inside and mind the house. Many an afternoon I stood by, watching the phone ring before the answering machine finally clicked on and the voice of Hat Lady or a personal shopper from Barneys or one of Clarice's editor cronies unspooled itself onto the tape. Other times there was nothing but what sounded to me like an exasperated mouth sound, expressly male, followed by an angry hang-up.

Clarice began coming down for our morning sessions increasingly late, sometimes not until noon. Now, however, I didn't go up to her bedroom looking for her but remained waiting in her study. Instead of sitting on my ridiculous little dictation stool with my spine straight as a plumb line, I tried sprawling across one of the ornate fauteuils in the corners, my legs dangling over its tufted arm. This feigned nonchalance would last about a quarter hour before I was sitting grammar-school straight again, reading Gayl Jones or Natalia Ginzburg or leafing through an art book, looking at pictures of Marys and saints and angels. But more often I just sat there dreaming.

A lonely chill blew through that room. I knew Clarice and I were beginning to play out our endgame, but I remained anchored to the house, inert, dilatory, mute. I was floating along, waiting for something to happen. At night I lay in Cornelia's bed, watching the patterns of light from passing cars dance on the ceiling.

One night Clarice came home very late and burst into the room.

I was sitting up reading when she stumbled through the door and plunked herself down beside me on the bed. Her face was a mess. She was mad drunk in that whisky way that seems to engender persistence.

She rocked and swayed, trying to get her balance.

"Is this what you wanted?" she asked me.

"What?"

"Is this what you always wanted?"

"Oh God, Clarice, you should go to bed."

She saw the book I was reading and picked it up.

"Sybille *Bedford*?" she said. "That woman is for *shit*." She threw it across the room. "Why are you *still here*?" she yelled at me.

"I don't know," I said.

All I wanted was to get away from her, but she caught my arm.

"No, you don't leave, of course you don't. I'm only joking. You know I'm only joking." She got to her feet, brushed herself off. "Come here," she said. "I need you to make a phone call for me."

"It's after midnight," I said.

"Come on, it doesn't matter," she said. She pulled me down the hallway and the stairs and into her office. She turned on the wall switch—nothing that had ever been done before—and light flooded the room from the huge chandelier. The effect was at once grand and dwarfing.

She swung me around the desk and put me in her seat. She indicated the black rotary phone.

"Algonquin four eight six two nine," she said. "Dial it."

"Clarice. That's *this* number."

She looked at me, sure she was being fooled.

"And so it is," she said. "And so it is."

"Clarice, you should go to bed."

"Never mind that. Call this number."

She recited a number to me and I slowly dialed it. The rotary seemed to take forever to spin back around after each digit.

It started ringing and I held the receiver out to her.

"No," she said, "you talk."

A male voice picked up in a moment.

"Clarice?" he said.

I could hear an entire world of smarm in that one word. Broyer Weatherhill.

"Hi," I said to him, idiotically.

Clarice held my gaze, nodding at me.

"Who is this?"

"It's Francesca Varani, Broyer. Clarice's secretary."

"What do you want? Is she there?"

"She is," I said. I went to pass the receiver to her, but she shook her head again.

"She doesn't want to talk to you."

Clarice nodded her head approvingly.

"So why are you calling?" he asked.

"So why are we calling?" I asked Clarice.

She smiled broadly at me but said nothing.

"Look, can I talk to her?" he said at last.

"No, you may not," I said.

"Can you at least tell her I'm sorry?" he said.

"He said he's sorry," I said to Clarice.

She let out a cackle of delight. Then she shook her head, took up her fountain pen, and began writing something. She held it up to me.

TELL HIM I HAVE A MESSAGE FOR HIM.

"Clarice has a message for you," I said.

"Okay," he said. "What is it?"

She wrote something else and then held it up to me, smiling.

"I can't say that," I said to her, talking into the phone.

"Can't say what?" Broyer said.

Clarice was nodding: *Certainly you can.*

"No," I said.

Clarice rolled her eyes and shoved the paper my way.

I cleared my throat.

" 'You're a scoundrel,' " I read, " 'and a rat.' "

"My God, please tell her I'm sorry," he said. He sounded more impatient than distressed.

"He says he's sorry," I told Clarice.

Clarice shook her head. She was writing something else, and she turned it around and showed it to me.

"'You're a dilettante,'" I read. "'You'll always be a dilettante. You're only fooling yourself and you have the writing talent of a grub worm. Of Dan Quayle.'"

"Okay, I get that she's angry," he said.

"Do you? Do you really? Do you understand what your irresponsible actions have done to this family? You come in here and do what to this family?"

Clarice was waving me down to stop, because I was off-script.

"Please tell her that I didn't mean to," Broyer said. "Please tell her that . . . I love her. Yes, I love her."

I pulled the receiver to the side.

"He says he loves you," I told Clarice.

She threw her head back and let out the biggest cackle of all. And then she began furiously scribbling.

"Hold on," I said, "there's more."

"What?" he said. "What is she saying?"

She turned the paper around to me.

"God, Clarice," I said.

She nodded, smiling.

I cleared my throat.

"'You have a penis the size of a lead pencil,'" I said.

He was screaming even before I hung up on him. I dropped the phone into the cradle and slumped back in Clarice's chair.

She walked slowly around her desk and came to me.

"Thank you, dear," she said. She leaned forward and kissed me on top of my head. Then she tipped up my chin to look into my face, smiling at me most tenderly.

"We win," she whispered.

She turned, sashayed across the room under the bright lights, and closed the door behind her.

*

Even before the sun was up the next day, I was gone.

Part III

20

Williamsburg in those days was like the Wild West. Its streets were amazing in their emptiness. Southside was a wounded place, a war zone of burned-out car chassis tipped on their sides, piles of inexplicable rubble rising to crazy heights in weedy lots, and stoops where crack vials crunched beneath your feet like peanut shells. Over by the water, the massive anchorage of the Williamsburg Bridge stamped itself down in front of you like some giant reminding you of your puniness, and the JMZ line, thundering high above, rained down wispy toxic fibers on your head. Standing by the East River, you'd wonder if that thing in the water out there was a shopping cart, a taxicab, a bag of garbage, or someone's severed torso. Farther inland, the utter quiet and odd slanting light was like nothing so much as a de Chirico painting: grand old columned buildings, forgotten statues casting long thin shadows, an inscrutable something just beyond your line of sight. The melancholy and mystery of a street.

But Southside was also Los Sures, and here it wasn't empty at all. You'd turn down one of the blocks off Marcy and *blam,* ten thousand Dominican or Puerto Rican flags would be flying from fire escapes and street signs and clotheslines strung from tenement to tenement, and the sweep and fervor would do something to your heart, like a Childe Hassam painting. You'd see lots of people hanging out on the sidewalks in these parts, and here was where I learned that in a pair of sunglasses I could pass for Hispanic, no problem. *Look at her,* some chick with her flossy hair in a topknot would say at me with that Boricua pop to her voice, *look at her all walking down the street—hmm.*

Farther east and past the nonstop racket of the Elevated over Broadway, you'd hit the Satmar Hasidic neighborhood, where no one particularly wanted to see me, while on the fringes of the Northside and up into McCarren Park it was pretty much already Polish Greenpoint. I traveled much in Williamsburg, always with my feet. The Italian section I couldn't help but be curious about, and here was where I formulated the idea that Italian Americans, with their twin lions flanking humble stoops and needless balustrades topping vinyl-sided houses, were fond of stone as a building material because it's hard and unchanging and thus reminds them of their heads. *Us* of *our* heads, I should say. These folks interested me in some kind of pining, regressive way, but their presence on the street proved elusive. You would be walking down Devoe or Conselyea and look around to see that you were the only person there. But on these blocks you knew that eyes were watching you. Mammas were making braciole behind closed front doors—the kind with the leaded glass insets, classy, that you got at Home Depot—while old Gs lurked at windows to make sure no one touched the still-wet Italian flag colors they'd just painted their narrow driveways. God help the skinny hipster who slapped an *Andre the Giant Has a Posse* sticker on the corner stop sign.

I'd been there a lot to hang out with Trina, and we'd go around to look at the great big signs shaped like scissors and glasses and thread spools along Metropolitan and wonder who made them and what they could have been made out of. Balsa wood? They crumbled in a way that reminded us of very old foam rubber. We'd buy semolina loaves at a bakery that had a sign from the 1930s and a curved glass display window, or walk down to Domsey's to troll for clothes. You could always count on Trina to score a green suede A-line miniskirt with three-inch-round tortoiseshell buttons for five dollars cash. In the field in front of Domsey's was a school bus that I remembered from the '80s, smack in the middle of an acre of rubble, burned to a carapace and covered with graffiti but otherwise perfectly habitable.

There was a handful of bars we'd go to, most of which hadn't yet been fully colonized by groovers priced out of elsewhere, those people who—even as we squirmed at the idea—must have seemed to the folks who'd lived in Williamsburg for years to be a lot like people like us. We'd sit and drink and talk while revolving pairs of cops, firemen, and fellows who worked at the neighborhood spinning-and-stamping shops chatted us up. We'd smile and graciously rebuff them and that would be it: no one was an asshole to us. There may have been no end of Beefy Art Dudes around, but somehow these guys tended to just sit and stare at us over their cans of PBR, swaddled in their Carhartt jackets, Jim Thompson novels sticking out of their cross-strapped messenger bags. The pizza man on Driggs who looked very much like the drawing of the pizza man on the universal pizza delivery box had taken a shine to Trina, and sometimes we'd order the penne alla vodka and get extra-huge portions, causing us to huff with effort lest we not finish our aluminum containers of food and thus hurt the pizza man's feelings. The pizza man was very attuned to Trina's moods, and if she ever went in there with a long face, he could always cheer her up by saying, *Who's your favorite pizza man? Come on, who's your favorite pizza man?* There was a notorious coke bar called Kokie's only blocks away, but this was no place we would ever go.

I had a friend called Kelly who was in her last year at Pratt—she was an old Brooklyn hand and was forever reminding me of this—and she did some work with a community group called El Puente, on the Southside. When I told her I'd found a beaut of an apartment for $250 a month right by Gabila's Square Knishes on South Eighth, she told me that if I moved there and planned on ever going out after sundown, it would only be a matter of weeks before I left the neighborhood in a body bag.

So I ended up moving in with Kelly in a sort of two-bedroom apartment right on Metro Avenue, $400 a month split two ways. This was off the third stop on the L, and there was something about the way the street zagged at that point, taking you past a White Castle and a gas station on the way to our apartment, just before you hit the spooky industrial expanse around Maspeth Creek, that made your heart sink. Sometimes walking home at night I felt like Charlton Heston in *The Omega Man:* the last person on earth. Other times, walking west toward the groover epicenter where Trina lived, more than once when I hit the dim section beneath the Brooklyn-Queens Expressway some dad in a sedan would slow down to ask me, was I working? Was I working? I had by now found a temp job at an entertainment conglomerate, nonsense work but decently paid, so yes, I was working. I would always thank him for his concern.

"Chess," Trina told me, rolling her eyes, "these guys think you're a *ho*."

Which you'd see many of over by Kent and Wythe, standing on those joyless low-rise industrial corners, always with short skirts and big bags. I wondered about their lives, what they had to kill off in themselves to get out there. And I was shocked to witness more than once minivans driven by Orthodox Jewish guys slow down to pick up one or two of them. *I don't understand,* I'd say to Trina. *They're not even supposed to touch women.* I was reading Daniel Fuchs's Williamsburg Trilogy by then, and loving these books so much, I was even more given to thinking of anything Jewish as automatically good. Hasidim picking up streetwalkers just didn't fit the picture.

I walked around Daniel Fuchs's old neighborhood in the Southside looking for traces of this past. I loved the old Yiddish signs, the ones in English but in wavy pseudo-Hebrew lettering, and I loved the still weirdly extant bits of Depression-era enticement: *Try a Lime Rickey, You Don't Like It, You Don't Have to Pay!* I loved the botánicas with their Chango Macho bath salts and El Jorobado de la Suerte perfume that smelled like Pine-Sol and was supposed to get you fat cash. I loved going by the tiny brick Leonard Library, Betty Smith's own, and seeing the banners of all the Brooklyn writers: Marianne Moore, Walt Whitman, Betty Smith herself. I loved all the faces you'd see, so different from what you got on Eleventh Street—drama-queen Latina girls with huge hoop earrings and starlet lips, ancient men dressed for temple like something out of Roman Vishniac, Polish drywall hangers with hard faces and blue-sky eyes. Less easy to say what all these different folks made of me and my tribe. My friends and I were in many ways the beginning of the disease that would all but destroy working-class Williamsburg, but I loved being there, and I loved Williamsburg for what it was.

Thinking back on those times, I really was always walking everywhere. I was in transit, literally and emotionally, and walking was the way I coped with everything that was roiling inside me. I was afraid that if I slowed down and let myself be alone with myself, the floodgates would open. It was better and cleaner and cooler to keep moving, not to give in. I thought of Kendra, drowning in her unhappiness, and Audrey, who was always on my mind even though I hadn't actually talked to her in forever. I felt for them, but part of me, some practical, hardheaded, peasant part of me, told me that *if they'd just kept better fucking control over themselves,* they wouldn't have slid down into their misery. They had arms to catch them, or else they wouldn't have let themselves fall. I wasn't like them. I'd grown up in a row house and my parents had had a combined income of $35,000 a year for a family of seven. These were the things that I told myself.

Anyway, the temp job I'd gotten was a quick skip from the L to the 4/5 to Madison Avenue, and the story I found there was half of the story that would repeat in my work life for years to come. That is, no one at the place did a lick of work. They might as well have been a crowd in a field flying a single kite. This stood in ridiculous contrast to what I'd eventually find in the architecture industry, where people cranked until all hours, bleeding out their talent over CAD drawings or the successful "value-engineering" of a broadloom "requirement" to a craftily similar carpet tile "solution." *This is not why I went to Yale Architecture,* a skinny, sexy older lady from East Texas once told me while we sneaked a cigarette in the mailroom in our company's offices at the World Trade Center, but that's another story.

Within a few weeks at the entertainment conglomerate I'd finished every last task given me, and I was mad bored. Mad, mad, mad, mad bored. Amazingly, my one foray into reading a book on the job had been met with a *word of advice* called in by my temp agency after being tipped off by an anonymous snitch. And so I began making the rounds of the other admins to ask, *Do you need a hand with anything?* At this they would have one of two responses: annoyance or stark, staring terror. After several days I was given to understand that I risked being the Goody Two-shoes who, if this were a prison instead of a corporate office, would get knifed to death by an unwitnessed mob on the basketball court. Everyone reveled in their inertia, their daily trips to the Duane Reade, their hours of deliberation over whether to order Cookie

Puss or Fudgie the Whale for Michelle in accounting's ten-year work anniversary. Greenhorn that I was, I'd risked messing up the natural order of things by my moronic diligence. And so I spent my days writing long letters to my friends, staring at the picture of the stupid cat with the stupid pince-nez, or just sitting there dreaming.

All this time I was trying so hard not to think about Clarice and Kendra and Jerry and the whole Marr-Löwenstein family that all I could do was think about them.

The night I left, I simply packed my bag and slipped out and showed up at Trina's door. I figured I'd go back for the rest of my stuff once things had cooled down—I just needed to get away from Clarice and clear my head. I'd left her a note, telling her I was sorry but this wasn't working out and I'd call her in a few weeks. I'd made it sound as bland-vanilla and un-blamey as possible, but I knew that whatever I wrote wouldn't matter. She would be furious regardless. I pictured her reading the note and then crushing it to her breast like Joan Crawford in extremis. Trina, Kelly, and I had just seen *Mildred Pierce* at Theatre 80 and were forever doing reaction shots from it, cringing in horror, lashing out in fury, or welling up with emotion like any good drag queen.

In these weeks, as I was working out this new scene for myself—neighborhood, apartment, job, hard-line attitude of unemotionality—I was also constantly wondering why Clarice hadn't tracked me down.

"You sound like you want her to," Trina said to me when I finally spoke this aloud, one night over a beer at the Charleston. The Charleston in those days was generally always empty of customers and thus where we'd go when we wanted near-absolute quiet, even if the scene was kind of like a lite version of Fellini's *8½*. It must once have been a nightclub of some sort, and the couple who ran it defied all notions of dignified old age. They probably looked like a million bucks in 1960, but thirty years on they were ghosts of themselves, the impresario an unreconstructed and slightly vicious carny in a wide-lapel suit and the missus, modeled on Jayne Mansfield, a flirty, dishy grandma with false eyelashes and who knew what else. It was like they were auditioning for *Broadway Danny Rose*. Booze seemed to be involved, in a maintenance-drinking way, as well as a certain professionalism that suggested that they were perfectly sincere, pre-ironic, and had no idea what their fascination might be for the new kids in town. This was the thing about Williamsburg in that era: all these folks had been doing what they'd been doing for years, in a close-knit-neighborhoody way, and then all these outsiders like ourselves streamed into town and merely by virtue of looking at them made them strange.

At any rate, Trina would always be the person to put me on the straight and narrow.

"Why would you want that?" she said. "Why would you *want* Clarice to track you down?"

"I guess I want to know that she misses me," I said, and as soon as I spoke I realized that I hadn't even admitted this to myself.

"Do you really care?" Trina said.

"I guess I do. I mean, I guess I want her to realize how fucked up she made things. How crazy and untenable. How crazy *she* is."

"And that would do what?"

"Make me feel . . . vindicated?"

"And that would get you what?"

"Make me feel . . . right? Get me the last word. Oh, not like that, not like in a door-slam way. Make her realize she was wrong. She was wrong and I was right." It sounded stupid even to myself.

"Good luck with *that*," Trina said. She tipped her cigarette into the ashtray, and we both sat looking at it. "Would that even change anything?"

"Jesus, Trina, don't you ever have a feeling of injustice and you can't get a hearing and it's like you could explode?"

"Sure, yes, of course I do! But this woman's a dead end. You knew how messed up she was when you first went into this. I mean? What do you want?"

"I want her to like me," I said miserably.

"But she doesn't like anyone!" she said.

"God, I miss Jerry," I said. It just spilled out of my mouth.

I slumped in my chair.

"*That* guy? You *do*? I thought you put that whole thing out of your head. Are you serious? God, Chess, why didn't you tell me?"

"I don't know. I don't know! I didn't want to seem pathetic. I didn't want to bore you."

"Oh, Chess—you can bore me anytime."

She reached out and rubbed my shoulder, and I guess it was that single touch that made all my hard-line pretensions fly right out the window. Right out the flipping window. I felt myself crumble and suddenly I had my hands over my mouth and tears were running down my face.

"Oh, oh, Chess, oh, Chess," she said. "Why don't you tell me these things? You don't have to be all Lord Jim on me. Geez! I figured you were sad, but it's like you don't let on. Look, don't worry, forgive me if I'm somehow telling you I don't want to listen, of course I do. Look, why don't I call her for you? Why don't I just call the bitch? You still have to get all your stuff—we can go together. She'll be on her best behavior. Hell, I'll ask if she knows where Jerry got to, do you think I care? For all we know he's joined an anarchist klezmer band in the former East Berlin. Sorry, I'm kidding—I just want to cheer you up. Jesus, Chess, you have to let this stuff out or it'll kill you." She grabbed a bunch of paper napkins and handed them to me.

I took them and was wiping my face, blowing my nose, starting to calm down and then breaking out crying again.

"Oh, Chess," she said. She kept rubbing my arm, comforting me.

"I'm sorry," I said.

"Nothing sorry in it, so please don't worry."

"But I'm sorry."

"Oh, Chess."

She leaned her face close to mine.

"Who's your favorite pizza man?" she asked.

"Oh God, please don't right now," I said.

"Come on! *Who's your favorite pizza man?*"

I wiped at my eyes. "I guess you are," I said.

"I can't hear you!"

"You are! Jesus Christ, Trina."

She tilted her head to the side and made a silly face—and her amber eyes were the most wonderful thing in the world to me at that moment.

*

The next day Trina called me at work—and the receiver was in my hand before the ring finished.

"Did you talk to her?" I said.

"The woman's a *freak*," she said.

"What? Why? What happened?"

"I don't know—she was all bubbly. Like she was on a talk show. She was all silver-bells laughter, ha-ha-ha-ha-ha, so happy! Total phonus balonus. I'm like, Hi, this is Trina, Chess's friend, and it was like she pretended she knew I'd be calling. Just all friendly and fakey and bizarre. Anyway, she said we can come by on Saturday to get your stuff. One o'clock, is that good?"

"What? She wasn't angry?"

"No, I told you, it was like water rolls off her back, it's nothing at all to her. Who knows how she really feels about anything? I asked her about Jerry and she was like, Oh, who knows, he's a grown man, he could be anywhere, ha-ha-ha silver bells. She's a got a nine-volt battery for a heart."

I was silent, looking up at the ceiling.

"This just doesn't make any sense," I said.

"Look, don't get all melancholy, okay? If this guy ever does show up I've got a million questions for him, like what is your sorry, purposely elusive behavior about and who died and made you Hamlet, okay? Look, Saturday we'll go by there and get your stuff, okay? Then we can come back to Williamsburg and drink our faces off."

*

That Saturday at exactly one o'clock I stood at the top of the stoop with Trina and rang the doorbell of the house on Eleventh Street. It seemed wrong to have to ring the doorbell.

Dolores opened the door.

"Girls, you come in," she said, waving us inside. She gave a scan up the street, down the street, and then suddenly jerked back and slammed the door. Trina and I looked at each other—what? When Dolores turned around again, I introduced her to Trina and she nodded gravely.

"Ms. Marr no' here," she said.

"Upstate?"

"Yes. She has a note for you. With your belonging." She stepped aside, and in a row down the entrance hallway were all my things, neatly packed by someone else's hands. There was an envelope on top of the first box, and I picked it up and looked at it.

FRANCESCA VARANI, it read. As if legions of other Francescas might be tramping through there. I ripped it open, and inside was a prorated check for the last four days I'd worked. Nothing else. I pulled the envelope around to make sure there was no tiny note hiding in there. Amazingly, Dolores and Trina both reached out to touch my arms at the same time.

"She has never been a nice lady," Dolores said.

"She's an A-hole," Trina said. "She's an ass-H."

"Did she say anything?" I asked.

Dolores shook her head.

"Oh. Oh, well. Well, thanks for packing up my things, Dolores."

"Oh, she does that," Dolores said.

Dolores insisted on helping us move everything out to the stoop. She and I shook hands good-bye, solemnly enough, and then Trina went to get the Chevy. Once the door was closed on me I stood alone on the stoop, surrounded by my bag-lady things.

I had been banished from the kingdom.

In a moment Trina pulled up and was honking the horn like a madwoman, jolting me back to earth. We managed to jam everything into the Chevy, and then it was whoosh down Eleventh Street, a full turn around to go east, and a careen down the Bowery to Delancey. *It's very fancy,* I sang, my heart suddenly lifting, and we waved like mad at a cute G in some kind of porkpie hat in front of Ratner's; we could have sworn he was blowing bubbles. Oh, was it ever April. The light changed and immediately we were spinning across the bridge, the big Xs of its struts to one side and the rickety, racing J train to the other, the view down the East River to the bay beyond all the bridges like a world opening up, and then we were across the bridge to the other side, to Brooklyn, the shortest journey ever when you go west to east, sailing by the great Renaissance pile of the Williamsburgh Savings Bank with its IT'S TIME TO SAVE sign nearly jammed up against the roadway and then the ad for Peter Luger Steakhouse peeling from its brownstone wall. Brooklyn felt wonderful, wide open, the loveliest punch line, like a million bucks. We blew down to street level by the bus turnaround and then we were spinning up Havemeyer and sailing, sailing down Metropolitan Avenue to my new place, to my new life. I felt like the most tremendous weight had been lifted off me and also I felt like crying.

We pulled up to the apartment on Metro and Trina slid the Chevy into the only open parking space, magically right in front. We got out of the car at the exact same time and slammed our doors in tandem, making each other laugh. A taxicab had stopped behind us and was idling, and I thought he must want the space we just took. Instead the light suddenly clicked on, and out of the backseat stepped a wild-looking homeless man.

Who was Jerry.

21

"Who is that *freak*?" were the first words out of Trina's mouth.

Jerry was slanting toward us, and though he wasn't in earshot suddenly he stopped, shook himself off like a cat, and reordered himself. He changed before my eyes. His coat was caked with dirt and he had a sprawling beard, fire-red and wild, but it was as if he straightened up, clarified himself, and became once again the young lord.

"My God, that's your Werther," Trina whispered.

He stepped up on the curb and put out his hand.

"You're Trina," he said.

I watched as Trina slowly answered with her hand, barely outstretching it as Jerry swept it up, raised it to his lips, and bestowed a kiss upon it. Trina was no pushover, but some idea corrected itself in her, and I watched her look at him, watched her understand now what was so solitary and strange and electric about this boy. And all of her million questions to him were stilled into silence; as were mine.

*

That evening he and I went up on the rooftop and looked out over Williamsburg.

We must have unloaded all my things from Trina's car and taken everything up to the apartment—I'm sure we did this—but it was like I was in a cloud. I remember him casting a look around the place, and how I was unable to read him at all. I couldn't believe he was there. I remember Trina hugging me good-bye and then I stood at the window, watching her pull the Chevy out of the space, out onto Metropolitan Avenue, and then drive away. I pictured her turning at the next block, by the Catholic church, to go back west. I was alone now with Jerry and somehow was delaying the moment when I would turn and look at him.

"Won't you look at me?" he said, as if reading my mind.

I turned, and he was standing in the middle of the floor, tall and unto himself, an unlikely incursion in that room. The apartment seemed to have shrunk around him.

"Is this yours?" he asked.

"I have a roommate," I said, and this might have been the first sentence I spoke to him.

"Is it a she?"

"Yes."

He looked at me, questioning.

"She's away. All week."

He came over and took my hands in his.

"I don't understand," I said, stepping back and taking myself away from him.

In a moment he bowed his head.

"It feels very small in here now," I said. The trucks rumbling down Metro were so heavy they made the windows clatter. It was all too close to the outside, too precarious. I had been thinking I had gotten away. But this was no place to live, I understood now.

That was what his unreadable look had been. No place to live without him.

"Let's go to the roof," he said.

Traffic seemed to be running east below us, trucks hauling things away, out into Queens. I could see the pigeon man on the Southside, the flocks of birds circling above him as he stirred them down from the sky. Looking west I could see the towers of the Trade Center and, turning again, Jerry, standing in the middle of the silver roof.

"Why did you leave?" I said to him at last.

"I told you, I had to."

"It makes no sense. You made it sound like . . . you would be back. You would be back for me."

257

"I'm back now."

"But you never *said* anything. You never got any word to me. It was months and months, and at some point I thought you were just gone for good. Why did you do that to me? Don't say you were testing me—"

"I can't explain," he said.

"That's nothing I can hear. You left and that was it."

"But I'm here now," he said.

"And what can I do with that?"

"I'm telling you, I'm here now."

"And then what?" I said.

"I thought you had faith," he said to me.

In the yard behind the building, sheltered from the noise and filth of Metropolitan Avenue, the landlord and his wife grew tomatoes in the warm months. Now it was a square of dirt was all, as I stood looking down at it. I was nowhere near the edge and there was a lip that came to my knees, but our feelings were too large for that small space and I turned too fast and did some kind of idiotic sprawl, and Jerry grabbed me and reeled me in. And then he was holding me and crooning over me and petting me as if I were some precious thing.

"I don't want to lose you," he said.

"It hurt me—you left and it hurt me," I said.

"I'm sorry," he said. "I'm sorry."

"God, I missed you so much. I hated how much I missed you. *I missed you so much.* Why did you make me miss you like that? Why did you come into my life and make me care about you and then leave? It was like you'd gone and died and I'd never see you again."

"I'm sorry," he said. "I never want to leave you. Never again."

"Don't say things you don't mean," I said.

"But I mean it," he said. "Believe me—please believe me." He closed tight around me, pulled me to him and would not let go. How can I explain. We were like this for hours, up on the roof, trying to understand this thing between us, trying to understand the two of us, the possibility of an us, and we were there so long evening went into night and then into morning. I remember the sadness in his green eyes, the pained way he held his mouth. He held my hands tightly in his and rubbed my knuckles almost raw, as if he were breaking down the composite of me. I remember how the sky changed, how the pink showed east and then streaked across the sky. And with the morning something was sealed for us. We would be together. That was how we would be: together.

What is impossible to capture here so many years later is the joy I felt at this. The joy, the bliss, the perfect kiss.

*

He told me that when he came back for me Clarice slammed the door in his face. The timing was impossible; it turned out I had left just one week before he came back. He told me he was seized by a kind of mania and he haunted the block, waiting for the door to open. The first time Clarice left he rushed the house and Dolores let him in, gave him something to eat. As far as she knew, I had left no address.

He didn't know what to do. He told me he was convinced that Clarice knew where I'd disappeared to but she was hiding it. He decided he'd just sleep in front of the house—he would advertise his presence. At first he slept under the stoop, but then he took to sleeping at the top of the stairs, in the tiny checkerboard space between the unlocked street door and the door of the house itself. Clarice would pull aside the curtain and rap on the glass to make him go away. She told him she would call the police. He said, *Good, call them.* But eventually he'd go away. There was a deli on Fifth that used to be the Lone Star, a place with a big iguana sculpture on its roof. They had a bathroom and tables upstairs, and he would go there and drink coffee and nod as he sat looking out the window. There were homeless people who hung out there, teen runaways and sad old winos. At some point he realized he was homeless too.

He always went back to Eleventh Street. He sat on the stoop and waited for me. Weeks passed and I never came. And then one day I did.

He wouldn't tell me where he'd been the many months leading up to these moments. I had a million questions that he would not answer. My words were left to float between us until they split into tiny particles and disappeared. He was trying to tell me something else, something important, that he'd stayed away until he knew he could come back and best his mother. He had come back to disgust her and embarrass her and wear her down. He was paying her back. He would never give in— but neither would she. And so they were exactly matched.

The battle they fought was over me.

But what I wanted to know was *how he lived* all that time, what he ate to keep himself alive, where he laid his head at night. Maybe who was there to comfort him.

Finally I learned to let it go. I didn't understand this way of relating with someone. This way of not relating. I didn't understand then that this would be the pattern of our life together.

*

We had fallen asleep in my room, on the thin mat I was borrowing until I could get a bed. We awoke in the early evening, and I found a can of soup for us to eat. I had become watcher and listener and tender. I felt like we were bandits, doing something illegal together.

"We can't stay here," he said.

"I know," I said.

"Cancel your job thing. Tell them you have the flu."

"But we'll need the money."

"Don't worry about that. There's always a way."

This time I didn't question him. We locked ourselves in, hung bedsheets against the sun, talked and prowled at night, drank endless coffee in three a.m. diners. These times were burdened and tentative but also they were lustrous. They were magic. Empty, except for us. We were always together and we learned each other's bodies. I loved the way he touched me. I loved to look at him. I loved to watch him as he slept, to study the curve of his closed eyelid, to put my arms around him and guard him from the world.

On one of the last days there I finally opened the boxes that Clarice had packed. It was as if I'd been afraid of contagion, of her hands on my things, I was afraid of bringing it into the temporary autonomous zone we were sheltering in together. From the last box I pulled out Jerry's flute case.

"Look," I said, handing it to him.

He set it before him, then quietly snapped it open. He drew back, reacting to something inside. And then he took it out and handed it to me. It was a thick envelope, with these words written on it:

YOU WIN, GERHARDT.

"Jerry," I said. "My God."

Of course we knew what it was. Jerry's murderer's smile spread across his face. I ripped open the envelope and shook out every last bill, all the money, all the dirty money—money so dirty that in a way it was absolutely clean.

*

We found a place on the Northside, $700 a month, a railroad that was one half of the top floor. Asphalt shingle and one of those old clotheslines on a wheel that attached to the building across the backyard, which was choked with ailanthus trees, bathtub planters, rusted bikes, and indoor furniture left outside so long it looked like Claes Oldenburg sculpture. Inside our apartment, the floor was old linoleum and the walls were painted with something that left a light, chalky coating when you touched it with your fingers. In the kitchen above the oven was one of those metal flue covers that sealed up the hole where the old stovepipe had connected to the wall, this one with a winter landscape scene printed on it in soft colors.

We had very few belongings and no furniture at all. I had my Abruzzese grandmother's spaghetti pot and cutting board, five wooden spoons, two bowls and two plates, a fry pan that Kelly gave me, a serrated knife from the grocery store, and a can opener. Jerry had sheet music, a metronome, a button accordion, and a full set of silver plate from the St. Regis Hotel. Our bed was a swaddling of old blankets. We camped out like children, ate dinner sitting on the floor with cloth napkins in our laps.

We made love and held each other, listening to music on the radio. Often I would read to him, his head resting in my lap. He told me he had stopped singing—his illness had done something to his voice—and so instead he played his flute for me. I was so happy to look at him. I close my eyes and think of this now.

*

I remember it was easy for me to find temp work. There were some agencies where, if they didn't have a gig for you right off, you could go on-call, show up at their office by 7:30, and sit reading your book as the calls came in. I was good at this kind of thing; you could throw me in anywhere and I'd figure it out. In certain stretches of Midtown I temped in every building, and even years later I could tick them off on my fingers: in the canyon of towers on Sixth Avenue, in skyscrapers all along Fifty-Seventh Street, down Fifth Avenue, across Forty-Second, up Lex and down Third. We had gone through the packet and whatever I had for our deposit and rent, and we needed money.

Mornings we'd go out the door together, and yet we were still in our own world. We would get on the L train, tight against the doors, our bodies meshed together and smelling of sweet sleep. We saw no one but each other; it was as if the outside, breathing world were not real to us, were invisible. At Union Square we would part, and every parting seemed to suggest terrible and irreparable loss. And so we clung in that moment of parting as if our hearts would break.

I would go to my temp job, doing my work diligently and yet dreaming of him all day long. He would go up to Forty-Second Street and busk, playing his flute with his case open on the ground before him. I picture him there, this improbable young man so dour in his clothing but with an absurd red silk foulard knotted around his neck. Often he would wear this scarf or some other odd, dainty object of mine, decorating his person with it. It was as if by this he were advertising his love for me. In the evening we rushed home to be together as if a year had passed, and we were each so relieved that the other had come back again. We haunted Williamsburg in the night hours, were thrilled to drag in old furniture off the street, would go to the rocks down by Grand Street and step around the crack vials to look out across the water.

There is great clarity and great opacity in remembering this now—clarity in the way I can still see it in my head, opacity in what I thought it all meant. For us in those days everything was extreme, nothing fair or middling. Somehow the stakes of us loving each other were so high that the smallest thing could become impossibly fraught. It was as if we immediately meshed together and became a third entity that actually represented neither of us. Or I went over to how he was, loving him as I did—but not knowing how little, ultimately, it reflected who I was.

But never mind that for now. Never mind that. I just want to see these two people together in their moment, as if they are people in fiction, in a story that speaks to my own. I see the young couple in *L'Atalante,* on the prow of the barge, so unlikely, so raw and so beautiful. I see the barge passing so silently up the waters of the canal, so dream-like and quickening, and so quickly gone.

22

I guess I hadn't ever known anyone who'd reached the age of twenty-four and never had a job.

In a way, it was part of the strangeness and specialness of him, something beyond the realm of questioning. The joke was, when Jerry busked, he averaged about $20 an hour, while my temp-worker hourly rate at that time was just about $12. So Jerry could actually pull in much more in a week than I could. Problem was, there was only so much flute-playing a person could do.

The world came intruding on us all too soon. Some days I would come home and Jerry was already there, waiting for me, drumming his fingers on the table as if I were late. Or I'd find him lying flat on the linoleum of the kitchen floor, staring up at the ceiling. What was the matter? He tried to explain, but his frustration made him inarticulate. It was something like this: I had helped to free him, and, now free, he had no idea what to do.

He had an at-large disgust for many things of the world: bourgeois behavior, hypocrisy, conformity, capitalism. But these were all abstractions, and his feelings needed to find an object. What was he doing, anyway? What was he *doing* with his life? He shouted this aloud to himself, looking at me as if I knew the answer. I had met friends of his by now, and just about all of them were involved in some kind of activism: the War Resisters League, homesteading, writing for one of the anarchist papers, making chili at a Catholic Worker house, protesting the gentrification of the East Village. But it was as if his own preco-ciousness in things like this had worn him out. He was done with the squatter scene, and he had a rap sheet from being twice arrested, once in the Tompkins Square Park riot of 1988, which kept him quiet on that front. He'd been going to protests since he was twelve. He had an enormous weariness, something he shared with Kendra.

They had seen and done too much, gone from child professionals to child dropouts. At his most desolate, this was what Jerry always returned to. He'd been a prodigy, a star, at the expense of having a child-hood, and then when he walked away from that he was left with what? He and Kendra, they were left with *what*? Their mother had not pro-tected them. She had given them *nothing*. At some point when Jerry would be talking like this, hopped up and pacing the apartment, he'd slump against the wall, exhausted from the effort of trying to represent what he was feeling. He angled his body away from me as if he were separating himself, as if he were not in the room or in the building or on the planet with anyone else.

"And what are *you* doing, anyway, always going to *work*?" he spat at me one day.

I stared back at him.

"My God, don't you think there's other things I want to be doing besides making spreadsheets for some gross CEO? Don't you think I want to be *writing*?"

"Then why don't you just do it then?" he shouted.

"How are we going to live?" I said. "What are we supposed to *live on*, Jerry?"

And it was as if some elusive idea of causality hooked itself up in his mind, some abstraction was finally brought home to him.

He had never been poor.

"We're stuck in this cycle and I hate it," he said.

"It won't always be like this," I said.

And it wasn't, it wasn't really. I was disciplined; I put myself in a chair most every night and weekend morning and wrote reams of stuff. Most of it was terrible, but I didn't realize this because I was young and on fire. I knew I could write my way out of this cage of working for a living;

I was special and talented. We were special, talented, and our life was a shimmer. We were potentialities waiting to be realized. We would turn a corner; it would happen any moment now . . .

But sometimes I'd sit at my makeshift desk, pick up my pen to write, and just stare at the Brooklyn sky outside the window. I *was* embarrassed at having to do something as mundane as work for a living. I felt shame over this, as if by doing so I'd dragged Jerry, the rare moonchild, sadly down to earth. I felt like I was not ready for this life together with him. I knew I was a fraud—I needed more preparing, more experience in order to match his knowledge of the world. I was gauche, I said embarrassing and foolish things, I did not speak French. I did not understand how to live. How do people *live*? I sought the answer everywhere.

I would close my eyes and think, We can get there, I know we can get there.

I remember the early heat wave of that first summer together, an incredible scorcher that killed old people on their couches and made children pass out in the street. At night we'd sit on the fire escape, legs dangling, to catch a phantom breeze. The backyard down below was invisible with tree cover, a canopy of green, and we'd be smoking cigarettes despite the filthy heat, tapping ash away from ourselves and watching it fall in nearly intact cylinders onto the treetops, the air so humid it acted as a kind of cushion. We tried not to lean against the wall, because even at night the asphalt still retained all the heat of the day.

Strange thing, one evening after days of this, so much intense heat had put us both in an almost giddy mood, and we phased in and out of this, joking in a way that was unusual for us. Because Jerry was always so deadly literal. We sat there, swinging our legs and goofing around. We had been together about three months.

"Clarice found us," he told me.

Neither of us had been in contact with her since the last days on Eleventh Street.

"What? How?"

"I'm sure through Cornelia. I suppose, I mean."

"But—what does she want?"

He looked out across the treetops.

"She says she wants to have me back in her life."

"Do you want this?"

I knew he'd say, *Of course not.*

"I hate her," he said instead.

We sat looking out over the treetops.

"I'm going to see her tomorrow," he told me at last.

I turned to him, questioning.

"Alone," he said.

He lifted my hand, and kissed it.

*

Almost as soon as Jerry left the next day, I stood at our front window in the heat-stilled afternoon, willing him to come back. I had a terrible feeling.

But Clarice was his mother, after all. They had their own relationship. I rolled this around in my head, trying to talk myself out of feeling anger, then out of feeling abandoned, and then giving in to all those feelings. Why didn't she want to see *me*? Didn't she care about *me*? It was almost a hundred degrees and the heat made me drowsy, so at some point I dragged a chair to the window and propped up my head in my hands.

It was Sunday. The crackhead couple who'd been arguing in front of our building the night before, yelling so loudly they'd entered my dreams, were long gone, and the block took on a melancholy aspect, silent but for the hum and drip of air conditioners and the whispering of a hundred oscillating fans. When would Jerry come back? Nothing changed for what felt like hours, and I was alone in the stillness of my thoughts. Sometimes I'd hear the sudden slap of a door slamming shut, and out in front of a building a figure would appear, always alone, pausing to blink at the sun. Sometimes it would be an old-timer and sometimes a new-school person, an invader from Manhattan. Once a small family walked the length of the block, eating huge lollipops that were actually mangoes cut like flowers, their voices soft and skittering at four stories up.

At some point I must have fallen asleep in the hot afternoon air, because the next thing I heard was the sharp clap of a car door. I lifted my head to see a cab idling below our apartment, its trunk open. In a moment the trunk closed with a slam, and I saw Jerry with a huge box in his arms.

I ran down the stairs to meet him, and he looked up, unsmiling over the box.

"It's an air conditioner," he said.

"What?"

"She wanted us to have it," he said.

"We'll give it back," I said.

"I don't want it anyway."

"Then why did you take it?"

"Fuck if I know," he said.

I pressed myself against the wall and he pushed by me and climbed the stairs. He put the huge box in the middle of the kitchen floor and turned to me.

"We took that money before," he said.

"And we said it'd be the last time we would," I said.

"I know," he said. "I can't think when I'm around her."

"Let's take it back."

"But that would mean seeing her again."

He sank to the floor. It was insanely hot inside our apartment, but he wore his jacket, a narrow black chauffeur's thing from the Paris flea market. He reached inside his breast pocket, pulled out an envelope, and threw it down between us.

"A thousand dollars," he said.

I sank to the floor beside him.

"What do we do?" he said.

He stared at the envelope, and so did I. Of course we had to give everything back. But why did he even *accept* these things, bring them here? I listened to the buzz of the old clock on the wall and it was as if I could feel the motion of its second hand spinning. I looked at Jerry, and I saw that the thing had overtaken him again, the uncanny thing where tears were running down his face but he remained as impassive as a stone.

"We have to get out of here," he said.

"What? We just moved in."

"We have to get out of New York. Out of the country. We have to get away from her."

I took his hands in mine.

"Jerry, we *are* away from her. We don't have to see her! We're grown-ups and we can determine what we do."

"No, I can't. I've never been able to. I've always had to get well the fuck away from her to live. When I came back I thought I crushed it out of her, I thought I won. I'm so fucking stupid—you never win with her. I lost."

"How did you lose?" I said. "We *are* away from her and we're together and why isn't that enough?"

"You don't understand," he said miserably.

"What did she *do* to you? Please tell me. What did she do?"

"It's just nothing I can ever explain," he whispered.

"My God, did she . . . ?"

He pulled his hands away.

"Everyone goes to that and it's nothing I can explain. Look, she was there and then she wasn't, not at all, and I hate her so much. I hate her so much. You come in and then you go out again and I want to know, why can't you always just be here? Why can't you always just be here?"

"Jerry," I said to him, "I'm here. I'm here! I don't understand."

"But you have to understand," he said, his eyes burning. "You *have to.*"

He slumped forward and I pulled him to me, gathered him together, collected him in my arms. He let himself collapse against me and I petted his head, wanting so badly to soothe him. I was looking up from there, up into the blank ceiling, up into the hot world above us.

And I understood our future then, as clearly as if it were written across the sky.

He would be ill, ill in his special way, for the rest of his life. I would care for him. Time would wash over us, years would wash over us. We would try, but we would never get away. She would always be there, the ruiner. Clarice in the flesh right up in his face or Clarice the idea always in his mind. The devil on her boy's shoulder, criticizing him, mocking him, steering his thoughts. Every choice he made, even counter to what she wanted, would be in response to the fact of her. I would take on this self-policing too—I would stand with him in everything, thinking it would make him feel less alone. When he railed against something she did, I would be right there with him. When he caved in, I would too. We would stand united in the face of this thing, letting it distract

269

us from our real life. She would be the limousine idling outside our window, the imprint across every word her son could not read. I would be her son's lover, but I would also be his caregiver and sometimes his warden. We would always be together, in the way that *always* can be meant so ardently when a young woman is twenty-three and so in love with a young man, but also maybe so in love with saving, with rescuing, with redemption. Because through this you prove your worth on this planet, a need that might never go away.

Or maybe it was just about loving him, even past the moment when there is nothing left to prove.

Sometimes he would just disappear. He would leave for days, the only explanation one of his charged, illiterate notes left on the table. *I AM FRIGHTED BY MY REALIENCE ON YOU.* I may have been the cure, but sometimes I was a shape that was too much like the shape of his mother. In times like these the world was too much with him, reality was something imposed upon him, and he resented the notion that he had to abide by it. I was part of that imposition, with my "practicality" and my "kindness," something that in his worst moods he ascribed to my upbringing, as if I were an acted-upon soft machine with no ability to form my own beliefs. *Le christianisme est par excellence la religion des esclaves.* Yes, I was one of these slaves. He needed to make up his own world, not live in this cave of received ideas.

And then, after he had disappeared for two or three or four days, he would come home, dirty, exhausted, guttered. I would have spent those days sick with worry, but when I'd see him again all I felt was gratefulness. His attitude would be one of depressing penitence. It was as if he wanted me to punish him. Sometimes he told me that I was the only one tethering him to this earth. I watched him melt before my eyes.

"What is it like to have faith?" he would ask me.

What is it like to have faith?

Sometimes he would say this with such sadness, as if I were a holy object to him, as if my belief somehow ennobled me. But sometimes it was as if he were spitting it at me, as if he needed to communicate to me that he missed nothing by not having this and in fact it disgusted him. Both attitudes were baffling to me. I could only tell him that it was not a choice I had made; and then, of course, I became to him once more the acted-upon peasant. I would try to tell him that faith was beyond words, and this, coming from me, seemed to him the worst insult of all. Because the space he lived in was the space beyond words.

If he pursued these black moods of his too long, inertia overtook him and he collapsed. It was as if it became a kind of pose, an enactment of his moods. In his worst posing he would say things like *of course* he was not supposed to live in the world; the world could only taint you; he was a kind of *poète maudit,* forever at odds with the world. The money he took, and still took and took, from his mother was the tithe she paid to him for ruining him. It was owed to him. It was a tax on her normalcy. That he was always funded by his mother and did not know how to walk away from it squelched his self-esteem, and he threw it back in the world's face, painting himself as all the more wretched and accursed.

And then sometimes Jerry could be the happiest man on earth. Expansive with joy, thrilled to be alive. It was as if two lenses came briefly together to produce an amazing focus. Times like this I didn't question; I was happy to see him happy, and happy to stay up all night and drink champagne on the roof, to ride the train with him the breadth of Brooklyn to Far Rockaway to smoke hashish and watch the sun rise. This would go into the next day, and his elation would only increase until the lenses crossed and moved apart again and it became mania, superhuman, unstoppable.

I was a dumb kid, loving and believing. I grew up surrounded by so many not quite sane people that I never believed in what was called normalcy. I took this other way of how it was to be in the world as the only way. If you are true of heart, you will suffer. And mostly I still feel this is true. But this also meant that despite my love and my care, I didn't know how to help this boy. And so the strongest memory I have of this early era of ours is the close of that chapter, when someone not me knew enough to get a doctor for Jerry, when I am walking him up Central Park West, my arms wrapped tightly around him because I know that if I let go of him, if I let go, the weary life force will spill out of him and he will be lost forever.

23

So one morning these many years later, I'm walking down the street to work, down that dingy Garment District street, and I see this guy across the way stretched out against the side of a double-parked delivery truck, his arms stuck out like Christ on the cross and his head hanging down at a crazy angle like something out of Matthias Grünewald. It's so striking that I stop in my tracks. And then an SUV goes by him—*Be-beep!* the driver nicks his horn at him—and I realize that the guy is just getting out of the way, mugging for the driver. In a moment another car passes, but now the guy's already blended into the crowd, the mass of humanity trundling swaying racks of garment bags down the street, lining up at the food cart for their bad coffee and worse doughnuts, or hustling down the sidewalk along with me to get to our chump-change jobs on time.

How much time had passed? I really couldn't say. The huge proposal had gone out the door, and right behind it a whole slew of other bidding opportunities had come into view, like Alps on Alps arising. Some of them were a bit of a stretch, some more far-fetched than not, some wholly absurd—as far as I knew, none of Acme's interpreters were willing to relocate to the Green Zone in Iraq—but Acme bid on them all.

It was spring. How could this be? I didn't understand it—somehow months had blown by. And maybe because it was spring, a rush of nostalgia overtook me. I found myself thinking of my younger self as if she were a person in her own right, with little to do with me. And it occurred to me that besides being clueless in just about a thousand other ways, what this young me didn't understand was how much sadness is in these words when an older person says them to you: *Time is really flying.* I found myself thinking of books I loved when I was young, the kind of books that maybe you can love only when you're young, *Le Grand Meaulnes, Sentimental Education, First Love, Novembre,* and it seemed to me that they were all about one thing: the first loss. And from that first loss you understand, for maybe the first time, the idea of time passing. There's a preciousness in this, in this realization; there is the exquisite ache of it. And there is the idea that maybe the first loss will always be the most painful one.

Well, I was mostly alone in these thoughts. Fitz was up at an artists' colony and I was by myself in the city. I'd been all over him to apply the year before, he'd been thrilled to get in, and then when the time came to go he managed to tear himself up with guilt because he was the one who got to go off and do art while I was stuck working the gig at Acme. Truly, I have to say that at first I had a private little life-is-not-fair temper tantrum in our four-foot-square bathroom, and then when I had finished screaming into a towel, I realized (with no small surprise) that I'd gotten all the stupidity out of my system and was simply happy for him. This seemed to be an index of some newfound grown-up understanding, and I stood blinking in amazement at myself as if at a genuine miracle.

At any rate, with Fitz not there I was having mad insomnia, so instead of trying to sleep, most nights I'd sit out on the fire escape above the East Village and look at the sky over Manhattan.

This should have been stirring and filmic, but half the time I'd find myself itemizing all the jerky things I'd done over the course of my time on this planet. And although some were ancient, I could still feel the full force of embarrassment around every last one of them. There was a particular cluster around college, and I lingered over loans I'd meant to repay but never had, phone bills I'd stiffed suitemates on, things I'd borrowed and completely ruined. I thought of how I'd always been a conscientious door-holder, and how sometimes in the tunnel system beneath the Barnard campus some stupid chick would sashay through as if I were her personal door-holding assistant. And this started to happen so frequently that one day I said, *Fuck it, I'm not holding any more doors for these entitled assholes,* and so I let the door leading to the underpass between Altschul and Milbank Halls drop behind me and then heard an *Oh!*—and turned to see that I had just dropped the door on the dean of my class year, Dean Deborah Deutscher. Oh, God. The worst of it was that Dean Deborah Deutscher was staring at me with a keenly, deeply wounded look in her eye. It was as if she were saying, *I'd heard you were a difficult person, Francesca Varani, and didn't think it was so, but here's all the evidence I need.* And I was so embarrassed and such an all-around spaz that instead of apologizing, I ran away.

It was on one of these insomnia nights when something occurred to me.

Maybe so many of my troubles started with the course I'd set for myself when I was still a teenager. Maybe my troubles came from the fact that I hadn't stayed down there in Barfonia and gotten a BA at a perfectly nice college in a town where they had one art-house cinema, one record store, and one professor with a cool, asymmetrical haircut, but instead had put on those big britches of mine, moved up here, and gone to Barnard College. You know? Maybe Barnard should have saved the tens of thousands of dollars it had spent on me for a worthier candidate, more of a go-getter, someone who had her eye on a career as an art curator, tenure-track Janeite, or commercial real estate broker. Someone who knew how to *plan.* Anyway, as the night hours sailed by, I got stuck on this notion and wondered if maybe it was all those twinkling stars in the Barnard firmament, all that Margaret Mead and Zora Neale Hurston and Laurie Anderson and Ntozake Shange business, that had put these ideas in my little peasant head in the first place. Maybe, no fault of its own, the school had given me false expectations about my course in this life.

I must have dozed off on the fire escape as I sat with these thoughts, because in no time at all I heard my alarm go off.

It was time to go to work.

*

I have to say, Qi-Shi and I had become pretty tight over the months. This was a great joy to me, and whenever I felt despair creeping over me, he could cheer me right up with his sweet, absurd ways. From time to time we'd go to lunch, and something about being offsite seemed to give us a new lease on life, helped us share intimacies that went beyond dissecting the Japanese concept of *mono no aware* ("the ahh-ness of things"), discussing the playing of Nim in *Last Year at Marienbad,* or hating on the wretched Nadir scene. At any rate, although I'd barely slept the night before, I was in high spirits on this particular day: it was Friday. Qi-Shi and I decided to go down to Soul Fixins' to partake of the day's $7.99 Bail-Out Special.

We lingered over our coffee after we ate, looking out on the parade of humanity going down Thirty-Fourth Street, many of them with huge boxes of booty from B&H Video. We both couldn't help but look at one family that had stopped directly in front of our window: a pair of chubby, benign-faced parents wearing identical periwinkle Michelin Man parkas, bright running shoes, and idiotic foam Statue of Liberty crowns. They were studying a smartphone while their daughter stood ten paces off, all Gothed out like early-era Siouxsie Sioux and glaring at the tops of her parents' heads like she would gladly set them on fire.

With an air of confessing, Qi-Shi began telling me just what freaks his own parents were. They were fire-and-brimstone Pentecostals, he said, and they did things like exorcise the mailbox and speak in tongues before meals at the neighborhood Applebee's. He said they believed in witches and demons and scary things flying around the room. Cap-E evil, he said, was a reality to them, just the same as orange juice or jumbo packs of Swiffer refills.

I found myself telling him that my mother was not really so different from that, that she'd been heavy into the Catholic Charismatic movement of the '70s and I'd heard her speaking in tongues when I was a child. And how weird it was—it really was like she had been seized by something. And I told him how after my father died, all this morphed into something much worse, much sadder, and she'd gotten increasingly credulous and superstitious until she was prey to every last right-wing hater group with a direct-mail stamp. And I told him how, ha, it's funny, but she was lost to Alzheimer's now. I had forgiven her for so much, forgiven her everything by now, but she didn't even know me anymore. One time she had rallied, though. She looked at me, her eyes had lit up, and she took my hand. *Ada, I'm so glad to see you. How is it that you're here?* Ada was the name of her best friend when she was a girl.

And maybe it had something to do with his mentioning Applebee's, I told Qi-Shi then, but I was thinking of the awful people around my mother in her adult life, and how she was sorely tested but always managed to treat others kindly. There was one horrible woman in particular, Mrs. Bacon, who was part of some interparish Catholic-Protestant sodality group and who loved having people over to admire her big, bloated, book-free house while she force-fed them entirely undelicious vanilla refrigerator cookies. Mrs. Bacon was the whitest person I had ever met in my young life, quick to condemn the behavior of others and certain of her supremacy in all things. She also happened to look like the Goodyear Blimp in a floral-print dress, but with a big, mean face. I told Qi-Shi about this one time my mother had taken me to Ho-Jo's after mass and how I'd been looking forward to spending some time with her, just the two of us, as well as eating a French dip sandwich, and then how suddenly Mrs. Bacon appeared from nowhere, pushed into our booth, and began, out of the blue, to lecture my mother about how she should be tougher, how she should be *more assertive, Rachele, and not let people walk all over you.* And I told Qi-Shi how my mother didn't say a word in her own defense, how she just deferred to the stupid woman, nodding and making helpful listening noises as this awful bully terrorized her, and how when our food came I couldn't even eat it but instead sat there fantasizing about reaching under the table to pull out a shotgun and blow Mrs. Bacon's fat fucking head right off. All these people, I told Qi-Shi, mistook my mother's compassion for weakness.

Qi-Shi was looking out the window when I finished, but he turned to me and said, "I used to weigh nearly three hundred pounds."

"Wait—what?" I said. "You?"

He took off his enormous groover glasses and gently swiped his hair across his forehead.

"I was eating myself into oblivion because I realized I was gay and I knew my parents would hate me for it."

"Oh, my dear! I'm so sorry. When someone's mean it's like I'll call them fat, but if someone's nice they're really just—"

"Oh, you don't have to say that, Frances! But yeah, I was fat. I was huge. Panda size. Then I came out to my parents, and I don't know, everything started to equalize. I told everyone I knew and everyone I didn't know—I was, like, running down Broadway in a rainbow bunting yelling, *I'm Qi-Shi, I'm queer, I'm not going away!* Then I met a guy and cooled it with the Taco Bell. Of course my parents don't talk to me, don't support me at all, and whenever I have the foolish notion to call them up, they love to tell me how I'll burn in hell. Anyway, I guess, like, in different ways, we both lost our parents."

We sat looking at each other. A wave of tenderness for this boy rose up in my heart.

"If you want, Qi-Shi, I'll be your mom," I said.

He tilted his head at me and smiled.

"Oh, thanks, Frances. But that's totally loco and unnecessary," he said.

Our moment was abruptly cut short when we realized we had four minutes to get back to the office. I slapped down some cash and we took off running down Thirty-Fourth Street, catfish jumping inside us like live bait. We raced up the avenue and into the building lobby and slid across the economy terrazzo flooring as Mr. Shah, who knew a frantic Acme moment when he saw one, slashed his hand between the doors of the just-closing elevator. We hopped in and sailed up and dove out of the elevator, through the door, and into the office—and the skinny hand on the clock showed a full nine seconds to spare. We held our hands over our racing hearts. And then, with one last tender look at each other, it was Qi-Shi back to his workstation and I back to mine.

When my young friend was called into Dee-Dee's office later in the day, I took no special notice. But suddenly Nikki materialized at my elbow, her eyes with their L'Oréal Paris Lineur Intense Liquid Eyeliner enormous.

Qi-Shi, she mouthed.

What? I said and then, "What?"

She drew her finger across her throat.

"What? What the *fuck*?" I said.

I leapt out of my chair and charged toward Dee-Dee's office. Just then the door opened and Qi-Shi shot out and slammed the door behind him.

"But we weren't even *late*," I said to him.

"Insubordination," he said.

"*What?*"

"General insubordination," he said.

Everyone sprang up from their seats and glued themselves to him.

"That's bullshit," Françoise said.

"That's fucking bullshit," Nikki said.

"Fuckers."

"Fucking fuckers."

"Fucking *fuck sticks!*" Nikki shouted.

Qi-Shi was locked out of the server, given ten minutes to gather his stuff—we all pitched in to help, popping off about what a cruel and skeezy fuck Dee-Dee was all the while—and then building security showed up to perp-walk Qi-Shi off the premises. We stood at the window of the locked card-key access door as he stepped into the elevator and then turned to wave a sad, fond hand at us.

Minutes later my phone rang. It was Qi-Shi, calling from the street.

"Are you okay?" I said.

"I'm fine. It's okay. I'm just standing in front of the OTB, having a good cry."

"Oh, honey, I'm so sorry," I said.

"It's okay, Frances! It's really okay. I should've got out of there a long time ago."

"Oh my God, I just . . ." I swiveled to my computer and watched as the FedBizOpps.gov procurement page, with its gradient-fade waving American flag header, went all fuzzy. "I just . . . so selfish . . . I just don't know what I'm going to do here without you."

"Awww, bitch!" he said. "Just stop being so employable!"

*

It was amazing how newly horrible it was at Acme with Qi-Shi gone.

Not long after, I was staring off into space over the copier when Cissy came of nowhere, leaned her witch face with its highlighter eyebrows into my face, and hissed, *Oh, do we miss our widdle fwiend?* I blinked at her, wondering if this might in fact be the most moronically cruel thing a grown-up had ever said to me. I grabbed my coat and fled the building. I had no idea where I was going, but I had to get out of there.

Somehow, I'm not sure why, I crashed through the doors of Macy's and found myself in the men's department. As I slashed down the aisles with my mind aflame, I thought of how Fitz would be home from the colony in a week—a fact I was crazy with gratitude about—and even though we didn't have the money, I suddenly thought, Buy him a gift! A sweater. Yes!

But it was all terrible. Everything looked wrong and misshapen and not like clothing people wore on their bodies. Everything had cinchy Euro waistlines, and anything that looked halfway good cost a million dollars. Really, Fitz was no kind of spendy, dressy fellow anyway. What was I doing there trying to find some probably sweatshop-made sweater for such a man? This place was *bullshit*. I turned and made for the door, and just then "My Funny Valentine" swept down from the PA.

"My Funny Valentine"! It was a big, heart-swelling tangle of strings, and it hit me like a ton of bricks. I stopped in my tracks as a huge rush of melancholy rolled over me.

What was I doing with my life? Why couldn't I get ahead? Why was I so incapable of being a proper, successful grown-up? *What was wrong with me?*

I pushed out of the store and blasted up Seventh Avenue. I had to get it together, not ooze around Manhattan like a walking wound. I had to find a way to cope. What could I do? Simone Weil might have offered up her labor to God as a kind of prayer when she was sweating at the milling machine over at the Renault plant, but what could *I* do?

I stopped in the middle of the avenue, "My Funny Valentine" still ringing in my head. I realized then. It was clear as day. I had to *transform the experience.* I had to do what everyone else did at a sucky job: I had to plug in! Put on some headphones, put on my music, and float away.

The next day I went in armed with an old CD player. I nestled the earphones into my ears, popped in a CD, and turned it on. I signed in to the procurement page on the New York State Contract Reporter, but then, as soon as the music started, a world of beauty swept over me.

It was Jorge Ben. How to explain this? As soon as I heard the first notes of the guitar of "Ôba, Lá Vem Ela" I could taste the music on my tongue like sugar. It was so strong that I had to put my fingers to my lips to contain it. And when I heard the pause in the strumming and

Jorge takes a tiny intake of breath just before he sings the first words, I felt the sugar explode in my mouth. *It was impossible that I was allowed to listen to such beautiful music in such a terrible place.* Oh, but all at once I wasn't there—I was in another world. The music carried me and I floated away, all time suspended. When the song I loved most began, when I heard the beginnings of the song called "Apareceu Aparecida," the lilting guitar and then the percussion comes down and Jorge starts singing . . . *ah!* He sounded like the most beautiful man in the world to me. It wasn't that I could understand Portuguese at all, but I could feel the joy in his heart at this song: he's seeing someplace beautiful to him, Aparecida, he's seeing it, it appears to him, *apareceu,* it must be a play on words, but I didn't want the translation, because to me it was simply about the realization of joy that you didn't know was possible. And my heart was ready to burst with this joy.

I felt this all over me, this perfect sound, the breath of life.

Oh, how could I complain? Now when I was at work and feeling any kind of way, I could always find the music to match it. I could put on The Fall and rock out to Mark E. freaking out like a crazy spaz, I could put on Memphis Minnie and shake my head around to the "New Dirty Dozen" while she whales on that big guitar of hers, I could put on Lys Gauty singing "La Chaland qui Passe" and float down the most melancholy canal in Paris with her. I could put on anything I wanted—it was all my world, mine. One day I put on my favorite Duke Ellington song, my favorite version of this song, Duke Ellington & His Orchestra, July 30, 1945, when he comes in with the piano in that massive, chiming, inimitable way, and then the whole band slides in and there's Johnny Hodges on the alto sax, that smoky, specific, magisterial sound, and then the coolest trumpet comes in, this is Taft Jordan, and things start to gallop and then comes in that fat big sound of the trombone and this is Lawrence Brown, and he brings the whole band up jumping, this is the hottest brass in all the world as they all slide back in together, they're so tight and it goes up up up until it's that beautiful tremendous controlled screaming that ends with a huge finish, the hugest finish, the song that will always kill me in the heart, a song about inevitable change and sad-sweet nostalgia and fleeting beauty, a song called "Time's a-Wastin'."

*

One night a few weeks later, I happened to be the last one left at work. Hating the place as I did, I'd been amazed that Petey should have entrusted me with a set of keys to lock up. But despite everything, when given a task, I remained a Girl Scout at heart; and being able to escape into music had made me newly pliant—quiescent to the point of being almost narcotized, in fact. I did the rounds, checking to see that nothing was on fire, making sure that the wheezing photocopier had been turned off and Nikki's hair straightener unplugged, closing all the windows. When I came out of Dee-Dee's empty office, something made me stop and look into the palm tree basket.

On top of the tangle of yellowed strips of paper, I saw this:

QI-SHI CHEUNG 4/24/09

And I thought, You know, feng shui might be some goofy white-people's stuff, but there's no way I'm going to leave this boy's name moldering in this wretched holding pen for all eternity.

I grabbed the slip of paper, pushed back into Dee-Dee's office, and heaved up the old sash window. I stuck my head out over the street. It was a tender night in May. I ripped Qi-Shi's name into tiny bits and flung them out into the night sky.

I watched as the pieces swirled together a moment in the breeze, then flew apart, freeing themselves over the sleeping Garment District.

24

Someone else should take this over now, tell the story of Jerry, the story of Jerry and me. My methods break down. Suffice it to say—to be entirely insufficient, actually—we were together for six years. A long time, in a way. In another, no time at all.

We figured out a way to live. Meds do wonders, it's true. After much trial and error, after mood swings as high as mountains and as low as cracks in the earth that send you plummeting, Jerry would become some new version of himself, functioning, slower, calmer . . . reduced. I don't know the right words; I am just saying what it was like. I would ask him to explain it, and all his metaphors were architectural. *There is a high wall, and I know I can put a ladder to it and climb up and see, but I don't care to find a ladder. There is a long hallway, with many doors, and I go and try a door and see that it is locked and I know I can probably open it, but I just keep walking down the hallway.* Sometimes his eyes seemed abnormally dull, as if occluded by his internal weather; sometimes their green was so bright he didn't seem human. Sometimes when he was in a bland period he didn't seem even to understand what was lost. He was like some nice, vague neighbor I didn't know very well. Sometimes he was so content he was like a baby, preverbal and unreachable. There was never any still point for long. He was always the same Jerry, but there were many differently calibrated versions of him.

When he was level and okay, the scales tipped, and I became the one who was uneven, discontent, questing. I took as a given that we would always be together, and I chafed under this even as I loved him.

Sometimes I would look at him sitting at the window in our apartment, the light washing over him, and he seemed closed like a book, slightly imbecilic and thus someone to protect. Sometimes he was arrogant and critical and he focused on everything wrong with me, corrected my terrible French pronunciation, was newly amazed at some foolish, malformed idea I had, reminded me how unworldly I was. Like Clarice, he was always trying to school me in the ways of his class, of the specific and rarefied class fraction that the Marr-Löwensteins inhabited. I was so much a bumbler and a boor. He took me to Paris and Rome and Barcelona on his parents' money and I was thrilled and greedy for experience, but then inevitably things would devolve until I was sobbing in a café on the Boulevard Saint-Germain, on a cul-de-sac in Trastevere, on a bench on La Rambla, exhausted by the errors I knew I would make.

The class thing grew huge between us. Sometimes I threw it back in his face, dwelled on the worst possible memories, wanted to punish him for it. Didn't he see what he'd been given, in contrast to what I hadn't been? Sometimes he did, and that was really the problem. At times he would become so aloof and withholding that I would feel crass and vulgar before him. I reminded myself of the scene in *Nana* when the two whores go on and on about their wretched past—although in my case it was things like government cheese and being smacked across the face in public—making the young aristocrats before them squirm.

The crucial, the heartfelt, the seeking nature of youth—that fell away from our lives. Or seemed off in the periphery, something we'd meant to get to eventually.

He found steady work, through Clarice, at a classical music label. He was valued for his listening, for his discernment. He was told how uncanny he was, and I made an equation in my head that traded his inability to process things visually for a heightened ability elsewhere. But he couldn't hear words, especially my words, so much anymore. He heard only music. With praise he grew pompous, and meds made him bloated; between these things, it was as if he had been zipped into an exaggerated, funny-suit version of himself. Sometimes when I was on the street and didn't expect him to be there, I walked past him like a stranger.

I always thought things would right themselves in the end.

No one spoke to my heart the way he did, even when he was not my perfect Jerry, the Jerry who was passionate and amazed and knew how to smile. Who looked at me with love in his eyes. The Jerry who, when we came out of a film that I loved terribly, instead of dismissing it as sentimental, sought to understand why I loved it. I was vain because I took pleasure in thinking I'd taught him compassion, but that came to seem like some fond old children's story, a relic.

He rose in his career while I bumped around from temp job to temp job, throwing out the pages of my Great American Novel as quickly as I wrote them. But I would catch up, I promised myself. I would catch up. Meanwhile, I built up so much rancor against him that I looked for criticism in every word he said to me.

This is what you do when you expect to be together always. You feel free to criticize a building that is standing, never expecting that your criticism might cause it to be torn down. You maybe do not understand that you will be the one to tear the building down.

I always thought things would right themselves in the end.

One Sunday morning I was reading the paper to him, an article about the letters of Kurt Weill and Lotte Lenya—*Speak Low,* the book was called. She was from a poor family, the daughter of a coachman, she worked as a domestic and sometimes a prostitute, and he was from a "good" background, the son of a cantor. This is how I remember it. Lotte was amused to find that Kurt had left his butter out so long that it had become rancid, but she didn't want to hurt his feelings and said nothing. And so after she stayed over one night, the next morning she ate rancid butter with him. At the end of the article, Jerry asked me to pass him the paper so that he could look at the picture of them. He looked at it for a long time before he said to me, *They are like us, they are just like us.* And I said, *I'm a prostitute?* It seemed amazing that we could have been together as long as we had by then and yet I was reducible to an outline.

Almost like I still was not real to him.

I banged out the door and walked the length of Manhattan Avenue to Newtown Creek, up at the top of Greenpoint where Brooklyn runs out. There was a big brick complex up that way, warehouses or manufacturing buildings, guarded by a pack of Dobermans straining their leashes and barking like they would rip you apart. I couldn't get to the water from there, so I cut over to a sad little park off the East River, where I sat on the back of a bench and looked across the water at Manhattan. I realize now I was looking into another version of our life together, us back those years before, when Jerry was sick in bed and I was the person who stole fire for him. When so much was about imagining. I missed the way we had been. I missed him. I realized, at the end, that I missed him even when he was there with me.

Love is pure gold, and time a thief.

*

So, swing it out, it's funny to remember these things now.

And it did end with a whimper. I left Jerry slowly, I drained the sweetness out of our relationship. I used another man to get away and then I left him too.

I went to another city for graduate school, and in the summer I came back to New York to temp and earn some money.

I had a friend from one of my earlier temp gigs, a woman named Max, a musician who had an apartment up on 106th Street on the West Side. Her roommate had disappeared into some leftist missionary work, and so I rented that woman's bedroom, which had in it a bed, a shoe-shine kit, and a chair with a well-read copy of Adorno's *Quasi Una Fantasia* sitting atop it.

Max had been dropped just weeks before by her girlfriend, a sallow woman called Natorah who looked like some tall, pole-bean cowboy with a line for a mouth. I never did click with Natorah or think she was all that, but I understood how much Maxie was devastated when it ended. It was a hot summer of sadness for us both. Our bedrooms were right beside each other and our windows looked out on the same view, a basketball court up on 107th, next to the Booker T. Washington School. In the evenings sometimes I couldn't sleep, and sitting smoking by the window in the hot breeze, I'd hear Max crying in the room beside. Other times I'd be the one crying and I'm sure she heard me too. We were there in our identical box bedrooms on either side of the same wall, both so crushed by our own sadness that we weren't able to comfort each other at all.

We were about the same size, and I remember there was an all-black sailor-style dress and a black silk shell that we'd trade back and forth to wear to our various boring temp gigs. *Do you have the dress?* one of us would say to the other, frantic and hungover in the morning, stray toothpaste on the eyelid. Max was newly out and went to New York Liberty games, women's health events at the LGBT center, and the weekly *Xena: Warrior Princess* party at a lesbian bar in Park Slope with a certain to-hell-with-criticizing-this-cliché resolve, determined to fight her way past her heartbreak. In time she started bringing women home, and one in particular stuck—an NYU junior Maxie called (not to her face) Baby Dyke. Baby Dyke looked like Hothead Paisan in a baseball cap and was always doing things like drinking our milk straight out of the carton, adjusting her crotch, and describing cunnilingus techniques in exquisite detail to see if she could make me blush. I kind of wanted to chuck her off the roof, but she was a nice distraction for Max.

As that summer went on Maxie was out of the house more and more, and I'd find myself alone on weekends, too sad, somber, and poor to make any plans. Sometimes I'd cry to Trina on the phone, but mostly I'd lie on the futon couch in the living room and read until the sun went down and I couldn't see the page anymore. The window shared an air-shaft with a battered women's shelter, bizarrely donated by the Duchess of York, if one were to believe the engraved placard on the front of the building, and come evening these women would start wailing out the windows:

Oh Lord
Why did you do this to me?
What did I do to deserve this?
Oh Lord
Please deliver me
I have been good
I am hurting so bad
I have been good

I would start crying along with them, at once feeling for these women, missing Jerry in a thousand ways, and thinking my hurt was bullshit in comparison. I'd think, Why don't I just go back to him? *Why don't I just go back?* Sometimes the cries from next door would get so heartrending that I'd turn up music way loud to drown them out, but Max and I had very different taste and I had no great love for her Righteous Babe CDs or copious lute music. I did find a Duke Ellington CD, and this I'd put on, up there on Duke Ellington Boulevard, and it was there that I first heard the song with the alternate title: "Things Ain't What They Used to Be."

Jerry had gotten Max's number somehow and he'd call me on the phone to talk. I was so close so many times to giving in. I was mad lonely and I did not understand what I had done to my life.

One day late in the summer I did give in. He'd been calling to tell me those random things you tell the person who has wounded you: something terrible has happened, I need to see you to tell you. He'd found out some news. He wanted to show me something. I said okay and he picked me up in front of the apartment building on 106th Street, in a car I didn't recognize.

We were so glad to see each other. Despite whatever the terrible something that he wanted to show me was, the drive had the feeling of a fine excursion. We left the city and drove through New Jersey and into Pennsylvania, talking all the way in an easy, holiday style. I remembered all the things I liked about him, and looking at his profile as he drove was immediately familiar, what had been done on so many trips together so many times in the past. It made all the sense in the world that we should be together like this. We stopped at an old modular diner clad in diamond-creased stainless steel and ate French fries and strange lettuce sandwiches, laughing easily, glad to be near each other. Comfortable. We talked about things upcoming in the future in a manner that suggested the future was something we would share. We were seduced into dreaming by the sight of each other.

We knew each other's bodies and gestures and smells intimately, microscopically. All the creature parts, the outside.

It was toward the middle of Pennsylvania, not so far, in fact, from where Audrey had grown up and disappeared back to. There is something about that part of the world that will hang you with loneliness. It was near a town that Jerry said had "closed," emptied of its people because it was on fire underground, the roads melting, forever burning from a coal-mining explosion. We were on the edge of Appalachia.

The road climbed into a hill town, and both of us grew silent. I looked out the window at the houses. Some of them were fancy but had an air of neglect, and the brick town hall looked permanently closed. It struck me that the town had been built with a hope that had never been realized.

"Why are we here?" I asked him at last.

"You'll see," he said.

We turned from the main road and climbed still higher. The houses grew more sparse and ramshackle; some were rusted old trailers. A big yellow dog ran out into the road and Jerry stopped short. I furiously waved away the dog with my hand, but he stood in the middle of the road, watching us as if fascinated.

We drove on up the road, passing in and out of wooded parts. Finally Jerry turned from the road, pulled up in front of a house, and cut the engine.

We sat in the car and looked at the house.

It was narrow and spindly and seemed pitched forward, as if it might throw itself off the hill. It was wooden, painted green around the windows, with skinny clapboard siding that seemed to have been once some kind of white, except the paint had been buffed off in a way that was fantastically total, as if it had been scrubbed all over with a huge wire brush. It had a warped porch that was fenced in with dirty plastic latticework nailed up all over it. It stank of hard luck and suspicion.

"What is this place?" I said.

"Let's get out and see," he said.

My hand shot out to stop him as he opened his door.

"They'll shoot us," I said.

Jerry laughed.

"No one's home," he said.

He got out of the car, and I didn't move until I saw him disappear around the side of the house. I ran after him.

He was standing in the backyard, looking up at a cheap add-on, even worse than the original house, with a swayback tarpaper roof.

"I guess that's their idea of a mudroom," he said.

"It's awful here—let's get away," I said.

"Aren't you curious?" He looked at me with mischief in his eye.

"I can feel the cold coming out of it. It's so cold. Please, there's something wrong here."

I tried to walk back to the car, but he went around the far end. I turned and ran after him, afraid to let him out of my sight. I found him on the front porch, looking up at something that turned out to be a hornet's nest.

"It looks just like pottery, doesn't it?" he said.

There were masses of junk out on the porch—bales of newspapers, old paperbacks turned to garbage from years of rain, a plastic laundry basket full of dirty toys, empty food jars, something that looked like a neck brace. Jerry reached in and selected a Barbie. Its hair was chopped short and its body was filthy with handling, naked and missing a leg.

"I guess she used to rent it out," he said.

"Please, Jerry, what is this place?"

There was a yellow sign in the window headed by large letters that read: CONDEMNED.

He turned to look at me.

"This? This is the house that Clarice grew up in," he said.

"What?"

He studied my face, reading the amazement there.

He was pleased.

"Yes, you heard me right," he said.

He walked to the edge of the porch and I followed. He turned and gave me his arm for the stairs, splintered and warped as they were. We walked some yards ahead, wordlessly, and then turned back to look at the house.

"I found a letter on her desk," he said. "I was over there for dinner and I went in to get a picture book and this letter was left out, almost as if she wanted me to see it. This was deeded to her—I don't know. I guess they tell you when they condemn a place. Except I guess she was hard to find, so it's been like this for years. In limbo, decaying like this."

He looked at the house as he said all this, not at me.

"Why did you bring me here?" I said.

He turned to me. His voice was filled with a sudden ardor, as if he could contain something no longer.

"Because now you can see we're not so different after all," he said. "You see? See how poor this is? This past is a part of me. Part of *me*, do you understand? You see, we're practically the same. Because look at how awful this is."

I looked at him. I looked at him, his hopeful face. And then I turned, walked to the car, and closed myself inside it.

I went back to school a week later. When months had passed and Jerry called me again, it was to tell me that there was a new woman in his life. To this my reaction was many things at once: *I am happy for you. I am worried for her.* And, in the fucked-up ardor of my own selfish heart: *But no one will love you like I do.*

*

Thinking on this so many years later, I realize how much I had taken for granted in getting away.

I treated grad school as a distraction, or as a kind of vacation from my life. I hadn't thought it through, and in a way it was about nothing so much as to be in a city that was not New York. In a city where there was no Jerry.

I'd gotten a full scholarship, a "free ride," and although it was at a fancy school, it was at a place known not so much for its creativity as for its genius-level gearheads. The going directive was "Eat, sleep, study—pick two." Judging by the towering stacks of pizza boxes outside the library and the suffering wretches walking the halls at all hours, the kids there went in for the first and the last. The school had the highest suicide rate in the country. But the degree I was there for was new, experimental, comparatively "soft," something called a SMACT, the ACT standing for architecture, civilization, and technology. The idea was to open the door for cross-disciplinary, hybrid work, but of course those of us in the tiny program were a hopelessly freaky, self-questioning, marginalized bunch. When we all came together for some fantastically awkward social occasion, everyone inevitably drank too much and fell into a kind of extensive, itemizing bitterness that would seem shamefully ungrateful to outsiders. We riffed for hours, saying we'd been smacked, were talking smack, had a smack habit, etc. One terrible evening at the dean's house, I watched as the smartest and kindest among us abruptly excused himself from a conversation about Ivan Chtcheglov's *Formulary for a New Urbanism* only to throw up violently in an umbrella stand. It just seemed a function of graduate school that you walked around feeling alienated.

I think this was also when I first understood the full meaning of the expression "imposter syndrome."

By the second year I had wised up somewhat and got myself well away from the grad-school complaint scene, finding an apartment not in Cambridge or Boston proper but up above Somerville in a place called Medford. One of my profs, when I told her where I'd moved, said, *Medford! That's where you're stuck living when you get your high school girlfriend pregnant.* It was no kind of cool place, but I had a very decent deal sharing the top apartment of a New England three-decker with the grown daughter of the building's owner, a woman who, once I told her my name, said the apartment was mine, sight unseen. *You Italian?* she said, and I sighed at the implications: *Sure, I'm Italian, ma'am, but I might also be an ax murderer.*

Mrs. Romano's daughter, Rosemarie, was not what you would call a dynamic personality, but we got along fine. She collected owl tchotchkes, smoked menthol Benson & Hedges, and was fond of crocheting potholders made to look like oversized citrus slices. Rosemarie worked up the road as a cashier at the Stop & Shop, and when I made what I thought was the inevitable Modern Lovers' "Roadrunner" reference, she looked at me as if I'd tweezed it out of a *Twilight Zone*–like receptacle of arcana. *There's a song?* Her most characteristic response was a kind of impressed *Tch!* noise, employed when I said something that thrilled or amazed her, which seemed to be at least five times an hour: *Chessie, God but you're smaht.* She was a true urban villager, someone who believed in all kinds of bizarre superstitions and had an enormous fear of the unknown.

Our block was a closed universe of Mary nooks, vinyl siding, and drawn blinds, and you could readily imagine all sorts of induction ceremonies going on behind closed doors, meaty trigger fingers being pricked, Saint Lucy prayer cards being burned, etc. I mean, it smelled pretty Mafia to me. But since I was living on about $23 a week—cigarettes, mostly—and my trip to the bus to the T to campus took forever, often I'd find myself staying hyper-local, kicking it around "greater" Medford. I became interested in the strangeness of the place, the quaint old Yankee stolidity with its grim Guido overlay. The town center, which always seemed to be almost completely depopulated, was a small miracle of bad city planning, a melancholy spaghetti of streets with ho-hum shops: credit union, storefront insurance company, doughnut shop, nails place, H&R Block. The gold-domed courthouse was cut off from sight by a long, cheerless medical building, but I liked going down to the old bury-ing ground on Salem Street. There I could spend hours amid the slate headstones with their dreamlike winged skulls, the leafy plane trees, and the glorious old bones of one Sarah Bradlee Fulton, Heroine of the Revolution. I'd hike up to the Stop & Shop with a big canvas bag to shop for my groceries (De Cecco pasta forever on special: three boxes for five bucks), and if Rosemarie was working, we'd stand out in the park-ing lot and have a cig together. It got so that we could talk shit about anything—the weather, the BoSox, the Big Dig—and we evolved it into an art form, "personal" in a particularly Italian American way, as if any of these things were cousins who were failing us. I liked that Rosemarie said the name of her hometown like *Meffid*.

And sometimes up there during the long nights I'd get my mad insomnia and slip out of the house round about three a.m., walk down to the park by the Mystic River, and sit on a hard bench to look at the stars. There was something beautiful in it. I realized come that last semester that I'd gotten over my ethnographic snobbery and I'd become fond of the whole scene, of Meffid, of Rosemarie, of the cranky old deaf guy in a hairnet at the antique, mediocre bakery. And that in some way I was at peace with the emptiness of it, I was *in love with modern moonlight,* and it would be an easy place for a peasant like me to put down roots.

Which could only mean that I had to get back to New York City right quick.

*

But when I finally came back to stay, it was as if an era had ended. Something had gone from my city, I can't tell you what it was.

My friendship with Fang had long tapered off, and any calls I made to revive it she left unreturned. On the other hand, Audrey called me so relentlessly from her parents' house out in Pennsylvania that I grew to dread the sound of her voice. I was the level one, the problem-solver and listening ear, so when I tried to tell her my own confusions she couldn't hear me at all. And she was so medded up that a simple conversation was like talking to a foreign-language speaker who despaired of finding an English equivalent for her words. I was in no kind of Mrs. Fix-it mood anyway; I was having trouble enough finding my own way. I had other friends, but really it was Trina who bore me up in these times. She was always there, with tart criticism or a loving word or some piece of goofiness that would distract me from my self-involved sadness.

They were still too much with me, the Marr-Löwensteins. I would think of us as still together. I'd see in my mind's eye all of us in a house that existed somewhere else in time, enacting the same things over and over again. I would be falling in love over and over again. I felt like I was supposed to have stayed with Jerry. *This was the way it was written,* and I had chosen to ruin it.

"Chess, God love your melodrama," Trina would say to me.

I got an apartment on the Southside, a big ugly place for $850 a month, got a job that was all right, felt embarrassingly overpaid for it, was surprised to be able to make new friends. Was surprised to find that people actually liked me. Guys I worked with would ask me out, and I'd demur or steer things to a friendly, meaningless lunch. Guys would chat me up in bookstores or bars or, in a strange spate that lasted for a few inexplicable months, in large-scale art installations at various museums and galleries. I wondered what they saw in my face that they were so quick to approach me while I read the graffiti on the walls of the Temple of Dendur. I fell into some dance of strangeness with an architect I worked with, and we would have evenings out that turned into endless talk sessions, but I'd always go to bed alone. There was something else going on in my heart.

I was slowly coming out of my disease of the past.

I remember that spring I felt my spirits lift. It was the first time I could "see" spring in years. I thought of a garden way up in Central Park, and how its allée of trees would be blooming pink just then. Though it was a long way from Brooklyn, one Sunday I felt like it was the only place I wanted to be, sitting under the blossoms amid so much beauty. I got on the subway.

What a day it was. The park was crowded, but I didn't mind, I was just glad to be around so much life and color. Couples in wedding clothes stood for photographs, and I walked the garden looking at the flowers, touched by the beauty of everything and how close at hand it was. Close at hand, and able to be shared by everyone: which I realized was my favorite thing in the world.

I sat down on a bench with my book, but instead I let my eyes close, grateful for the sun on my face.

"What are the chances?" a voice was saying.

"What are the chances?" the voice was saying again.

I opened my eyes and saw who it was.

"Fitz," I said.

"Well, hello," he said.

We beheld each other.

"I never come here—and *you're* here," he said. "I just had this feeling, it was such a beautiful day, I don't know, it's so strange, I just felt like being here." He looked as I remembered him, thoughtful, kind-eyed. But even more open than he had been—artless, and frank.

"I never come here either," I said.

He spoke to me so plainly.

"I can't believe how happy I am to see you."

I felt a rush of emotion. Words came tumbling out of me, joyful, unmediated, unequivocal.

"I feel so happy to see you too. I feel like . . . I *missed* you. God, I really missed you, Fitz."

He sat beside me on the bench and peered into my face.

"You're different," he said.

"What do you mean?"

"Do I tell you this? God, do I tell you? Yes, I think I do. You don't know this, but I used to see you around all the time. I remember I saw

294

you on the West Side one day, walking on the bike path with him. I saw you all over the East Village. I was at a table right by you in Veselka one day—you were with him and a woman with a skunk stripe in her hair. I know, I sound like a freaky stalker, but this was just the way it happened. You never would see me. I'd see you and him all over the place, I saw you at Sun Ra and Sonic Youth at Summerstage, I saw you at that DeLillo reading at the Ninety-Second Street Y, I saw you at the Richter show at Marian Goodman. And you never saw me at all."

"I'm sorry," I said. "I'm so sorry I never saw you."

"Don't worry. It's those cagey moves of mine—I can make myself disappear. And maybe I didn't want you to know I saw you. You seemed . . . sad, to me. You always seemed sad. You're different now, somehow."

I sat looking at him, feeling my heart beating.

"You're not with him anymore, are you?" he asked.

"No," I said.

He looked away, looked up at the sky, the trees blooming above us, and then back to me, trying not to smile.

"I don't know," he said. "Would you like to go get a coffee or a beer with me? Or a glass of wine? Or a carton of kefir or a shot of elderflower liqueur, like maybe right now? Maybe right now or tomorrow or the next day? Sorry, sorry, I'm just so glad to see you again. No pressure! Look, I've been in therapy for years, I'm doing everything I promised myself I wouldn't do when I saw you again. But I just feel so happy!"

*

After we got together, I was amazed by how lucky I was. It was as if Fitz were the only person who could have pulled me out of the wreck of the past. But before I got there, for too long after it all ended, I still had the Marr-Löwensteins living in my head, driving my observations, my opinions, coloring my world. I'd dwell on the mystery of this both there in my mind and aloud to Fitz, hash things out endlessly, looking for an answer.

He was as patient as a foot soldier, until one day he was not. We were coming out of the Met at closing time, walking with the vacating throngs through the first-floor galleries, when I saw a chair. It was a nineteenth-century *sedia savonarola,* and it was up on a stand with a velvet braid running from its back to its cushion in case someone was tempted to make the mistake of trying to sit on it. I stopped and looked at it. This chair, this very same hundred-and-fifty-year-old chair, had stood in the entrance hall of the Marr-Löwenstein house. Where you could drop your coat on it, lean on it as you took off your shoes, actually sit on it.

I cut away and pushed through the crowd and out of the building. I ran down the stairs and then Fitz caught me by the arm.

"What is it?" he said.

"Why are they still in my head? Why can't I get rid of this by now? My God, I look at that stupid chair and I think of Clarice and it's a million years later but all I can think is, My God, was I so terrible? Was I really so terrible? Why didn't she like me?"

Fitz held me hard by the arms and leaned down so that his face was right in front of mine.

"There's no answer to that," he said. "She's fucked up and I'm sorry for that. I mean, I am and I'm not. Because if she weren't so hateful, would we be together? I know you have to do this, I know it, but do you understand how you make me feel when you do this? And Chess, sometimes, guess what? There *is* no answer. Not one that will satisfy you, at least. It's a puzzle that can't be solved. And you just have to walk away and save yourself. Which is what you did. You have to find a way to not let it hurt you, because you're only torturing yourself. Chess, please. *Sometimes there is no mystery.*"

And this did not switch it off forever, that's just not the way I'm made, but somehow this was the thing Fitz gave me that allowed me to put this past mostly away. When I was finally able to put it away, so many other things came to the surface, things that I had avoided, things that I pretended didn't hurt me anymore. I had so much grief over the sadness of my family, over our anger and our estrangement. I had so much grief over the cruelty of my father, over my mother's refusal to see reality, what it did to my sisters and my brothers and me. I would spend years with this, trying to understand it and learn how to live with it, and this would be my new life course for a long time.

One night I had a strange dream. I was driving with my father in his beater car; we were driving through broken-down old Hilltop, past all the ruined houses where he used to live. We crossed a bridge called the Augustine Cut-off and then we drove through the ineffable, wooded neighborhood called Alapocas. Then we were driving up the Concord Pike, past the immense field where a cryptic old dairy farm sat crumbling and forgotten, left desolate and alone. And I saw that everything around us was encased in ice. I realized that the tide had risen and then frozen over, and that all of the places around us were—

—*submerged*, my father wanted to say. He wanted to supply the word for me, but he could not. Then I understood. *He had been dead for so long that he had forgotten language.* He turned to look at me, and his pale blue eyes were so sad. And I realized he was trying to say to me, *I am sorry. My daughter, I am sorry I hurt you.*

There was a great thaw, a great thaw in me, plenty of pain to come but somehow never like the past. I had this man now, a man who gave me so much, who listened and never made me ashamed of my childhood, never made me feel like I had something to hide. He just saw me, there in front of him as I was. And in time the story of the Marr-Löwenstein family and what they were supposed to mean to me diminished and turned itself inside-out. Until it occurred to me that maybe I met them not because they were to dictate my life, not because they were some impossible ne plus ultra, but because only through them would I find: Fitz.

Epilogue

After I read about Clarice's death, I found myself thinking of the last word I'd had of each of the Marr-Löwensteins.

Some years before, Fitz and I had been at the Chelsea Flea Market on a Sunday afternoon. He had wandered in one direction and I in the other, and I found myself looking at a collection of odd things on a vendor's table: letter openers disguised as Gothic daggers, jade page-cutters, tiny pistols that shot out flame for a cigarette. Everything was beautifully laid out, nestled in thick crushed velvet in fine old wooden display cases. I looked up to compliment the vendor, who stood on the other side of the table rocking on his feet, hands behind his back, wearing a narrow British-style three-piece suit, which was very well made and which he was a bit too plump for. When I saw his florid Pre-Raphaelite face, the compliment died on my lips.

"Bertrand Marr-Löwenstein," I said.

"Yes?" he said. He didn't know me.

But neither did he seem the disdainful old jerk of the past. He was still Bertrand, but he looked indistinct, his face stretched to sagging by time, alcohol, marrons glacés.

"Hey," Fitz said to me, coming up to the table.

"Fitz!" Bertrand said, lighting up.

They slapped their hands together in a shake like they were great old pals.

"Bert," Fitz said, "old Bert Marr!"

"Still grinding knives?" Bertrand asked, and I realized he must have had some kind of crush on Fitz in those ancient days.

"God, no! I'm back in school finally to get my degree."

"That's grand, that's just grand," Bertrand said. "You always seemed like the brightest boy around, and yet so self-defeating in your *maison de Goodwill* clothes, really!"

"How about you—what are you up to?"

"I've been all right, up and down, you know? I had to give up the business in London, it was failing *spectacularly*. I had some losses. Many, really. My partner—well, we went our separate ways."

It occurred to me that Bertrand had been made nice by disappointment.

"I came home a few years ago to check on the mater, and I've just kind of stayed. She's, well, she's had a hard time of it lately." He looked at me now. "I remember you, dear, of course I do now. You were Kendrick's great friend."

"How is Kendra?"

Because she had disappeared into the ether. All the years I was with Jerry she never came back. For a long time I'd assumed she was dead, that she'd died a junkie, and I comforted myself by thinking that in the end, even if she was in some kind of squalid, wretched place, when she departed this earth her chemical mind would have been filled with the deepest bliss.

"Kendra's joined the Krishnas!" Bertrand cried out.

"You're *kidding*," I said.

"Clarice was thrilled about it, to tell you the truth. Kendra was living like a slug in the rumpus room, all pizza and Seconal and Dumas novels. Now at least she has a *hobby*."

"God," I said. "God."

"Yes, dear, it is very funny, isn't it? You know what old Mr. Marx said about history playing out the first time as tragedy, the second as farce? She'll always be Kendra, I'll give her that.

"Cornelia's not done very well for herself either," he went on. "None of us has the faintest knack for making what you'd call *money*. She was canvassing for—who was that man, ran for president? The one who

299

screamed like a queen on television and so of course they had to tear him down?"

"Howard Dean," Fitz said.

"That's the one!" Bertrand said. "Poor little Nelly. Cornelia's back in her adopted state, doing public relations for some artisanal sausage concern. She doesn't have two sous to rub together, but she goes with a man who wears a beard and Eddie Bauer, and I suppose she's happy."

"Wow," I said.

"You're both looking so *well*," he added.

He himself was not looking remotely well, but he was so friendly and soft that I was quick to lie. Fitz was looking at me, urging me to ask what he knew I wanted to ask.

"How is Jerry?" I said at last.

"How is Jerry?" he said. "Well, I suppose Gerhardt's fine. He was in France for some time, you did know that? And then he landed back home again. I suppose that's the curse of us all, the silver cord. He's had another of his breaks, but you know he'll be fine." He smiled at me, but I couldn't take it in.

We said good-bye, Fitz speaking for me because I was plunged in my own thoughts. As we turned, Bertrand gave me a parody of a funny uncle's wink, this rotund man who had nothing for himself but a few lovely things under glass.

But you know he'll be fine.

*

One day not long after, Fitz and I were hustling across town when we ran smack into a parade going down Fifth Avenue. We were late for some theater event on the West Side and annoyed by this loud festival clogging the street—I had my New York Get There face on, deaf to interruptions. But then something made me see what was in front of me.

It was a Hare Krishna festival, the Ratha Yatra, huge and colorful, when the believers pull an enormous chariot down the street. Everyone was dancing to a loud, clanging beat, all of them chanting together in a multitude of ecstatic voices:

Hare Krishna Hare Krishna
Krishna Krishna Hare Hare
Hare Rama Hare Rama
Rama Rama Hare Hare

All of them moved as one mass, up and down to one beat, caught in a single moment. I was hypnotized, and Fitz caught the moment of it too. And instead of darting through, we stood there.

I was fascinated to see believers of all kinds, people who looked Indian or Bangladeshi but also all types of others, the East Village temple-goers and guys who looked like Jewish doctors and blond women so totally Upper East Side but for their saris and wide-open faces and the fact of them dancing down the middle of the street. It struck me how happy they all looked, how genuinely and deeply adoring they seemed. Oh, what is this bliss, I thought, what is this bliss?

The chariot, canopied in red, came toward us, surrounded by believers. Some were pulling it, some holding loosely on to its yellow rope. A beautiful girl with paint on her face passed in front of me and pressed something into my hand. I didn't know what it was and I wanted to give it back, but she kept going and I called out a thank-you. I looked at it, expecting some magical relic.

It was a tiny plastic zip-lock bag, with a label that read: COCONUT BUNS PRASADAM.

"Damn, it's a cookie," I said to Fitz.

"Promise me you won't eat that," he said.

When I looked up again the chariot had passed. I saw a woman from behind, pulling the rope that dragged the chariot down the street. And I knew it was her. It was Kendra. And I knew I had to run down the street and get in front of her so that I could see her face, see her face so that I could finally see her happy. See her blissed out, thrilled to be a part of this thing—finally content.

I started to move through the crowd, Fitz calling my name. The parade suddenly sped up and I did too, manic with the idea of catching up to Kendra.

And then I stopped.

The parade was beautiful and alive, but the people pulling the chariot suddenly seemed corralled. They were self-tethered, but still they were tethered like cattle, like beasts of burden.

Not free at all.

Fitz was at my side again. He took my hand and we silently decided together to ditch the event across town. I needed to stand there and watch this thing to the end somehow. And we stood on the curb, unspeaking, amid the clanging and the chanting. We watched as the heart of the parade passed and then it thinned out into stragglers. I looked at them all. There, that woman—actually, was that Kendra? Or that woman—that was Kendra, of course! It had been years since I had actually seen her.

All of them were Kendra, and none of them was Kendra.

At the end of the parade, a vehicle rolled into view. It was an enormous Humvee, a war machine, but it was bedecked with flowers and carrying a group of Krishna men and women. All of them looked old and exhausted, and as they passed they turned their unsmiling faces to gaze at Fitz and me.

*

So what's fascinating, in an anthropological sort of way, is that I stayed at Acme long enough to see just about everyone else go down around me.

Trash-mouthed Nikki got the ax, Vinny the lecher got sacked, poor agreeable salesman Walt got the boot—and walked out whistling "Hey, Look Me Over," so relieved was he to finally get the bad news he'd been so long dreading—and the curly-haired dispatchers each got a visit from the Turk in rolling succession. The young IT kid Jacob, impeccable Françoise, the acid-casualty speaker of Modern Standard Arabic, and money guy Will were all fired together one sunny morning. Somehow even Cissy—*porco Dio!*—got chopped down like a stout tree for firewood. She particularly did not go gentle into that good night, and strange to say, when she got the news, she grabbed me in a hug and wailed into my bosom, her highlighter eyebrows bleeding orange all over my shirt. Poor Mr. Shah from security attempted to pry her free as she clung to me, he and I looking into each other's eyes like people in a horror movie trapped together in a broom closet.

I had somehow become the office agony aunt.

Each day I yearned to be fired, but somehow I remained bulletproof. New people came and went, and one day I realized that besides sinister Petey and Dee-Dee himself, *I* was the person with the longest tenure there. How had this come to pass?

On that day of revelation, late on a midsummer Friday, I came to remember something a boss had told me back in the day.

It had been during the clueless era after the winding-down of the "arrogant years" of my twenties and the beginning of the slow-dawning clarity of my thirties. I'd had a gig writing a brief history of a cast-iron building in SoHo for its owner, a motherless, overfed millionaire who was at once ragingly suspicious and as tight as new shoes. I must have done something above the call of duty for him, however, because one day he asked me to come into the office, promising me a "surprise." There he offered me a chair, leaned across his broad Chippendale desk while yanking at the neck of his Phish T-shirt, and said to me with a smile, "Frances, I've always found that Catholics make the best workers."

His smile was almost salacious. And right then I understood that what he was telling me was no kind of compliment, but actually this: *Frances, I've always found that Catholics know how to eat shit.*

In thanks, he gave me a $10 gift certificate for Bath & Body Works, which I swiftly regifted to a homeless woman on the corner of East Seventy-Second Street.

I remember I was aware of many things in that moment. I was aware that I did not want to become my mother. I did not want to forgive, I did not want to be kind, I did not want to consider other people's limitations and adjust my own expectations accordingly. I simply wanted the millionaire dude to stand still so that I could scream in his face.

That had been, what, ten years before Acme, and I knew myself to be not nearly the angry woman I'd been. I'd mellowed. "Mellowed," what the heck? Who was I kidding? I didn't even like the word! I had no business "mellowing." Why was I always the good girl tiptoeing around people, the hard worker, the sport, the *nicener*? The caregiver, the "understanding" one? Why was I always in the role of the person *reacting*, why was I never *doing*?

Of course these thoughts cast me back to Kendra. I mean, here was a woman who took up as much space as she wanted. She was a slob and a jumble sale and she dazzled and made big, big mistakes, she stole and connived and she was always looking for *transcendence* and she manipulated and charmed you and ate up the oxygen in any given room. But through it all, Kendra was always *herself*. She never gave in.

Suddenly it seemed imperative that I get some news of her. Where was she? What had happened to her? It'd been ages since I'd looked up anything after Clarice's passing, but now I turned to my computer and typed in Kendra's name.

And, how crazy . . .

Kendra had been appointed executrix of her mother's estate. Of all the siblings. Not only that, but she was calling herself not a former dancer, not a survivor, not a "denizen of the downtown scene," but a *writer*, having published something I'd totally missed: a weight-loss/ self-help/mystical hybrid how-to manual that, from what I could see, had sold stunningly well. Maybe I'd missed it because she was married now and had used the man's name: Weatherhill. She had married Broyer. She had married her mother's old lover.

I found their wedding picture in the *New York Times*. I stared at them, Broyer looking out-of-his-mind happy at his good luck while a poised woman stood beside him. *Kendra*. How could this be Kendra? She was coiffed and thinned and deflavorized into pretty blandness, smiling a greet-this-beautiful-morning smile and wearing a good Chanel suit. I stared and stared at her, not believing this could possibly be the real Kendra, my Kendra, the Kendra of my past.

And so she had turned herself into a *successful parasite*.

I leapt from my chair and went to the window. I looked out over the sooty Garment District at the wig store, Rock the Fashion Hut, trimming shop, decaying deli, what the hell, because in reality I was seeing nothing. All I saw was *her*, the new and final Kendra. The image spread in my mind like ink in water. Maybe the past was the true misunderstanding. Maybe Kendra always knew she would end up like this, claim her inheritance, move into her entitlement. My image of Kendra with her blue hair and damaged eyes standing on the corner of 116th and

Broadway melted into air. And with it, I felt something else leave me that I hadn't even understood had any power over me still, some part of my heart or my body that, if pressed, would be found to yield no pain anymore.

I would be who I was.

I shut down my computer, picked up my bag, and looked around me. No one was paying any attention to me at all. I put my set of office keys on the desk. I was done there.

Downstairs in the lobby, I said good-bye to Mr. Shah.

It was a day of almost insane sun outside, and I found myself wanting to walk east. I realized that I wanted to go to the water, to the East River, I wanted to walk the hot day of Manhattan and mark the clarity of this moment.

Because this was the day when youth finally died for me.

Going east, I felt a criminal lightness, I felt myself a wisp of flame. And as I walked, this walk became a thousand, a thousand walks across the city, a thousand trips and wanderings and *dérives*.

Some years later I would get out of the train at the new and nearly empty Hudson Yards station and amaze myself to be completely disoriented at the street level, just me and some tourists looking for the *there* there and a few affectless skater kids riding fakie on a dead-end street. I would find my bearings and head east, walk into the morning sun and in those blocks way west see the dark old Hell's Kitchen aspect still somehow preserved, that real meagerness of resources, that desperate outsider savvy. I'd see a textbook energetic crazy man in inexplicable headgear walking around hollering and waving his arms, and once I'd crossed the feeder roads to the Lincoln Tunnel, I'd see a dozen no-frills chain hotels and a shiny-sad Irish pub where a bored girl in a smock top stands smoking outside. And then the tourist glut picks up, everyone spilling north from Penn Station, and at the corner of Eighth Avenue by the T-Mobile store the most violently delicious onion-ring smell fills the air. There's a storefront with headless mannequins, their hips out with cheap-chic attitude, there's the headphones-wallets-watches-pashmina-perfume store, there's the dollar-slice pizza place and the soot of a hundred years, and as I go by I'm thinking about how all this fabulous old sleaze soon will pass into nothingness. *New York—you shoulda seen it in the old days.* I'm on the Acme block when I realize I can't even recall which building it was; the memory has left me, it's somehow faded into the anonymity of lost time.

A boy in front of me throws his losing Take 5 ticket into the air—*Aww, man!*—and whirls around, and when he sees me starts singing that song about not being able to feel his face when he's with me. But then he sees me better, sees that I'm old enough to be his mother, and politely trails off his song to a hum. I smile at him.

Age has taught me patience.

I've crossed over to the East Side, I'm all the way to First Avenue, and I realize that what I want to do more than anything is go up to the UN. I'm not even sure why. I love the feeling of mystery here, something left, the empty, pitched landscape of weedy lots just south with their smell like an endless childhood afternoon, chickweed and crabgrass, something slightly rasping and forlorn. The strange lonely wealth of this city. But then it's perfect when you clear the curve of the library and the tall, slender Secretariat springs into view. I run across the street, run against the light. I want to read the words on the Isaiah wall, read how we will beat our swords into plowshares, I want to be there at what's maybe my favorite moment in all of New York City. Because despite a hundred stupid realities, the city still feels to me like hope.

I climb the stairs and look out over the edge of Manhattan.

And then, I keep walking.

Acknowledgments

My thanks to everyone who inspired me, helped me, and kept the faith along the way:

Kim Sullivan, Thomas Glave, Sarah Hill, my hero Gerry Howard, Colette McDonald, Sharon Corso, Carole Maso, Ann Reinhard and Ken Koton, the inimitable Nancy Frick Battaglia, Ken Gangemi, Caroline Stern, Kathy Hipple and Alberto Zayden, Lisette Wesseling, Wing-Sze Ho, Phil Graziano and Michael Spirito, Claire Chafee, Patti Kelly, Erik Ryding, Adrienne Fitzgerald, F. S. Rosa, Neill McKenna, Barry Allen, Erika Rosenfeld, Clara Arthur, Steve Bleiweiss, *il miglior fabbro* Michael Daddino, and the wonderful Susan Golomb. Shout-outs to Marian, Cecily Joyce, Jen Fuqua, Alarice Joyce, Lily Wang, Pato Fernandez, Kathleen Hill, Sandy Opatow, William Chapman Sharpe, Ira Silverberg, Linda Yablonsky, Joan Acocella, Ela Basak, Jacob Forman, Cole Heinowitz, Daniel Rios, David Hess, Charis Conn, Lydia Salzman, Vicki Gestwicki Murphy, Devin Fitzgerald, and my friends at work, especially Carol Giffen, Cami Lee, David Florio, Howard Allen, Aris Carlot, Hilary Whittier, and the endlessly inspiring Lynn McClouchic, who may never know how much I've learned from her. Shout-outs as well to Mike Cohn, Anthony Delmar, and my other friends met through the late, great Manhattan Stuttering Support Group. My gratitude to the New York Public Library system and the New York Foundation for the Arts, as well as to Yaddo and the MacDowell Colony for early support. All props and respect to Malka Burton and Smadar Yaish. To Glen, to my dear Mr. Brent, to my mother, Colette, I wish you were here.

About the Author

B. G. Firmani is a graduate of Barnard and Brown. Her short fiction has been published in *Bomb, The Kenyon Review,* and the *Bellevue Literary Review.* She is the recipient of a New York Foundation for the Arts fellowship and has been a resident at the MacDowell Colony and Yaddo. She lives in New York City, has a day job, and writes on the weekends.